Sally Stewart's childhood in London was shared with four older brothers and briefly interrupted by a sojourn in the country as an evacuee. She returned in time for the Blitz but completed her schooldays in Kent.

It was at school that she first began to write and then, in 1983, she won a *Woman's Weekly* competition for unpublished authors. Since then Sally's stories have frequently appeared in magazines, and she has now had more than ten full-length novels published. She lives with her husband in Somerset and is currently working on her next novel for Headline.

D1137565

Playing With Stars

Sally Stewart

HEADLINE

First published in 1998 by
HEADLINE BOOK PUBLISHING

First published in paperback in 1999 by
HEADLINE BOOK PUBLISHING

10 9 8 7 6 5 4 3 2 1

ISBN 0 7472 5984 4

Typeset by Palimpsest Book Production Limited,
Polmont, Stirlingshire

Printed and bound in France
by Brodard & Taupin.
Reproduced from a previously printed copy.

HEADLINE BOOK PUBLISHING
A division of Hodder Headline PLC
338 Euston Road
London NW1 3BH

Playing With Stars

Chapter 1

Kate crept downstairs in the half-light of dawn and let herself out of the house. To be abroad alone so early that London's air still smelled fresh and cool was something she hadn't experienced before. The sleeping giant was beginning to wake – she could hear a boat's siren hooting on the river, and a train rattling over the points at Borough Junction – but for the moment there were no living things to see except a couple of cats returning home after the excitements of the night. Then the hot, acrid smell of burning coke came floating on the air. Round the corner, sure enough, was a nightwatchman's canvas hut, but he was too busy brewing tea on its glowing brazier outside to notice her.

Because it was the way she always walked with William, she crossed Bankside first of all, to inspect the river. No gulls fighting over pickings on the wet, shining mud . . . the tide was high this morning. The water looked quiet, coloured the same soft grey as her grandfather's best waistcoat, but the sky above it downstream was touched with pink. She thought it looked pretty with its scattering of silver fish as well. Not fish really, of course; everybody knew they were barrage-balloons, floating up there to keep out the German aeroplanes that wanted to hurt London. In a way they were the reason she was out here now, instead of in her attic

1

bed at home. This morning she wouldn't be there to squint through closed eyelids and make patterns with the first rays of sunlight to reach her little window. Aunt Lou would go downstairs to put the kettle on for her first cup of tea of the day, not knowing that the attic was empty. It made the unfamiliar world about her seem suddenly lonely, and she was glad to see a tug go by, pulling its string of barges. She waved to the man at the wheel, but if he saw her he didn't wave back, and it occurred to her for the first time that perhaps adventures were better shared.

She turned away from the river and discovered that she wasn't entirely alone after all. A tall, helmeted figure was making its way towards her at the slow, deliberate pace she recognised. There was nothing wrong as a rule about a friendly chat with a policeman, but she thought she wouldn't have one this morning . . . just in case. Instead, she crossed the road and dived into the network of alleyways beneath the railway arches.

A familiar smell hung about them at any time of the day, whether the market was open or not, but already the first traders were arriving to set up their stalls. She was used to them – rough, kindly men who wouldn't mind her being there as long as she didn't get in their way. However hard they worked they could always talk as well – a rapid crossfire of Cockney grumbles and jokes that sometimes seemed to mystify the slower-talking country men who came to sell them fruit and vegetables. She wandered about, dodging vans and barrows, watching what went on, and pondering the strange names stamped on sacks of potatoes and crates of cauliflowers . . . what sort of people lived in Spalding and St Ives?

Slowly the sun found its way into the Borough alleyways.

The smell of labouring men, squashed fruit, and trampled cabbage-leaves grew strong in the warm air, and she was getting tired and hungry. The shining half-crown piece left in her purse at home would have been useful, but it hadn't seemed right to bring it with her now, knowing that Aunt Lou had provided it for a different purpose.

'Aintcher got no 'ome, nipper?' The question was launched at her by a Mr Fred Potts of Bermondsey, whose name was beautifully painted on the stall she was now lingering by for the third or fourth time.

''Course I have,' she answered with dignity. 'But I like being *here* . . . I might want a barrow of my own one day.'

Fred shouted to his neighbour on the pitch next door. ''Ear that, George? Seems we'll be 'aving some more competition before we're much older!' Then he grinned at the small threat to trade standing in front of him. 'Better scarper now all the same, else yer mum'll be gettin' in a stew. You can 'ave a banana on the 'ouse, but no nickin' anything else soon as me back's turned.'

She thanked him for the banana and accepted his hint as well – it was time to find another refuge. No difficulty about that, though, because neighbour to the market was another place she often went to with William. She might go into the cathedral, or she might not, having no coin to drop in the box by the door, but there was a little garden in the precinct outside where no coin was needed – the benches were free. The banana, even eaten very slowly, didn't last long, but the morning's good-fortune wasn't over. She discovered in the lining of her blazer the remains of a bag of acid-drops that had fallen through a hole in the pocket. A coating of navy-blue fluff had to be removed; apart from that they

3

were as good as new. She was carefully picking off the wool when a young man emerged from the church door and made for the seat beside her.

He said a polite good morning, then opened the sketching-book he carried and began to draw the great, grey building in front of him. She edged a little nearer along the seat, inspected the outline growing under his hand, and shook her head. As if he felt the gesture, he turned to stare at her.

'You've missed out the angel,' she said kindly, 'just *there*, see?'

Her companion looked again, and saw. The carved stone angel was the worse for London wear and tear, but she was undoubtedly there beneath her covering of soot and grime. He smeared away a charcoal line or two, redrew them, and the angel appeared. His instructress smiled and held out her dingy paper bag as a reward.

'Do you fancy an acid-drop? They taste better than they look.' It was a sacrifice in her present circumstances, but Aunt Lou always said that giving didn't count unless it hurt. The young man accepted the offering and studied it through gold-rimmed spectacles that she hadn't seen anyone wear before. William sometimes screwed a monocle into his bad eye, and her friend next door, Elsie Manners, favoured rimless lenses that slid down her long, thin nose.

'You seem to know the cathedral very well,' the artist beside her suggested. 'It's new to me . . . I haven't been to Southwark before.'

A small sigh warned him to expect another correction. 'Its proper name's the Ward-of-Bridge-Without, but William says no one seems to know that but us.'

He apologised for the general error, and offered a pleasant

smile. 'Shall we introduce ourselves? I'm Sam – Samuel Anton Maitland, if you like names in full.'

She held out her hand with huge aplomb – a duchess condescending to the hoi polloi couldn't have done it with a grander air, he thought – then changed her mind and clapped both hands together. 'The initials *spell* it, too . . . now I call that clever!'

Her thin, plain face was suddenly bright with pleasure, and it seemed even more unlikely than before that she could be a typical example of a Southwark child, although she certainly looked like one. Her blazer and cheap cotton dress were over-big – to allow for growth, Aunt Lou would have explained – and she'd found nothing better than an old brown shoelace to tie back a mop of dark hair. But average street-urchin she could scarcely be when her accent was so unexpectedly pure.

'I hope your parents found something equally neat for you,' Sam suggested curiously.

She shook her head. 'I don't think they could have tried very hard. I'm plain Kate . . . nothing to boast about there at all.'

He smiled again at the regret in her voice and tactfully changed the subject. 'If your William knows a lot about the Ward of whatever it was, perhaps he could tell me where Shakespeare's Globe Theatre was?'

''*Course* he could – we live on top of it . . . well, practic'ly; only the street's called Paradise Walk now.' She defluffed another acid-drop before releasing her next piece of information. 'You can't see William's theatre from here . . . you need to walk along to Blackfriars for that.'

'William's? . . . you mean Will Shakespeare's?'

She looked disappointed in him. 'No, silly . . . my grand-father's, William *Cavendish*. He and Granny were ever such famous people – everyone in London went to clap and cheer them at the Swan. It's on the other side of the river, but sometimes we can see the flag still flying.'

Sam searched his memory for an echo from the past . . . yes, there'd been a husband and wife team treading the boards together for years after the Great War, performing the drawing-room comedies of Frederick Lonsdale and Gerald du Maurier.

'It was a little bit before my time, and I haven't been long in London in any case,' he said hastily, 'but of course I've heard of the famous William Cavendish.'

She nodded, not doubting it; the story of her grandfather's brilliant career was something she'd been brought up on. But the thought of him was a reminder of home, and her face grew troubled. Sam registered the change and suddenly wondered what she was doing there alone. He wasn't practised at guessing children's ages, but she couldn't be more than ten, perhaps only a long-legged eight or nine.

'Have you mislaid someone? Or should you be *inside* the cathedral, listening to your teacher?'

'I haven't 'zactly mislaid her,' Kate answered with care, 'but I'm not quite where I'm supposed to be.' She studied her companion and decided that he might safely be trusted with the truth. 'I *told* Aunt Lou I wasn't going to be a 'vacuee in the country, but she just went on putting all my clean vests and knickers in a suitcase. She'd got a label ready, too, with my name on it, and my gasmask . . . and a packet of digestive biscuits so's I wouldn't be sick on the train journey.'

'But . . . but you decided not to go,' Sam commented.

He made it sound so reasonable that she smiled gratefully at him when she nodded.

'When it gets to past dinner-time I can go home – no point in dragging me to the station once everyone else has gone.'

He felt sorry for the unknown Aunt Lou, landed with the unenviable task of standing in for parents who seemed to be missing. With a vague hope of being helpful to her, he suggested that people often spoke well of the country . . . Kate might even like it if she gave it a try.

She shook her head; he noticed that she seemed to favour gestures, positive or negative as the case required, to emphasise what was coming next. 'I belong in Paradise Walk. P'raps I'll look at the country some other time; not now.' Then her voice suddenly changed. 'But I'll no get an egg to my tea today, and I'm fair clemmed already.' Sam's bemused expression made her grin, but she was kind enough to explain. 'That's not how Aunt Lou speaks – she's a Campbell, you see! At school I talk same as me friends, but I ain't allowed to at 'ome!'

He listened to the swift, sure mimicry and smiled himself. 'I know . . . you're going to be an actress, like your grandmother.'

'William hopes so,' she agreed, 'but I think I'd rather do what my friend Elsie does.' Then with a suddenness that took him by surprise she seemed to decide that the conversation was over. There wasn't even time to ask her what it was that Elsie did before she'd sprinted away on long, thin legs, leaving him feeling strangely bereft. He went back to his half-finished sketch but it seemed uninteresting now – he wished he'd insisted on delivering her home, regretted not being introduced to William and poor Aunt Lou, and a place unbelievably called Paradise Walk in the run-down back streets of the Ward-of-Bridge-Without. He added a smile to the face of Kate's angel and closed his sketching-book, wishing something else as well. It would have been nice to know whether she won her battle *not* to be a 'vacuee.

The next morning Mr Chamberlain's voice announcing over the wireless that Great Britain and her Empire were at war with Germany was solemn enough, but his message was driven home almost at once by the banshee wail of London's first air-raid warning. It seemed more necessary to stand and stare at the sky than hide in the dank little shelters that were now humped in every patch of garden, and in any case the warning turned out to be a false alarm. The war itself seemed just as unreal, too, as the months went uneventfully by. No heroics were called for, apparently . . . only good-humoured patience with an ever-growing burden of restrictions on normal life. They must learn to eat less, and see in the dark, because there would be little food and no lights; they must know where they were by instinct because there would be no place names or sign-posts to guide them; and they couldn't even rely on the ringing of the bells in future to tell them when to go to church.

Kate stayed in London and refrained from pointing out, when most of Southwark's children returned home after a month or two, that she'd been right not to go at all. By the late summer of the following year, when the war had finally become very real and dreadful, she was still in Paradise Walk; then it was Aunt Lou who refrained from pointing out that she owed that fact largely to her friend next door. Elsie Manners had asked William to consider what would happen

8

to his granddaughter if he and Louisa Campbell should both
be killed.

'*I*'d take care of her if I could, but it's no use relying
on me either,' she said bluntly. 'One bomb here during
the night and the whole Walk would be blown to kingdom
come. Then Kate would be left with nobody except those
God-fearing, hypocritical relatives of Fanny's up north who
couldn't get rid of an orphan baby quick enough when her
mother died.'

William was forced to agree and to do something he hated
doing – remember not the triumphs but the unhappiness of
the past. He and Fanny Campbell had met and fallen in love
when his touring-company played a season in Edinburgh.
Her stiff-rumped parents never forgave him for luring her
away to London, but there was worse to come – Fanny
herself embarked on a licentious career on the stage, and
the only child of the marriage, Marguerite, grew up to be a
Gaiety Theatre dancer. The Campbells grudgingly accepted
Marguerite when she was pregnant and anxious to escape
from London, but her only friend in the cold north was her
Cousin Louisa, the daughter of Fanny's brother. Then still
only twenty-five, Marguerite was tragically dead in a street
accident, and Louisa brought the three-month-old Kate back
to her London grandparents. There was no lack of love from
William and Fanny, but Louisa couldn't see them looking
after a baby when they were at the theatre every night. She
stayed on to do the job herself, always meaning to go home
but never quite managing it. She was still in Paradise Walk
when Fanny fell ill and died, and after that there was no
question of going back to Edinburgh. She was by now the
linchpin of the household, gruff and undemonstrative and
totally reliable.

William gave a little sigh that put away the past, then tried to grapple with the difficult present again. With his stern-faced friend, Elsie, on one side and Louisa on the other, he knew how a sailor felt trying to negotiate Scylla and Charybdis. There existed between the two ladies no love at all; only complete respect and a strong mutual inclination to tell him what he ought to do.

'Lou still thinks Kate should be away from here,' he said miserably. 'Of course she should, but if she wouldn't go when everything was quiet, she certainly won't be talked into leaving now.'

'Let her be,' advised Elsie. 'Children are tougher than we like to pretend. My guess is she'll grow up pleased with herself for having lived in London in 1940.'

William allowed himself to be convinced. School after school south of the river was being blasted or bombed to ruins, but he took comfort from the fact that at least in the things that mattered Kate's education wasn't suffering. Their long nights weren't really passed in the air-raid shelter at all, but in an imaginary Globe Theatre. William threw himself into the parts he hadn't had the chance to play at the Swan – Jacques, Benedick and Prince Hal – while Kate, Lou and Elsie comprised the rest of the company, with two more old friends who also lodged, as Elsie did, in William's other house next door. Mildred Pearce had been Fanny's protegée but was mostly to be found 'resting' these days; her brother, Percival, was still in steady demand as a player of the bit-parts that more ambitious actors didn't want. The air-raid shelter might give no scope for action, but they could fairly let themselves go in the readings. A very youthful Juliet regrettably collapsed in giggles when her Romeo – plump and balding Percival – delivered his more impassioned speeches. Still, William could fairly claim that his granddaughter was learning to love what most children only accepted by forced feeding.

The imaginary glades of the Forest of Arden and Illyria were always sunlit, but outside the real world seemed dark enough. The RAF had fought and won the Battle of Britain, and the expected German invasion hadn't come; but most of the continent of Europe was in the Wehrmacht's grip, and the only battles being fought now were at sea, or far away in the deserts of North Africa. For weeks at a time Londoners could sleep in their own beds again because the German bombers were heading for cities like Birmingham and Plymouth and Coventry. Then, in the dying moments of the year, they were suddenly back again over London in the most terrible raid of all. There was no play-reading that night, and when morning came they crawled out to breathe air that was thick with smoke and the dust of shattered masonry. William muttered something about walking as far as the river to stretch his legs, but found when he got to Bankside that Kate had followed him.

Holding hands, they stared at what had been the City of London. Fires were still burning, and the stench of terrible destruction hung over them, choking and obscene. Unable to speak, William looked at Kate's white face beside him, wet with tears like his own. But suddenly she pulled her hand out of his and shook her fists at the sky.

'Sodding Germans . . . I hate you . . . *hate* you.' Then her voice broke and she had to turn her face into his coat while great, shuddering sobs racked her thin body.

He held her tight, but tried to scold. 'Katey love, you've been hobnobbing with those Bermondsey women in the market again.'

She nodded without lifting her head and he struggled to find some gleam of hope that would penetrate the horror an exhausted, overwrought child was wrapped in.

'It's not as bad as it might have been . . . they missed our dear old friend – if you look you'll see St Paul's is still there.'

She nodded again, and smeared away her tears, but she was careful not to look across the river as they turned towards home. And later that day William was equally careful not to tell her the news that Elsie brought back to Paradise Walk. There would be no point in going down to Blackfriars in future to look for a crimson and white flag floating above a theatre stage-house – the Swan was now a smoking ruin, too.

Chapter 2

The years of war dragged slowly past, but a month or two before Kate's sixteenth birthday an exhausted world stumbled into peace. Absorbed in more global happenings, she'd scarcely perceived that her own adolescence was being left behind, but suddenly it was time to think about the future.

As usual, it seemed advisable to take the problem to her friend next door. William preferred reality softened by the coloured veils of fantasy, while dear Aunt Lou marched straight towards life's certainties, stopping to look neither left nor right. Elsie Manners, on the other hand, though sometimes harsh, was also ready to deal in what *might* be possible. With her rimless glasses, and black hair scraped back tightly in a bun, she looked type-cast for the part of spinster school-mistress. But Kate knew that behind her high forehead lurked a mind as intricate as the rich, strange costumes she fashioned for the theatre. Mostly she worked away from the house next door, but sometimes she could be found at home, frowning over a designer's sketch that had to be converted into a working paper pattern. When Kate went in one morning she looked up, then nodded at a wicker basket in the corner of the room, overflowing with bright scraps of material.

'I suppose you've come looking for something to wear. You can have a rummage if you like, but you'll have to make it yourself – I'm busy.'

She sounded cross and, for once, looked tired. Noting the fact, Kate suddenly realised that she couldn't even guess at her friend's age. Elsie refused to admit to birthdays, but Mildred downstairs occasionally hinted that *she* wasn't the only one to touch up the colour of her hair.

'I wanted to talk to you,' Kate said now, 'but I'll go away if you've got to finish that.' She dropped a little kiss on Elsie's head in passing, then knelt on the floor to sift through the latest additions to the remnant basket. It had been a favourite game in childhood, making dolls' dresses from Elsie's leftover scraps of material. Nowadays, Kate found that the pieces came in useful for her own meagre wardrobe.

Elsie suddenly laid down her pinking-shears. 'Talk if you want to. Ophelia's shift can wait – she's only going to drown in it, poor thing.'

Kate sat back on her heels, grinning at the familiar dryness, but she seemed in no hurry to speak. There was time for Elsie to stare at her and realise that a lanky schoolgirl was growing up. But she wasn't growing up in the least like her mother. Marguerite Cavendish had been beautifully compact . . . beautiful altogether, in a golden, fragile way. She'd been a good enough dancer as well to grace the stage of the old Gaiety. For the moment, at least, Kate had no beauty at all, being thin and awkwardly angular, with features that were too big for her face. But in Elsie's considered view Marguerite had fatally lacked character, whereas no one, thank God, could say that of the girl who sat watching her now with bright, observing eyes.

'It's about the future,' Kate said at last. 'I'll be taking Matric soon, and I've got to decide what to do after that.'

'I suppose your grandfather can't make up his mind – one day it's to be a scholarship to Oxford, and the next you're going to take RADA by storm!'

Kate nodded, not smiling now because the matter was serious. 'Something like that, although he knows as well as I do that Aunt Lou scrapes and scrimps to make ends meet as it is. I need to *help* as soon as I can, not involve them in more expense.'

'What does your aunt recommend?'

'Anything but the stage – it's a den of every known vice to Aunt Lou. She thinks a nursing career would be nice, or a safe, respectable job in some Civil Service typing-pool! But I don't *want* to be a typist, and I think I might be a bit too argumentative, don't you, for any hospital sister to stomach? Besides, I *do* want to be in the theatre.'

'You fancy yourself as the new Sarah Bernhardt, I suppose?'

Kate's expression registered sudden sadness. 'I would be if I could, because it would make William so happy. But what use is an actress who clean forgets all her lines the minute she gets in front of an audience? I've done that in every school play so far, and they won't have me any more. In any case, I don't have the right face for it.' She considered a square of crimson velvet left over from some medieval tunic, and then looked up at Elsie. 'As a matter of fact, I'd like to be something like *you*! I'm good at making clothes, and I always have an idea in my head of how a play should *look*. I wondered if your designer might need someone to fetch and carry for him? That way I could work and learn at the same time.'

'I'll put it to him if you like,' Elsie agreed after a pause, 'but I can tell you now what he'll say: "My dear Miss Manners, please advise your young friend to go and do her learning somewhere else; after *that* I might offer her the privilege of letting me work her into the ground!"'

Kate frowned, unfolded her long legs, and stood up. 'Well, I don't much like the sound of him anyway. Never mind . . . I'll get a job in a provincial theatre and make a start there.' She gave Elsie a farewell grin and went back home to consider which province should see the beginning of her brave career. Elsie resumed the cutting out of Ophelia's dress, but she hummed tunelessly while she worked, a sure sign that she was thinking of something else at the same time. In the end she gave a little nod, having decided what she was going to say to William Cavendish, and the outcome of the conversation was that Kate didn't set off after all at the end of the summer for theatrical lodgings in Chelmsford or Doncaster or some other sad place that William could scarcely bear to mention. Instead, at Elsie's suggestion, she was to enrol at the Lambeth College of Art and become a student of scenic and costume design. When she asked how they could possibly afford the course, William waved the distasteful subject away with an old actor's graceful gesture. But, pinned into a corner, he finally had to admit that the College fees would be paid for with a small sum of money provided by her father.

'You've never mentioned the money before, *or* him,' Kate pointed out incredulously. 'Are you sure you're not fibbing? If it really means using up your or Aunt Lou's savings, then I refuse to go.'

'Since savings are something we don't have,' said William, sounding very convincing, 'you needn't fash yourself about *that*, as your dear aunt would say. There was no point in mentioning your father's little nest-egg before, and you don't have to worry about it now . . . it's dealt with by some lawyer's clerk.' Another wave of his hand dismissed the clerk, but his mobile features expressed sad regret. 'You're quite sure about this Lambeth place, Katey? There's still time to change your mind. Think of the power that comes with holding an audience in the palm of your hand . . . think of *playing* on a stage, instead of painting the scenery.'

Kate smiled but shook her head. 'Think of standing there unable to remember a word of what you're supposed to be saying! Anyway, I've heard *you* say that a production is only as beautiful as its setting and costumes.'

'True, but no designer, however exalted, ever got his name in lights. I hoped I'd see "Kate Cavendish" there before I died.' He managed to sound so wistfully frail that she had to remind herself that he was in excellent health.

She had always been taught by Aunt Lou that the past, being full of anguish, was not for mentioning. Now, her father's astonishing gift prompted a question that insisted on being spoken.

'Gramps, why should the name in lights have been "Cavendish"? Why wasn't I given my *father's* name?' She could see that the question was unwelcome even now, but whether the unknown man had been someone to feel proud of or not, he'd existed in their lives to the extent of fathering her. She knew beyond a doubt that it was time she was told about him.

'He was an Italian, by the name of Arturo Contini,' William said reluctantly. 'You knew that already. Like a lot of Italians, he came to live in Clerkenwell after the Great War – there were so many of them there in those days that it was called "Little Italy". It was the centre of the jewellery trade, you see, and Contini's family were jewellers in Milan. He saw your mother dancing at the theatre, and went every night after that.'

'It sounds a romantic story, but I can see you didn't like him,' Kate observed, watching her grandfather's expression. William hurried on, ignoring the interruption. 'When . . . *after* our dear Marguerite was killed in a street accident, he suddenly went back to Italy and you became *our* child. But in case there should be any legal quibble later on, I made sure of having your name changed by deed poll. *That's* why you're a Cavendish.'

Kate tried to imagine a man who, however distraught he might have been over a dead young wife, could have abandoned his own child. Nothing that she could think of lessened the feeling now of having been rejected by her father, and it was on the tip of her tongue to say that *she* would reject his money. But William's ravaged face prevented her. She'd been a burden to him long enough, and if she refused to make use of what was hers *he* would still make shift to help her.

'That's all I want to know about my father,' she said quietly at last. 'It's old, sad history, and I'd rather think about the future. I'm going to that college, dear Gramps, and when I've become successful I'll earn huge sums of money, and wrap you and Aunt Lou in luxury in your old age . . . see if I don't!'

William agreed that they would look forward to it and, in the relief of getting through a difficult conversation forgot to raise any more objections to his granddaughter's choice of career.

*　　*　　*

18

The Lambeth College of Art might not have struck many people as a hidden paradise, but to Kate for the next three years it represented Shangri La. There she forgot the drabness and austerity of post-war Britain, with its continuing shortages and frequent financial crises. But at home Aunt Lou still wrestled with the task of feeding them on rations that seemed to dwindle rather than improve; and William inveighed bitterly against a Labour Government that, having impudently unseated Winston Churchill, was doing its incompetent best to change the traditional ways of England. Elsie more generously maintained that it wasn't all the Government's fault. Everyone was tired, and disinclined to be goaded into working harder on less food; their reward for having won the war was *still* no jam for tea today, and not much chance of it tomorrow, according to the cheerless Sir Stafford Cripps. Thanks to the ungrateful Americans who had cancelled Lend-Lease, it was still the Age of Austerity.

But amid all the gloom and greyness of daily life the lights of theatre-land shone with exciting brightness. For the sum of half-a-crown enchantment was available to anyone prepared to queue for a gallery seat; and, as Kate pointed out to William, queuing was something they were very good at by now. More Saturday afternoons than not, Aunt Lou having refused the treat they offered her, the two of them would set out hand in hand like school-children for the West End.

All the great ones of the London stage seemed to be playing there in those intoxicating theatre years just after the war – Olivier, Gielgud, Richardson, Guinness, Peggy Ashcroft, Edith Evans – the roll-call was endless. Then there came another afternoon when they finally got in to see something else that all London was flocking to. Theatre critics said that the production was flawless and the settings superb, but for once Kate didn't notice these things. She sat, scarcely breathing, as Harry, King of England, flung back the French Dauphin's challenge, and wept as he put heart and courage into his raggle-taggle army before the battle of Agincourt. She listened to Shakespeare's words, but fell in love with the fair-haired, golden-voiced man who made them come alive. His name, her dazed inspection of the programme said, was Jeremy Barrington, restored to them after war-time service in the Navy. So doubtless he was a hero in real life as well. Walking home afterwards she merely nodded when William announced that he'd asked for his congratulations to be sent round to Mr Barrington's dressing-room.

'Even the biggest and best of us like to be appreciated, Katey,' he explained. 'It's the way actors are made, always needing to be reassured . . . and perhaps a word of praise from a fellow-professional may count for a little more than most; I hope so.'

The modest afterthought would normally have made her smile, but for the moment she was still a French princess being wooed and won by Henry. Her grandfather was imagining a different scene – a tired man in a dressing-room, creaming make-up off his face and trying to wind down after an electric performance. Yes . . . a little pat on the back was always welcome then.

The reality of William's imagined scene was slightly different, because Jeremy Barrington in fact sat talking to two friends. Angus Macdonald, the director of the play, was complaining that the pace of the evening's performance had been allowed to drag a little. 'Am I not right?' he asked of the other visitor.

'Perhaps Jem did linger a trifle too long over his "little touch of Harry in the night!",' Sam Maitland agreed. 'Still, it riveted the audience to their seats, so who are we to complain?'

Angus grinned but sounded firm. '*I* can complain – I'm the boss, let me remind you, and I'm not going to let our leading man slide into self-indulgence, however much the gallery applauds him.'

He wouldn't either, Sam reflected, with the knowledge born of long friendship. When did an awkward, stubborn Highlander ever listen to anyone else's point of view? Angus and Jeremy Barrington were more recent friends, since they had found themselves serving in the same destroyer. Jem told very funny stories against himself about his naval career and claimed that he wouldn't have survived it without Angus's help. Sam could imagine that he'd made a hopeless sailor, but at least he hadn't tried to duck the ordeal. Now, resuming a career that had begun at the Birmingham Rep before the war, he was coming to the height of his powers to hold an audience mesmerised; but he was an unexpectedly vulnerable, humble man. Sam often found himself watching over him now as Angus must have done during the war.

'Slowing down or not, it's still a stunning production,' he reminded both of them, and saw Jeremy's tired face break into a smile. 'It could run for ever if Jem didn't want to do anything else.' A thump on the door interrupted them and when Angus opened it he found the stage-door keeper standing there.

'Sorry about this, Guv – got overlooked when the boy brought programmes round for Mr Barrington to sign.'

'This' was a small visiting-card that Angus handed to

Jeremy. The message on the back was brief but beautifully inscribed, and it made him smile again.

'Whatever anyone else may think, Mr William Cavendish is kind enough to assure me that tonight I must have given the performance of my life! He calls himself a fellow-thespian, but he lives in SE1, so I suppose the poor old boy has fallen on hard times.'

'Not Paradise Walk, SE1, by any chance?' Sam asked suddenly.

'Well, yes – here, see for yourself.' Jeremy flipped the card across, but stared at Sam. 'Why did you think it might be? Are you going to say we should have *heard* of William Cavendish?'

'Too young, both of you,' Sam said kindly. 'He was a great man in the twenties.'

'You're too young as well. I suppose you bumped into him in some sleazy pub or other on one of your prowls round London,' Angus suggested.

'Not at all . . . I met his granddaughter,' Sam explained slowly. 'It was right at the start of the war, because she was trying not to get herself evacuated to the country, seeing as how she belonged in Paradise Walk with William.' He smiled at the recollection. 'She was such a mettlesome little piece that I even found myself pretending that of *course* I'd heard of her grandfather! I'm glad he survived the war – he might easily not have done in Southwark.'

William might also never have heard from Jeremy Barrington afterwards, but Sam's story about the Cavendish family prompted him to send a charming note of thanks to Paradise Walk. William was touched by it, and Kate confirmed in her belief that she'd been entirely right to fall in love with him.

Chapter 3

The long years of trudging across a bombed wasteland to Lambeth every day were over. At nineteen and a bit, Kate surveyed the peculiar, exciting world she was to conquer and found it good. William might still hanker after another player in the family, and Aunt Lou – long-exposed to the artistic temperament at close range – might yearn for something safer; but her friend next door would perfectly understand the value of the precious diploma she had now gained.

But Elsie was working night and day, Mildred Pearce dramatically explained, on an important dress rehearsal. It was left to Milly herself to weep happy tears over Kate's triumph.

'You're one of *us* now, darling . . . well, sort of . . . part of the *theatre* anyway.' She sighed over the thought, and became emotional. 'I knew you'd be their star student. I said so to Percival – I *told* him the sacrifice was bound to be worth it in the end.'

A sudden stillness in her visitor went unnoticed, but actresses are trained in the matter of voices and even Mildred couldn't miss the change in Kate's.

'What sacrifice? I mean, *whose* sacrifice?'

Milly's rich colour faded a little, but she did her best to retrieve the mistake. 'A . . . a figure of speech, darling. You know how I run on – more hair than wit, Percy always says. You've slaved away for years when you ought to have been having a good time. *That* was a sacrifice, I'm sure.'

'I *was* having a good time,' Kate said firmly, knowing that Milly would yield nothing more, having been frightened into total silence. It was time to hand over a large folder and leave.

'Here you are, Milly, my prize-winning costume sketches for Lady Macbeth. They're for Elsie to see as well when she gets home. I let myself go a bit with the Celtic necklaces!' It was a temptation to say that perhaps she'd been inspired by her unknown jeweller father; but she thought better of it and went home in search of William instead.

He was reading in what he was pleased to call the conservatory at the back of the house. The word conjured up visions of elegant wrought-iron furniture, potted palms, and warmth, but 'William's lean-to', as Aunt Lou preferred to describe it, lacked all these things. Since the Blitz it had also lacked many of its panes of glass, and although a little extra ventilation in the summer was no disadvantage, he was still hoping to convince a tight-fisted official at the town hall that it came under the heading of bomb damage the Council had a duty to repair.

He smiled at Kate as she went in, but noticed that she was looking stormy . . . a little brush with Louisa perhaps; not infrequent since they both held strong opinions. His dear Fanny had been a very different sort of woman, always sweetly reasonable, he remembered sadly.

'Gramps, now that I've finished at Lambeth I should like to write and thank the lawyer's clerk.' She saw the sudden blankness in his face and felt a small twinge of remorse.

Despite his upright figure, and the beautifully brushed, thick hair of which he was so proud, he *was* nearly seventy – too old, perhaps, to be expected to remember every fib he'd ever told. 'The clerk who looked after my nest-egg,' she prompted him.

'Oh, the . . . the nest-egg, of course! It's all used up now, my dear. I think I told you that it didn't amount to very much. Still, it came in useful . . . no doubt about that.' William gave a flustered little nod and then retired behind his newspaper. A moment later it was tweaked out of his hands and he was left facing Kate.

'The clerk's name and address, please,' she insisted quietly.

He tried to smile, tried not to remember Louisa's grim prophecy that one day the truth would out, because it always did.

'No . . . no need to write, Kate. Clerks don't expect thanks for doing their job. It would be quite . . . quite supererogatory, believe me.'

She knelt down beside him and took hold of both his hands. They were beautifully tended, like his hair, but freckled with the signs of age that reminded her to be gentle with him if she could.

'Shall I tell you what *I* believe? There never was any money from my unknown father, nor any clerk to deal with it, because you or Aunt Lou scraped together enough to pay for my college fees. I'm not moving from this spot until you tell me *truthfully* which of you it was.'

There was no chance that she would let him off. A Southwark childhood and the rough and tumble of street games had taught her how to hold her ground, and she'd forgotten none of the lessons learned then. Her Italian father might have passed on to her his dark eyes and hair, perhaps even some of her sure artistic taste; but her stubbornness and pride hadn't come from Contini. William took comfort from the fact before accepting that a confession was now unavoidable.

'It was Elsie Manners who suggested the college and paid for it,' he finally admitted. 'She knew you'd get no sort of scholarship, but she was determined that you should have your chance. You were not to know, and she wanted no thanks.'

Kate was silent for a while. Then, with the tenacity of a terrier at a rabbit-hole, she returned to the earlier rigmarole that William was desperately hoping might now have been forgotten.

'I don't suppose you've ever even heard from my father since my mother died, but do you know where he lives?'

William's suddenly anguished face almost made her retract the question, but she'd asked for the truth and must accept it now.

'I don't know, and don't *want* to know,' he said slowly. 'Marguerite always insisted that he was ordered back to Milan by his father before they knew she was pregnant, but I was never sure whether that was true or not. All I'm certain of is that he destroyed her happiness and finally her life, because she couldn't go on living without him. There was no chance that he would return and marry her; his future was already arranged for him in Italy – that was why he went back.'

Kate looked for a moment at the truth: she was the bastard child of parents who had had no thought for her at all. It seemed to matter less, though, than the desperate despair of a woman she had no memory of. 'You mean the accident wasn't an accident after all?' she asked in a voice that scarcely trembled.

'The driver of the bus maintained that she just stepped off the pavement in front of him. I think I believe him.'

'You should have told me the truth before,' Kate suddenly shouted. 'I've been feeling grateful to my father for the money . . . I should have been *hating* him instead.'

'The right moment for telling you never seemed to come,' William said miserably. 'We moved to Southwark, and just explained that you'd been orphaned. At the time you were too young to understand and then the longer I left it, the harder it seemed to become. But Lou always said that once you needed your birth certificate you'd realise that Contini didn't marry your mother.' He stared at his granddaughter's white face and thought that the past refused to die – its power to haunt and hurt the present seemed to be never-ending. 'You're illegitimate in the eyes of the law, my dear, and you've had to do without parents,' he admitted, 'but you've been greatly loved for all that. It's why Elsie thought of the nest-egg story – she was afraid you'd refuse her help otherwise.'

Kate nodded, and then leaned forward to lay her hand against his cheek. It was a gesture she'd used since she was a very small child, and now it made him want to weep.

'I think we'll forget about the Continis . . . I'd much rather be a Cavendish.' Then she stood up and managed to smile. 'You'll be feeling better, I dare say, now *that* skeleton's not rattling in the cupboard any longer!'

He wanted to ask her not to go and talk to Elsie, but decided that it would make no difference whether he asked or not. It was a long time since she'd let anyone else tell her what to do.

But, knowing that her friend would come home late and tired after a long dress rehearsal, Kate went for a walk instead. Once through the archway that separated the Walk from Thrale Street, she was in the thick of Southwark's noise and bustle. The High Street was the usual seething mass of traffic, but its air was heavy with familiar, unexpectedly rural smells – fruit and vegetables from the Borough Market, and the warm, yeasty aroma of the hop warehouses. She stood for a while looking across the river, pierced by a sudden shaft of memory. Just here she and William had stared at the smouldering ruins of the City. Its skyline was altered now, and there remained many painful gaps, but at least St Paul's still heaved itself up into the clouds like a great, grey whale. Tired of walking at last, she came back to the peaceful precinct of the cathedral and sat down to think about a young mother's wasted life, and an unhappiness so despairing that even a child of her own hadn't seemed worth staying alive for.

A late gleam of sunlight caught the grey tower in front of her, and suddenly her strained face relaxed into a smile. Her angel was still there, wings pointing the way to heaven. A child she scarcely now recognised as herself had sat here, talking to a friendly young man. His name had been lost in the byways of her memory until she'd glanced at a treasured old theatre programme the other day. It starred Jeremy Barrington, the great man who'd taken the trouble to respond to William's congratulations. But this time another name in the programme had registered with her – the sets and costumes had been the work of someone called S. A. Maitland.

Elsie was trimming the Emperor's nails when her visitor

arrived the following morning. She still looked short of sleep, but for once unharassed and serene.

'No disasters at the rehearsal last night?' Kate guessed.

'The lights failed, and the leading lady had to be prompted three times, but no disasters of *my* making,' Elsie admitted.

The Emperor, a tabby of immense proportions and awesome dignity, abandoned his toilette to settle himself on Kate's lap. She scratched the spot on his back that he found difficult to reach himself, while she considered what she'd come to say. Elsie watched her downbent head and decided to say it herself.

'I suppose that fool Milly let the cat out of the bag. I was afraid she would, sooner or later. I didn't *tell* her about the college fees but she saw some receipted bills on my table, and made an intelligent guess for once.'

Kate lifted her head, and fixed large questioning eyes on a woman who managed to sound as if she'd been caught out in some shameful misdemeanour.

'She dropped a hint, without meaning to. I wormed the rest out of my grandfather,' Kate said briefly.

Elsie pushed sliding spectacles higher up her nose and gave a snort of disgust. '*Everybody* talks too much . . . simply can't keep their mouths shut at all.' She clamped her own thin lips firmly together and glared at Kate, who suddenly began to smile.

'It's no good, Elsie dear; you can't stop *me* saying my piece either! I shan't ever be able to thank you properly for lavishing your life's savings on me, but at least I must try. I shall always be so . . . so *very* grateful, and as soon as ever I can I'll—'

'Pay it all back, I suppose,' Elsie interrupted fiercely. 'Well, you just listen to me, Kate Cavendish. That was a

gift, and I won't have it thrown back in my face like . . .
like some rotten kipper.'

The affronted Emperor was suddenly dumped on the
ground so that Kate could get up herself. Elsie didn't
normally accept demonstrations of affection, but for once
she was overruled and enfolded in a loving hug. Then Kate
smiled rather tremulously.

'I also got the rest of my history out of William. Did *you*
know about it? I suppose you must have done, you've lived
in this house so long.'

'Yes, and I knew your mother as well – she was a pretty,
graceful thing, engaging and sweet and not very intelligent.
I saw her with Contini several times and knew there was
much more to it than Fanny ever supposed.'

'William said yesterday that she . . . she wanted to
be killed.'

'I dare say. Her lover was gone, and so was her dancing
career. A child born out of wedlock was something to be
hushed up twenty years ago so she was desperate to escape
from London; but I doubt if Fanny's Bible-thumping relatives were much help to her; she hated them *and* Edinburgh.'
Elsie stared at Kate's pale face, and gave it a brisk little
pat. 'It's done with, child . . . no good weeping over it, or
wishing you could run Hamlet's bare bodkin through the
man who fathered you. His blood is in you whether you
like it or not, *and* his talents, whatever they may have been.
You're anything but a fool, so you won't value yourself any
the less for having no legal father.'

Kate gave a faint wry smile. 'Are you going to say that
other people won't value me less either? I doubt that, Elsie
dear – I'm afraid it's still customary to be legitimate!'
Then, to her friend's relief, she put the awkward subject

aside. 'Before I left college I went through a list of theatre vacancies. The Birmingham Rep needs a design assistant, and I need practical experience. If they'll have me, I think that's where I'll make a start.'

'You'll be worked into the ground, paid a pittance, and robbed by some provincial landlady,' Elsie observed. 'I could probably hear of something going nearer home.'

'Thank you, but it's time I began to stand on my own feet,' Kate said firmly. 'Aunt Lou needs a rest from looking after me as well, but I shan't stay away for ever, because London's where I belong.' Then she grinned at Elsie. 'What did you think of my Lady Macbeth dresses, by the way?'

'*Very* splendid, but I pity any poor actress who had to lug them round the stage. You might give a thought to *that* in future!'

'There you are, you see . . . the voice of experience . . . *exactly* what I need to learn.' She dropped a kiss on her friend's cheek, bowed to the Emperor, who watched her with one baleful eye open, and finally went home to write a letter that a theatre management in Birmingham would be unable to resist.

Three weeks later she left Paradise Walk for the first time in her life, sent off by the rest of the inmates as if she were going not merely as far as the Midlands but to Ultima Thule itself.

Sitting in the train on top of an old gaberdine raincoat that smacked too much of schooldays, and trying to look well-accustomed to travelling alone, she felt very lonely. She didn't want to go to Birmingham at all, and Falstaff's question, reasonable enough to any dyed-in-the-wool Londoner, kept fitting itself to the rhythm of the wheels. 'What a'devil doest thou in Warwickshire?' She fought down panic and tried to find an answer. It had been time to venture away from Paradise Walk . . . to take stock of herself, and of what she now knew about the past; and a repertory theatre founded by the great Sir Barry Jackson was just the place to start the brilliant career she was planning on.

Feeling calm enough at last to read, she opened the newspaper William had thoughtfully provided for the journey. The theatre page informed her that Angus Macdonald's record-breaking production of *Henry V* was at last ending its run. He was to start work in Stratford, and Jeremy Barrington was being lured away from London too. New York would see him play alternately Shakespeare's and Shaw's partner to the Egyptian queen. Kate stared out of the train window, down which, appropriately enough, sad raindrops were now trickling. The golden-voiced man who still haunted her dreams would act Shaw's world-weary Caesar wonderfully enough, but he'd been born to take the part of Mark Antony.

The early-autumn sun glinted on Manhattan's glass towers, and flung swathes of brilliant light along the caverns down below. Jeremy had been there for several months now and could scarcely call to mind the shabby old city he'd left behind. Its wounds and shortages seemed unreal in a brave new world like this one, where nothing was in short supply and nobody seemed tired or disenchanted. He'd found it intoxicating to begin with . . . something to be proud of, too, that an Englishman could make even hard-nosed New York critics dust off their superlatives. To begin with – then one day when he heard himself say yet again how much he loved being there, he knew it was no longer true. He was getting very homesick for grey and rainy London.

In this melancholy frame of mind he was taken to still another cocktail-party, and heard amid the drawling Yankee voices around him a clipped English accent. It was his hostess speaking – Mrs Jacob Stein – and he called to mind what he'd been told about her. She'd arrived as Margot Sheridan with her schoolgirl daughter at the beginning of the war – already a widow, because Nicholas Sheridan had killed himself spectacularly driving a very fast motor-car. Young and beautiful enough to attract a lot of attention, she'd chosen to marry a middle-aged millionaire. Jeremy saw smiling at him now a woman whose perfectly groomed elegance only wealth could provide, but Margot Stein's welcome was warm and sincere.

'I did so want you to meet my daughter, Anna, as well,' she said. 'She's an actress too – rehearsing out of town at the moment. I know . . . come for Thanksgiving dinner – that's a holiday that even actors are bound to be given.'

He accepted the invitation, and was then accosted by his host, who pointed to the untouched glass in Jeremy's hand.

'You don't care for cocktails, I see. Come next door and I'll give you a decent drink.'

He was led out of the rich, crowded room into Jacob Stein's own sanctum – a place where real work was done because it was almost spartan in its furnishing except for one small, perfect landscape hanging where it could best be seen.

'A little piece of self-indulgence,' Mr Stein explained, pointing to the Sisley that Jeremy stared at. 'If a thief tried to rob me of it I think I should probably kill him!' He smiled as he said it, leaving no less an impression that what he said was true. The smile rearranged more pleasantly features that were ugly in themselves but redeemed by intelligence and humour. All in all Jeremy thought his host looked a very formidable man.

'I shall be unpopular for hiding you away in here,' Jacob said, pouring Matthew Gloag whisky into old, hand-cut glasses. 'But I thought you might need rescuing – adulation can grow very wearisome.'

It was something a millionaire might be well placed to know, Jeremy thought, but instead of saying so he waved the word away with a modest gesture.

'No one would complain of being received with the sort of kindness I've been shown here, and I'm afraid actors thrive on praise!' He smiled with unexpected sweetness, and sipped the best whisky that he'd ever tasted, while Jacob Stein watched with a connoisseur's ungrudging pleasure a guest possessed not only with male beauty to a rare degree but charm of manner as well.

'Will you be staying on after the run of these two plays?' he asked. 'I'm sure you could take your pick of offers.'

'I'm going to Hollywood – I'm not sure why except that making at least one film seems to be something one has to do. After that, I shall go home.' Jeremy looked up and met Jacob Stein's interested gaze. 'Perhaps that sounds ungrateful – stupid even, when so many advantages seem to be *here*. But I miss my old friends, and whatever else London lacks at the moment it isn't theatre quality.'

'I wouldn't call anyone stupid who wanted to go back there,' Jacob said quietly. 'It's a place I have a great fondness for.'

They were still smiling at each other when Margot Stein

came into the room to find her guest, and end the conversation.

Jacob had to be absent from his wife's Thanksgiving dinner, but when Jeremy went again to the huge apartment overlooking Central Park, Margot's daughter, Anna Sheridan, was there. He thought she made more of less than her mother's perfection of feature, perhaps because she was an actress trained to make the best of herself. Her colouring was remarkable too – a mane of red-gold hair, white skin, and eyes of a darker blue than usual. Careful not to play the part of the established star condescending to a beginner, Jeremy had reason to be thankful for this when it turned out that she wasn't a beginner at all.

'I know *you're* in the business too,' he said with a charming smile, 'but . . .'

'You haven't seen my name on Broadway,' she calmly helped him out. 'We open with an out-of-town try-out, next week – something new and rather heavy for me . . . Strindberg's *Miss Julie*. Your prayers are asked for!'

'When you come to New York I shall eavesdrop at a rehearsal if you'll permit me to; otherwise I shall never get to see it at all.'

She nodded and smiled, and seemed happy to remain with him after dinner, but he had the strange and disconcerting certainty that it wasn't because she was personally interested in *him*.

'The *New York Times* critic saw your last play in London and went wild over it. He was also rather ecstatic about Angus Macdonald's direction.'

'Then I hope he made a complete job of it and commended the sets as well; he should have done. They were by another good friend of mine, Sam Maitland.'

She seemed not to be interested in Sam's contribution. 'You're a friend of Macdonald's?'

'We served together for a time during the war. More truthfully, *he* served and I muddled through, thanks to him!'

'I knew him here,' she suddenly confessed. 'After he was wounded and taken off active service he was sent to Washington to do some liaison work with the US Navy, but he spent all his spare time visiting New York theatres. My step-father liked to entertain anyone from England, so we might have met anyway; but I was playing my first real part – Irina in *The Three Sisters* – and Angus came backstage afterwards. It had been a dreadful production, he said, but I'd been quite good!'

Jeremy's shout of laughter made heads turn towards them, but for the moment they had forgotten the other people in the room. They were engrossed in their private world of the theatre. 'Poor Anna . . . it sounds *exactly* like him, and I can tell you that he hasn't changed. He's still the same awkward, stubborn Highlander, with an unfortunate habit of being almost always right.'

'He wasn't right about me,' she said ruefully. 'We fell headlong in love almost at a glance, and got engaged. I had it all perfectly worked out – I was going to become the darling of the New York stage, and Angus would direct plays here or write his own. Jacob thought it all happened too quickly – we should wait six months and marry on my twentieth birthday, but by then the war was over and it wasn't perfect at all. Angus only wanted to go home, and I refused to give up New York. We had a huge row, and that was the end of our brief little love-affair. I haven't heard from him since.'

'Poor Anna,' Jeremy said again quietly. 'I knew he'd finished up the war over here, but he's never talked about you. He's become a fiercely self-sufficient man, and perhaps the broken engagement explains why. Women find him a challenge, of course, but the dear things flutter their wings in vain – I doubt if he even notices them.'

Anna's mouth curved in a faint, sad smile. 'He used to say that one day he would make a great stage play out of Henry James's novel *The Portrait of a Lady*. He promised not to give the part of Isabel Archer to anyone but me. I suppose he's too busy now to even think about doing it.'

Jeremy felt glad to be able to give her news that might dispel the shadow in her beautiful blue eyes.

'Not according to Sam Maitland, who works with him most of the time. Sam kindly keeps me up to date with all the gossip, and his last letter mentioned that very thing. Angus has begun work on the book – which means, for a start, cutting out about half of it. I dare say he'll do that brilliantly, never using two words himself where one will do.'

Anna nodded, but seemed to be staring into the past at the young man Angus had been and the headstrong young girl he'd fallen in love with. Then she refocused her gaze on Jeremy. 'I know you're going to California soon, but will you be blessedly kind and . . . and keep in touch? I should be so grateful to have news of Angus. It's important to me to know what becomes of him.'

He solemnly agreed to relay Sam's bulletins, and wondered whether for all these past months Angus had been hoping that he would also render the same service about Anna. If so, it would be just like his Highland friend never to have mentioned the fact to him.

At Margot's invitation, he became after that evening a frequent guest at the Stein apartment. It was flattering to rub shoulders with the rich and the mighty who congregated there, and it amused him to regale Sam Maitland with his progress through the higher reaches of New York society. But he'd left Manhattan and was working in Hollywood in the spring of the following year before he could give Anna news about *The Portrait of a Lady*. Angus was ready at last to cast his dramatised version of it, and Sam was already beginning to sketch Isabel Archer's wonderful Victorian dresses.

Chapter 4

Birmingham might have been a million miles away and all about them instead was a landscape clothed in the brilliant colours of spring. Kate turned to smile at the young man beside her.

'The Malvern Hills on a fine April morning!' Gilbert Forrest said with a wave of one hand. 'Nothing on God's good earth could be lovelier.'

She didn't mind agreeing with him, but registered a small objection. 'All the same, it's rum to have England's beauties pointed out to me by an American.'

'Not rum at all,' Gilbert insisted. 'You take them for granted; I'm still getting used to them.'

He was staring at the gentle folds of hill and valley around them – a charming American actor who was getting so used to England that four years after the war he'd come to fight in had ended he was still determined not to go home. She looked at him with affection, thinking that about Gil Forrest there was no deception, no unpleasant surprise to be discovered. He *was* the man he seemed, and he'd been her friend ever since she'd arrived in Birmingham.

'I used to think the "country" was just for all the poor things who didn't live in London,' she confessed, 'nothing to do with me at all. I never admitted to my friends at school that I hadn't been born there – I longed to be a proper Cockney, the same as they were.' Then she gestured to the springing greenness all around them. 'It seems less important now.'

Gilbert was looking at her now, still disinclined to believe that he could have been unaware of her existence six months ago. Nothing had warned him one wet September morning – no pricking of his thumbs, none of the actor's breathlessness waiting to go on stage – that Kate Cavendish was about to fall into his life. She'd done just that, tripping over a cable in her haste to fetch or carry something.

'Everything seems *more* important to me now, not less,' he said simply.

She flushed, but frowned at the same time, aware of being inexperienced for the situation she found herself in. Male students at the college had got short shrift from her; daft, soft creatures she'd thought them, who'd have done better to remember why they were there; it certainly wasn't to keep trying to distract *her*. But Gilbert Forrest wasn't daft, and she had been aware from the beginning that their friendship was important to him.

'Gordon isn't going to renew my contract,' she said suddenly. 'It's no surprise . . . we haven't exactly hit it off.'

'How could you have done? He's a little, vain, averagely talented man who's afraid you're going to run rings round him.'

She smiled with pleasure at the compliment but allowed something for partiality. 'I can't run rings yet, but I might do later on. My trouble is that I argue with him, and he thinks I'm only there to be his willing slave.'

Gilbert watched her, thinking that she'd lost weight working for Gordon Fleming. She was driven too hard, and probably didn't eat enough of the wretched food her landlady supplied. He'd regretted the cutting of her long, brown hair soon after she arrived but she said it got in the way. Now that he was used to it cropped as short as a boy's, and slightly curling, he liked the way it revealed the shape of her head, and slender neck. Thin as she was, she was nothing like a boy, and his eyes lingered as usual on her mouth. A little mole above her upper lip always seemed to be directing his attention to it, but he hadn't tried to kiss her yet; she was a girl to be gone slowly with.

'I remember your first appearance as Gordon's slave,' he said abruptly. 'The dungarees you wore were several sizes too large for you, and your face was streaked with dust. I had the feeling you'd been weeping.'

'I had – with rage! Instead of helping to design splendid beautiful sets, I spent my first week in the store, crawling round stacks of dusty old flats looking for bits of Elsinore Castle that Gordon insisted were there. It would have been far quicker to make and paint a new one.'

'Since when you've put in the sort of working day that would bring an automobile factory out on strike. Actors in fortnightly rep have to work hard enough, but this is the first full day *you've* had off since you arrived. I should have let you sleep, not dragged you all the way out here at break of day.'

Kate smiled and shook her head. 'Dear Gil . . . I think it was very good of you to bring me; I needed a little change from Birmingham.'

He was accustomed now to the rapid changes of mood that her conversation reflected. Being with her was like being on one of Chesterton's merry, mazey, English roads . . . you might end up in Beachy Head instead of Birmingham.

'What will you do next?' he asked. 'Go home and take a rest with your grandfather?' He'd been told about William, and the great days at the Swan, and didn't understand why she smiled.

'I shall go home and find another job. Gramps hasn't worked for years, and he and Aunt Lou live on the small rents he charges his tenants next door. I have to pay my way, but having survived Gordon's baptism of fire, I think I'm probably worth employing now.'

But Gilbert wasn't smiling, and his hands suddenly gripped hers, warning her that she'd landed herself in a situation she wasn't prepared for.

'It's all wrong,' he burst out. 'You shouldn't be slaving away in cold, filthy basements for men like Fleming. I know I'm in the world of the theatre, but you shouldn't be, Kate. You should be looked after . . . cherished as my mother is cherished back home. My father's a dull sort of man, you might say, but he owns a fine factory in Westchester County. He's hard-working and upright, and greatly respected, and I guess he hopes one day that I'll get the theatre bug out of my system and be content to learn how ball-bearings are made! How do you feel about ball-bearings, sweetheart?'

'I hope you never do any such thing, Gil. You're too good an actor for that – I've heard our Great Director say so!' Kate insisted earnestly.

His hands released her, but only so that they could cup her face, and she could feel them trembling. She was conscious suddenly that they seemed to be alone in an empty world. Any moment now, carried along on the excitement of that sense of isolation, Gil would do or say something she didn't want, couldn't deal with, was even deeply afraid of.

'You're wrong about me,' she said slowly. 'The theatre

is where I belong. My mother was a dancer before I was born, but she killed herself rather than live without a lover who deserted her and married someone else instead. I was given my grandfather's name, but it isn't really mine at all – my father was an Italian.'

Gilbert was an actor, trained to pretend to what he didn't feel and to conceal what he did. Even so she was aware of a change. His hands released her, and she knew he'd lost the urgent longing to kiss her. Probably the upright gentleman in Westchester County hovered in his mind . . . the good, dull man who cherished his wife and would be horrified at the thought of a bastard daughter-in-law. It was no surprise – hadn't she *told* Elsie that it was customary to have a father who gave his child a name? She didn't love Gil Forrest, although she liked him very much. She would have felt betrayed if he'd launched himself headlong at her. But it was shockingly painful to discover that he now no longer wanted to.

He smiled at her bravely, though. 'I'm sorry about your mother, Kate, and who cares whose name you've got? As soon as I can persuade some London management to take me on I shall follow you there. It's high time you introduced me to William and Aunt Lou, and I shall hate Birmingham without you.'

He did lean forward and kiss her then – a gentle, friendly kiss that raised no alarm in her nor any desire in him. It simply concluded a conversation that seemed to have brought them to a dead-end, and she was deeply relieved when he suggested that it was time they started walking again.

A converted warehouse – at least, what remained after it had been much reduced in size by a German bomb – had become

Sam Maitland's dwelling-place. He liked explaining to his friends that the Ward-of-Bridge-Without was packed with London's history, and although Angus Macdonald arrived looking unimpressed, the huge studio windows on the first floor kept him standing there, staring at the view.

'Beats your Bayswater Road hollow,' Sam pointed out with pride. 'All you see is a river of filthy, choking traffic; old Father Thames here changes mood and colour every time I look at him. Think of it, Angus . . . I live almost on the spot where Shakespeare crossed over every day to come to the Globe Theatre; I walk down Tabard Street and imagine the pilgrims setting off for Canterbury; and I patronise a local pub still called the Blue-eyed Maid! This is the real London, and I dote on it.'

'I hope you still dote on doing some work occasionally, as well. We haven't got time for you to sit mooning at the river.'

'I've made a start on the sets for *The Portrait of a Lady*, but there's a lot of other stuff on hand as well at the moment. A wardrobe-lady friend of mine insists that I need an assistant. I think she's probably right and, knowing dear Elsie Manners, she'll probably come up with one in due course.' Sam took off his spectacles and ran a hand through thick, springy hair that grew in tight curls like a lamb's fleece when he forgot to get it cut. He was more solidly built now than in student days, but it was the only change Angus could detect in all the years they'd known each other.

'I'm having difficulty with the costumes, as a matter of fact,' Sam suddenly confessed. 'It's no use seeing Isabel Archer in my mind's eye if the actress you finally choose turns out to be a different sort of girl altogether.'

'I'm having difficulty too,' Angus said with a touch of

grimness. 'There are half-a-dozen actresses who could play the part adequately, but speaking it is another matter. English women simply can't manage a convincing American accent. In fact, the business of casting the whole play is a nightmare. Daniel Touchett and his son, Ralph – both key roles – must sound as if they'd lived here for years, but *they're* still Americans from Vermont too.' Angus sounded irritable, and his dark frown blamed Henry James for making a director's lot so difficult. Then a rare, charming smile changed his face. 'Still and all, it's going to be worth it . . . I can't help feeling that it might just turn out to be rather a good play!'

After he'd gone, Sam frowned once more over the unfinished sketches propped up on his drawing-board, then put them aside for more urgent work. But he had to apologise for being behind-hand with it when Elsie Manners called on him the following morning. She looked critically round the huge room, then at him, and spoke her mind as usual.

'Disorganised, Sam . . . that's your trouble, and you also take on more work than one man can handle. I suppose you think that *your* late designs are still better than anything that arrives on time from other people.' Her severity melted into a faint smile. 'I dare say you're right – it's why everybody puts up with you.'

They put up with Elsie, too, he reflected, for much the same reason – she was simply the best at her job in London. His shy, sweet grin said as much, and then they got down to work. But later, when they were drinking the coffee together that Jeremy Barrington thoughtfully sent over from America to his still-rationed friends, Sam found himself describing Angus's problems with the new play. Elsie listened with interest, storing up the conversation for the dinner-table talk in Paradise Walk that evening. Meals there were still a communal affair – had been since Louisa took over the catering at the beginning of the war, in the belief that shared rations might seem to go further. The habit, like the rationing, remained; and the inmates of William's two houses had long since become one family. But tonight it was to be a celebration, because Kate was home from Birmingham.

William bemoaned her short hair, Milly her thinness. Lou said that clearly she'd been neglected as well as much put upon. Kate only smiled, and Elsie watched her, wondering why the others didn't comment on the only change in her that was important. The past six months in Birmingham had given her the confidence and poise she hadn't had before.

There was a great deal to talk about, but at last Elsie got the chance to air the subject of Macdonald's new play. William grandly brushed aside the casting problems.

'Every director thinks he has those, my dear. They solve themselves in the end, in my experience.'

Milly thought she could have played the part of Isabel Archer very well, but wistfully feared that she was a little too plump for it now. Percival brushed up his moustache and saw himself in the rôle of dashing Lord Warburton. Kate said nothing at all until they rose to go home, but then she asked Elsie quietly where Sam Maitland could be found.

'Not a million miles from here nowadays . . . I suppose you could even call him a neighbour since he's come to live on Wharfside. Why do you want to know – thinking of asking him for a job?'

'No . . . I've got a better idea.' Kate smiled at her friend, but for once didn't tell her what it was.

She dressed with care the next morning, remembering all too vividly herself an earlier impression that she hoped Mr

Maitland had long since forgotten – the dilapidated blazer, and dreadful, over-long cotton dress that had hung unevenly not far above her ankles, although memory kindly obscured the acid-drops. Elsie's instructions led her to Wharfside easily enough, and there no choice was necessary; for some distance all round, only one building seemed to be habitable – Sam Maitland certainly wasn't troubled by too-immediate neighbours.

The ground floor of what had been the warehouse was used, apparently, only for storage – an assortment of pieces of wood and stone, discarded doors, furniture, and steamer-trunks; anything that Sam had seen and thought might come in useful. But over the strange collection hung something altogether more exotic, because for generations before the war the warehouse had been a spice store, and the faint, pervasive odours of clove and cinnamon still scented the dusty air.

Smiling at the idea, Kate banged on the upstairs door. That was how Sam Maitland saw her again – a thin, smiling face under a cap of brown hair. It belonged to a slender, long-legged girl in a distinctly stagey velvet jacket and a patchwork skirt of as many colours as Jacob's coat. She'd toyed with the idea of wearing a feathered Robin Hood hat as well, left over from Birmingham's Christmas pantomime, but decided that it might be too much of a good thing. One should always know, as Aunt Lou was fond of saying, when enough was as good as a feast.

'I've seen you before,' Sam said at last. 'You've changed a bit since then, but you were playing truant from school.'

She returned his stare with interest, feeling less nervous about her mission now that he seemed familiar himself – the gold-rimmed spectacles and the shock of curly hair hadn't changed at all. But he'd smiled at her that day in the cathedral garden, and he wasn't smiling now; in fact they were still standing in the doorway, as if he were reluctant to invite her inside. 'I hope you don't mind my coming,' she said a little nervously. 'Elsie Manners told me where to find you.'

He gestured her in at last, but she had the strong impression that, although he might normally be a peaceable, unruffled man, she had made him angry by coming. It didn't seem a very promising start; still, she was there now and might as well be hung for a sheep as a lamb – another of Aunt Lou's invaluable sayings. Then she almost forgot everything else in wonder at the room she was shown into. The end of it that they were in was clearly his studio, full of drawing-boards and paints and rainbow-coloured swathes of material; the rest of it seemed to be sleeping and living quarters combined – a divan-bed hid under bright camel blankets, the armchairs looked deeply comfortable, and there were books everywhere. Best of all, along the width of the huge room windows looked directly out over the river.

'It must seem like living at sea,' she said with a tinge of envy in her voice.

'It suits me,' Sam said briefly. 'Now, shall I make a guess as to why you're here? Our mutual friend, Miss Manners, thinks I need an assistant. Had she warned me that she was going to encourage you to hurry round here, I could have told her that I'm much too busy at the moment to teach a student. I'm sorry if that sounds very blunt, but it would be more unkind not to tell you the truth.'

He disliked the idea of having his hand forced, and would have to tell Elsie so the next time he saw her. But for the moment he was faced by a girl whose expression he couldn't read, and whose silence was so disconcerting that he was forced to go on himself.

'Elsie never talks about her private life, nor even about where she lives; but I know it's here in Southwark, and you did say she told you where to come.'

Kate gave a little nod of her head, and even that gesture he found he remembered, although her cropped hair no longer needed tying up with shoelaces. Then at last she spoke.

'Elsie lives next door to us in Paradise Walk, but I'm not here about a job. I'll find my own when I want another one. You seem rather snappy about that, so you'll probably object to *this* as well, but she told us what you said about Angus Macdonald's new play . . . about the difficulty of casting it.'

'You've got a suggestion to make?' Sam enquired politely.

'Yes, I have . . . two, in fact. If Mr Macdonald can be bothered to travel as far as Birmingham he'll find an American actor called Gilbert Forrest playing there in the City Rep. Gil served in the US Air Force over here, but liked being in England enough to stay on after the war. He's a very good actor but he'd scarcely need to act the part of Ralph Touchett; except that he isn't dying of consumption, he *is* Ralph – kind and gentle and humorous.'

There was a long silence, but Sam Maitland's face had relaxed into pleasantness now. 'I'm sorry if I snarled at you to begin with. What's your second suggestion?'

'Well . . . well, I'm not quite so sure about this one, but Ralph's father *is* supposed to have been in England for thirty years, so I don't see why my dear William shouldn't make a lovely Daniel Touchett.' She saw the expression on Sam's face and hurried on. 'I know he hasn't appeared on the stage for years, but old actors are like circus-performers – they never lose their nerve or skill . . . only some of their stamina, perhaps; but this wouldn't be a very long part.'

'You seem to know the book very well,' Sam observed.

'It's one of my *best* favourites, so you can tell Mr Macdonald, if you like, that I shall be very critical of what he does to it.'

'I shall be sure to pass on *all* your messages,' he said gravely.

Her business there concluded, Kate gave another longing look at the view but could think of no excuse to linger, just to watch the river. She almost didn't hear what Sam said next.

'If you've had a job already, what was it? Were you in the company at Birmingham as well?'

'Not as an actress; I was the designer's – Gordon Fleming's – assistant. I needed theatre experience after getting my diploma, but I'd have to be starving to sign on with *him* again.' Her smile suddenly reappeared. 'He wouldn't have me anyway – we didn't get on!'

'A point in your favour, I should think,' Sam said judiciously. 'I've heard talk of him.'

He thought that what he was about to do next was to wish her good morning. Instead he heard himself say, 'I've always regretted not taking you home that day . . . to meet William and Aunt Lou. Will they be there if I come to call in Paradise Walk?'

'Of course . . . and my grandfather loves visitors, especially anyone connected with the theatre.'

'If I come tomorrow, will that give you time to draw me a sketch of a dress for Isabel Archer?' Her face was suddenly vivid with delight that couldn't be put into words, and she simply nodded and went away. But he had the impression that his light-filled room had grown a little darker, and across the span of years came back another memory. Kate Cavendish had left him once before, and then a cathedral garden had suddenly felt empty.

Chapter 5

On an April Sunday morning the Bayswater Road didn't deserve Sam's description of it. There was little traffic to negotiate, and on one side of it Kensington Gardens reminded city-dwellers joyously that the season was spring. Angus stared at a fountain of gold beside the path, and read its label in passing. They were indebted, it seemed, to an eighteenth-century, globe-trotting gentleman called William Forsyth for introducing this bright shrub to England. But Angus didn't care; he had more personal matters on his mind.

Damn Sam Maitland for inveigling him into saying that he'd go to Birmingham on what would turn out to be a fruitless journey; and damn him still more for another time-wasting promise – to interview the elderly and super-annuated actor who was his Southwark neighbour. But these were mere pinpricks of irritation beside the ordeal he was on his way to now; the telephone was an instrument of the devil, never giving warning of being about to ring and turn the world upside down.

He trudged morosely across the park into Piccadilly, and arrived at the stately entrance of the Ritz Hotel with five minutes to spare. It was something else to feel angry about; although he hadn't hurried, his heart was pounding and the palms of his hands felt damp. He wiped them on the rough tweed of his jacket just in time, because a moment later Anna Sheridan was coming down the stairs towards him. No longer pounding now, his heart seemed to stop beating altogether.

Four years ago, when not quite twenty, she'd been lovely, but not the head-turning vision she was now; he could see the other people in the lobby staring at her as well. She was an actress, for God's sake, he told himself savagely . . . enjoying an entrance and an audience. But her smile . . . oh, dear heaven, her slow, remembered smile.

'Dear Angus . . . it's so *lovely* to see you again, and to be back in London.' She sounded calm, and completely Americanised now – needlessly so, he reckoned, when both her parents had been English. With shining hair, and tended skin, and beautifully casual clothes, she looked a creature from a different world that knew nothing of rationing and shortages. That offended him, too – she had no damned right to make the London women around her seem shabby.

He found his voice at last. 'What brings you back now? A little shopping trip . . . just a stop-over on the way to Paris?'

She shook her red-gold head, and her smile said that she didn't mind waiting for him to get over such childish hostility. It rammed home the fact that she was managing this reunion better than he was.

'I came to *London*, Angus . . . to see *you*.'

'Unexpected,' he managed to say. 'I thought we'd agreed only to bump into each other by accident in future.'

Her eyes were fixed on him, registering changes in a face that had once been familiar to her – sensitive and interesting then, though never conventionally handsome.

It gave nothing away now and its lines were more deeply etched – she thought he probably frowned more and laughed less than before.

'You've been making quite a name for yourself; word of Angus Macdonald has reached us in New York.'

'Kind of you to say so, but I doubt if you came three thousand miles to tell me that I'm making progress.'

She was saved from answering by the appearance of the head waiter at their side, eager to conduct her in person into the dining room. It was a respite that she needed. According to Jeremy Barrington, Angus hadn't changed, but it wasn't true. The young naval officer, still limping from his wound, had been a different man – fun to be with, and so easy to know and fall in love with. *This* Angus Macdonald was an intractable man, glowering at the huge, pre-war-sized menu that offered a small post-war meal.

'We like to play this game over here – it's called keeping up appearances,' he explained sourly. 'Nothing has changed so long as we don't *admit* to any change.'

Uncharacteristically, Anna fidgeted with her handbag for a moment, then plunged into speech before he could ask her again what she was doing there.

'I met Jeremy Barrington in New York. My mother and step-father liked him, so we saw quite a lot of him before he went to Hollywood.'

'He mustn't stay there too long,' Angus commented. 'It's the ruin of any good theatre actor, and the theatre is where he belongs.'

'He used to pass on news of . . . of what was happening in London. He'd even heard from another friend that you'd finally managed to write the stage play you'd always wanted to make of that Henry James novel.'

There was a long silence before Angus spoke at last between gritted teeth. 'All my dear friends seem to have the unfortunate habit of talking too much. Do I understand *now* why you came hurrying to London? Surely not. The brilliant Anna Sheridan can take her pick of parts in New York.' There'd seemed the remote possibility for a moment or two that she'd come because she wanted to see him. Disappointment made his voice savage, not sad.

'She *can* take her pick, as it happens,' Anna agreed quietly, 'but she wants more than anything else in life to play the part of Isabel Archer!' A rueful, pleading smile suddenly touched her mouth. 'Do I get just one tiny good mark, dear Angus, for at least being honest with you?'

He lifted his shoulders – denial or agreement; she didn't know – but she risked putting a hand on his arm so that he would have to look at her. 'Four years is a long time; we've both moved on from being so unthinkingly young and in love that we believed life was certain to offer us nothing but happiness.'

'Four years is certainly a long time,' he agreed, 'but you've come all the same to remind me of a promise I made then.'

'No . . . I can't hold you to that promise now. But if you haven't already decided on an actress, will you at least let me read the part for you? I couldn't have done Isabel Archer justice four years ago, but I think I might be able to now.'

Her face was pleading and beautiful, and everything about her voice – accent, timbre, inflections – was absolutely *right*. Resentment could still wall up his stubborn heart, but his mind was working again. He might dread the danger of getting involved with her all over again, but to find the right, the only, Isabel, he must even be prepared for fresh hurt.

'A reading, if you like . . . just to see how it goes,' he agreed brusquely. 'And now for God's sake eat up your delicious Vienna steak. If you find yourself having to get used to food like this, it will bloody well serve you right for not knowing where you were well off.'

She picked up her fork, smiling at the strange object on her plate because it was almost certain now that she would win. No bitterness about the past would blind Angus to what was best for his play, and she would *be* the best; that certainty had brought her all the way to London.

Should she warn William of the true reason why Angus Macdonald was going to call on him? Kate debated the question anxiously in her mind until the very morning of the visit. Sam Maitland had been to Paradise Walk several times to listen to the reminiscences of a man who had his place in London's theatre history, and surely Macdonald – if he didn't lack all vestige of grace and humility – might also be expected to take a little interest in the past? In the end, Kate decided to advertise his visit in this way, rather than put into her grandfather's head the dangerous idea that he was about to be inspected.

As usual, William was turned out almost too nattily for the occasion. His wardrobe, left from the days of past success, identified him as a man who belonged to a world in which visitors had never dressed in shapeless tweed jackets and baggy corduroys. Kate stared at Macdonald's dark, reticent face and abandoned hope of grace or humility. He looked arrogant, impatient, and regretful of being there at all . . . not the sort of man to encourage her grandfather to make his best impression. Still, William began well enough by lavishing praise on 'a great – I think I might say flawless –

production of *Henry V*. And Mr Barrington's performance
. . . something to match the giants of the past.'

Macdonald's mouth twitched in a smile, but Kate decided
that she preferred him frowning. 'Your giants of the past
were often dreadful old hams, I'm afraid – ranting hard
enough to bring the gallery down about their heads!'

Ready to put this mistaken young upstart in his place,
William caught his granddaughter's imploring eye and
remembered that courtesy, however undeserved, was always
a guest's due. But from then on, it seemed to Kate, the
visit went from bad to worse. Macdonald spoke less
and less, William more and more – tacking between the
stagey grand manners of a bygone age and obsequious
agreement with anything Sam Maitland's taciturn friend
did bring himself to say. She thanked the gods above that
at least she hadn't mentioned Macdonald's present search
for actors; but then, as if plucking the thought out of her
mind, William's fancy suddenly lighted on a conversation
he remembered.

'You can put Hamlet into plus-fours, my dear sir, and
Macbeth into battledress – the Bard can survive what any
misguided idiot does to him; but it's a different matter with
what I understand you're now working on. Take the part
of Daniel Touchett, for instance – squarely in the Victorian
tradition you seem to despise; the actor who plays *him* will
have to understand that.'

Pleased with this final shot from his locker, William
glanced at his granddaughter, expecting an approving smile,
but her expression, instead, was agonised, while Sam
Maitland was staring at the floor. There was a silence that
no one seemed able to break, and it suddenly told William
why Macdonald was there. Kate saw her grandfather's face

change, and went to stand behind him, so that she could wrap her arms about his neck.

'Dear Gramps, I'm afraid a great director isn't obliged to take our advice,' she said as coolly as she could. 'We'll just have to wait and see whether he makes a mess of it or not.'

This time Sam forced himself into speech before worse could befall, and the speechless Angus gather sufficient breath to demolish both William and his granddaughter. With a vice-like grip on Macdonald's arm he steered him towards the door, mumbling that they were already late for another appointment.

In the silence they left behind Kate and William stared at one another.

'You put them up to that visit, child, and I played the scene very badly,' he said finally. 'Macdonald will have gone away thinking me a stupid old fool who doesn't understand that the theatre, like everything else, has changed.' He smiled as he said it, but she felt as if it had been her own, the soreness of his failure.

'Macdonald's the stupid one,' she shouted. 'He's arrogant and unkind . . . and certain to ruin *The Portrait* if he can't see that you'd make the perfect Daniel Touchett.'

Angry tears trickled down her cheeks and William sacrificed his carefully-folded silk handkerchief to wipe them away.

'No need to take on so, Katey. The truth is probably that I'm too rusty to start again. It's better this way . . . you and I can go on thinking how perfect I'd have been, and we shall never be proved wrong.'

She nodded reluctantly, trying to smile, and made up her mind that Sam Maitland could whistle for any more sketches. In future she'd have nothing to do with him, *or* his friend.

Outside in the street Angus stared into space as they marched along, apparently unaware of his companion. At Wharfside Sam broke the heavy silence only to offer some coffee, and assumed when he was followed up the stairs that his invitation had been accepted.

As visitors always did, Angus made for the windows and stood staring out at the river. Sunlight was a bright dazzle on the water, and the trees along the Embankment opposite edged it with brilliant green.

'She's an impertinent piece, your evacuee friend,' he said at last, using the Scottish word Sam had employed once before. The 'great director' gibe still chafed, Sam could see, but he thought Angus had deserved it.

'Think yourself lucky she didn't heave something at you instead. You scarcely went out of your way to put old William at his ease. I don't know why not . . . you're not usually so high and mighty.'

'It didn't occur to me that he'd have been told why we were there – *that's* what put the ghastly finishing-touch to it.'

'He *wasn't* told – neither by me, nor Kate . . . but I'm afraid he guessed in the end.' Sam disappeared into his galley at the end of the room to make the coffee. When he returned with a mug in each hand, Angus hadn't moved, and his face looked so tired and preoccupied that Sam spoke more gently.

'Here you are . . . courtesy of our distant friend, who occasionally remembers his starving colleagues in London. Would you rather be left in peace, or do you want to tell me what's wrong?'

The diffident question, so typical of Sam Maitland, made Angus turn and look at him. 'William Cavendish couldn't adapt to the style of playing I want . . . he was reared in a different tradition altogether, and I think he understands that. But I *could* have let him down more gently . . . I'm sorry I didn't.'

'Handsome,' Sam acknowledged with a faint grin. 'I'll tell Kate, if she ever gives me the chance.'

'You can also tell her something else. At least she was right about her American friend. I watched Gilbert Forrest give two performances and invited him to London on the strength of them. So that's one problem solved.'

'But not your worst one?'

Angus took a long time to answer. At last he said, 'I don't know whether it's solved or not. Someone from the past has suddenly turned up in London – thanks to Jem shouting from the roof-tops over there that I was casting *The Portrait*. Anna knew I'd do the play one day, and always wanted the part of Isabel Archer. She still does, apparently.'

'Anna . . . Anna *Sheridan*, do you mean? Broadway's darling, everybody's dream leading-lady? My dear Angus, what did you do to deserve her?'

'I offered to marry her once upon a time,' Macdonald said grimly, 'but our engagement foundered as quickly as it had come about. Anna refused to give up New York; I knew that I had to come back and get started over here. She still wants the part of Isabel, and I'm bound to say she looks and sounds perfect for it. But God knows whether I've done the right, inevitable thing in letting her stay, or been the worst kind of bloody fool.'

Sam had no opinion to offer, but he understood now the frame of mind that had made their visit to Paradise Walk so disastrous. Macdonald was a man who didn't take kindly to uncertainty – his own or anyone else's. On top of that, Anna Sheridan was probably not the kind of woman that a one-time lover could feel half-hearted about. If another thing that Angus was unsure of was whether he loved or hated her, getting this play ready for opening was going to be even more fraught with danger than usual.

'Remember what you said yourself a little while ago,' Sam suggested gently. 'We've got the makings of something very good.'

'Provided we don't "mess it up", of course!' Angus suddenly shook his dark head. 'No . . . I'm damned if we do, and give Kate Cavendish the pleasure of saying she told us so. First run-through next week, Sam, assuming that the cast is complete by then. You've got a lot of work to do if we're to open six weeks from now.'

'I'll manage – for the first time in my life I'm getting organised!'

Slightly comforted, Angus took away with him the knowledge that whatever his friend promised would somehow be delivered. But by the next day Sam's optimism was looking misplaced. He waited for the visit he expected, understood by the second evening that it wasn't going to happen at all, and on the third morning felt obliged to set off again himself for Paradise Walk. Irritation with Kate dwindled and died as he went under the archway from Thrale Street, because each visit there gave him renewed pleasure. The Walk's more obvious bomb-damage had been made good, and it had been spared a direct hit that would have ripped a hole in its lovely, shabby symmetry. Just as it had been built a hundred and fifty years earlier, it still looked today; and the people who lived in it were there because they belonged to the Ward-of-Bridge-Without.

Kate opened the front door to him and would have closed it again if her caller's foot hadn't been in the way. She was dressed in working overalls, and a blob of white paint had found its way onto her nose.

'My grandfather is out, and I'm extremely busy,' she said coldly. 'You're welcome to come in and entertain Aunt Lou if you like.'

'Thank you, but I'm not a performing flea, and it's you I need to talk to.'

She remembered that she'd stubbed her toe once before on this unexpected streak of cussedness in a man who looked and sounded persuadable. It seemed unfairly misleading that his voice should be so slow and gentle, and his smile so kind. She led him into William's conservatory, and he saw that she was in the middle of painting its battered wooden frames.

'A little more glass, perhaps?' he suggested helpfully.

'That comes next. What have you come for?'

'The other sketches . . . you promised them.' Her brevity was catching – he as well only seemed able to produce one sentence at a time. Most of his mind was engaged in thinking that she was absurd in her shapeless overalls, but touchingly gallant as well in the sharing of her grandfather's wounded pride.

'I changed my mind about the sketches . . . I'm sorry, I should have let you know.'

Sam moved towards her, pulled the paintbrush out of her hand and put it in a waiting jamjar. She was forced to look at him, and to register the fact that it would always be a mistake to underrate a man who insisted so little that he was formidable.

'Listen to what I'm saying, Kate. It wasn't Macdonald's fault that William guessed why we were here – it just happened. My friend gave one of your suggestions a try, but he had the right to turn it down if he believed it wouldn't work. Your other idea was more successful – Gilbert Forrest has been hired.'

Her stony expression relaxed into pleasure for a moment, but then hostility was back in place again. 'Your friend can do what he likes – he's the Guv'nor. But my grandfather served the theatre faithfully for longer than Macdonald has – that entitled him at least to respect.'

'Angus knows that; it's partly why I'm here – to apologise on his behalf.'

Kate considered this and gave a little sniff. 'It's *particularly* irritating to be apologised to – it quite takes the wind out of one's sails.'

'Maddening,' Sam agreed. She glowered at him, suspecting that he was laughing at her, but his mouth was serious, and so was his voice. 'Kate, I ought to be in the studio working hard, not talking you into a reasonable frame of mind. There are huge sets to be drawn, made and painted, and so many costumes to be ready in six weeks' time that even *I* must now agree that Elsie Manners is right . . . I need help badly. I don't know how awful you'd find me to work with, but I couldn't be any worse than your experience in Birmingham. What do you say to a six-week trial?'

She thought for a moment, then gave a firm little nod. 'I must finish here now that I've started, but I could report for work this afternoon.'

They shook hands solemnly on this arrangement and Sam left her to go back to William's woodwork. He loped back to the studio half-inclined to smile, and half-inclined to wonder whether he wasn't in the same boat as Angus, having been either clever, or very stupid indeed. To make up for William's disappointment as much as anything else he'd offered Kate a job. For years now, he'd chosen to think of himself as an observer of life, not a player in the hectic game, and he thought he could safely expect his new assistant to provide him with interest and entertainment. But even now he had the disconcerting suspicion that she might in the end provide much more than this.

Chapter 6

Beyond hoping that her path wouldn't cross Macdonald's very much, Kate embarked on her new job with no anxieties about the future. But when Elsie Manners was told about it, she looked thoughtful.

'What sort of man do you take Sam Maitland for?' she asked after a moment. 'Clever at his job, but otherwise not amounting to much in the exciting theatre world of tantrums and temperaments? Too ordinarily decent to be interesting?'

Kate considered the dry questions with care before she answered them. 'I take him for someone you approve of . . . that makes him unusual for a start! I'll let you know later on what else I think about him, although I can tell you now that he's not just clever; he's brilliant at his job.'

'Artistic Viennese mother . . . a singer who died young,' Elsie contributed briefly.

'Hence Samuel *Anton*, I suppose?' Kate hazarded. 'I wondered about that.'

'He mentioned her once – obviously adored her but doesn't have much in common with his father, who's a brain-surgeon in Edinburgh. The conversation's never been referred to again, so maybe he regretted telling me. No need for you to mention that I've told you, but it won't hurt for you to know that he's not as uncomplicated as he seems.'

Kate agreed that it certainly wouldn't hurt, but on the whole she foresaw no difficulties. In fact as the days passed she was enjoying herself too much to worry about anything at all. As Sam had said, there was an immense amount of work to do, but they could see it growing under their hands each day and knew that what was taking shape was good.

The theatre in St Martin's Lane that Macdonald's play was destined for was still occupied by another production, so Sam's sets were being constructed on the ground floor of his studio. Kate couldn't decide which of them she loved working on the most – the English country house and garden of the first act, the terrace overlooking Florence, or Isabel's final, grand apartment in a palazzo in Rome.

While the carpenter, Pat O'Donovan, hammered and sawed, she painted her way round the finished sections, according to Sam's designs. To add her mite of noise she sang cheerfully but rather out-of-tune all the Victorian music-hall songs that William had taught her as a child. She was embarking on 'My old man said follow the van' for the third time one morning when Sam descended the staircase, with coffee for them both, and to beg for a change of repertoire.

'If the songs of Marie Lloyd are all you know, I shall have to take you to hear some real music,' he suggested.

'They happen to be all I can sing,' she answered with dignity, remembering just in time that she wasn't to mention the Viennese lady who might have guided his own musical taste. Instead, she said, 'I can't decide which act is going to have the loveliest set, but each of them should make any right-minded audience gasp with pleasure.'

Pat O'Donovan sipped from his mug and grinned, and Sam found it hard to remember that he'd regretted the impulse to take Kate on. For once impulse had been right, and anxiety wrong; she worked until she had to be driven home at night, sketched costumes for him that showed exceptional flair, and so far hadn't argued with him at all. In fact, the truth of the matter was that he liked having her there. It was also clear that she was happy, and he supposed that the young American Angus had brought to London was the cause of that.

'Your friend getting on all right?' he asked. 'I gather from Macdonald that rehearsals are going well.'

She nodded as she picked up her paintbrush again. 'Gilbert still can't believe what's happened – instead of years of playing provincial second-leads, he's got a chance to make his name in the West End. Apart from that, he also thinks the play itself is very fine.'

Sam grinned at the reluctant afterthought, but asked another question.

'Have you told him how he came to get the part?'

'Of course not – in any case, he got it because he deserved to.' She spoke more sharply than she intended, but Sam persisted, and his next question was one that she took time to answer.

'Does he enjoy playing opposite Anna Sheridan?'

Kate carefully coloured in the sweeping curve of a garden balustrade on the backcloth she was painting. 'It's crucial to the story,' she said at last. 'They've got to enjoy each other.'

*   *   *

Within another week they had moved their fragile completed flats into the theatre, and were having to hurry on, now, with wardrobe work. It was the moment for Kate to meet Macdonald's chosen leading lady. Looking at Anna Sheridan, her first instinctive certainty was that he couldn't have found anyone who more perfectly embodied Henry James's beautiful, wayward heroine. Even in rehearsal clothes, this girl moved and looked and spoke like Isabel Archer, but in her dressing-room afterwards, examining the sketches Kate had brought, she sounded much more like a successful actress with wealth and high connections behind her. She approved of everything except the colour of her first-act dress.

'*Much* too insipid, I should have thought. Sam must change that for something more interesting.'

'That's how it's described in the text,' Kate pointed out with reason, 'white muslin, with black ribands – on account of her dead father, I suppose.'

Anna's smile faded. 'Text or not, I don't propose to make my first appearance in *that*, so please tell Mr Maitland so.'

'You need only tell me,' said Kate gently; 'it's my design.'

She was aware of having erred, and knew that she would have done better to hold her tongue. When it came to a pecking-order in the theatre, the designer's assistant was dust beneath the feet of the leading lady on whose shoulders the brunt of a production was to fall. The work of taking measurements went on, but it was done in silence unless words were absolutely necessary.

She went away warned by the incident, but described it amusingly to Gil Forrest the following evening. Whenever rehearsals broke up early enough he came to Paradise Walk to share their supper, and to add to it – much to the delight of Milly, who was always hungry – the contents of the food parcels that arrived from Westchester County. Afterwards more often than not he and Kate would walk down to Bankside, to watch the river flow past, and talk about the progress of the play. Tonight she was disappointed that he didn't seem to enjoy the story of her meeting with Anna Sheridan. His disapproval was as noticeable as the breeze that blew coldly off the river, reminding her that she couldn't feel quite confident now of this man who knew her history.

'Anna wasn't to know that you weren't just Sam's messenger,' he pointed out with what seemed to Kate to be unnecessary fairness.

'True, and in any case you don't think I ought to poke a little fun at the leading lady,' she suggested with a smile. 'Miss Sheridan is too important for that!'

Gilbert still wasn't satisfied that justice had been done. 'Too important to the production, but too nice as well, Kate,' he said earnestly. 'She's being wonderfully kind and helpful to me.'

'Then I shall make her look wonderfully beautiful,' Kate promised. She knew that she had just been reminded of something else: she was part of the theatre, and without the work that she and Sam and Pat O'Donovan and his crew did, there would be no production. But it wasn't they who had to bring a play to life, and actors couldn't help thinking the rest of them barely necessary.

She suggested that it was time to go home and for once Gil didn't disagree. He kissed her good night as usual, and smiled his shy, sweet smile. But the knowledge was in her mind, sharp as the prick of a swallowed fish-bone in her throat, that when he held her he was still Ralph Touchett imagining himself kissing the beautiful Isabel.

The six weeks Macdonald's schedule had allowed them shrank alarmingly. Small setbacks that could have been laughed at a month ago became full-blown disasters when opening night was less than a week away. Even sweet-tempered Pat O'Donovan was heard to swear when a stagehand put his foot through a beautifully painted canvas wall, and the chief electrician went about searching for maverick wires with the quiet frenzy of a man who knew the stars in their courses were fighting against him.

Sam surveyed his own kingdom, feeling reasonably sure that the play was going to look beautiful, and the costumes would be ready on time – thanks to Kate and Elsie Manners sewing for dear life in the wardrobe room. The sweeping Victorian dresses had required a great deal of making, but Anna would have no cause to complain about what she was given to wear. Too busy with his own problems to watch rehearsals, Sam merely caught occasional glimpses of Macdonald, looking tired and fine-drawn. That was normal; but there were things about this production that certainly weren't normal.

A typical theatre man would have found relief in talking about them, but that wasn't his Highland friend's way – Angus would have chosen torture, given a choice of that or the horror of having to explain himself. Then one evening when the theatre had at last fallen quiet, Sam stopped on his own way out to stare at the hugely enlarged photograph of Anna Sheridan, installed in pride of place in the foyer. It had been framed to resemble a real portrait, and she was wearing her third-act dress –

black velvet, collared with delicate white lace. Sam was aware of not having made up his mind about her yet, but one thing was certain – she possessed, pressed down and brimming over, that magnetic power to attract that all true actresses must have.

'Beautiful, wouldn't you say?' a voice behind him suddenly asked. When he turned round Angus was standing there, not frowning for once, and not smiling either. His face gave nothing away, but for lack of any evidence to the contrary Sam decided that he was being invited to be honest.

'Certainly she gives the illusion of great beauty,' he answered slowly. 'We both know that *that's* what matters in a theatre.'

Angus nodded, but seemed to have nothing more to say about Anna Sheridan. 'How is your mettlesome piece making out? My impression is that she climbs into a cupboard whenever she sees me coming. I suppose she thinks the play's a mess, but finds she hasn't got the brass nerve after all to tell me so.'

Only a man, Sam thought, immersed in his own affairs could take such an unlikely view of Kate Cavendish; still, he saw no point in saying so. 'She crossed swords with our leading lady once or twice,' he admitted instead, 'and she reckons you're not keen on having her here either. For the moment she's trying to stay out of trouble.'

'You didn't answer my question. Is she going to be any good?'

'She's good already,' Sam said with certainty, 'but she'll be better still with a little more experience. Added to that, she only has to smile at them and the most bloody-minded stage-hands turn into sweetly reasonable men. It verges on the miraculous!' He stared at Macdonald's face and decided to risk a question of his own. 'I haven't had time to stop and listen . . . are rehearsals going all right?'

'So well that if I'm not very careful I shall fall into the trap of thinking we can't fail next Thursday. Then I'll have a posse of theatre critics baying for my blood and it will damned well serve me right.'

'But the gamble has paid off,' Sam persisted. 'You were right to let Anna stay?'

'If we're still talking about the play, yes, I was right.'

'And if we're not?'

Macdonald's faint smile faded. 'Then the question becomes unanswerable. Leave it, Sam, and go home – poor old Bert Trotter's waiting to do his rounds and lock up.'

Since Bert spent the night in his basement cubby-hole at the theatre, it wouldn't have hurt to let him wait a little longer, but Sam accepted that he wasn't going to be told how matters stood between his friend and Anna Sheridan.

The next day, though, he thought he knew. The complete run-through of a play before the dress rehearsal was normally a brisk, mechanical affair – the cast deliberately saving themselves for the desperate exertions to come. It wasn't how Anna Sheridan tackled a run-through; for her it had to be played at concert pitch. Watching from the front of the house, Sam was aware of several things at once: even in rehearsal clothes and without a vestige of make-up on her face, Anna *became* Isabel Archer – beautiful, passionate, and doomed by her own nature to make the mistakes that would ruin her happiness. Whatever verdict the critics and the public might pass on Macdonald's play, they would have to marvel at the emotional charge of this performance. It was exactly what any other playwright-director would pray for . . . exactly what Angus himself would have asked of heaven above, except for one thing – he happened to be body and soul in love with the girl concerned. His face as he sat watching her gave him away once and for all, but he knew better than anyone else that she must be first, last, and always an actress. A lover or a husband might be remembered from time to time . . . enjoyed, even, between plays, when she wasn't otherwise engaged. Some men might find such a life tolerable, but not this all-or-nothing Highlander. Sam got up and left the auditorium, and thought Angus didn't even notice when he walked away.

The dress rehearsal went so badly that even the customary brave jokes fell flat. Missed lighting cues, fluffed lines, stage doors that either wouldn't open or wouldn't stay shut – all conspired to try everybody's nerves; and so that nothing should be lacking the young actress playing the part of Pansy, Isabel's step-daughter, rocketed into hysteria, having broken a sacred taboo by stepping through a doorway onto the stage with her right foot instead of her left.

It was the director's job to restore the morale of his tired and jaded company. Watching him set about it when he looked exhausted himself, Kate was obliged to admit to reluctant admiration for a man she'd found it easy to dislike.

Afterwards in the wardrobe room, putting to rights the disorder left by a hectic day, it took her a moment to realise that she was no longer alone. She might have expected Sam, but it was Macdonald propping up the doorway as if he

75

would collapse if he moved away from it. He didn't make a habit of visiting them, and she steeled herself to hear that the leading lady wanted still one more last-minute alteration.

'Sam sent Elsie home with a bad head. I can stay if something has to be done,' she said briefly.

'There's nothing to be done except go home yourself – you look like Orphan Annie in a thunderstorm.'

She remembered that she'd been in the theatre continuously for sixteen hours, had eaten very little, and given no thought to putting fresh lipstick on her mouth or tidying her hair. A bedraggled wreck was almost certainly how she looked, but she thought he might have managed not to tell her so.

'Nah if you'd tole me it was goin' to be inspection-time, Guv, I'd 'ave powdered me bloomin' nose!' The perfect mimicry of a Cockney stage-hand, half-comical and half-impertinent, made his mouth twitch, but she was too busy winding up reels of cotton to notice.

'It was a dreadful rehearsal,' he said next, 'probably what you thought I deserved. Don't spare me – I'm sure you reckon I've ruined *The Portrait*.'

She was forced to look at him, registered his extreme fatigue, and was surprised by the rueful smile that seemed to be asking her for reassurance. From the recesses of her own tired brain she dragged the memory of his visit to her grandfather. The arrogant stranger who had come to Paradise Walk was scarcely this depleted man who stood in front of her now.

'The rehearsal doesn't matter,' she said gravely. 'You've made a fine play out of a great novel – that's quite enough to have done.'

He didn't answer and they stood staring at one another

until at last he nodded, accepting what she'd said. Then he spoke, more roughly than he meant to. 'It's after midnight. Leave those bloody cotton-reels alone and go home. That's an order from the Guv'nor.'

She nodded in her turn, and finally he pulled himself upright and walked away. But when Sam came to collect her for their shared taxi-ride back to Southwark she was still standing at the work-table, doing nothing at all.

Angus climbed the stairs to the dressing-rooms, calling good night to anyone still there. Anna's door was half-open and the lights were still on. When he went in, she was out of costume but sitting at her make-up table as if she couldn't bring herself to leave.

'I asked Gilbert Forrest to see you home,' Angus said sharply. 'Why are you still here?'

She smiled at him in the mirror. 'Don't blame Gil – he was touchingly anxious to take care of me, but I declined with as much gratitude as I could manage.' Her voice trembled and her hands were suddenly lifted in a little gesture of appeal. 'Dear Angus, I needed *you* with me, not that very charming American.'

As always when she managed to get through his defences, Angus told himself that she could no more stop performing than she could help breathing – it came naturally to her. But there was nothing contrived about the exhaustion that shadowed her huge eyes, and made her skin seem transparently pale against their blueness.

'I know the rehearsal was a mess,' he said with rare gentleness, 'but there's nothing to worry about. You are sublimely wonderful in the part, and I'm even assured by Sam's Southwark waif that the play is all right as well!' He smiled at the memory of that conversation in the wardrobe room, and Anna knew with a sharp stab of jealousy that he was remembering something about Kate Cavendish that had pleased him.

'It must, of course, make us *all* feel much more confident that an inexperienced assistant approves of what we're doing,' she agreed sweetly.

Macdonald's raised dark eyebrow was a wry exclamation. 'Only a small joke, Anna . . . you weren't meant to take it seriously.'

She stood up and held out her expressive hands to him this time. 'Sorry . . . did I sound *very* bitchy? It's because I'm very tired, and still rather apprehensive about tomorrow night, no matter what our little below-stairs oracle says.'

Angus took hold of her hands because he couldn't help himself. Success or failure tomorrow depended to a large extent on her, and she was entitled to be on edge, or downright unreasonable if she chose.

'Of course you're tired, my dear, and now your equally apprehensive director is going to take you home.'

The short journey back to Anna's Chelsea apartment was made almost in silence, but at her front door she emerged from thought to smile at him.

'A nightcap, Angus . . . just one small glass of whisky?'

'Thank you, but I think not – I should probably fall asleep with it still in my hand. I shall take myself back to the Bayswater Road that Sam despises so much!'

'There's no need to – you could try Cheyne Walk and see if you like that better?' she suggested softly.

He stared at her in the discreet glow of the hall lights, uncertain of what she was offering until her slow smile confirmed it for him. They had been carefully formal with each other ever since she'd arrived in London, but now her hands suddenly fastened themselves round his neck and her mouth was very close to his. It was four long years since he'd felt her melt against him, and now it was more than flesh and blood could bear not to pull her into his arms and kiss her smiling lips. His body seemed to be disintegrating with sheer longing for her, but some small remnant of common sense said coldly in his mind that this wasn't the moment to give in to raging desire. He lifted his head and managed to put her away from him.

'I think I'm being turned down,' she murmured. 'Let that be a lesson to you, Anna my girl!'

Angus tried to smile, but the smile went awry. 'You'd tempt a hermit-saint,' he said unevenly, 'but I make it a rule never to sleep with my leading ladies just before opening night.' His hand beneath her chin forced her to look up at him. 'You *must* go to bed and rest, my dear, for at least the next twelve hours. I shall see you at the theatre tomorrow evening, and then God please help us all.'

Chapter 7

Anna went very early to the theatre the following evening, according to her habit of arriving in time to think herself into the character of the woman she was soon going to have to become. It was easier with this rôle than any other she'd known – proof that she'd been entirely right to come to London, and that her mother and step-father's objections had been entirely wrong.

For once her mind was less than biddable; it insisted on hurrying on ahead. The immediate great adventure was enough to think about, but she couldn't help dwelling on how she intended the evening to end. To pretend that everything was normal she leafed through the pile of well-wishing telegrams and cables waiting on her dressing-table, but even here all was not as usual after all. There were charming greetings from Jeremy Barrington, still in California, but for the first time that she could remember no message from Margot and Jacob Stein. It was so hurtful that she couldn't allow herself to think about it now; for the moment all that mattered was becoming the woman that Henry James and Angus had created.

Outside the quietness of her dressing-room the theatre was gradually coming alive. The excitement of opening night, different and unmistakable, was beginning to float like a shimmering mist into every backstage nook and cranny. It was in the voices of the people she could hear calling to one another, and in the air they breathed, adding an intoxicating new chemical to the old, stale atmosphere. In an hour or two it would even spread to the front of the house, and the people starting to take their seats would be infected by it as well.

Everything had been left in readiness by her dresser – make-up laid out, first-act gown waiting to be slipped into. It was the one Kate had had to change – no white muslin now, but a dramatically skirted dress of grey taffeta shot with mauve, iridescent as a pigeon's wing. It was Anna's favourite among all those she had to wear, but she had seen no reason to tell Kate so.

A knock at the door seemed to be what she'd been waiting for, but the man who stood there wasn't the one she needed to see. Sam Maitland shyly offered her the posy in his hand – orange rosebuds rimmed with gold and sparkling with tiny water-drops.

'Just to wish you a triumphant night, Anna,' he explained diffidently, when she looked at the flowers and then at him.

'I'm taken by surprise,' she said at last. Her charming smile removed offence and for the first time he could see how easily she might ensnare a man. 'Dear Sam, I've always had the impression that you didn't quite approve of me! I'm being honest, you see, so you can be as well.'

Sam removed his spectacles and stared at them, feeling rather at a loss. But still, Anna had invited frankness.

'I couldn't make up my mind whether you'd come to be a help to Angus or a torment to him,' he admitted finally. 'He and I have been friends a long time, so I was bound to be thinking of him, not you.'

He had no idea what he would say if her next question asked whether he'd now decided one way or the other; but he was saved from this dilemma by the arrival of Macdonald himself. Sam smiled thankfully to his friend, saluted Anna, and hurried away, taking with him the impression that the atmosphere in the hot, bright, little room had suddenly become charged with electricity.

'Roses from Sam . . . so sweet of him,' Anna said, vaguely waving the posy in a gesture quite unlike the usual controlled grace of every movement she made.

Macdonald's rigid face relaxed a little. 'I believe they have to be put in water, if you're trying to think what to do with them.' Then his voice changed. 'Darling Anna, I haven't brought you anything at all except my love, and every good wish and prayer in the world that I can think of.' His arms suddenly enfolded her and she could feel the steady beating of his heart. When he slackened his hold she smiled at him more tremulously than usual.

'*Just* the cue I needed! I've known ever since I got to London that I should have to say this sooner or later, although I didn't imagine I'd choose an hour before opening as my moment. But I know now what a fool I was four years ago – too young, too spoiled, and too inflexibly certain of what I thought I wanted.'

In the silence that filled the room Angus heard the busy noises of the theatre around them. It seemed to him that he should be out there among his people, doing a dozen things that might otherwise get left undone. But Anna, on whom so much depended, had decided to resurrect the past and lay it in front of them. She was waiting to hear what he would say, and the words came at last.

'My dear . . . nothing has changed, except that while

you have grown a little older I seem to have become as old as time. This production apart, your life is still in New York; mine is in this country. I can't do anything to alter that, even loving you as I do. So you see our equation doesn't work out now any more than it did four years ago.'

'You weren't listening,' she complained gently. 'I didn't understand then what really matters; now I do. I love working in London, but the truth is that it's mostly because I'm working with you.' She stood away from him a little, and smiled again. 'There . . . I've said it, and you who've grown so old and wise, my darling, don't have to say anything more at all.'

He had a split-second vision of himself answering her bravery with a grateful bow and a retreat back to safety. Even if she hadn't remained the only woman he had ever wanted, it couldn't be done. God alone knew whether the situation they were in would lead them to happiness or disaster, but they would have to go on with it now.

'Anna, shall we try again?' he asked gravely. 'Will you live with me and be my love, and send to the devil anyone who says that theatrical marriages never work?'

Her smile was radiant but her eyes filled with tears. 'I was afraid I'd been turned down for good last night! Oh, my darling, I'll send the rest of the whole world to the devil if you like.'

Macdonald's arms enfolded her again, but dropped to his sides as another knock sounded at the door. The messenger outside nursed a huge sheaf of flowers, and the card attached to them made her catch her breath.

'Oh, Angus, my mother and Jacob are *here* . . . in London for the opening! I was trying so hard not to feel upset because

I hadn't heard from them, and they've been planning this all the time.'

'Jacob's carefully timed little shot of adrenalin,' Angus said with a broad grin, 'just to get you over the hurdle of first-night nerves.'

Anna blew him a kiss. 'It can't compete with the shot I've just had, but it was dear of them all the same.' She was so alight with happiness that his own small worm of doubt turned over and died of shame. Then she held out her hands to him in a charming gesture. 'Will you promise not to misunderstand if I say that I feel sorry for all the people who were unable to get a seat in the theatre this evening?'

He kissed her hands before he let go of them. 'Of course I understand. They're bound to regret for the rest of their lives missing what they might have seen tonight.'

They smiled at one another, but the call-boy's voice outside shouting the half-hour made her expression change. It was time to become Isabel Archer.

'Dora will be coming to help me dress and I haven't made up yet, so you must go, my dearest.'

He nodded and walked out into the clamorous excitement that was reaching fever-pitch. For the moment even his renewed engagement didn't seem to matter. The play he'd agonised and sweated over was finally about to become a reality – to be exposed to curious public eyes, and left naked to the critics' knives. The memory of Anna's beautiful, confident smile should have been what reassured him, but he heard himself listening instead to the voice of Kate Cavendish gravely informing him that out of *The Portrait of a Lady* had been born a fine play.

There was nothing more for Kate to do . . . no small task

left to remind her that she'd had a share in a hugely exciting enterprise. The actors were paramount now, but even the crew – flymen, 'lights', and humble scene-shifters – still had parts to play; only she seemed to be entirely surplus to requirements. The thought was so mournful that it made her smile, and she told herself that this stage in a production was something she should have got used to by now.

She'd come to the theatre far too early, but another glance at her watch confirmed that time *was* crawling by; soon the call-boy would be making his first round of the dressing-rooms. 'Beginners – half-an-hour, please.' Gil would almost certainly be dressed and ready now, and perhaps grateful not to be left alone.

He managed to greet her when she went in, but she knew that it wasn't just his stage grease-paint making a stranger out of her dear, familiar friend. It was Ralph Touchett looking at her now, unable to conceal disappointment that she wasn't the girl his heart and soul waited for. She held out her gift all the same – it was what she'd come for, to give it to him and wish him well.

'It's just for good luck . . . nothing much,' she mumbled. 'I found it in a street market the other day.'

At last he stirred himself out of whatever paralysis held him still and opened the little package. Inside he found a black china cat, sprightly tail curled over its back, green glass eyes sparkling in the bright lights of the dressing-room. Gilbert's sweet smile reappeared for a moment, but then he looked remorseful.

'I'm a selfish heel, Kate. This is *your* first London show too, but I didn't remember to get *you* anything.'

'Mine doesn't count,' she said gravely. 'It's your big

night, and I'll be praying very hard that everybody realises
how lucky they are to be watching you.'

'I'm the lucky one,' he contradicted her, 'playing *here*,
opposite Anna, when I might have been stuck in Birmingham
Rep for years. I asked Angus once how he came to be there,
but he just said a friend had suggested he might find the
actor he was looking for.'

'And so he did,' Kate pointed out, smiling at him.

'Well yes, but it was getting Anna that really mattered,'
Gilbert said earnestly. 'I think we all realise that, but I'm
bound to understand it better than anyone else – because of
Ralph's closeness to Isabel in the play.'

Because he was besotted by a woman who absorbed
adoration as a sponge soaks up water, she might have
said, but she was saved by the call-boy's knock at the
door. 'Half-hour, please, Mr Forrest.'

'Soon be curtain-up; I must go, dear Gil, but I'll see you
when it's all over.'

She smiled at him wholeheartedly, but went away weeping a little in her heart for a friend who'd once come close
to believing that he loved her. But it was Anna who held him
mesmerised now. From sheer force of habit she wandered
back to the wardrobe room, only to find that it wasn't empty
as she expected. Sam Maitland was hovering there but, in the
unaccustomed glory of dinner-jacket and black tie, it took
her a moment to recognise him.

'You're looking very grand,' she complained, sounding
put out by the discovery.

'You too,' he said politcly, cvcn though it wasn't quite the
word for her. She looked simply, not grandly, beautiful. He
was accustomed to seeing her in shapeless, working overalls,
not in a sleeveless dress of coral-coloured linen, whose only

ornament was a sash of striped silk that was probably one of William's old ties. But it was Sam's expert opinion that his assistant had the rare quality of style. He thought he could guess why she also looked sad.

'As a matter of fact, I'm feeling a bit left over,' she confessed. 'Are you?'

He smiled at the typical turn of phrase, but sensed her feeling of loss. It wasn't Anna's fault that she'd bewitched Gilbert Forrest, but he couldn't help wondering whether it ever occurred to her to limit the damage she could do.

'We're both a trifle *de trop*, Kate,' he agreed. 'But our moment will come when the tabs open and the paying customers see Gardencourt in all its sunlit glory!'

She smiled, but faintly, and he tried again. 'There's distinguished company out front, by the way – Aunt Lou and Milly, flanked by your grandfather and Percival Pearce, sitting in the dress circle.'

Her eyes searched his face, but it was amused, not teasing. 'You mean they're all *here*? They've bought tickets without even breathing a word?'

'William thought it would be nice to surprise you by an informed discussion of the play at breakfast tomorrow morning. No tickets were needed, by the way – Macdonald invited them here.'

It was well-known that opening nights were emotional affairs. She hoped that might account for the fact that her eyes were suddenly full of tears. But then Sam himself made matters worse by putting in her hand a shabby little jeweller's box.

'Nothing compromising . . . don't go imagining it's a diamond ring,' he said hastily, seeing her startled expression.

She blinked her wet eyes and stared at what lay inside

the box – the tiny figure of a laughing boy sitting against a rock, boy and rock carved out of a piece of ivory no bigger than an inch square.

'No well-dressed Japanese gentleman would be seen without one dangling from the end of his sash,' Sam explained. 'Perhaps not a very suitable memento of our first working partnership!'

She smiled at him and licked at a tear that trickled past her mouth. 'It's . . . it's just about perfect, I'd say.'

For the first time in their acquaintance she felt shy of him, and unprepared for his knack of springing surprises on her. There was nothing showy about Sam Maitland; in fact she sometimes thought he'd deliberately decided never to compete with the colourful, temperamental creatures of the theatre, who needed constant attention as ordinary people needed air. But the truth was that he was quite as impressive as any of them in his own quiet way.

Then he suddenly disconcerted her again. 'Our trial run together is up, Kate . . . or had you forgotten about that?'

She examined his face and it told her nothing. 'Won't I do? Do you want to get rid of me?' The questions were jerked out of her and hurled at him because it was the only way she could ask them at all.

Sam took off his glasses, stared at them, and put them back on again. 'I was hoping we could make it legal . . . a proper, permanent partnership.'

'M . . . Maitland & Cavendish, you mean?'

He smiled at her. 'Why not C . . . Cavendish & Maitland? It sounds better that way.'

She nodded helplessly, now too overwrought to be able to thank him for his kindness; all she could do was stroke the face of the little ivory boy before she closed the box and hid it in the pocket of her skirt.

'I think I'm finding this evening altogether too much for me,' she muttered at last.

'Well, it's by no means over yet,' he said as matter-of-factly as he could. 'But if we don't soon go and hide somewhere out front we shall miss that audience gasp you promised me.'

Three hours later the celebration was in full swing. First-night parties could sometimes seem no different from a wake, but there was no mistaking the joyous orgy of mutual congratulations that followed a triumphant opening. Pent-up doubts and anxieties melted in the warm exchange of kisses and compliments . . . a long, long run was being magisterially predicted by even the crustiest critic, now a little flown on Jacob Stein's champagne. Kate watched and listened and wondered whether she would ever feel at home with this aspect of the theatre. She tried not to look in the direction of Anna Sheridan, almost hidden in a throng of people that of course included Gil. But it was no use denying the fact that their leading lady had earned every scrap of the adulation she was being showered with.

Still, for Kate the night had lost its magic and she hoped it wouldn't be long before Sam remembered he'd promised to escort her home. The noise and heat and glare of the overcrowded room drove her downstairs at last to the quietest, dimmest place she could find – the now-deserted stage, with the last-act set of Isabel's Roman salon still in place. She collapsed onto a velvet footstool with a little sigh of relief, then nearly jumped out of her skin to find that she was being observed; someone else had sought the same retreat and was sitting in a large, winged armchair. Angus Macdonald was stretched out, long legs crossed in front of him, as if he proposed to spend the night there.

'Excitement too much for you?' he enquired.

Kate gave the matter thought. 'I don't mind excitement when I'm part of it,' she decided finally. 'But what's going on upstairs doesn't seem to have anything to do with me.'

'Nor me,' he said unexpectedly. He smiled at her in the dim light, and instead of being a tiresome assistant he would rather have done without she seemed to have become a friend – newly discovered but met on equal terms. 'Shall we agree not to say one more word about the play?' he suggested. 'In fact, not talk at all? Shall we just stay here and quietly admire the view from Isabel's windows? Can *you* see St Peter's too, or is it only visible from where I'm sitting?'

He was either light-headed with relief from strain, or he'd been drinking too much champagne. Kate thought he was entitled to both excuses.

'I'm afraid I do have something to say,' she murmured apologetically. 'Two things, in fact. The first is that it was very kind of you to invite my family tonight. Aunt Lou isn't exactly enchanted with what she calls the Stage, but she'll have loved being asked, and my dear William will have been in his element.'

'Thinking how much better he'd have played Daniel Touchett?'

She grinned, but answered honestly. 'A little bit of that, perhaps, although it might *not* be true; but he just feels at home in a theatre.'

'And the second thing you had to impart?'

'Thank you for not telling Gil Forrest how you came

to go to Birmingham. He . . . he did very well tonight, didn't he?'

'Excellently well.' Angus stared at her downbent head and surprised himself by saying something else. 'He's also fallen slightly in love with his leading lady. It's almost obligatory, you know – there's nothing very important or permanent about it.'

Kate's mouth twisted in a wry grin – it took understatement of a heroic kind to describe Gil's intoxication as slight. But on this very remarkable night the most astonishing thing of all was that she didn't mind Macdonald knowing that Gil's recent change of heart had hurt.

She wasn't sure what to say next, but while she was still making up her mind another voice spoke behind them.

'Darling Angus . . . so *this* is where you're hiding. Everyone is looking for the hero of the evening, and I'm very much afraid Jacob wants to make a speech.'

Anna Sheridan had arrived, gravitating naturally to the only stage-light left on, so that it would shine down on her – red-gold hair gleaming, and white skin excitingly veiled in black chiffon. Kate stared at her, admitting her beauty, and knew that she couldn't blame Gilbert Forrest, whatever his degree of infatuation.

But she stayed where she was, resisting the temptation to creep away as if caught out, like some maid being familiar with the master of the house. Anna offered her a faint, cool smile but spoke again to Macdonald.

'My sweet, I *know* you're exhausted, but the sooner Jacob says his few words, the sooner we can go home to bed!'

Angus heaved himself to his feet, but still looked at the girl sitting on her velvet stool.

'You come too, Kate – you'll like my future father-in-law; I rather like him myself, as a matter of fact.'

But when he'd been led away by Anna she still stayed in the quietness of the stage. She now knew what Jacob Stein was going to say, and didn't want to watch Gilbert's face when he said it.

Chapter 8

On the other side of the Atlantic a man who was sick of Hollywood's mad unreality and California's eternal sunshine decided that at last he could go home. But Jeremy Barrington broke the long journey back to London with a night in New York, and used his empty evening there to call on Margot Stein. For once he found her alone in the apartment's huge drawing-room.

'I've been selfish,' she said, 'and made no plans to entertain you because I wanted you all to myself.'

Jeremy smiled his famous smile, then discovered himself doing it and stopped with a little grimace of self-disgust. 'Dear Margot, you see a creature stuffed, surfeited, fed to the very eyeballs even, with glossy Hollywood parties. I crave a quiet evening where I don't have to shout myself hoarse, and grin and grin and *grin*!' He sipped from the glass she put into his hand and thought that if he'd given himself away, Margot Stein would understand. 'Is Jacob not here, though?'

'He's still in London, tying up loose ends of business, but I came back alone for some prior engagements. We didn't know when we left New York that we should be staying away long enough to see Anna married to Angus Macdonald by special licence. There'd been no whisper of it in her letters.'

'Nor in the news I've been getting,' Jeremy agreed. 'But I'm not really surprised. Anna talked to me about Macdonald before I went to LA, and I had the feeling then that if anything took her to London at all, this is how it might end.'

He watched Margot Stein's face and risked a question. 'Aren't you pleased about it? There's no reason not to be – they've had long enough to be sure they're happier together than apart.'

'I know, and no couple could have looked more satisfied with life than they did on their wedding-day. The play is going marvellously as well, but I couldn't help wondering what would come next . . . I mean, how they'd be able to continue working together; and it's important because long separations spell the death of marriage.'

'Are you still wondering?'

Margot's beautiful smile suddenly lit her face. 'No, because my dear, clever Jacob found the perfect answer. He bought a theatre in London!'

Jeremy blinked at a statement made in the tone of voice most people would use for owning to the purchase of a book, or a new hat. 'A . . . a *theatre*, you said?'

'Well, it's only a derelict one at the moment,' Margot insisted, as if hoping to lessen the extravagance. 'They were deep in plans when I left – ownership to be shared between Jacob, Angus, and Anna, and a repertory season there with a permanent company as soon as the theatre can be got ready. Don't you think it sounds magnificent?'

'Magnificently quixotic on Jacob's part,' Jeremy agreed, smiling with complete naturalness at last. 'I've never heard of a more generous wedding-present.'

'Well, it's *that*, of course, but other things besides . . . a little thank you to London among them, I think, for its brave performance during the war.' Margot's face was thoughtful as she refilled Jeremy's glass. 'Jacob's grandfather came here seventy years ago – a Polish Jew, with very little to help him except his quick brain and the fixed determination that he was going to succeed. His son, Benjamin, built on the foundations Isaac laid, and in his turn Jacob has converted solid wealth into a huge fortune – part of it as a direct result of the war. He's not stupid enough to feel guilty about that, but he looks for chances to say thank you when he can – for his family being *here* and not wiped out in the Holocaust, for Europe not being permanently under the jackboots of the Third Reich. Jacob doesn't pour money out indiscriminately on all the hangers-on and undeserving causes that swarm around a rich man; but nothing gives him greater satisfaction than seeing money well spent on making people happy. A beautiful theatre salvaged from a bombed ruin would strike him as money *very* well-spent.'

Jeremy lifted his glass and smiled at Margot. 'Then we'll drink to Jacob, and to happiness for Anna and Macdonald.'

He'd been away almost a year – long enough to grow accustomed to the space and pace and plenty of America. London seemed a cramped, discouraged city by comparison with New York, and an occasional break in the grey sky scarcely made up for the sunlight of California that he found he'd already begun to miss. People here saddened him, too – the porters and waiters and taxi-drivers he met all served him with the puzzled discontent of men who thought they'd earned a better time than they were having.

Feeling depressed himself, and uncertain of the wisdom of having come home, Jeremy set out one morning to trudge from his Strand hotel, across Waterloo Bridge, according to the instructions he'd been given over the telephone. Trust Sam to establish himself in some godforsaken, riverside wasteland and expect his friends to find him there. South of the river, he turned downstream, despondently recognised Bankside Power Station as the local beauty-spot he'd been told to look out for, and found himself at last at Sam's bright-yellow front door. It was flanked by a strange collection of old chimney-pots that spilled greenery instead of smoke into the air, and a scented orange rose clambered up the wall, undiscouraged by the neighbourhood. So typical of his friend was the arrangement's haphazard charm that Jeremy was looking less disgruntled when Kate opened the door to him. She saw a half-familiar man whose eyes were intensely blue in a sun-browned face; his bright hair was sun-gilded as well. He wasn't wearing stage chain-mail now, or a velvet tunic emblazoned with the royal lion and leopard, but when he smiled and spoke she knew for certain who he was.

'May I make a guess and say "Good morning, Kate"? Sam's letters mentioned a charming new business partner!'

Thoroughly flummoxed for a moment, she could only stare at him. The experienced hand capable, as she'd thought, of dealing with whoever might arrive on Sam's doorstep, had suddenly become a stage-struck adolescent again. Hot colour flooded her face, and regret at her appearance made her hotter still. Whoever in his life had seen a fully fledged business-woman in paint-splashed dungarees and a shirt that Aunt Lou had washed at least once too often?

She found her voice at last, but sounded brief and unwelcoming. 'I'm afraid Sam's out – perhaps you'd like to call again?'

'I'd rather sit down, if it's all the same to you,' Jeremy said plaintively. 'I made the mistake of *walking* to this extraordinary outpost of civilisation!'

The hint of affectation restored her to normality. 'I live in Southwark too, and we don't see anything extraordinary about it. If you're thinking of staying, there are still stairs to climb – do you reckon you can manage them?'

He smiled bravely. 'Onward and upward, Kate. Where you lead, I shall follow.'

They climbed the stairs in silence, he unexpectedly amused by her air of disapproval, and Kate fearing that she'd been sadly mistaken in Jeremy Barrington. But when she led him into the huge, airy room his affectations fell away. He walked over to the windows, and looked at St Paul's across the river. The clouds had parted at last, and the light was soft and misty – London sunlight.

'I see now why Sam lives here,' he said quietly, 'and I apologise for casting the smallest slur on Southwark, Kate.'

Mollified, she smiled at him, and he saw that he'd been wrong about *her* as well . . . she wasn't plain at all.

'Well, it suits us,' she agreed, 'but I expect it looks a bit different from the places you've been used to.'

He nodded but seemed disinclined to talk about America. 'I thought Sam would be here this morning – he said he would when I telephoned last night.'

'Something urgent must have cropped up; he doesn't normally forget appointments. I could make some coffee if you like – there won't be any sugar, and the milk's dried, but otherwise it will be all right.'

'It sounds,' he agreed solemnly, 'just what I should like.'

At ease with him now because he hadn't lost the English habit of making jokes with a straight face, she retired to the kitchen and hoped that Sam wouldn't remember his appointment too soon; she was beginning to enjoy herself. Jeremy was inspecting a model on her work-table when she came back.

'Cinderella's ballroom,' she explained. 'It's early to start on pantomime work, but we need to have November and December clear for other things.'

'It looks as beautiful as spun-glass – just as a fairy-tale ballroom *ought* to be.'

Her face flushed with pleasure at the praise. 'We need some fantasy, I think – life's still rather grim and grey here at the moment. Even the Government understands that, so instead of being told to work harder and burn less coal, we're to be cheered up for a change – with a festival! I expect that's why Sam isn't here. He's part of its design group, and they're always needing to have urgent meetings, because things keep going wrong. It took the festival committee years to settle on a site, and the one they finally chose was the boggiest stretch of the South Bank. It's a headache for architects and designers.'

Jeremy sipped his bitter coffee with every appearance of enjoying it, and changed the subject again. 'Shall I stand a chance of getting in to see Macdonald's play? I know it's a huge success.'

'Oh, the Guv'nor will find you a seat,' she said definitely. 'I seem to think you're old friends.' She hesitated a moment, then threw diffidence to the winds. 'Before you went to America my grandfather and I saw you in *Henry V*. You probably won't remember, but he sent round a note afterwards, congratulating you, and you were kind enough to write and thank him for it.'

'I don't remember *you* congratulating me,' he said, half-teasing, half-serious.

'I didn't . . . but I shan't ever need to see that play again. That ought to be praise enough for you,' she answered gravely.

He was silent for so long that she feared having said the wrong thing and offended him. But then he smiled at her – not the practised, charming smile of a man confident of making an impression, but something altogether more sweet and simple.

'I came back to London, believing it was where I really belonged. But everything seemed so shabby, and everyone seemed so cross, that I was beginning to regret leaving New York. I've been away from the theatre here a long time, and I even got to thinking that the public would have forgotten me – a desperate thing for an actor to contemplate, Kate!'

His beautiful voice held an inflection of humour, but she looked at him and knew that it had been an effort for him to seem amused. This talented, celebrated man was actually asking to be reassured. She wanted to do the very best for him that she could, but knew by instinct that mindless adulation wouldn't do; she must sound calm and very convincing.

'My Aunt Lou insists that actors gorge themselves on praise like caterpillars on lettuce-leaves, but William would know how you feel. It comes, he says, from always being someone else. The rest of us aren't always having to jump in and out of our own skin.' She smiled at Jeremy with all the warmth in her heart. 'Still, you'd be just plain daft to imagine we could possibly have forgotten you!'

They were still looking at one another with contentment when steps sounded on the stairs. Then Sam burst in, harassed and apologetic, but neatly dressed for once in a grey flannel suit. He grinned when Jeremy looked visibly impressed.

'I know . . . I feel like a tailor's dummy, but it's the result of hobnobbing with civil servants nowadays! Dear Jem, it's very good to see you, and I'm sorry you went clean out of my head until half an hour ago. Then I decided that you'd probably prefer talking to Kate, so I didn't rush out of the meeting. Does Angus know you're back?'

'Not yet – I tried last night; no answer. And you're entirely right – your presence here hasn't been missed at all!'

Remembering that they'd got off to a less than brilliant start, Kate smiled gratefully but thought it would be tactful to leave the two old friends alone together. Their stocks of drawing-paper were getting dangerously low, she announced, and she would go out and replenish them. Sam didn't try to dissuade her – Jeremy Barrington wasn't an unscrupulous man, but he couldn't help using the unfair share of charm the gods had given him. A walk in the fresh air away from him would do Kate nothing but good.

When she'd been tenderly escorted to the door by his visitor, Sam resumed the conversation. 'I suppose you were trying Macdonald's old number. Perhaps my last letter has been following you around and you don't even know that he and Anna are now married. They're both living in Anna's apartment in Cheyne Walk – she didn't seem to fancy the Bayswater Road, but I can't blame her for that.'

'I did know about their marriage, but not from you,' Jeremy explained. 'I saw Margot Stein before I left New York, and heard about Jacob's idea of a wedding-present as well. Angus must think he's strayed into the kingdom of heaven – Anna for a wife, and a theatre of his own to do what he likes with – no unreasonable management breathing down his neck, and no greedy impresario swallowing up the profits.' He stared at Sam's downbent face and was reminded of his friend's habit of walking away from the private lives of other people. This least self-revealing of men was also the most reticent when it came to the exchange of the endless gossip that theatreland indulged in.

'I decided it was time to get back onto a London stage again,' Jeremy went on abruptly. 'Your kind Kate assures me that I still have a place here . . . I hope to God she's right; otherwise it's a rather pointless gesture to have come at all. Margot said that Angus has a permanent company in mind – perhaps he'll take me on for old times' sake.'

Sam smiled, even though his manner still seemed hesitant. 'My dear Jem, any management in London would want to take you on! But you should talk first to Macdonald – I'll give you his new number. If you're at a loose end for lunch come back here, but I expect you'll go to Cheyne Walk. I hope so, for your sake. With Anna's Spanish maid, the catering's much better there!'

Taking the hint that his friend was desperate to get back to work, Jeremy rang the number he was given, and heard Anna's voice – Anna Macdonald, as he must now try to think of her – at the other end. After a brief conversation he returned to Sam, already busy at his drawing-board at the far end of the room. Jeremy was faintly smiling, and almost unable to remember that an hour ago he'd been regretting coming back to London.

'No matinee today, so I *am* invited to lunch. Anna seemed delighted to have company . . . Angus is on his way to

Edinburgh, apparently, and the poor girl was feeling rather lonely. She'll get me in to see the play this evening. Au revoir, Sam – I'll be in touch.'

With a buoyant wave and a graceful farewell bow, he was at the door, already confident of beginning to feel at home again. He'd been a fool to let himself get depressed; it was the actor's unfailing philosophy: if today looked bad, there was always tomorrow.

Sam watched him go, then returned to his own work again. But his frown was not for the design that refused to grow under his hand. For once he was thinking of something else altogether.

At Cheyne Walk there was a servant, polite but unsmiling, to open the door. She ushered him into a room that, like the studio he'd just come from, offered a dazzling river view. But it had nothing else in common with the untidy comfort of Sam's home. Here, instead, were gleaming mahogany, glazed chintzes, and expensive flowers that were forbidden to drop petals onto polished surfaces. Jeremy decided that the décor would suit a celebrated actress very well, but he found it harder to fit Angus into this temple of discreet good taste.

He was still wondering about his friend when Anna walked into the room. He'd last seen her nearly a year ago – since then she seemed to have grown more beautifully self-assured, more completely confident that any movement she made would be the right one. Her certainty pleased him – he thought it was how Anna Macdonald *ought* to look.

'Jeremy darling . . . we'd almost given you up – decided we'd lost you to Hollywood for good.'

He kissed her cheek and took the hands she held out to

him. 'All my congratulations, Anna – marriage suits you, and so does great success. You're looking beautiful, and I hope Angus realises how little he deserves you!'

She smiled as she poured sherry from a heavy old decanter and handed him a glass. 'Two weeks married and already I'm without a husband. He's living heart and soul with another woman – Shaw's St Joan. He'll rush back from Edinburgh occasionally to check up on our performances in London, but it's creating the still unborn production that counts.'

Jeremy thought it was probably true of most dedicated directors; it was certainly true of his all-or-nothing Highland friend, but better than anyone else Angus could have married, Anna would understand the complete absorption that was necessary and not feel hurt by it.

'I saw Margot before I left New York . . . heard about Jacob's theatre, of course. My dear Anna, what a gift!'

She looked, he was surprised to see, faintly discontented. 'Wonderfully generous,' she agreed, 'but I must confess that I couldn't see why it had to be quite such a *dilapidated* gift! There are other theatres he could have bid for, but they wouldn't do. He's still here, goading lawyers, architects and builders into working at quite un-English speed.' She registered the slight disappointment in Jeremy's face and at once offered a charmingly rueful apology. 'I'm an ungrateful cow, you're thinking! So I am . . . consider my objections withdrawn.'

He obligingly dismissed them with a wave of his hand, but sounded serious. 'I was remembering something Margot said to me . . . Jacob's reason for wanting to salvage beauty out of desolation.'

Jeremy's voice turned the simple sentence into poetry.

Anna listened to it with the detached pleasure of a professional, and realised at the same time how unexpectedly happy she was to see Jeremy Barrington back in London. Beneath the surface Californian glow he looked tired and world-weary for the moment, but her impression was strong that as soon as he recovered he would be the actor she most wanted to play against. She dragged her mind away from the thought and remembered that they'd been talking about her step-father.

'What my mother said about Jacob is true,' she agreed, 'but it isn't the whole truth. He's fascinated by anything that isn't perfect – it allows him to do something with it!'

Jeremy grinned, recollecting the sight of Jacob Stein in his study at home, engrossed in the pieces of a venerable clock that could be made to work again if he reassembled them with sufficient love and care. For him the broken clock, the shattered theatre would be the same – things that should be made to fulfil their true function again. Instead of saying that the principle seemed to be a good one, Jeremy tactfully changed the subject.

'Are you going to settle down here, Anna?'

His gesture merely indicated the formal room they sat in but she chose to recall their conversation in New York.

'I must . . . I'm married to Angus now – *blissfully* married to him when he doesn't desert me! We *work* perfectly together, too, so I hope he won't often go rushing off to direct other people . . . I'd like him to stay here, of course, writing wonderful new plays for *me*!' Her lovely smile robbed the words of selfishness, asking Jeremy to understand that although she meant what she said, she needn't be taken seriously.

'Life's still a bit grim and earnest here, don't you find?' he suggested. 'Depressingly so after New York.'

'Well yes, but I cheat, I'm afraid. Margot sends me nylons and silk underclothes, much to the disgust of the tiresome girl who works for Sam Maitland – I could feel her silent disapproval while she was measuring me! It's another black mark that I didn't spend the war in London, but I refuse to wear darned lisle stockings and petticoats labelled "utility", just to regain Miss Cavendish's good opinion.'

Anna watched Jeremy's mouth curve in a reminiscent smile and thought she knew the reason for it. 'I met her this morning when I called on Sam,' he said inevitably, 'made one gaffe straightaway, but managed to retrieve my error. After that we got on rather well. Sam says she's very good at her job.'

'I should hope so – why employ her otherwise? It isn't quite enough that the stage-hands adore her.' Anna's shrug disposed of a subject she found uninteresting. Then her expression changed and she smiled at her visitor with entrancing warmth. 'Dear friend, I want to hear about *you* – what exciting play have you got lined up?'

'No play at all as yet,' he admitted. 'The truth is that I feel drained after a year of non-stop work, and nervous about starting again in London. It's important to make the right choice now, and I wanted to talk to Angus about that. Damn him for hiding himself in Edinburgh!'

Anna's gloomy Spanish maid appeared to announce that lunch was ready and they moved to another grandly formal room. It was a far cry from bachelor discomfort and the squalor of theatrical lodgings. Again Jeremy wondered to what extent Angus felt comfortable in his wife's elegant home, but he could find no tactful way of asking her.

They talked instead of New York and Jeremy's time in America.

'I loved Broadway at first,' he concluded, 'and grew tired of it in the end, but from start to finish I hated Hollywood. Angus is right – I belong on a stage, a London one for choice, playing to a live, responsive audience.'

Anna nodded, smiling a little. 'Of course, there speaks the man who can't help but be a theatre actor. Ordinary, sane people fail to understand *us* as much as they're mystified by writers and painters who choose the lives they do. We're something to be grateful for but still very odd in their view.'

Jeremy's blue glance held hers across the table, acknowledging that what she said was true. It accounted for the fact that they were two of a kind, at ease together. Anna was still talking, but he had the strong impression that her mind was not on what she said; something else was at work in the quiet room, binding them in some secret, shared harmony.

'You'll find London audiences wonderfully receptive,' she said almost at random. 'My theory is that it's because their lives are so grey, and hedged about with restrictions and eternal shortages. People here *need* the fantasies we offer them.'

'The Government think they need a festival too, so I'm told. Sam's even made the mistake of getting involved in it. The poor misguided chap wears a collar and tie nowadays and goes to committee-meetings!'

They both smiled at the absurdity of this new vision of Sam Maitland, even while they knew they scarcely considered it. Their minds were more engrossed in a vision of the future that looked full of dazzling promise. It was Anna who was brave enough to put it into words when

Jeremy announced that he must leave her to rest before the evening performance.

'Jacob's determined that his phoenix shall arise from the ashes in time to greet the New Year. That gives you a month or two, my friend, to idle away if you need a rest, or to play Hamlet, the Master Builder, or whatever else takes your fancy.'

'And after that?' he enquired, although he was sure of the answer.

'After that you and I must appear together. We can give London something unforgettable, Jeremy . . . you're as certain of it as I am!' Her smile was triumphant and intoxicating, but he tried to keep his head.

'Darling Anna, certain as we may be, Angus has to agree. He's in charge, and he may want you to go on with your present leading man – Sam says he's very good.'

Her expression immediately changed, triumph mixed with sorrow now. 'Gilbert is *quite* wonderful, for the simple reason that in *The Portrait* he's obliged to fall in love with me. But we can't go on feeding him parts that suit him so well!'

Jeremy kissed the hands she held out to him, but felt sorry for a man he didn't know. The poor, enraptured swine hadn't stood a chance, of course; only long experience taught an actor how to keep reality separate from what happened to him on stage.

'You're dangerous to know,' he said truthfully. 'If I had as much sense as I *think* I have, I'd paddle my little canoe as far away from you as possible.'

Anna reached up to kiss his cheek. 'Nonsense . . . I never hurt my friends . . . I love them too much. Shall I see you after the performance?'

'Of course.' He smiled and went away, to waste the rest of the afternoon sitting by the river. His excuse was that he was trying to guess which play Angus would choose for the reopening of Jacob's theatre. But rational thought stood no chance against an avalanche of doubts and fears about the future, and tremors of insidious excitement. As often as he decided that life would be safer alone, he was tugged in the opposite direction. And in any case if Fate *meant* him and Anna Macdonald to act together it would arrange things accordingly for them in due time . . . it was the superstitious belief of every player that 'the ripeness is all'.

He was even more convinced of it after seeing Anna's shattering performance as Isabel Archer. When he finally went back to his hotel room it seemed to him that the future had already been settled in some way. But he fell asleep at last to dream of a girl who had Kate Cavendish's smile. She was pointing to an endless flight of stairs he had to climb, and asking him if he thought he could manage them.

Chapter 9

Jacob waited for Angus to return from Edinburgh before he left London himself.

'I've given everyone a target,' he explained. 'They work better like that in my experience . . . move heaven and earth to prove that what you expected them to fail at they *can* do after all.' Jacob offered this philosophy cheerfully, but the tired-faced man who received it didn't look particularly impressed. Angus merely nodded, and said that they would do their best to open on Anna's twenty-fifth birthday, two weeks after Christmas Day.

'You probably haven't had a chance yet to decide what you'll open with,' Jacob suggested. His ugly face creased into a smile. 'But I can see that it's important for the two of you to agree!'

Angus hesitated for a moment, tempted to confide his dreams for the new theatre in a man who might understand them better than most. But there'd been no time yet to get them clear in his own mind, and Jacob Stein wasn't the man to air some untidy, half-baked notion to. The moment for talking slipped past and by the following morning had gone altogether; Jacob was on his way back to New York.

That evening Angus dressed without enthusiasm for a soirée at the American Embassy. He took little pleasure in the social world that his marriage had introduced him to, but it couldn't be avoided now; Jacob's influential friends were Anna's too, and she seemed to have been born with the knack of feeling at home in the company of the rich, the famous, and the powerful. Finding no such knack in himself, Angus was content to watch her shine, and marvel that the gods had finally permitted *him* to have possession of her. But they had so little leisure to enjoy together that he resented the loss of a fine, free Sunday evening they could have spent more enjoyably alone.

'You don't care for German Lieder, I take it,' Anna suggested when at last they were in a taxi going home. 'You've been unable to do anything but scowl the entire evening.'

Angus turned towards his wife, more than ready to smile at her. 'My darling, to please you I'll dote on German Lieder if you like, but not when the soprano is of Wagnerian proportions and has a persistent tendency to sing ever so slightly off-key.'

Anna still tried to look severe, but it was unarguable that the singer had been both large and flat. She found Macdonald's face exciting when amusement lurked in his eyes and mouth as it did now, and she couldn't help but know with secret pleasure why he'd considered the evening wasted. The truth was that she agreed with him. The nights he'd spent in Edinburgh had seemed very long, and she wanted very much to go home and let her husband make love to her. She thought that in his face now she could see the same impatient need.

But need must wait, it seemed. When they were back at Cheyne Walk Angus kissed her neck as he removed her coat, but his voice sounded deliberately matter-of-fact; if passion troubled him, it wasn't being allowed to get out of control.

'A nightcap if you're not too tired, sweetheart?'

'I'd rather not!' Her meaning was clear but, although he smiled, he shook his head, refusing the blatant invitation.

'There's nothing I'd like better than to take you to bed this instant, my love, but we have to talk a little first. I've got to leave before you're likely to awaken in the morning.'

'Not Edinburgh again *already*, Angus,' she said sharply. 'You're only just back, and you promised that one visit would be enough for the moment.'

'So it would have been, but Robins got through to Sam this morning when we were out saying goodbye to Jacob. There's a little crisis up there that I *must* go and see to. I'll be away two days at the most, I hope.' He stared at her stormy face and tried to speak lightly. 'It's lovely to be missed; I miss *you*, sweetheart, and hope we never get used to being separated, but I'm afraid it's part of the job we do.'

Anna offered him a thin, unforgiving smile. 'That's why Jacob bought the theatre, of course – so that we *shouldn't* have to keep going in different directions. Once it's ready we can be fixed there . . . not shunted about between managements, selling ourselves to people who don't care about us or understand the first thing about our strange profession.' She waited for Angus to rise to the bait she offered him, because already their only discussion of the new theatre had hinted at the prospect of them disagreeing about it. But for once he chose discretion as the better part of valour. He was tired and Anna was angry; it wasn't the time to start trying to persuade her of something he knew she would be reluctant to accept.

'Let's leave the future a bit longer,' he suggested, 'but I want you to promise me you'll let your understudy play for a night or two while the Edinburgh Festival is on. There's a brilliant newcomer in the cast of *St Joan* for you to see – I think you'll want him snaffled for our new company.'

'I doubt it,' she said coolly. 'With Jacob leaving, there hasn't been a chance to give you my news. Jeremy is back from the US. He's anxious to talk to you about what to do next, but whatever it is he can only do it for a little while. I've told him that we shall need him ourselves after that.'

There was no lingering vestige of amusement or desire in her husband's face now. Angus simply looked thunderously angry.

'Then you may also have to tell him that you've made a mistake,' he shouted. 'God dammit, Anna, we don't even know yet what we're going to open *with*.'

She studied her fingernails and frowned at the sight of some chipped polish. 'Whatever we choose, I shall need a leading man; whatever we choose, Jeremy will play it better than anyone else.' She abandoned the nail and stared at her husband instead. 'You won't be allowed to make all the decisions, Angus; it's as much my theatre as yours.' Her expression was coldly unfamiliar, but her resolve was not – he was acquainted with that.

'Oh, it's much *more* yours, my dear!' he said ironically. 'Don't hesitate to remind me that it's bought with Jacob's money, and is being refurbished with more of the same. Perhaps that qualifies you to choose your own director as well?'

'Now you're simply being childish.' She said it with dignity and with the confidence of knowing that he would have to recognise it as the truth. Having boxed him into a corner, she was content to look sad, knowing that she also looked beautiful and desirable.

'Anna love, I'm sorry.' He came to stand in front of her and put his hands on her bare shoulders. 'We mustn't let Jacob's marvellous present get us at odds with one another. I'm not saying that Jem isn't a magical actor; it's just that I saw the chance to do something different – instead of "stars" always hogging the limelight in plays chosen simply to show them off, I wanted a real ensemble company with everyone sharing the work and the credit. Taking on someone like Barringtom immediately scuttles that idea.'

'Taking on *me* – as I'm afraid you're bound to – scuttles it as well,' Anna said coldly. 'I'm not ready for a long time yet to play bit-parts in my own theatre so that some little unknown ingénue can have her chance. And I'll tell you something else, Angus, before we end this futile discussion. The people who crowd into the theatre that Jacob wants to make beautiful again will come to see players like me and Jeremy – they don't want dreary, well-meaning ensemble playing; they want the ice and fire and brilliant sparkle that only comes from performers like *us*.'

It was a telling exit-line and Anna didn't make the mistake of spoiling it. She swept out of the room, leaving him seething with a complicated mixture of fury, regret, and very uncomplicated desire. He sat for a long time in the over-furnished room that still didn't seem to be his home. They would have to do something about that eventually because he hated living in it, but it wasn't important now. Somehow he must see Anna's point of view as well as his own. They were committed to each other, and it would be unthinkable to fall at the very first fence.

At last he fumbled his way to bed in darkness so as not

to disturb her, and understood that he was not forgiven. She was curled up as far away from him as possible, and apparently deeply asleep. He lay beside her, sleepless, and disquieted about a future that seemed ominously hung about with shadows. Moonlight invaded the room, touching her pale face and the red-gold hair that streamed across her pillow. She was normally a generous and passionate lover and his body cried out for her, but all he could do was to get up and draw the curtains to protect her from the disturbing brightness of the moon.

When he came back to the bed she was awake, and suddenly holding out her hands to him. In the dimness he thought he could see that she smiled; or was it just that her voice sounded amused?

'Darling, all that fuss about nothing! I've been doing a lot of thinking and I'm almost certain I know what we should open with . . . *Much Ado*. Don't you agree that I shall deserve the part of Beatrice after months of being poor tragic Isabel Archer? I *promise* I'll play Lady Disdain for you more beautifully than she's ever been played before.'

She would, too. He could see her in his mind's eye. As naturally as she breathed she would become the most enticing, sparkling, warm but brilliant woman Shakespeare ever painted.

'*Much Ado* it shall be,' he agreed helplessly.

He heard her laugh, and knew himself forgiven. She drew him down to bury his head against her breast and for the moment defeat didn't seem too high a price to pay for love-making that left him spent, but at peace again. With desire finally satisfied, Anna slept in his arms, but he remained wide-awake as the dawn light slowly seeped into the room. She would be a Beatrice to remember, but for certain playing opposite her there would be his great and glorious friend, Jeremy Barrington. He must bury in some unvisited corner of his mind the idea he'd had of a different kind of theatre, and accept that happily married men couldn't expect to dream private dreams and see solitary visions. Full daylight came at last and he slipped out of bed without waking her, but he got ready to leave with a feeling of relief. The worrying sense of having come close to disaster would surely have faded by the time he'd returned to London.

More often than she needed to, Kate found reasons for walking past the Swan. Each time there was more progress to report to William. Already the roof was intact again; now the smoke-blackened walls and stone columns of the lovely portico were being scrubbed clean. The workmen, to whom she always said good morning, complained, of course, about the inhuman speed at which they were being made to work; but it was forced grumbling, she felt – their hearts weren't in it. They were pleased with what they were doing.

From Sam's model she could guess at the transformation taking place inside. Her grandfather resurrected for her fond memories of crimson plush and ornate Venetian chandeliers, but she knew that the new interior had been planned differently. Dark blue velvet against a background of white and gold was the scheme Sam Maitland had chosen, and she didn't doubt that it would look inevitably right and beautiful. The Swan was a gracious playhouse with a long history, but Sam had decided that it wasn't to be mummified by the past. When she tried to explain this in Paradise Walk Milly looked hurt and William claimed a trifle dramatically that an unstable world cried out to heaven for the balm of tradition and continuity.

'He's quite right,' Sam said when she reported her lack of success with them. 'All the same, the Swan will have to manage without the past if that means tons of vulgar Murano glass cascading from the ceilings.' He was about to hide himself again in the report he was reading, but for once she didn't take the hint. They shared the Wharfside studio very amicably but she was more conscious nowadays than she had been in the past that the longer she knew Sam Maitland, the less she could guess what he was thinking.

He was still only thirty-three – much the same age as Macdonald, and seven years younger than Jeremy Barrington. Sam made no effort to insist that women should take notice of him, but in Kate's interested observation, his effect on them was unusual. Other men could find them exciting, witty, or beautiful; they seemed anxious that Sam should like them.

She had never been tempted to repeat the confession made to Gilbert Forrest about herself, reckoning that Edinburgh might run Westchester County a close second when it came to the effect left behind by conventional upbringings. All too likely an episcopalian streak in Sam Maitland would have to disapprove of poor, desperate Marguerite Cavendish, but she couldn't be sure when she was so often made aware of how little she knew about him.

'How do you come to be *here*, when you might be anywhere else instead on the planet William reckons so unstable?' she asked suddenly.

He looked surprised at the question but ticked off facts for her on his fingers. 'Conceived and born in a cold stone house in Edinburgh while the "war to end wars" was raging. Reared in the same, but escaped from time to time to be educated in a cold stone school instead. Afterwards sent to an even colder Swiss sanatorium to be killed or cured of TB. It turned out to be the latter, as it happened, but I decided then to forsake Edinburgh for good, and became a student in London. Angus Macdonald was in the same lodgings in Bedford Square – another thankful exile from the frozen north. He went away to fight, but I did not because of my suspect lungs. When we met again we found we were still friends. That brings us up to date, I think, except that the lungs now seem to be perfectly all right.'

It left some huge gaps, Kate thought, and she couldn't help staring at the simple pen-and-wash drawing that hung above his desk. It was the face of a woman, delicately featured and appealing, whose only resemblance to Sam seemed to be the dark eyes that looked consideringly at the world.

'My mother,' he said briefly. 'She didn't die until I was fifteen, so I was much luckier than you.'

Kate didn't argue with him but doubted if it was true. She had always had Aunt Lou; Sam had lost someone he'd adored so much that he couldn't talk about her even now, and then been shipped, heart-broken and alone, to a mountain sanatorium. It explained why the warmth and gaiety that had surely been the legacy of his Viennese mother was the façade Sam Maitland hid behind. No one got past that protecting screen to the survivor of so much grief.

Kate took the hint and returned instead to what they'd been talking about earlier. '*Is* it such an unstable world?' she asked suddenly. 'William only thinks so because people don't attend the theatre in evening dress any more, and we've given India back to the Indians – he fears that Disraeli and poor Queen Victoria must be turning in their graves about that. But I don't feel inclined to be so despondent. I'd rather take the Swan as an omen for the future – a fresh start that it's up to us not to spoil.'

'Hurrah for the optimism and bright courage of youth . . . hang on to them, Kate!'

Sam smiled as he spoke, but she decided that he wasn't laughing at her. Better still, for the first time in weeks he was looking at *her* again instead of at another wad of committee papers that he was required to read. She didn't know, because he managed to conceal the fact, that he was always aware of her; the paradoxes she presented intrigued him. Her working outfits still made no concession to glamour, but they unfairly accentuated all the same the slender body and beautiful long legs they were supposed to hide. Her cropped hair should by rights have looked unfeminine, but it merely drew attention to the delicate bone-structure of a face that vividly reflected whatever she was thinking. Only in that inability to hide her feelings did she now remind him of the gawky schoolchild met in a cathedral garden long ago. It pleased him that she moved with such quick grace, and sang – always out of tune – because she was happy. Even amid the smell of size, hot glue, and paint that frequently floated up to the studio from the floor below he could detect the faint flower perfume she wore. He knew that he would miss her beyond words when the time came to dissolve their partnership.

But she was staring at him, wondering what made him look so thoughtful.

'You don't exactly have one foot in the grave yourself,' she pointed out. 'Is it wrong to feel optimistic and happy? Are we to sit and wring our hands, and wait for the end of the world to come because a bomb has been invented that can destroy us all?'

The sudden question made him shake his head. 'No, we put all the faith we can muster in God, or in each other, and until the worst happens enjoy every day as it comes.'

Kate smiled at him approvingly. 'That's what I think too. Gilbert is rather inclined to gloom, especially about the Russians, but I expect it comes of being an American. He can't help feeling that every other country on earth should love the USA and understand that its motives are entirely pure!'

Sam agreed that Americans were still sadly thin-skinned in such matters, but his own impression was that Gilbert Forrest had more personal cares on his mind than the alarming deterioration in East-West relations. With Anna's marriage to Macdonald he'd been rudely shaken out of fantasy. It was one thing to revere his leading lady as a brilliant actress; quite another to go on pretending she was a woman he might possess when she belonged to the very man he was indebted to. Sam thought Gilbert Forrest would recover in time; more worrying was Anna's power to attract a different man. Jeremy *might* keep his head, but they would soon be playing closely together, and their future depended on a dangerous situation not getting out of hand.

The prospect made Sam give a little sigh that caused Kate to look at him again. Whatever he might say about enjoying life, at the moment he seemed both tired and sad.

'You're quite sure about the lungs . . . being all right, I mean?' she asked with sudden anxiety.

'Yes, I'm sure, but thank you for asking.' Sam confirmed it solemnly, but then asked a question himself. 'Do I gather that Jem Barrington has taken to calling in Paradise Walk?'

Kate's smile reappeared. 'It was to meet William at first, and bandy quotations from Shakespeare with him, but now he seems to enjoy the rest of the household as well. Elsie is still holding out, but Milly giggles and blushes like a schoolgirl again, and even Aunt Lou is beginning to smile on him. He charms people without trying to.'

'Does he charm you?' Sam enquired. He watched faint colour touch her cheekbones, and for once she answered without looking directly at him.

'He's very kind . . . *that* charms me about him.'

The need to warn her seemed so imperative that it put unthinking words into his mouth.

'Jem's kind, Kate, but at a loose end until rehearsals start; what's more, he's lonely and having to find his feet again in London. Will you remember that?'

She lifted her head and stared at him, colour higher now and her eyes bright with anger. 'Why not say what you mean? He's a celebrated, glamorous figure; we're a bunch of oddities that he finds it amusing to be nice to while he has nothing better to do.'

Sam wondered whether she would be more or less angry if he said what he thought was true – that Jeremy's desperate need was not for amusement but for an antidote to the pull of Anna Macdonald. Kate was appealing, vivid, and conveniently to hand; better still, she was eager to think well of him – especially if he seemed to appreciate the other inmates of Paradise Walk. Sam was tempted to cravenly retreat, but she wasn't nearly as experienced as she thought she was, and Jeremy could do her much more hurt than Gil Forrest had done.

'Jem is an actor, Kate – *that*'s what I mean. He needs an audience, and can't help giving the impression that it's the best he's ever had . . . until another one comes along.' But her stormy face confirmed that his advice was getting the reception all such well-intended officiousness deserved.

'You must think we're gullible fools,' she shouted. 'We *know* about actors in Paradise Walk. But Jeremy doesn't come just to strut and prance and talk about himself; he comes to . . . to be part of the family.'

For once, he thought, she wasn't being honest, and the fact goaded him to unaccustomed rage. 'All right . . . let him be anything you like – Harry, King of England, or any other idealised hero your imagination fastens on. But don't ask me to feel sorry for you when he suddenly forgets that Paradise Walk exists.'

It was an even worse mistake – an error he wouldn't have believed he was capable of making. But the words were out of his mouth and couldn't be taken back again.

'I shouldn't dream of discussing this subject with you again . . . ever,' Kate said distinctly. 'And now I shall get on with some work. Perhaps you should do the same. We have a meeting with Angus Macdonald in a week's time.'

She went home that evening without her usual good night and eager 'see you in the morning, Sam'. He worked until he fell asleep at his drawing-board and woke, cold and stiff, in the dead hours that follow midnight. It didn't seem to be a promising beginning to the bright new start she had insisted on.

Chapter 10

Macdonald's meeting had to be held in the studio at Wharfside. Only around Sam's huge work-table could the company be assembled while the theatre itself was still full of plasterers and painters. Anna went under protest, still complaining during the taxi-ride from Cheyne Walk that there was no necessity for them to go at all. They had patched up their quarrel but her husband's quiet insistence on the meeting had made her irritable.

'Talk to the cast if you must,' she said sharply, 'but I fail to see why wardrobe women and carpenters have to be persuaded in advance that they're going to enjoy what they're asked to do.'

'One wardrobe supervisor and one head carpenter,' Angus pointed out, 'both of them essential members of the company. They're going to have to work damned hard. I want them to feel valued, and involved in our adventure.'

He was tempted to plead with her – ask her to be as charming to them as only she could, but she had turned away from him to stare out of the window at the Borough High Street.

'God, what dreariness! How can Sam Maitland bear to sink to such a neighbourhood?'

'He happens to like it, and so do the other people who

live here. If you air your opinion in front of Kate Cavendish she'll quote you chapter and verse on Southwark's long, proud history. There is also the guts of its citizens to remember . . . it took a pasting during the Blitz, which explains all the empty spaces we're driving through.'

'My dear Angus, I'm sick of hearing about the war, and even more tired of Kate Cavendish. If our designer can spare the time from all his other pressing and important commitments, I should prefer *him* to sketch my dresses for *Much Ado*.'

'Then you'll be making a mistake, Anna. Sam is the first to say that his partner may outstrip him when it comes to period costumes. On the showing of her designs for *The Portrait*, I think he's right.'

In fairness to Kate it had had to be said, but he knew that it had done nothing to improve his wife's temper. They drove in silence and arrived outside Sam's yellow front door. The climbing rose no longer bloomed, but winter jasmine made a tracery of bare twigs and buds against the wall, and the chimney-pots were still filled with greenery. Anna's tight mouth suddenly relaxed at the sight of them, because they gave her a graceful excuse for climbing down. There had been time in her marriage to Macdonald to learn when climbing down was necessary; mostly she had things her own way, but there was a core of granite in him which even her female adroitness left untouched.

They were the last to arrive. Jeremy was keeping the four other principal members of the cast entertained – Jane Carlisle, Gilbert Forrest, David Kent and his wife Judith, grouped next to the empty chairs left for the director and the leading lady. Then, true to theatre hierarchy, came the front-of-house manager, Walter Fairbrass, facing Macdonald's unflappable stage manager, John Clarke. Beyond them Pat O'Donovan stared bashfully across the table at his friend and lighting colleague, Ernie Williams, while Kate watched Elsie Manners unnerve Gil Forrest with a fierce stare – too far away to explain to him that her friend was only calculating how much material would be required to make him a velvet doublet. Sam, uncaring of hierarchies, simply sat where there remained an empty chair left at the foot of the table. Anna smiled and waved them to their seats again, but it was Macdonald who called the meeting to order and took charge.

Kate listened critically and decided that he did it very well. Clearly and with no wasted words the coming season was explained to them: three plays introduced in sequence running, if the gods and the paying customers agreed, until the next mid-summer; then a much-needed break for everyone concerned, followed by a fresh programme of three plays in the autumn to take them round to Easter. They would open with *Much Ado About Nothing* just after Christmas, as soon as the theatre was ready; Shaw's *Pygmalion* would be the second production of the season; and Noël Coward's *Private Lives* the third.

Sam listened to Macdonald's final choice of plays and wondered how much he'd been governed by the need to provide plum parts for his two leading players. They would do them beautifully – there was no doubt about that; but he knew that such a programme of obvious box-office winners wasn't what Macdonald had hoped for in a theatre of his own.

'There'll be a huge amount of work to get through for everyone concerned, I'm afraid,' Angus was saying, 'but I hope you'll grin and bear it knowing that what we create between us will justify it in the end. We've all worked together long enough to know that we can rely on each other, and we shall have one enormous comfort – the knowledge that we're a permanent company with our own beautiful home, thanks to Jacob Stein.'

'When can I make a start on publicity, Angus?' Walter Fairbrass asked.

'The theatre box-office will be habitable in a week's time – so reckon to start then. Rehearsals will have to begin in our usual church hall, because there's still too much hammering and banging going on. But opening night, God willing, *can* be on Anna's birthday, as we planned – twelfth night after Christmas. I hope that doesn't mean we've chosen the wrong play!'

'Cast, dear boy?' asked Jeremy, as if there would be the slightest doubt about it.

'It writes itself – Anna is Beatrice, of course; Jeremy, you're Benedick. Jane here shall be our Hero, and Claudio goes to you, Gilbert. It's usually allowed to be a thankless bloody part, I'm afraid, but between us I don't see why we shouldn't make something better of it.'

Gil Forrest half-rose in his seat and looked around the table. 'To be part of *this* company, Angus, I'd even play Nana in *Peter Pan*.'

Jeremy led the applause for a tactful comment that made everybody smile happily, and Sam told himself that he'd been over-anxious; the omens for a bright new start were looking reasonably good after all.

'Kate and I have started work already on the opening production,' he confessed. 'There'll be no gimmickry, no fashionable and inexcusable mucking-about with the text. The curtain will rise on what Will Shakespeare said it should rise on . . . a nobleman's house and garden in seventeenth-century Messina. In other words, the sets and costumes will be beautiful, elaborate, and extremely difficult to make.' He smiled at Elsie and Patrick O'Donovan. 'Just what you expected, in fact!'

They looked pleased not to be disappointed, and it seemed that the meeting was coming to an amicable end. Then Anna gave a little rap on the table and they all looked in her direction.

'Angus has settled everything that needs deciding except the all-important matter of a name. My darling step-father believes in never wasting anything – it's thanks to that philosophy that a sad, old, derelict building is being made useful and beautiful again. So I decided to take a leaf out of Jacob's book and not waste my own small contribution. My playwright great-great-great-grandfather has done some small service to the stage, so I hope you'll agree that it would be the perfect choice to call our new theatre the Sheridan.'

There was a little silence round the table. Looking first at Angus, Sam saw that Macdonald's expression had the deliberate blankness of a man who had been taken completely by surprise. Sam's gaze travelled along the table and came to rest on Kate. No blankness there – her face had gone very white and still, but he knew as surely as night followed day that she was simply gathering every ounce of self-control that she could muster.

'The theatre doesn't need a name,' she said quietly at last. 'It has one already.'

Anna smiled at her from the far end of the table.

'The *old* one, you mean? My dear Kate, I don't really think we need remember that. An old-fashioned, failing theatre called the Swan succumbed to flames. Let it rest in peace, and let us make a brave new beginning.

Sam prayed, but uselessly – because his partner was on her feet now, flushed and fierce-eyed where she'd been pale a moment before.

'My grandfather's theatre didn't fail or succumb – it got *bombed*,' she shouted. 'Can't even *you* see that there's a difference? It's always been called the Swan, and must go on being that till it finally falls to dust. Three hundred years of London's history would say so, even if it wasn't still in spirit William's theatre.'

Sam cleared his throat, about to suggest that since in a very real sense it would now also be Jacob Stein's, they might ask which *he* favoured: continuing theatre history or making it. But Anna got in first, appealing not to her husband but in a direction where she felt more certain of support.

'Jeremy darling, I'm at a disadvantage with Miss Cavendish, who likes to think me a renegade American. Do you suppose *you* can convince her that half our audience won't have heard of the Swan, and probably none of them at all will have heard of her grandfather?'

She smiled as she said it, but it was clear to everyone around the table that the battle-lines had now been drawn, and no quarter would be asked or given. The silence was so complete that Sam supposed they all, himself included, had stopped breathing. He waited for Kate to be vanquished – not by the error of her argument, but by the warm, intimate smile that Anna was using to embroil Jeremy in the fight on her side. Together, it said, *they* were the theatre that was being born again, and it was the future that mattered. The quaint Edwardian past was dead, and Kate Cavendish was not only impertinent but absurd.

Jeremy looked at Angus, but his friend's eyes were fixed steadfastly on the papers in front of him; he looked at Elsie Manners, who stared impassively back at him, offering no help either. At last there was Kate, still standing arrow-straight and tense at the foot of the table. She gave a faint little smile that seemed to forgive him in advance for the blow he was obliged to deliver, and he found that he couldn't deliver it after all.

'Anna my dear,' he said, clearing his throat, 'I don't think you quite understand how famous a play-house the Swan has been. I suppose I didn't either until William Cavendish told me its history.'

Her smile didn't falter, and Sam watched it with reluctant admiration.

'My mistake,' she said softly. 'I had no idea you were on such intimate terms with the Cavendish family.'

Angus came to Jeremy's rescue at last – not before time in Sam's opinion – to make the very suggestion he'd thought of himself.

'The man to decide on the theatre's name is not here. I suggest we leave it to Jacob Stein, and start work now on all the urgent matters that *do* concern us.'

Anna lowered her sword, infuriated by Jeremy's defection, but confident that she could rely on Jacob to see that she won in the end. She said a charming goodbye to everyone but Kate, and allowed herself to be led away by Macdonald.

The studio seemed very quiet when the rest of them had gone, but despite all that there was to do Kate still sat at her place at the table, not doing anything at all. Sam disappeared into his kitchen and returned with a mug of coffee in each hand.

'Here you are. Drink up, partner, and then instead of looking pale and wan, sketch me a dress so stunning that no Beatrice worthy of the name would be able to resist wearing it.'

Her strained face almost broke into a grin. 'All right, I *will*.' She gulped down the coffee and thought of something else that needed putting into words. 'Sam, I'm sorry if I'm more trouble than I'm worth.'

She hoped he'd laugh away the possibility, but 'I don't think I'd go so far as to say that' was what he muttered finally.

There was nothing to do but go back to her own drawing-board feeling both chastened and disappointed. It was a comfort to remember a moment when Jeremy Barrington had done his best for the Cavendishes, but Sam had offered her a challenge and she must rise to it or die in the attempt. She took a piece of charcoal and began to draw. Slowly tension faded from the air and the studio was its familiar self again.

The autumn of the year merged so dolefully into winter that a festival to celebrate the achievements of a still-rationed, regimented Britain seemed daily a more and more ludicrous idea. But Kate was struck by a curious fact: the louder grew the Jeremiahs' shrill cries that the idea should be abandoned, the more doggedly Sam and his colleagues went on working. If people didn't want a festival, it seemed to prove that a festival was what they needed most. With logic stood so perfectly on its head, Kate found herself in favour of it after all, and vigorously defended not only the whole mad venture but Sam as well for ever getting involved in it.

She was still in the studio late one evening when Angus Macdonald arrived unexpectedly. He frowned as usual at the sight of her, and she decided she must have dreamed a few quiet moments in the hurly-burly of a first-night party when they'd talked as friends.

'Sam not here? Is he *ever* here, instead of being embroiled in that bloody stupid festival? We have a production to get ready. It would be reassuring if he could remember that occasionally.'

The Guv'nor was in such fine, vituperative form that she decided the day's rehearsals had gone badly. Macdonald was the sort of impatient perfectionist for whom the smallest delay or mishap seemed a disaster and, like his actors, he lived with nerves at full stretch. She could forgive him irritability, but not unfairness.

'The production *will* be ready on time,' she said firmly. 'Sam may not be getting much sleep at the moment, but everything he's said he'll do is being done.'

'All right, but where is he now . . . lolling about over port and cigars with the rest of the fools who've got involved in a charade we don't want and can't afford?'

Kate forgot that they'd been her own sentiments six months ago. She felt like a tigress with a sick cub, or a mother with an ailing child that was being ridiculed.

'It's not a charade,' she shouted. 'It's not a waste of public money, either. We need a little harmless gaiety, and it won't cost a fraction of the millions that are poured into buying guns and bombs to keep an insane world on the edge of yet another war. You're also way off the mark with your sneer about rich living. Sam's reward for an evening's work will be a sandwich and a cup of coffee if he's lucky.'

Startled by the unexpected attack, Macdonald lifted his hands in surrender. 'All right . . . all *right*. I retract the sneer – unconditionally!' She examined his faint smile carefully; there was no derision in it, but she wasn't entirely won over.

'You don't have to consider *us*, of course, but there are plays you could have chosen that aren't set in umpteen different rooms in the same house, and a garden, church, and prison. And it isn't even as if any of them will be the slightest bit of use afterwards for *Pygmalion*.'

'Put like that, I'm afraid it does sound unreasonable,' Angus agreed meekly. Then he asked a question that took *her* by surprise. 'Do you regret being part of the company, Kate?'

She stared at him, puzzled by what seemed like stupidity in a far from stupid man. 'That's *daft* . . . of course I don't.'

Then remembering that he must be aware of his wife's reluctance to acknowledge her at all, she tried to apologise. 'I sometimes regret not knowing when to hold my tongue,' she admitted. 'Aunt Lou is always telling me I should, but I forget again when the moment comes. At getting on for twenty-one you'd think I could do better.'

Angus shook his head, having apparently considered the matter. 'No change can be expected now; I'm afraid we shall have to take you as you are.' He didn't smile as he said it, and she was left with the impression that they might one day decide not to take her at all.

'Can I give Sam any messages?' she asked, anxious to be helpful if she could.

'No – you can go and get some food and sleep. I'll see him at the theatre tomorrow.' He walked to the door, then stopped and stared at her. 'By the way, it's settled now. Opening night at the Swan will be on January the sixth.'

She thought the date had always been fixed, nodded politely, and then took in the rest of what he'd said. Her eyes asked the question she stumbled over putting into words.

'The . . . the *Swan* . . . you d . . . did mean to . . . to say *that*?'

He nodded and watched the tiredness in her face melt away. 'The judgement of Solomon – or, in this case, clever Jacob Stein – is that we should call ourselves the Sheridan Company as a bow in the direction of Anna's ancestor; but the theatre will come to life again under its old name.'

She tried to keep from smiling, afraid that it would seem too much like crowing over his wife; tried to think of something to say, and in the end could only mutter, 'Oh, William *will* be pleased when I tell him.'

Macdonald's hand lifted and seemed about to touch her cheek in an unexpected gesture, but dropped to his side again without touching her. 'It's nearly ten, Kate. For God's sake go home.'

She would have liked to thank him for asking Jacob Stein, wished that she dared apologise for the irritation that Anna must surely be feeling; but while she fumbled for words that would be safe to say he let himself out and walked away.

Christmas was approaching much too fast; twelve days after it they must somehow be ready. The finished theatre looked as beautiful now as Sam's sketches had promised, but it waited expectantly; the first breath of its new life would only come when an audience filled its dark blue seats and the gold-swagged, velvet curtains swung open on Leonato's home and sunlit garden.

Sewing for dear life now in the wardrobe room, Kate left Elsie Manners to conduct the fittings in the actors' dressing-rooms. Elsie would return from time to time to say that small adjustments were required, but she was useless as a judge of what was happening above-stairs. The play as such didn't interest her, and nor did the actors very much. But she loved the materials she handled, and touched them as other women touch flowers.

Kate's impression that all was not going well with the rehearsals came first from Gil Forrest. There was little enough leisure for any of them now, but he'd resumed the habit of coming to Paradise Walk on Sundays in the hope of finding Kate at home. It was an irritating new development to find that more often than not he was left to make do with William and Aunt Lou – Kate having already been collected by Jeremy. Gilbert deeply resented what he thought of as up-staging, although he tried to explain that he was thinking only of Kate.

'You see, ma'am,' he said earnestly to Louisa, 'she may not understand a man like Jeremy Barrington. He's years older than she is . . . sophisticated, and experienced. I'm not saying he'd do her any harm, but then again he might, because he's used to always having what he wants without considering the rights or wrongs of it.'

Aunt Lou looked undisturbed. 'If it's a seduction you're thinking of, I don't think you need worry. Kate grew up in Southwark, not Cheltenham, and it'll take more than Spam fritters at the Savoy to make her lose her head.'

William also watched the visitor's face, more inclined to think there might be something amiss in the company than to worry needlessly about Kate. 'You don't approve of your fellow-Thespian, Gilbert? That must make playing with him rather difficult.'

'Oh, I like him for myself . . . of course I do,' Gil said hastily. 'He's got perfect stage manners – never tops someone else's lines or hogs the limelight. People tend to look at him all the time of course, but that isn't his fault; he's just so damned watchable.' Gilbert drove a hand through his hair, then stared at William. 'Did you ever have the feeling at rehearsals that something was wrong you couldn't put your finger on? I'm sure that's what Angus is thinking, although he's careful not to say so for fear of making us worse.'

William thought of the tension he'd sensed in Jeremy Barrington as well an hour ago. It wasn't unusual at this stage of rehearsals, and it wasn't important as long as the actors didn't begin to think that it was.

'Nothing to worry about,' he said with immense assurance. 'In fact, better a little strain now than the feeling that you're home and dry, with nothing to strive for on the night.'

Gilbert agreed that this might be so and went away to tramp mournfully around Hyde Park, trying not to think of Kate being seduced by a practised charmer even despite a Southwark upbringing.

In fact Jeremy Barrington could have explained that it was the last thing on his mind. Seduction required confidence for success. At the moment he was feeling too depressed and unsure of himself even to try an assault that would certainly end in failure. Kate had agreed to come out with him today but he didn't make the mistake of thinking she was flattered by the invitation. He'd chosen a restaurant where he was likely to be recognised, but it had been for his own reassurance, not hers. She looked around with clear-eyed relish, but he knew she would have enjoyed just as much the Lyons Corner House that some hard-up escort might have taken her to. It was absurd but true that of all the women he knew she was the one who gave him the most comfort at the moment.

'Thank you for taking pity on me, Kate,' he said suddenly. 'I don't think you enjoy these pretentious places very much – you only put up with them to please me.'

Her eyes twinkled at him although she tried to keep her mouth serious. 'Blame a Southwark upbringing, where a meal out is likely to be at the cockle and winkle stall. If you feel comfortable and at home here, that's all that matters at the moment.'

Jeremy glanced round the ornate room, and then suddenly burst into speech. 'At *home*? My darling Kate, home was never like this – that's exactly why I come.' He paused for long enough to pull out cigarette-case and lighter; but she thought he was giving himself time, trying to make up his mind whether or not to go on talking. Then, suddenly, the floodgates were open; having begun, he couldn't help but talk now. 'Home was in a terrace house in one of the seedier streets in Birmingham. The amount of refinement my mother desperately insisted on was a paper-doily on the cake-plate at tea-time. My father used to poke fun at her for it and I wanted to kill him, but in the end it was *him* she sided with. He was an unskilled worker in a car factory and thought that was what I should be as well. When I told him I was going to become an actor he said some things I won't repeat, but have never forgotten.'

'Why not forget them?' Kate suggested gently. 'Your father must feel pretty silly now, if he remembers them.'

'He died during the war, but I'd left home long before then. At fifteen I got taken on as a call-boy at the Birmingham Rep – doing anything, desperate to learn, going to school at night; but even then, grim as life was, I knew it wasn't always going to be like that. Somehow, sooner or later, I was going to be an actor, and a very good one.'

Kate watched him staring down the years at the past and wondered if he was even aware of talking aloud. But he stretched a hand across the table to take hold of hers.

'It happened, largely with the help of a fairy godmother I found at the theatre. She fed me because I was half-starving most of the time, coached me, taught me how to speak and move, and finally told me when I was ready to walk out onto a stage and act.'

'Your mother must have been so pleased then,' Kate murmured, 'surely she must have come to watch you succeed.'

'I wrote and asked her, but she refused. I'd changed my name by then because my dear friend had also said quite rightly that billed as plain John Bagg I probably wouldn't get very far. But my mother was a stubborn, simple woman who couldn't understand that the young man who'd become Jeremy Barrington remained her son. She's still alive and still unable to understand. I send money to an account in Birmingham for her but she never draws on it. For her Jeremy Barrington doesn't exist.'

Kate searched for something to say, but not finding it could only put her free hand over his, offering its warmth and comfort.

'I sometimes think *I* don't exist,' he said desperately. 'I'm like one of those beautiful pieces of stage scenery you and Sam make . . . flat, and completely two-dimensional.' He tried to smile at her, but it was a rictus grin, begging her to help him if she could.

She prayed for guidance and took a deep breath.

'William would tell you it's an occupational hazard for actors – a crisis of identity, he calls it. If you're playing a part that fits into modern life it doesn't matter very much – you can go on being it off-stage as well as *on*. The trouble comes when all your heart and soul have to be poured into playing something like King Lear or Oedipus; suddenly there isn't enough left for being just plain *you* afterwards.'

'So what does this poor unfortunate remnant do?'

'He learns to understand that labels – Bagg or Barrington – don't matter, and that all the truth and beauty and power of what he creates on the stage come as much from inside him as from the playwright who provides the speeches. In other words, dear John-Jeremy, you exist all right and only an idiot could doubt the truth of it.'

He saw in her steady gaze nothing but complete conviction, and felt in the clasp of her hands complete, unselfish affection. Then unexpectedly she smiled, inviting him to share a change of mood.

'It's a pity I'm not good at love scenes. With a rip-roaring seduction in your chambers we could have *proved* easily enough that Jeremy Barrington undoubtedly exists!'

He gave a shout of laughter, despair transmuted into gaiety with the suddenness she was familiar with in actors. 'Sweetheart, it's not too late – we could soon add the love scene!' His eyes lingered on her mouth, but she shook her head so definitely that he knew better than to persist.

He was aware of what he'd sensed before in their outings together – a warm and loving heart, but a strange reluctance in her to wade into the deeper waters of physical desire. Even a light kiss on her mouth had sent her scuttling back inside her shell. One day, he told himself, when he wasn't quite so burdened with his own problems, he would discover the reason for that.

Kate, now feeling burdened too, wondered who else knew about the past humiliations that weighed on Jeremy. Not Anna Macdonald, probably. It was one thing to confide in a Southwark back-street brat, but quite another to take his chance with the step-daughter of a millionaire. Wanting desperately to help him, she offered another piece of advice.

'You could try feeling proud of yourself. It isn't everyone who can get the better of that fearsome Brummy accent!'

He burst out laughing again, aware as he did so that there had never seemed to be anything remotely comical about John Bagg before.

'Gil Forrest thinks that rehearsals aren't going very well,' Kate said suddenly, airing a problem of her own. 'If it's because Anna is upset about the naming of the theatre, I shall feel very responsible.'

'But not remorseful?'

She considered the teasing question and shook her head. 'No, not that. The Swan will still be standing long after this production is part of theatre history. As Aunt Lou would say, I ken fine what I think is right, and I can't help feeling glad, not remorseful, that Mr Stein kenned it too.'

Jeremy smiled at her, but no longer teasingly. He was becoming more and more certain that inside the slender form of Kate Cavendish lay some strength that he might always need. It even began to seem possible that in her company he would find peace of a different kind as well. If he clung hard enough to *her*, Anna's siren voice and body would lose their power to make his blood race and haunt his dreams.

'It's time I took you home, sweetheart; otherwise I might kidnap you and rush you back to the Albany.' But when they got up to leave he stood holding her hands. 'Don't fret about the rehearsals. They have a habit of coming out right on the night.'

Chapter 11

Elsie Manners got through the Christmas festivities more grimly than usual, but she almost convinced herself that the 'indigestion' she was plagued with was getting better, not worse. Kate, watching her friend, got her head bitten off for daring to ask if something was wrong. She tried again when the brief holiday was over, and was told more sharply still to mind her own business. But Elsie was counting the days until they were over the hurdle of the dress rehearsal; after that she'd go and see the doctor.

But an infected appendix wouldn't be ignored any longer. On the morning of the very day Elsie had waited for, Kate came into the wardrobe room and found her slumped over the table, ashen-faced and on the verge of collapse.

'Indigestion,' Elsie whispered, still clutching the unfinished little cap of starched muslin and imitation pearls that Hero was to be married in. 'I'll be all right in a minute.'

Kate bent down to kiss her clammy face. 'Of course you'll be all right, my darling duck, but not as soon as that, I'm afraid.'

Fifteen minutes later they were in an ambulance summoned by Macdonald, on their way to Charing Cross Hospital. Kate waiting for her to be admitted and sedated, was told that an emergency operation would probably be needed, and that for the moment she might as well go home. On her way out she found Sam, making his way in.

'Angus told me,' he said briefly. 'How's our poor girl?'

'Lucky not to have a ruptured appendix; she's had warning of it for days but, being Elsie, thought she could put up with it until after the dress rehearsal. They'll probably operate on her this evening. Much ado about *something*, for a change.'

'Don't agonise . . . Elsie will be all right,' he said gently. 'Bert Trotter was in his cubby-hole when I left the theatre and we have his word for it that she's a "real old trouper" – words of high praise and reassurance in Bert's philosophy. I was also to tell the "nipper" – I'm afraid that's *you* – not to get into a taking about her.'

Kate gave a little sniff and managed to smile herself. 'It's just like belonging to a family . . . theatre people are very kind, I think.'

It was a quality she set much store by; he'd noticed that about her before. And it was also typical of her that the Swan's stage-door keeper was reckoned as much a part of it as the Macdonalds themselves. He found himself thinking that he would have liked to kiss her pale face for comfort, but instead of doing so he merely said instead that they had a dress rehearsal starting in an hour's time.

'So we have,' Kate muttered. 'Well, angels and ministers of grace will have to defend me from too many disasters, that's all.'

Watching intently a little later, Kate found herself forgetting her own responsibilities. She hadn't ever had time to watch a run-through of the complete play before, but now she could understand Gil's reservations about it. Hard as it was to put a finger on what was going wrong, she was nevertheless sure that the Guv'nor must be feeling anxious. The production *looked* beautiful, *sounded* grand; but it simply failed to spring to life. Macdonald's drawn face reflected her own disappointment, and she knew that he must be praying for the miracle the following night that Jeremy had insisted would happen.

The rehearsal was over at last, complete except for the last line of the play, traditionally and superstitiously never spoken until the night of the first performance before an audience. She went into Walter Fairbrass's office to ring the hospital. Elsie had been operated on – the offending appendix had been removed, and there was no reason why she shouldn't be visited the following day. Kate went smilingly backstage again to tell Sam, and walked into the middle of a scene much more packed with real emotion than anything she had just been witnessing on the stage. At the centre of it was Anna, still in stage make-up, but out of costume and wearing a cream silk dressing-gown instead. Her sumptuous last-act dress of violet-blue velvet lay on the floor where she must have thrown it. Her face was starkly white against the vivid red-gold of her hair, and she was on the verge of uncontrollable rage. The sight of Kate was apparently what she waited for.

'So *good* of you to appear at last, Miss Cavendish. Sam thinks you've had a trying day and should be allowed to go home. But sorry as I am about poor Elsie Manners, I will *not* go on stage tomorrow wearing a dress I fall over every time I move. It doesn't fit and it's too long. Either you alter it for me or our designer must find himself a new assistant who can.'

There was a moment's silence. Kate looked from Anna to Sam, saw him about to speak, and quickly shook her head at

145

him. Then she bent down to pick up the beautiful discarded dress. With its richly coloured mass cradled in her arms as if it could feel the sting of rejection, she turned to Anna Macdonald again and spoke in a voice that didn't tremble.

'I expect you're very tired, but if you'll put the dress on for me, I can see what needs doing.'

Instead of the tirade she expected, Anna simply nodded and swept off to her dressing-room. Sam took a deep breath. 'Leave me to tell her that it can be done tomorrow, Kate.'

'Leave it to *me*,' cut in Angus Macdonald. '*I*'ll tell her.'

'Neither of you will,' she said sharply. 'Please don't argue, because I'm going to do it now. Anna is entitled to be certain by tomorrow morning that it's all right.' The expression on their faces made her give a faint, tired grin. 'It's safe to leave us alone together. We shan't murder one another!' About to walk away, she suddenly stopped again. 'I came to tell you, by the way, that Elsie's had the operation – I can visit her tomorrow.'

Anna was creaming make-up off her face when Kate went in. She went on with the unhurried, practised routine, staring at her visitor in the mirror.

'Did you take the trouble to watch the rehearsal, Miss Cavendish?' She saw Kate nod, and asked another question. 'I hope you were suitably moved and impressed?'

Almost certain that she was damned either way, Kate decided that she had nothing to lose by the truth. 'No, since you ask, I wasn't moved at all,' she said calmly. 'But Jeremy has promised me there's nothing to worry about, and I expect you've promised your husband the same thing.'

Anna's eyes glittered like blue steel in the pallor of her face. 'Perhaps I no longer care whether the Swan has a fiasco or not! Have any of you considered that?' If she expected horror she was disappointed; Kate merely shook her head like a teacher whose pupil had just been stupid.

'Not for moment! You're a true professional, for one thing; and for another Beatrice is the part above all others that any actress must crave to play. You couldn't bring yourself to spoil it.'

As if that ended the conversation, she held the dress for Anna to step into. 'You've lost weight since rehearsals started,' she decided. 'That's why it's dipping at the back. But it will be ready for you tomorrow.'

In silence Anna climbed out of it again. Then, for a moment that seemed longer than it was, they stared at one another: a woman dressed in hand-made silk underclothes, to whom glamour would always adhere as if by natural right; and a tired-faced girl in shabby working trousers and sweater. At last Anna spoke in a different tone of voice.

'I hope Elsie Manners is all right?'

Kate's fleeting smile acknowledged the change before she answered. 'Thank you . . . yes, she is.' Then she walked back to her work in the wardrobe room.

It was very late when Bert Trotter appeared, carrying a mug of nearly black tea and a doorstep sandwich with a slab of tinned meat inside it.

'Guv'nor's orders,' he said between wheezes. 'You're to get it orl dahn, else it's me that'll get the blame.'

The tea was hot and sickly sweet, tasting of condensed milk, but it put fresh heart into her, and she wolfed the awful sandwich, suddenly realising that she hadn't eaten all day. Bert watched approvingly.

''Is nibs is waitin' for you . . . but till you're ready 'e's 'avin a kip in the fwoy-yea.' Having brought out the word with triumphant relish, he winked and went away, leaving

Kate blinking tearfully at the velvet in her hands. Two hours later the hem of Beatrice's dress had been lifted and the waist taken in. She was free to go home.

Sam still slept and it seemed cruel to wake him. But when she did she sounded cross. 'I don't know what you think *you*'re doing here.'

'Waiting for you, partner, and you came very timely on the hour . . . I was dreaming that just as His Majesty declared the festival open every one of our pretty little domes and kiosks sank with an ironic gurgle into the Thames-side mud.' Then he stood up and touched her cheek with a rare, shy gesture. 'Come on, I'll take you home before *you* fall asleep . . . it's been a long and rather dreadful day.'

Elsie's greeting from her high hospital bed the following evening was nothing if not typical. 'You're not supposed to be here till seven o'clock, and you look much worse than I do. If things have been going wrong I want to hear about them.'

'Sister *said* I could come early, and you'll hear what you're told,' Kate said firmly. 'I suppose you know you frightened us half to death?'

Her friend looked grimly pleased for a moment. 'Ambulances and emergencies . . . a lot of unnecessary fuss if you ask me. But that's theatre people all over – everything has to be a drama, and twice life-size.' She pointed to a huge basket of hothouse white lilac on a table in the middle of the ward. 'Who d'you think sent *that* in January?'

Kate looked at it and smiled. 'Jeremy, I'd guess. Never mind . . . just to even things up I've brought you the smallest flowers I could find.' They were very small indeed . . . cold, pure snowdrops whose tiny bells were exquisitely striped with green. Elsie tried to frown but she wavered on the verge of tears, and the fingers that she touched the posy with were trembling.

'I'm a stupid, ungrateful, old fool. Why can't I just admit that my friends are much kinder than I deserve?'

Kate leaned over to kiss her cheek. 'Well, you *have* admitted it now, so that's all right. Sister says she's pleased with you, and if you don't misbehave she thinks you might be convalescent in a week from now.'

Elsie watched her friend's face, which looked more tired now than any amount of cheerfulness could conceal. 'I'm sorry, my dear . . . what a time to let you and Sam down like this.'

'Rubbish – all the work is done on this production, and the dresses for *Pygmalion* won't be nearly so heavy. So if you're thinking of sneaking back before you should, you can forget it. Sam will only send you home again.'

'All right, I hear you; there's no need to shout. Now tell me how the dress rehearsal went.'

Kate scarcely hesitated. '*Much Ado* looks ravishingly beautiful. Everyone thinks so – even our demanding leading lady who, by the way, asked after you very kindly!'

'Much obliged, I'm sure. So what else is wrong with it?'

Kate stared with troubled eyes at the regulation white counterpane in front of her but saw instead a man and a woman dressed in sumptuous period costume, confronting one another on a lavishly set stage.

'I ticked off in my mind all the things that were perfect about the production,' she said slowly. 'What I was left with was the one aspect of it that we'd have said couldn't fail.'

'Jeremy and her ladyship? I can't say *I*'m surprised,'

Elsie observed unexpectedly. 'They're too busy competing with each other – that's not how good acting partnerships are made, or any others for that matter.' She was tempted for a moment to add that Anna's marriage partnership might eventually suffer from the same problem as well. But she respected Angus Macdonald enough to believe he'd probably find a way of dealing with it. In any case when did chattering about people's difficulties do anything but make them worse?

'Curtain-up in two hours' time,' she said, looking at the clock. 'You must go. Give all of them my best wishes, Kate, and stop Milly Pearce from coming here to visit me if you can – she'll pretend I'm dying so that she can weep all the time.'

'She's coming with William tomorrow afternoon and I shouldn't dream of stopping her. All through breakfast she was trying to decide what she ought to wear!'

Kate went away smiling at Elsie's snort of disgust, but also thinking of what had been said about partnerships. Benedick and Beatrice were required to compete in the play; they were beautifully matched fencers in a duel of unacknowledged love. But it had to end in mutual surrender. What Jeremy and Anna had been trying to outdo each other in was never really capitulating at all, so that the heart of the play had remained cold. She could see no reason why that should change tonight, in which case Macdonald's crucial opening venture was surely doomed.

Still, her heart lifted at the sight of the theatre, waiting expectantly at the bottom of the little hill that led down from the Strand towards the river. Its portico lights were already shining through the January darkness, and someone – surely Sam – had remembered the perfect finishing touch.

A crimson and white flag, cunningly illuminated, floated above the stage-house once more. Nearly ten years ago she had stood with William on the other side of the river and wept with rage at the devastation; but the Swan was there to prove that evil didn't win in the end.

Inside the theatre the inevitable first-night excitement was growing. Walter Fairbrass, already kitted out in evening-dress, scurried out of the front office to ask about Elsie, and to check for the tenth time that nothing had occurred to mar the perfection of the foyer since he last looked.

'Big night, Kate,' he said proudly. 'I dare say the old Swan saw some grand occasions in its time, but nothing to outdo tonight – the American ambassador's being brought by Mr and Mrs Stein, and everybody who's anybody at all will be in the audience as well.'

She agreed that it would be an evening to remember, and then wished she'd found something else to say, with a less ominous ring to it. Uncertain where else to go and be safe from unanswerable predictions of triumph or disaster, she took refuge in the wardrobe room, and tried without much success to visualise her next task – the picturesque rags that Shaw's Eliza Doolittle might wear. It was no good – her mind wrestled with the problem of whether or not to visit Jeremy in his dressing-room. What free time she had he'd monopolised in the past few weeks; they were friends – she'd even begun to think he would have liked them to be more than friends. She had retreated from that, but she was aware of offering *something* he needed, and felt proud that it should be so. But Sam's warning hadn't been entirely forgotten – great and famous actors didn't always remain constant to their friends. Jeremy might have since regretted that rash confession about John Bagg, and a few weeks' close companionship gave her no permanent claim on him. At last she put the problem aside, certain at least that there was one member of the cast who needed visiting.

Outside the tranquillity of the wardrobe room she walked at once into a feverishly mounting backstage temperature of first-night nerves and desperate gaiety. Gilbert Forrest was sitting at his dressing-table, locked in fear, when she went in.

'Oh Christ, Kate . . . I can't even remember my first line. I must tell Angus that the understudy will have to go on.'

She went to stand behind him and began to massage his rigid shoulder muscles until they relaxed under her hands.

'Gil dear, of course you remember – the others who open the play go off and you're left alone with your friend. You've been dazzled by seeing Hero for the first time, and you say exactly what *would* come into your mind, having just clapped eyes on a beautiful girl.'

'Benedick, didst thou note the daughter of Signor Leonato?' Gilbert spoke the line himself, and gave a shuddering sigh of relief. 'Yes, of course . . . it is *exactly* what he'd say.'

'It's all securely in your memory,' she insisted gently, 'and once the current is flowing between you and the others on-stage, you need only let yourself be carried along by it.'

His hands covered hers where they rested for the moment on his shoulders.

'*Is* it going to work this evening, Kate, or not?'

The quiet question was more difficult to deal with than his desperation had been, but she forced herself to answer it with some certainty finally dredged up from her innermost heart.

'Yes, it will work beautifully, because no one is going to allow the Swan to be let down.'

His mouth twitched into a grin at last. 'Why didn't I think of that? I suppose because actors are so busy worrying about themselves. You're right, sweetheart – it's the Swan that matters tonight. I promise you I'll give it the best I have.'

He sounded himself again – earnest, nice, and inevitably dramatic; it seemed safe to leave him now, and she kissed him for luck and walked away.

At a bend in the corridor, leading to the star dressing-rooms, she hesitated and then suddenly decided that *not* to deliver her good wishes was no way to treat another friend. She turned towards Jeremy's door, then stopped again because Anna was already standing there, in the act of knocking. Kate saw him open the door, and knew from the expression on his face that he didn't need Kate Cavendish now after all. She waited for the door to close behind them and then bolted back to the wardrobe room like a hare regaining the safety of its form. Here was the only place she had any right to be, but the empty room felt very lonely. If only Sam would remember to come looking for her . . . *any-one* would be welcome to intrude on her isolation, even old Bert Trotter, but he'd be too busy, taking in telegrams and messages at the stage door. She decided that she wouldn't stay for the party – feeling tired and sad and unwanted was no way to go to Mr Stein's festivity, even though Macdonald had taken the trouble to invite her very civilly.

A shadow fell across the table in front of her and she looked up, expecting to see Sam. But a shorter, thicker figure stood there, and she knew whose it was – he'd been glimpsed once before at another opening night, and Jacob Stein's face once seen was not easily forgotten.

'Kate? Kate Cavendish?'

She nodded and he held out his hand. 'Angus told me I should probably find you in here.'

For once she was at a loss for something to say. She would have liked to thank him for saving the Swan from demolition, but it seemed presumptuous – he'd done it for reasons of his own, not to make the Cavendishes happy. Feeling tongue-tied and gauche, she hoped he was used to witless subordinates who just stared at him; it probably happened all the time to rich and powerful men who could change other people's lives with a wave of their wand.

'I'm sorry your grandfather isn't going to be here this evening,' Mr Stein said unexpectedly. 'I rather felt he should be.'

Kate's taut face suddenly relaxed. 'He's already been given a tour of inspection of the theatre by Sam, and he'll certainly come and see the play later on; but he decided that tonight it would be more . . . more *fitting* to leave the Swan to you.' Her transforming grin appeared, causing Jacob to wonder what had made her look so sad when he arrived. 'William's a great one for the right gesture – one of life's grace-notes, he calls it,' she announced with pride.

Her visitor nodded calmly, as if this was the kind of conversation he was accustomed to having. 'He's right, of course, but in a fast-dwindling minority, I'm afraid; grace-notes are going out of fashion.'

Having decided that Jacob Stein's intimidating features were misleading, Kate promptly spoke to him as a friend. 'Is it why you let us keep the name of the theatre – because that was fitting too?'

He nodded again and she realised something else about him: there was no need to tell him how much it had mattered because he already knew. Then a wave of his hand indicated her working clothes.

'I expect you're still on duty for the moment, but I hope you're coming to the party afterwards . . . I should like you to meet my wife.'

In the face of such courtesy it seemed impossible to refuse. Instead, she agreed that she could appear at the celebration looking reasonably festive when the time came. His eyes, under hooded lids, suddenly opened more widely – the better to stare at her, it seemed.

'I'm glad to hear you use the word celebration, Kate. Everyone else has been sounding uncommonly cagey about how this opening is going to go.'

He spoke as if the impression he'd been given hadn't worried him, but she was trapped by his intent glance, and thought she knew now why he'd come looking for her.

'I expect you've been talking to the actors,' she said as firmly as she could. 'It's a theatre superstition – unlucky to brag in advance in case the gods who like to punish mortals happen to be listening.'

He smiled, and gave her a formal bow that reminded her of his European ancestry. 'Until later then, Kate.'

He walked out of the room but she stayed where she was, still sitting at her work-table. Tiredness was a physical weight clamping her to the chair, but if one more human being required her to sound confident about the Swan's opening night she would find the strength to run screaming from the theatre.

Chapter 12

Angus prowled about like a hungry leopard, looking for the relief of something to do. But John Clarke, keeping his head as usual when all about him were losing theirs, had everything well in hand. Before the safety curtain was lifted, he was on stage making a final check that every last detail was correct. His assistant was in the prompt corner, call-boy at his side, ready to flick the switches that would bring everyone to the starting line. With fifteen minutes to go before he need be in the foyer with Jacob to greet distinguished guests, there was absolutely nothing for Angus Macdonald to do except decide whether a visit to his wife's dressing-room would make matters better or worse. This close to curtain-up, he knew that she preferred to be left alone, especially with the ordeal of a first night in front of her. He knew also that throughout the rehearsals there'd been something wrong with the way she and Jeremy played together, and with his own ability to remedy the error, or to reach her. It was much too late now to do anything about it but all the same he suddenly found himself knocking on her door.

She was ready to go on – fully made-up, and costumed in gleaming turquoise silk; red-gold hair elaborately coiled and held by jewelled pins that caught the light.

'My dear, no Beatrice ever looked more beautiful,' he said unsteadily.

A little nod acknowledged that she'd heard the tribute, but he felt sure that it scarcely mattered to her. She *knew* how she looked; the important thing was knowing who she *was* – the girl who must both infuriate and enchant Benedick, and who, in a sudden switch of the play's mood, must require him to kill Claudio for the unforgivable insult of impugning her cousin's virtue. All this was in front of her, and for the moment the woman called Anna Macdonald had almost ceased to exist. It was the separation that always occurred at this moment between the actors and everyone else involved in the production, even himself. Knowing it, he still felt lonely and excluded. He touched her hands briefly and then turned away, but he'd reached the door before she spoke.

'It's going to be all right, Angus. Jeremy and I understand one another now . . . I went to see him a little while ago.'

He scarcely speculated what their misunderstanding might have been in the knowledge that her intention was to offer him comfort. The unexpected kindness of it seemed to close the gap that had separated them for weeks past and suddenly it was easy to smile at her.

'Not just all right . . . it's going to be marvellous,' he said with sudden certainty.

And so it was. The hushed, enraptured audience, released as from a spell, finally confirmed the miracle with wild applause. But the players themselves were already certain of it. From the moment of Benedick's first encounter with his Lady Disdain, fear of failure seemed absurd; theatre magic was in the air.

Kate stood in the wings, smiling occasionally at Sam

who came and went upon errands of his own. But by the time the final scene was working towards its climax she could safely abandon her post. She regretted her promise to Jacob Stein but, having given it, must keep it. She missed the curtain-calls and the speeches while she changed her clothes. Then, ready at last, there was no reason not to emerge . . . except that she couldn't bring herself to leave the comforting familiarity of the only place where she seemed to belong. Nobody would miss her . . . not Sam nor Jacob Stein, and Jeremy least of all. She had just persuaded herself that she might decently escape when the call-boy came in with a note.

Darling Kate,
    Please come to my dressing-room at once from wherever you're hiding. I insist that we make our entrance to the party together!

It was signed with Jeremy's flamboyant initial.

The kindness of it almost made her weep. He needed no one's help in making entrances, but in the midst of triumph he'd bothered to guess that perhaps she did. What had seemed impossible a moment ago would be easy now.

Their entrance was made to some effect. From his post of duty at the side of the ambassador's wife, Sam heard the faint hiatus in the hum of conversation. He looked, as everyone else did, at the couple standing in the doorway. Jeremy, golden-haired, smiling, and dressed now in faultlessly tailored evening clothes, was his perfectly presented self; but it took Sam a full moment to be sure he recognised the vision of sophisticated elegance whose hand Jeremy held. Dear God, it *was* Kate – slender as a wand in a sheath of black silk so simple that its only ornament was the narrow straps that tied in a bow on her bare shoulders. A little veil of stiffened black lace was held in place by a velvet bandeau, and beneath it her eyes had been dramatically accentuated. His churchyard waif had finally emerged from her chrysalis, and he watched the moment of transformation with startled and unselfish pleasure. But Jeremy broke the stillness by leading her to where Anna, resplendent in an oyster-coloured gown and a stole of emerald satin, held court. Wonderful as she looked, Sam knew that she understood in one brief glance the foil she accidentally provided to Kate's quite different kind of beauty.

'Most dear Anna,' said Jeremy in his richest voice, 'we come to add our mite to the ocean of praise.' He kissed the hands she held out to him and then, it seemed to Kate, put affectation aside. 'I may never deserve any other claim to fame, but I shall have been Benedick to your incomparable Beatrice.'

A flicker of emotion disturbed Anna's face for a moment, but then she was in control again – the radiant, gracious leading lady.

'Thank you, darling, but we *all* did it together . . . and my marvellous wizard probably did most of all.' She tucked her hand in Macdonald's arm and smiled at him as if to say that *here* was her whole dependence and delight.

It was Kate's last clear recollection of a long and feverishly gay night. She was aware of being introduced to many people, among them certainly Jacob Stein's wife; she thought she drank too much champagne, and smiled too frequently; but mostly she was conscious of Jeremy's tight grip on her hand. He and Anna had just perfectly realised the magnetic attraction that pulled a man and a woman together almost despite themselves. Now, they seemed to be saying that it was all make-believe; the attraction didn't exist. She coupled herself only with Angus, and Jeremy as clearly coupled himself with Kate.

Sam watched, and wondered; but as Kate's face grew pale with exhaustion under its charming little veil, he decided that even the most dedicated observer of events could occasionally take part in the drama. He waited for a moment when Jeremy was entangled in another conversation and ranged himself alongside Kate.

'Ready to go home, partner? You look as if you've done enough celebrating, and I'm tired of shouting at people who don't even listen to my pearls of wisdom.'

Her strained smile reappeared but although she glanced at him, she quickly looked away. 'Thank you, Sam, but . . . but don't worry about me. Jeremy is going to take c . . . care of me himself. I tried to protest, when he's so very tired, b . . . but he insists.'

'Turned down,' Sam said flatly. 'I suppose I should have expected that, given that the hero of the evening is who he is. Of course, you could always just walk out with me now.'

She was forced to look at him and see once more in his face the sternness that had sometimes disconcerted her in the past. He disapproved of her intimacy with Jeremy, it seemed, but he certainly had no right to.

'I shouldn't dream of walking out on a very dear friend,' she pointed out with some heat, 'and in any case I'm *proud* that Jeremy seems to need me a little at the moment.'

Sam's grim expression didn't relax. 'My dear girl, he's on a pinnacle of success, surrounded by fulsome admirers, and acolytes eager to flutter round the shrine. I doubt if he needs you to dance attendance on him as well.'

'Pinnacles are lonely, exposed places,' she pointed out. She couldn't explain, and wouldn't have done even if she could, that beneath tonight's surface gaiety and exhilaration Jeremy was afraid, and probably always would be. Today's triumph could be tomorrow's dismal flop, and the memories of that pre-war beginning as poor John Bagg still haunted him.

'All right, partner. Stay and minister to the lonely toast of London; but I hope you're half as sophisticated as you look in that very fetching rig – otherwise I'm afraid you're misleading people. Now I'm going home to bed.'

He gave an ironic little bow and walked away. She was glad to see him go – Sam Maitland had got far too much in the habit of telling her what to do. When Jeremy reappeared at her side her smile for him was all the more warm and welcoming.

'Sweetheart, shall we follow Sam's sensible example?' he suggested. 'We've done the pretty here long enough and I crave peace and quiet again, don't you?' She could see that he did; his eyes were feverishly bright, but his voice was hoarse with tiredness.

Ten minutes later they were in a taxi travelling, she assumed, towards Paradise Walk. It was a shock to glance out of the window and see that they were going west, not south. Jeremy's grip on her hand tightened.

'Kate, I haven't eaten for hours, and I doubt if you have either. My trusty doorman promised to leave sandwiches for us – don't you think that sounds nice? Just the two of us having a quiet little supper together after all that racket and fuss.'

The memory of Sam's parting shot was very unnerving but she tried her level best to sound calm.

'It seemed to me you were quite enjoying the fuss. Is it really such a hardship to have an audience completely at your feet?'

'In other words, you're telling me not to be so damned affected and actorish! Darling Kate, you're *very* good for me. I've known it since the first moment you appeared at Sam's front door, trying to make up your mind whether you'd let me in or not.'

He lifted her hand to his lips, and already her poor little garment of sophistication was in tatters. Sam had been unforgivably right – she had no business at all to be where she was, still misleading a charming, experienced man who now thought he'd been given clear encouragement to proceed. She had meant well, but the road to hell was said to be paved with good intentions. Wanting to help Jeremy, she'd missed the sign that said she was running into danger, but she could see it now, all right. If she went inside his rooms tonight and tried to eat his little supper it would be tantamount to saying that she was ready to sleep with him as well. The effect of Jacob's champagne had worn off, leaving her with a headache, and feeling more tired than she'd ever felt in her life before, but she had to find something to say before it was too late and she humiliated Jeremy and herself.

'Jem dear,' she began hoarsely, 'I'm afraid I'd be sick if I tried to eat anything. It's been too long and fraught a day. I'd just like to go home, and *you* must need sleep even more than I do.'

The light from a street lamp slanted in, showing him her bone-white face and desperate eyes. Exhaustion was there, but something else as well that he recognised as fear and knew he mustn't ignore. It seemed a long time before he spoke but when he did she sensed no anger in him – it might have been the moment, she decided afterwards, when she began to love him.

'I'm sorry, sweetheart – I was being very selfish, as actors always are.' Then he tapped on the glass and directed the cabbie to change direction and take them first to Southwark. Outside her front door, he gently kissed her mouth.

'I meant what I said about you being good for me, dearest Kate. Shall we promise always to be friends?'

'*Best* friends,' she agreed gravely, and saw a smile light his exhausted face. Then he climbed into the taxi again and she stumbled thankfully indoors to bed.

They were a month into the run of *Much Ado*, with everything running smoothly. It was time, Angus knew, to start rehearsals for the next production . . . if only he could find the right moment to tell Anna so. But their lives never seemed to coincide for long enough nowadays to do more than smile and wave at each other. She always woke late, and breakfasted in bed after he'd left the flat. By the time he got back to it she was getting ready to leave for the theatre. It was a strange, unnatural marriage, even though their nights were spent in a shared bed. Anna saw this as no place for a leisurely, comfortable conversation. Either she would be deeply asleep before he could join her, or in a mood to be made love to. Then she would offer herself so urgently that their other lack of communication scarcely seemed to matter, and he could almost convince himself that there was nothing wrong with their marriage after all.

Sundays should have been something to look forward to, but somehow they had become the days when social life took over. The flat in Cheyne Walk was a meeting-place for the people Anna called her friends. They were fashionable and brightly amusing, and Macdonald found himself disliking most of them very much indeed. One afternoon he made the mistake of saying so when the door finally closed behind the last of them.

'It's indecent for anyone invited for a pre-lunch drink to be still here at four o'clock,' he said savagely. 'Too much trouble to go home, I suppose, between us and their next free-loading port of call.' He saw Anna's mouth tighten and knew that he was meant to apologise, but for once irritation elbowed discretion aside. 'My dear, be honest . . . admit that they're vapid, gossiping women and self-satisfied men obsessed with making money. You can't really enjoy them any more than I do.'

'Since I invite them why not assume that I find them worth knowing?' she asked coldly. 'What else do you suggest we do on a grey February day in the middle of London – sit and stare at the Sunday newspapers or at each other?'

Angus gave a disparaging glance round the room, but when he looked at his wife her set face made him speak in a more gentle tone of voice.

'We shouldn't be here at all when we're not working. Anna love, let's find ourselves a little cottage to escape to – near enough to reach after the Saturday night performance. We could have a log-fire to sit by when it's cold and wet, a hill to climb when it's fine, and peace to find contentment in each other. That's what we need, not a round of noisy cocktail-parties.' His dark eyes were not fierce now, but sad and pleading. Almost she was tempted to wonder whether perhaps he might be right; some still, small voice of reason urged her to admit that now or never they must weld their marriage into something real and lasting. But the excitement she craved was here in London – reality had become the time she spent on stage with Jeremy, being someone else. Who could she be in a cottage in the country, with no one but this self-contained husband to play to? The prospect was so frightening that she spoke more sharply than she meant to.

'Arrive exhausted after midnight to find that the water-pipes have frozen and the plumbing doesn't work? My dear Angus, I don't think so. I happen to *like* Cheyne Walk.' His face had become expressionless again and she was obliged to give a little ground. 'If you want a place to write in, by all means find your cottage. That way we might have your dramatised version of *Anna Karenina* in time for next season.' It was an ambition of his that she was eager to share; the part would be a gift to any actress, and she couldn't help but realise how beautiful she would look decked out in Russian sables.

'I'm afraid there's more immediate work to think about,' he said, seizing the moment that had arisen. 'It's time to start rehearsals for *Pygmalion* if we're to put it into the repertory in a month from now.'

There was a little silence before she got up, slowly and gracefully as she'd been trained to do, and moved about the room switching on the lamps. The winter dark had certainly closed in, but he suspected that her real purpose was to gain a little time while she decided what to say.

'I know I agreed to that play,' she said at last, 'but I should prefer not to do it next, Angus. It's a huge part to learn, and poor Jeremy's would be even worse – Professor Higgins never stops talking. Let's change the programme round . . . do *Private Lives* next, please.'

He took a deep breath and promised himself that he wouldn't shout at her.

'We *can't* just "change the programme round" now. My dear girl, be reasonable. Walter Fairbrass has published the opening date and started selling seats for Bernard Shaw, not Noël Coward; I'm afraid that even your bird-witted friends would be able to tell the difference. Apart from that, Sam and Kate have been slaving away at *Pygmalion* for the past month.'

'Of course . . . consider Sam, and the indispensable Kate Cavendish . . . think of poor Walter Fairbrass, if you must – think of anyone, in fact, but me!'

Quietness fell on them again, only faintly disturbed by Sunday's occasional traffic noise from the street outside.

'I thought you *wanted* to play Eliza Doolittle,' Angus said at last. 'Anna, it's a plum of a part in the best play Shaw has ever written; but if the work is too heavy for you on top of *Much Ado*, I could find someone else . . . you don't have to drive yourself.'

'If we do it, *I* shall play Eliza; let there be no mistake about *that*. But I've reread the play recently and I'm left with the feeling that the great George Bernard Shaw is a prosy old bore who has no right to be writing plays when he doesn't understand the first thing about flesh and blood men and women.'

On sure ground now, Angus moved across to her and took hold of her hands. 'I'll prove you wrong, sweetheart . . . just let us get rehearsals started and I promise I'll *prove* to you what a play it is.' No longer angry, no longer bored, his dark eyes shone, and she couldn't help but yield because his certainty was irresistible, and his theatre instincts not to be argued with. He felt her resistance crumble, and leaned forward to kiss her in sudden gratitude. Then he cupped her face in his hands.

'I get frightened sometimes that we might lose each other in this mad life we lead. We must be very careful not to do that, mustn't we, Anna?'

She smiled faintly but released herself and said that it was time to write her weekly letter to New York. When she'd gone out of the room he was left alone to reflect on things that gave him no comfort. As with all their disagreements, nothing had been solved. She hadn't answered his last question, and he had come no nearer to changing the pattern of their hated London Sundays.

Chapter 13

Sam Maitland shared Anna's lack of enthusiasm for *Pygmalion*, although his reason would have been difficult to admit to – he thought the principal actors would be miscast in it. Playing against their natural grain very occasionally resulted in remarkable performances, but the strain on everyone concerned was great, and the risks of failure very high. He suspected that Jeremy himself might take the same view, having a very clear idea of what his talents fitted him to do. Sam would have liked to ask him, but intimate conversations seemed difficult nowadays. Constraint had crept into their friendship, and since it hadn't happened before, Sam was inclined to put the blame on Kate. Perhaps even without knowing it, she was the catalyst in their midst, causing changes without being changed herself. Come rain or shine, come triumph or disaster, she would remain stubbornly, unalterably herself. He could imagine circles in which this quality would be a virtue, or at least do no harm. But in the volatile, mercurial world of the theatre, among people who liked to believe and then discard the fantasies they were continually creating, she was as dangerous as an uncharted rock to passing sailors.

He was sure of this about her now. Observation – honed

and dagger-sharp – informed him that thanks entirely to her, Gilbert Forrest had recovered from a harmless infatuation for Anna, and now less harmlessly disliked Jeremy instead. Their leading lady, who wouldn't permit another woman to upstage her, was as much irritated by this defection as she was by her husband's changed attitude towards Kate. Macdonald hadn't snarled at her for weeks, and had recently been seen to smile very pleasantly in her direction. Worse still was the case of Jem himself, whom Anna now counted on as her personal property. Instead of that, he seemed committed to a death or glory assault on Kate that must end in grief for one of them. Either Southwark obstinacy would prove too much for him, or he would win in the end. Sam tried to pretend to himself that he didn't much care which the outcome was. But Jem's charm and wealth and fame would almost certainly capture her eventually, and then he would soon lose interest in a girl who suddenly became no different from all the others who offered themselves.

In this litany of anxieties Sam carefully didn't include a sadness of his own. Since the night of the *Much Ado* party when he'd as good as accused her of cheating Jeremy, his partner had withdrawn her confidence from him. Of course it didn't matter; but the joy had gone out of their work together. They'd been used to arguing about anything under the sun – the Cold War, poor squatters, rich spivs, the new verse drama of Christopher Fry, or the old sublimities of Shakespeare; now they only spoke when words were necessary.

In this atmosphere of cool formality he finally managed to enquire of her whether Jeremy was enjoying the rehearsals of *Pygmalion*.

'Why shouldn't he be enjoying them?' It was a feminine trick she normally despised, answering a question by asking another one, but the query underlined an anxiety of her own – Jeremy looked strained and unhappy, despite the continuing success of *Much Ado*.

Sam gave a little shrug. 'It occurred to me that the part of Professor Higgins is one he might not be happy with, that's all. Jem's genius is for creating a character that the audience can take to its vast collective bosom and adore. Shaw doesn't care whether we like Henry Higgins or not; in fact, we're *supposed* to see him as a charming but tyrannical egoist, blind to everything but his own overruling passion.'

Kate wished she could disagree, but as usual Sam was right – both about the play, and about Jeremy who, more than most actors, needed to be admired and loved. She did her best all the same to sound convinced of what she said.

'*Pygmalion*'s a challenge, but that's all to the good. Jeremy is too fine an actor to want easy parts all the time.'

'I bow to your superior knowledge then,' Sam said pointedly. 'But if it isn't the play, some other little problem must be causing that "lean and hungry look".' He went on considering the model in front of him as if he didn't expect her to answer, but after a moment or two she picked up the challenge she knew he'd thrown down.

'Why not say what you mean?' she asked carefully. 'Why not blame *me*? I'm misleading . . . I think that was your expression . . . a lovely man who ought to be given what he wants.'

Sam watched her downbent face and came to the conclusion that in one important aspect he'd been wrong about her. She certainly looked different now, and it was no wonder Jem had got himself in such an emotional tangle. New-found poise added to the old elusive charm was a potent enough combination to bewitch any impressionable man. Sam, who thankfully knew himself to be quite *un*impressionable, was nevertheless not blind. A girl with Kate's eyes and mouth couldn't escape love for long. She'd been reared in Aunt Lou's Calvinist code of right and wrong, but it would crumble in the end. When it did, the dangerously taut mesh of relationships that held them together at the moment would finally be ripped apart.

She looked across the table at him, still waiting for his answer.

'If I've ever talked of blame I must have been unbearably interfering,' he said with the formality of a stranger. 'Neither you nor Jem need concern yourselves with my opinions. We all have to make our own choices – that's quite enough of a responsibility without worrying about what outsiders will make of them.'

It was a statement so reasonable that she could see no way of taking exception to it; there was nothing to do but go back to her task of designing the balldress that would allow a transformed Cockney ragamuffin to take polite London society by storm. They worked in silence for a little while, but suddenly Sam spoke again.

'Kate, I'm going away for a week or two. I wasn't sure it could be fitted in, but we're ahead of schedule, and my festival work is up-to-date as well; so I've finally decided to go.'

She stared at him again, this time noting the signs of tiredness she'd ignored before. He'd grown up in cold, inhospitable places and been very ill, she remembered. They'd fallen out of friendship, but she didn't want him to be ill again. Perhaps he *was* ill already, and concealing the fact from her. The thought was a jolt under her heart, because however irritating she found him, he was still Sam, and somehow important to her.

'Of *course*, go away and take a holiday . . . have a rest for as long as you can, but for goodness' sake find somewhere *warm*, though, for a change.'

The impulsive little speech, sounding more like the girl he had known, almost made him smile, but he shook his head. 'It's only a busman's holiday. I've been invited to go to Milan – new sets are required for a production of *La Bohème* at La Scala. Renata Tebaldi's to sing the part of Mimi, and with a bit of luck we might at least hear her rehearsing.' He was surprised by the 'we' he'd just said, but suddenly pleased as well. The psychoanalysts were right after all; left to itself, the subconscious came to some sensible conclusions. But Kate was looking blank and he had to explain.

'I thought my partner might like to be in on the job.'

After what seemed a long time the answer came. 'I'm afraid she wouldn't like it at all.' It sounded ungracious even to her, but she couldn't explain the sickening recoil within her heart and mind at the mere mention of the place where presumably her father's family still lived. It would have relieved her agitation to be able to shout at Sam, but she forced herself to speak quietly.

'I have no wish to go to Italy at all . . . *ever*.' The pained astonishment in his face made her bend over her sketch again. 'In any case La Scala wouldn't be my cup of tea – I like Nellie Wallace, remember?'

The sketch was dragged out of her hand and she was left staring at Sam again, but this time his face was alight with a bright, rare flame of anger.

'I thought it was a joke . . . something you'd copied from Winston Churchill during the war, because we needed to share his amused contempt for the Italians. Perhaps their showing *wasn't* very heroic, but you can't seriously refuse to go and see what the country has to offer. Dear God, Kate, you're a *designer*, and they have more than their fair share of the world's greatest art and architecture – not to mention music and literature besides, and the sheer irreplaceable beauty of the countryside.'

This outburst came from the heart, and for a moment he couldn't believe that she had scarcely listened to it. They'd disagreed often enough but never before had he seen in her face this mulish determination not to even hear what he said. He reached across the table to clamp her shoulders in a painful grip while he raged at her.

'Listen to me. You're too intelligent to behave like a bigoted fool and go on hating people who found themselves trapped on the wrong side in a war they didn't want. Mussolini ranted them into thinking they'd enjoy being Fascists. They didn't enjoy it, but he's dead, and they realise their error. That's the end of the story.'

'Stop shouting at me and leave me alone,' she shouted back. 'I'll hate them if I want to – they're cruel, cowardly people. There are plenty of other paintings and palaces to admire; I'll see them instead.'

His hands were hurting her, but what she registered more intensely was the fact that he had never touched her before. She'd always been treated with an outdated but charming courtesy. Now, the naked emotion in his face was frightening, and even more so was the strange physical response she felt within herself. Here, unsuspected and unforeseen, was the danger she must beware of, because suddenly there was nothing left to breathe except this frightening exhilaration that could lead her heaven knew where. But Sam had seen the terror in her face, and let go of her so abruptly that she almost fell. The sudden storm was past, and even if he had been driven by it too he was only intent now on watching the grey, seaward-hurrying river.

'Hate or love whomever you must, Kate,' he said quietly. 'It's nothing to do with me.'

Breathing fast, as if she'd just been running a gruelling race, she stood and watched him – a familiar, shambling figure dressed as usual in paint-splashed sweater and corduroys, dark hair curling on the back of his neck because it needed cutting, hands jammed in the pockets of his trousers. Nothing to disturb her after all . . . no reason to feel so immensely sad because she'd just been told that anything she thought, or said, or did, made no difference at all to Sam Maitland.

'I've got plenty of work to be getting on with here,' she muttered at last. 'I hope you enjoy Milan and get to hear Renata-whatever-her-name-was.'

'Generously said, partner!' His taut face relaxed into the ghost of a smile when he turned to look at her, so perhaps friendship wasn't quite dead after all. But she saw him very little in the next few days before he left for Milan, and she had the sad feeling that something precious had been lost for good; he would come back the polite stranger who had said goodbye to her. She didn't know, because Aunt Lou neglected to inform her of the fact, that he called at Paradise Walk before he left London.

There was reason to be grateful he'd gone away when the storm that had been brewing at the Swan finally broke over them. The rumpus was considerable, but at least its echoes couldn't reach as far as Milan. Without quite knowing why, she had the feeling that Sam held *her* responsible nowadays for whatever went wrong – even probably including the ruptured appendix from which Elsie was still recovering. It seemed a very unreasonable attitude, given the explosive temperaments around them, and unlike a man who was in general fair-minded. The present furore was certainly not of her making – only by sheer bad luck and Pat O'Donovan's urgent SOS was she in the theatre to get involved in it at all.

'I'm sorry, Kate, but a great ham-fisted fool of a stage-hand put the end of his steel ladder through a flat – and it's slap in the middle of the set, too,' Pat said apologetically when she arrived. 'I've cut out the torn canvas, and fitted a new section, but Leonato's terrace looks a mite odd now, I'm thinking. Do you reckon you can get it painted before tonight?'

'I'm afraid I shall have to! It *would* be my beautiful balustrade that got ripped, though – making the curves match is a laborious job.'

She was at the back of the stage roughing in an outline on the stretch of blank canvas when Gilbert Forrest appeared. It was rare for them to meet now that her spare time was spent with Jeremy Barrington. She felt a twinge of guilt, remembering Gil's kindness to her in Birmingham, and a stronger twinge of astonishment that his brief infatuation for Anna had caused her so much unhappiness. It all seemed to have happened a long time ago. His obvious pleasure at seeing her made her smile, but she fended him away from her with the long ruler in her hand.

'Why am I not allowed to kiss you nowadays?' he asked intensely. 'Is it because I'm not the all-conquering great man himself?'

She frowned over a question that irritated her. 'No – it's

just that I haven't time for kisses from anyone – I'm working against the clock. If *your* being here, dear Gil, means an on-stage rehearsal, I'm afraid Macdonald's going to have to put up with me as one of the noises not quite off.'

'Well, first of all he'd like to know what the hell you're doing here at all,' said a disembodied voice from the wings beside her. A moment later its owner loped onto the stage in time to see her blush. The world of the theatre dealt as a matter of habit in the coinage of Christian names; but in his case she couldn't manage it. He remained for her simply Macdonald, or the 'Guv'nor' as the stage-hands called him.

'There was a slight mishap to some scenery,' she explained quickly. 'Nothing we can't repair, but if I don't get on with the painting, it won't be dry by tonight.'

His brows were pulled together in a straight black line, but she doubted if she were the cause for once of his short temper. Her impression was that he drove them and himself hard nowadays, not to be disagreeable, but simply to stifle some inner distress. He was a difficult, unsociable man, but in an unexpected way she had come to find him likeable.

'We shall be reading this morning, not moving about,' he said at last. His hard mouth showed no inclination to relax, but all the same she thought he'd found something about her that amused him – perhaps she'd already got paint on her nose. 'If you don't clank paint-tins about or otherwise draw attention to yourself, we shan't mind you being here.'

About to promise that she wouldn't clank, or even try to distract them by standing on her head, she was saved by the arrival of the rest of the cast – Anna, Jeremy, David Kent and his wife who would play Colonel Pickering and Professor Higgins's mother respectively, and a newcomer who was to take the other key rôle of Eliza's father, Alfred Doolittle. Jeremy had told her that he was shaping very well as Shaw's talkative, subversive specimen of the undeserving poor, and Kate went quietly on with her work, glad to have the chance of listening to him.

Macdonald seemed to be anxious to avoid interruptions; the point of the run-through was to establish the crucial timing of Shaw's dialogue correctly, and to get its rhythms right. But they hadn't got very far into Eliza's visit to Professor Higgins to negotiate for elocution lessons before he broke in.

'Anna love, your vowels are slipping! She's still the Covent Garden guttersnipe – you're making her sound as if she's half-way to the genteelness of the flower-shop already. More Cockney rasp, please . . . in fact more impudent spirit altogether. Remember that it's taken courage for her to invade the classiness of Wimpole Street.'

There was a little silence before Eliza's lines were repeated again . . . almost shouted this time in Anna's determination to produce sufficient spirit.

Angus waved her on even though it still wasn't right, and they probably all knew it. He was reluctant to add to her dislike of these early scenes by pulling her up again, but five minutes later he had to. She had listened with a trained ear to the recorded sounds of Cockney speech, and was more or less reproducing them; but the end result was as little like a flower-girl from Hoxton as Bert Trotter would have managed to sound like a peer of the realm.

'Anna . . . no! I'm sorry, but we'll have to go over that again. Sweetheart, remember who you *are*. Eliza's cheeky, independent, and fiercely proud, but she's still impressed in spite of herself by Professor Higgins. She's not his equal yet, and knows it – she's still his "squashed cabbage leaf".'

'A moment ago I wasn't spirited *enough*,' she said coldly. 'Make up your mind, Angus. I'm not the reincarnation of some East End street-urchin, only an actress doing her best; if that isn't enough for you, you must say so.'

'It's exactly what's wrong,' he explained with the gentle patience he only showed towards her. 'Of course you're an actress pretending to be a street-urchin, but you mustn't *sound* as if you are.'

By now it was impossible for Kate not to turn round and watch as well as listen. It was safe to do so; they sat with their backs towards her, facing Macdonald. Even so, she could feel their unease, and the crackle of tension in the air. She could see Macdonald's pent-up frustration, and guess at Anna's infuriated, wounded pride. A lesser actress was bound to take this kind of criticism in her stride, would even be grateful for it, but to someone of Anna's reputation it must sound like a public humiliation.

'Let's try that last speech once more,' Angus was asking. 'Don't *think* about it . . . just *be* this wonderful guttersnipe who so passionately wants to better herself.'

But no sound came at all from his wife; she seemed to be locked in silent confrontation with a man who instead of being her husband might have been an inimical stranger. It was a trial of wills that threatened to become unbearable, an aching silence demanding to be filled. Jeremy took a deep breath, about to try to save the situation by suggesting that he and Anna could work on the difficult scene by themselves. Then from the back of the stage came the lines Macdonald had been waiting for, only now they rent the air in the true accents of Shaw's street-urchin – raucous, defiant, and completely authentic.

'Oi know what's right. A lydy friend o'mine gets French lessons from a real French gennelman for eighteen pence an 'our. Well, you wouldn't 'ave the face to ask me the same for teachin' me me own language, so I won't give more'n a shillin'. Take it or leave it.'

The echo of the words died into an even profounder silence. Then Kate stepped out of the shadow of a piece of scenery, having remembered too late that she'd been told not to draw attention to herself.

'That was Southwark, not Hoxton, I'm afraid,' she said hesitantly, 'and Professor Higgins would certainly have been able to tell the difference.' She would have gone on to apologise for the interruption but Anna couldn't permit her to hold centre-stage any longer. She stood up herself, tense and tragic – but with eyes as unfriendly as naked steel in the pallor of her face.

'*Now* I understand,' she informed them all. 'Hiding behind the scenery, our little seamstress sees her chance. She might never hope to play another part, but this is one part she thinks she *can* play because she doesn't have to act at all. She need only be herself!' Then she stared at Kate. 'It was a clever try, but it won't work. *I* am going to be Eliza Doolittle, Miss Cavendish, not you.'

The biting insolence in her voice made Jeremy's hands curl, waiting for what might happen next . . . with Kate God knew it could be anything. But she only stood watching her adversary, trying to remember that Anna's anger had been justified.

'I wasn't hiding behind the scenery; I was painting it,' she said distinctly. 'And I have no chance even in *this* play, because I can only remember lines when it doesn't matter. The other drawback is that I can't act. *You* can be Eliza *and* the dazzling creature who gets taken to the ball. I should have to remain as I began – the Cockney street-urchin. I don't mind that in real life – in fact, I'm rather proud of it; but it wouldn't do for Eliza.'

Anna looked round the circle of intensely watching faces. She offered *them*, but not Angus, a faint shrug and a charmingly rueful smile. 'My dears, I'm sorry, but I can't continue this wearisome rehearsal *and* perform tonight. Let me off now and I promise to do better tomorrow.' Then she smiled beautifully at Jeremy. 'Darling, I need a restoring drink at the Savoy, and after that you can take me on an East End pub-crawl. If we spend the afternoon listening to the natives' wood-notes wild, perhaps *that* will turn me into a convincing guttersnipe!'

He took the hand she offered him, glanced in Kate's direction but looked away again, and then walked with Anna off the stage. Kate stared after them blindly for a moment but at last remembered what it was that she was supposed to be doing there. In front of Leonato's half-finished balustrade again, she heard Macdonald dismiss the rest of the cast, and listened to their subdued voices fading into the distance. All *she* had to do was get on with her own work and not remember a time when Jeremy had taken her side, not Anna's. At least it was a mercy Sam hadn't been there. He'd have said she'd got what she deserved for forgetting that even the smallest competition with Anna wasn't allowed.

'I'm afraid the Savoy wouldn't be tactful, but I could offer you a restoring drink somewhere else,' Macdonald's voice suddenly suggested behind her.

She swung round, afraid that she might complete her ruin by bursting into tears.

'Thank you, but I'm not in need of restoring,' she said hoarsely, 'and even if I was, Bert Trotter's tea would do the trick. He'll be bringing it any time now.'

'And you wouldn't want to disappoint *him*, of course. It doesn't matter about hurting the Guv'nor's feelings.'

She wished she could be sure whether he was serious or not; decided in the end that he couldn't be, and risked a grin. 'Guv'nors don't have feelings – that's an article of faith with the rest of us!' Then she suddenly grew serious again. 'I'm truly sorry about this morning . . . I didn't mean to ruin the rehearsal, or upset your wife; but you were waiting for those lines and because I knew them they just came out.'

'The rehearsal was ruined already . . . or are you going to pretend you hadn't noticed?' He sounded discouraged – no, worse than that, she thought – deeply sad. It wasn't surprising; he'd just had to watch his wife turn to another man in a moment of difficulty they should have shared together.

'Anna *will* get hold of Eliza,' she said earnestly. 'She's too good an actress to fail in the end.'

Macdonald didn't answer for a moment, then smiled with the warmth that came so rarely to soften his hard features. 'I hope to God you're right; but I'm certain of something else – she's a less generous fighter than you are, Kate.'

Then he walked away, and this time she was indeed alone until the wheezy rattle of Bert's asthmatic lungs announced that tea and meat-paste sandwiches had arrived.

Chapter 14

The two weeks Sam allowed himself in Milan were hectic but memorable. Humbled by the way in which a war-ruined opera house had been magnificently rebuilt, he was also nonplussed by his colleagues' mixture of slapdash brilliance and unreliability. His co-designer, responsible for the production's costumes, explained that it was how Italians preferred to work. They were not as the Anglo-Saxons were, he said truthfully. Something had to be left to chance and the inspiration of the moment, because life struck them as more interesting that way.

'And if inspiration fails to arrive in time?' Sam asked his new friend, over a very late dinner one evening.

Giorgio di Palma gave the shrug that seemed to be an essential part of any conversation. 'Then we manage without it,' he admitted with a charming smile. 'At least a troubled history has taught us one thing – how to survive disasters!'

He considered the quiet-voiced foreigner opposite him, whose coming had been objected to with so much sound and fury, because it was well-known that the English had no love of music in their arrogant, matter-of-fact souls. But the *direttore* had been adamant and the Inglese had arrived – speaking adequate Italian, as it turned out, and apparently knowing his *La Bohème* quite as thoroughly as the rest of them. Two days had been enough for everyone to agree that his work was brilliant – unanimity so rare in an Italian opera house that it came close to being a miracle.

Giorgio watched his guest sipping wine with the thoughtful relish that seemed to be his approach to life, and made another confession.

'We were stupid, Sam . . . didn't want you to come, because we thought you were bound to hate us for being with the Nazis during the war. And if not that, at least you'd despise us because we fought so badly. We *can* do better, but not when our hearts aren't in it, you understand.'

'Well we're not fighters, either, unless our hearts are in it, and we never make good haters,' Sam pointed out. A gleam of amusement shone in his face. 'Far from despising, you could say I came to praise Italy, not to . . .'

'Not to bury it!' Giorgio pounced on the misquotation with joy and finished it off.

Sam raised his glass, acknowledging a master-stroke, but it was time to broach a different matter that haunted his mind.

'Giorgio . . . if I wanted to look for someone here, not known to me, how would I set about it?'

'You know his name, of course . . . you're sure he lives in Milan?'

'I'm sure of nothing except his name, but it isn't listed in the telephone directory. He rejoined his family here after living in London but that was twenty years ago.'

Giorgio's hands sketched an expressive gesture. '*Dio mio*, it's not very much to go on, my friend. If he was a theatre man, that might help.'

'Nothing to do with the theatre . . . he was a jeweller, I believe. The same surname appears in the directory, but not *his* name or initial. I don't want to disturb a dozen people unless I have to, to enquire whether they have a relative called Arturo.'

Taking another sip of wine, Sam slowly became aware of Giorgio's fixed stare. Then the Italian cleared his throat and spoke in a low murmur. 'You don't by any chance refer to a man called Arturo *Contini*?' He smiled at Sam's expression of astonishment. 'I only know of him because one of my sisters married into the family – she worked for a fashion house that bought costume jewellery from the Continis. Arturo, her husband's uncle, was sent to live in London after the First War. You didn't find him in our telephone directory because he now lives in Florence. When he became head of the firm he decided that the centre of the jewellery trade was there, not in Milan. If you wish to see him Graziella will help me arrange for you to make a visit.'

'If your sister will give me his address, I should like to take it back with me to London,' Sam said, aware of Giorgio's curiosity. 'The enquiry concerns someone else . . . it's nothing to do with me. But if you could tell me a little about him, I should be interested.'

It occurred to Giorgio that for a man whom the matter didn't concern, his guest was showing unusual interest, but he assembled in his mind what he knew about Graziella's uncle by marriage.

'He was the younger son of old Cesare Contini. The family had been gold- and silversmiths for generations, but Cesare was the one who made the firm known far beyond Milan. His elder son, Paolo, would eventually have taken over, but when he died at the beginning of the war, Arturo became the *padrone* instead.'

'He married . . . added to the family, I expect?' Sam suggested casually.

'He married as soon as he came back to Italy. By then the girl Cesare had picked out for him was old enough. But it seems not to have been a happy marriage, right from the start; perhaps Arturo had changed during his time in London. There was only one child, a son called Alessandro. He was killed when he was fifteen, running messages for the guerillas who were helping to drive the Germans out of Florence. Arturo's wife never forgave him – he was a leading figure in the Resistance; she blamed him for not keeping the boy safe, even though in such terrible times nobody was safe. Now he's left with a wife who seems to hate him, and no child. Paolo's sons will take over the firm when he dies.'

Sam thought of that story in relation to the one he'd listened to in Paradise Walk. Perhaps William was right to blame Arturo for his daughter's death, and perhaps Kate was justified in hating a man she didn't know; but nobody could say that he'd escaped punishment.

'What kind of a man is he? Do you like him?' Sam finally asked.

Giorgio gave the expected little shrug. 'I meet him on family occasions once or twice a year . . . perhaps see him if he visits Milan. We exchange remarks about our work and grumbles about our politicians. It isn't very much to base an opinion on when the man is an unusual Italian who doesn't talk about himself. All I can tell you for sure is that he still hates Germans, and that he's very clever . . . an artist as well as a craftsman. What he does, other jewellers copy.'

Sam nodded and abandoned the subject of Arturo Contini before Giorgio's longing to ask questions of his own finally got the better of him. The subject wasn't mentioned again for the rest of the visit, but on the day he left Milan he was handed a Florentine address written in a girl's flowing hand.

'My sister was curious,' Giorgio admitted, 'women always are, *non è vero*? I told her that someone in London wanted to get in touch with Arturo again.'

Sam thanked his friend but let the subject drop. Then having been invited with the utmost cordiality to think of Milan as his second home, and finally waved good-bye, he made the journey back to London wondering what the chances were that Kate would decide to get in touch with her father – small to non-existent, he decided, as the plane touched down with a bump and he was back on English soil.

Watched over by Kate, Elsie Manners had started working again at home. She was decorating the brim of a battered velvet hat with purple ostrich feathers – Eliza Doolittle's smartest headgear for a visit to Wimpole Street – when Milly Pearce conducted a visitor upstairs. It was a climb that made her pant a little nowadays, but she didn't grudge the effort for Sam Maitland. He was kind enough to slow his pace to hers, and treated her with the gentle courtesy that a middle-aged lady found agreeable. She would have liked to stay and help entertain him but Elsie, caustic as usual, pointed out that she needn't bother, because it wasn't likely to be a social call.

Sam admired the hat, and smiled at the rest of the out fit Kate had sketched – voluminous dark skirt, tattered shawl, flowered purple blouse to match the feathers, and buttoned boots.

'Eliza's Sunday-best for calling on Professor Higgins,' he guessed. 'She's good, isn't she, our Miss Cavendish?'

'I'd say so,' Elsie agreed, sounding faintly surprised that he'd bothered to come to Paradise Walk to tell her something she already knew. He was only just back from Italy, too, with heaven knew what urgent work waiting to be seen to.

'Kate will be glad you're back – she's been run off her feet with you away.' Elsie's black eyes surveyed her visitor. 'You look a bit tucked up yourself. Why not try saying no to people for a change?'

'We like to be in constant demand,' Sam explained solemnly, 'it makes us feel important.' He smiled at her customary snort. 'I'm glad to find you so obviously yourself again, Miss M!' But then his face grew serious. 'But what I really came for was some advice. Before I went to Milan I asked Aunt Lou to explain some things that puzzled me about Kate. She finally decided to tell me the story, and said that you had always known it, too. I went to Italy thinking that I'd like to trace Arturo Contini, because it seemed to me that Kate has been damaged by not knowing the full truth of what happened twenty years ago.'

'You *found* her father . . . talked to him?'

Sam shook his head. 'My interference stopped short of that, but I have his address, and what I know about him now suggests that he should be told he has a daughter.'

'Only you can't make up your mind who should do the telling?'

Sam took off his glasses and stared at them. 'It must be Kate, if she chooses to acknowledge him; but I'm almost sure she'll say no. On this one subject her intelligence doesn't get a look-in; she goes by irrational, stubborn instinct. We had a row when I merely suggested that she should go to

Milan with me – she'd wipe Italy off the map of Europe if she could.'

'But you've come back feeling sorry for Mr Contini.' Elsie considered the matter a moment longer, then shook her head. 'You said you wanted advice; well, here it is – forget him! Kate won't change her mind; she never does.'

Sam replaced his glasses the better to stare at the matter-of-fact woman in front of him. It was true that appearances were never safe to judge by, so perhaps beneath even Elsie's primly buttoned bodice had once throbbed a passionate heart. However inhumanly detached she looked, she *might* understand if he said that the past was crippling Kate. Loving a man, allowing herself to be loved by him – both would be resisted and spoiled unless she could come to terms with what had happened to Marguerite Cavendish.

'I'm afraid you're right,' he said at last to Elsie, 'but so is the Bible, unfortunately – the sins of the fathers do get visited on future generations, even to the third or fourth.' He was about to say goodbye when another question occurred to him. 'All well at the Swan?'

'How should I know? Kate says the buses are crowded enough without me trying to find a seat on one, which is her excuse for bringing work to me here.' Elsie frowned at the purple fronds beneath her fingers. 'Something *isn't* well, all the same – I always know by what she doesn't say. My guess is that she's troubled about Jeremy Barrington. Without meaning to, she's grown very fond of him – well, no surprise in that, of course. But he used to haunt Paradise Walk and now he never comes near. Actors . . . not the most reliable of God's creatures, I'd say.'

Sam smiled at a typical conclusion but went away thinking she was right about that too. He got back to Wharfside in time to be unlocking his front door as Kate arrived from an early visit to the theatre. For a moment he thought pleasure shone in her face, but then he decided that he was mistaken – she was merely relieved to see him back.

'You're very welcome,' she said amiably enough, but without the warm smile she would once have offered him. 'Poor Pat O'Donovan's having trouble with the set for the embassy ballroom scene – not enough doors, according to Macdonald, but there's another problem: Anna fancies making her entrance down a grand staircase. Did you enjoy your trip, by the way?'

'Thank you for asking . . . yes, I did. And thank you for leaving everything in such apple-pie order for me last night. As partners go, you're a pineapple of perfection!'

She grinned fleetingly at the echo of Sheridan's Mrs Malaprop, but then her face grew serious again as she preceded him up the stairs. At the beginning of their association she'd been merry of heart; that had changed now, but he didn't know whether Elsie was right to blame Jem Barrington. She'd been very definite, too, about not raking up the past, and certainly nothing in Kate's brisk, businesslike concentration on the work in hand encouraged him to launch into the subject of Arturo Contini.

With a heap of mail and messages and missing doors and impossible staircases to attend to, the memory of his conversation with Giorgio di Palma lost its sharpness. The slip of paper with the Florentine address remained in the folder of notes and sketches he'd brought back from Milan. His tired mind often worried at the problem in the cold, dark watches of the night but he came always to the same conclusion – another quarrel with Kate would strain their partnership to breaking-point, but he couldn't bear the idea of her out on her own in the cut-throat world of the theatre. For the moment, therefore, he must leave the subject of her father alone. With his mind made up, he added a casual postscript to his letter of thanks to Giorgio – there would be no point in Arturo Contini hearing of his enquiry, because nothing had come of it after all.

The following day he got to the Swan only in time to see the crowds pouring in for the evening performance of *Much Ado*. He watched the opening scenes from the back of the auditorium, and walked thoughtfully backstage at the first interval, not sure whether he wanted to find Macdonald there or not. He chatted for a moment with John Clarke, poring over his panel of switches in the prompt corner as usual, and listened patiently to Ernie Williams's mournful prediction that trying to work out the lighting for a rain-sodden night in Covent Garden – the opening scene of *Pygmalion* – would probably be the death of him. Ernie bustled away at last, having talked himself into cheerfulness again, but Sam was left frowning at a canvas flat that would soon become the stained-glass window of a church on-stage.

'What's wrong – *you* designed it,' said Macdonald's voice behind him. 'I suppose they damn the expense and run to real glass at La Scala?'

Sam turned to smile at him. 'My profound thought at the moment was only that nothing is quite what it seems in our little make-believe world of the theatre.'

'You've always known that – why get depressed about it now?'

'I was taking comfort from the idea,' Sam corrected him gently. 'It means among other things that I can ignore the faint impression you give that the director's lot is not a happy one.'

Macdonald answered with a nod in the direction of his own small office. It was chronically untidy, and the smell of stale tobacco smoke hung in the air. Sam remembered the exquisite apartment in Cheyne Walk and thought he could guess which setting Angus preferred. He accepted the dram of whisky that his friend poured for him but before he could find something safe to talk about Angus shot a question at him.

'Did you watch any of the performance tonight? If so, I want to know what you thought of it.'

With most other men a superficial comment, a brief compliment, would have done, but it wasn't, Sam knew, what Macdonald was asking for.

'I thought it would be a good thing when you're ready to open with *Pygmalion*,' he replied at last.

The perception of the answer and the obliqueness of it were both typical of Sam Maitland, but Angus needed him to be explicit for once. 'You mean that rehearsing one play and performing another at night is too much of a strain on the cast?'

It was something actors often had to do, both men knew – in fact it helped them not to grow stale during a long run. Sam stared at the golden liquid in his glass and wished himself back in his peaceful studio.

'I think it's only a strain if the mood of one play jars on the mood of the other,' he admitted reluctantly. 'Maybe Henry Higgins and Eliza don't chime happily with Benedick and Beatrice.' It gave away where he thought the trouble lay – with Jeremy and Anna – but he made an effort to sound more confident. 'Once *Pygmalion* opens, it won't matter at all, of course.'

Macdonald seemed to be searching for something amid the litter of papers on his desk. Finally he unearthed a packet of cigarettes and slowly lit one. 'I'm afraid it *will* still matter, because it was entirely the wrong choice of play. No one's fault but mine, and there's not a thing I can do to change it now.'

Remembering a past conversation with Kate, Sam found it hard to put conviction into his voice, but he did his best. 'It's a marvellous play, almost failure-proof even in the hands of some fool of a director, which is not what *you* are. It'll be all right, Angus.'

A wry smile touched Macdonald's mouth, then faded again. 'So Kate kindly assured me after a more than usually painful rehearsal while you were away. The truth is that no amount of hard work or clever acting is going to turn Anna into an ideal Eliza; my only comfort is that she becomes less miscast as the play goes on.'

'Then why worry? It's the final impression the audience take home that they'll remember.'

'It's the final impression that's most wrong,' Angus said bleakly. 'Shaw's intentions are quite specific – fairy-tale this may be, but it's *not* meant to have the obvious happy ending; the battle between Higgins and Eliza is more subtle and more interesting than that. But for the life of them Jeremy and Anna can't help playing the parts as if the playwright got it wrong. The professor and the guttersnipe are Benedick and Beatrice all over again, deeply in love even when they're lambasting one another, and bound to end up in each other's arms.'

After a long silence while he searched for something that could safely be said, Sam eventually found it. 'It may not be what Shaw intended but audiences will prefer it that way. Jeremy and Anna are right – a happy ending is what the paying customers like.'

'I don't care what they like – I'm offering them an intelligent and beautifully crafted human drama,' Angus roared suddenly, 'not a bedtime story for lovesick adolescents.' He saw the expression on Sam's face, and wiped a hand across his eyes before he apologised.

'Sorry . . . God knows why I'm shouting at *you* – your contribution, and Kate's, is beyond praise. Go home, old friend . . . I've got a script to read while I wait for Anna.' He smiled with wry humour and gestured to the whisky bottle. 'It's all right – I shall still be sober by the time the performance ends. Anxiety doesn't drive me to drink!'

Sam accepted the hint and said good night, but then chose to walk all the way back to Southwark. He stopped on the Embankment to stare across the river; arc-lights shone down on the churned-up chaos of what might, against all sane predictions, one day be a festival that Britain could take pride in. But meanwhile it looked as muddily cheerless and uninviting as the river that flowed past. He stood there until the biting night wind off the water made him shiver, but he felt cold because he was thinking of something Angus had said . . . Jeremy and Anna couldn't help but play their parts in a way Shaw hadn't intended. Sam thought it was true, but not because an audience preferred a happy ending. What two highly disciplined players really couldn't help was the spark of sheer physical awareness of each other that ignited whenever they shared the same stage. Did Macdonald, who was married to Anna, realise that? Did Kate, who loved Jeremy, understand what she was up against? Sam turned up his coat-collar, called good night to a looming police constable who seemed to wonder why he loitered there, and finally resumed his trudge home.

Chapter 15

Giorgio's slip of paper remained where Sam had hidden it – not entirely out of mind, he told himself; just deferred until he and Kate could talk again as friends. Meanwhile he knew she was at the theatre every night, patiently waiting to share the late supper that Jeremy insisted on when he could relax after the performance. One morning, because she looked so pale and tired, he made the mistake of saying that Jeremy was being unreasonable. At once, her dark brows drew together in a frown to warn him that he was venturing onto forbidden ground again.

'William and Aunt Lou will think I'm overworking you,' he explained, to lessen the offence.

'Don't worry,' she said coolly. 'I'll let them know they needn't blame *you*.'

She bent her head over the model she was working on and at that angle he couldn't miss the new, sharp definitions of her face, the hollows at temple and cheekbones. She wasn't just slender now, but over-thin, and the fragility of her wrists as she glued together pieces of Mrs Higgins's elegant drawing-room angered him. It would have been a pleasure to hate Jeremy Barrington if he could have convinced himself that Kate was just one of the many girls who fluttered round a spoiled stage idol. But it wasn't like that at all – Sam had seen Jeremy's eyes searching for her in a crowded room. He was a man tormented by the hold that another man's wife – as woman and actress – had on him, but Kate was keeping him sane, and for as long as she was certain that he needed her, she'd go on as she was going now.

At last Sam broke the silence that had fallen between them. 'The truth is, partner, that I wasn't worrying what William or Aunt Lou might think – I was anxious about *you*.'

She looked up then and met his grave stare. It sent colour into her face and made her fleetingly beautiful.

'Sorry to have snapped,' she mumbled. 'You must give me the push if I get more uppity than you can bear.' She smiled and suddenly became the girl who'd first knocked at his door. 'I'm not sure that a lot of high living agrees with me. Jeremy's grown accustomed to it, but I never shall.'

Hearing no defensiveness in her voice for once, Sam risked a question. 'For fairness' sake, couldn't he try living your kind of life occasionally?'

She considered the idea but shook her head. 'I'm afraid it wouldn't work that way round. You can go on as you began, living high or low, which is what most of us do. If you're talented enough you can go from low to high, as Jeremy has done. But unless you're driven to it, you can't put things into reverse. Apart from anything else it muddles other people. They *expect* Jeremy Barrington to be dining at the Ritz, not eating cockles off a Bermondsey stall.'

Sam's eyes gleamed with laughter, but he asked his next question seriously. 'Poor Kate . . . is *that* what you hanker after – a dish of choice cockles soaked in vinegar?'

'Not specially,' she admitted, trying not to grin, 'but I hanker after the sort of people who do. You must understand that because you live among them.'

'You mean their learning is mostly what they've picked up themselves, and their vocabulary would make a sailor blush; but they're quick-witted and kind and real, and you can't say as much for the patrons of the Ritz.'

She nodded, pleased because he did understand after all, but his next question took her by surprise and astonished himself as well.

'Would you consider coming with me to Covent Garden tomorrow night? They're performing *La Bohème* there as well, and I had to leave Milan with only fragments of it ringing in my ears – I couldn't even wait for the dress rehearsal.' He thought he saw rejection in her face and hurried on. 'I know how devoted you are to the peerless Nellie Wallace, but would it hurt to listen to Victoria de los Angeles as well?'

After a long time she found something to say. 'It wouldn't hurt at all, but I can't, I'm afraid. Ralph Richardson is opening in a new play at Wyndham's . . . there's the usual party afterwards . . . Jeremy promised we'd go.' She stared down at her hands, frowned because her fingers were trembling, and hid them in the pockets of her dungarees. 'I'm sorry – I'm sure it's high time I learned to tell Puccini from "Rule, Britannia".'

He wanted to call Jeremy the names that his Southwark neighbours had taught him, and shout at her to let him go to the bloody party alone for once, instead of being a willing, mindless slave. But even in the middle of his rage he knew that she was neither spineless nor a fool. She understood exactly the nature of the charade they played, in order that their whole bright adventure at the Swan shouldn't fall apart in ruins.

Anger couldn't survive, but disappointment made his

voice cold. 'Enjoy your party. If you're lucky it might be marginally less noisy and boring than the usual first-night free-for-all.' He flung together papers, glanced at his watch, and spoke again in the same level tones.

'Oh God, I shall be late as usual, and how I hate committee meetings.' He shrugged himself into an ancient Burberry because rain was being driven against the studio windows, and glanced briefly in Kate's direction; but she was staring at her model as if her life depended on it. A moment later she heard the door bang; silence was left behind, and an emptiness more painful than she had ever known.

The party the following night was probably just like any other; it only *seemed* more noisily unbearable because she was tired and starting to catch a cold . . . or so she tried to tell herself.

The critics were unanimous for once, although for different reasons. The gentlemen of the gutter press made merry at the expense of a Cockney Eliza who was known to live in Cheyne Walk; higher-browed colleagues despised so cheap a gibe, but regretted some serious miscasting. One of them even put his finger on Macdonald's worst anxiety – there was much to enjoy in the production, but surely it was the leading players' *Pygmalion*, not Bernard Shaw's?

Angus pushed the pile of newspapers aside, aware that he didn't want to concern himself with any of the things that required his attention. Even the Swan itself – *his* theatre, as he always privately thought of it – seemed for the moment a suffocating millstone round his neck. He hated the sight of the darkened stage, waiting expectantly for the failure of another night's performance. The rows of gaping seats in the auditorium were no longer empty, but filled in his imagination with booing, jeering spectators shouting down the actors on the stage. The dreadful vision lasted only a moment or two, but left him wiping perspiration off his face.

'A cup of coffee, Guv'nor? It won't taste very good, but I could brew some up in the wardrobe room.'

He opened his eyes to see Kate standing a yard away from him. She'd done her best to sound unconcerned, but he saw her little frown of worry and knew he'd left himself too clearly revealed. He shook away the memory of his nightmare and tried to smile at her.

'I need more than coffee, having skipped breakfast to buy the morning papers. It was a sacrifice the reviews don't seem to have justified, by the way.'

'Perhaps you skipped dinner last night as well,' she suggested, with another glance at his pale face. 'Never mind – I'll take you to some friends of mine; they're only just round the corner.'

He found himself following her meekly, not minding that she had witnessed his moment of despair. Five minutes later he was shepherded into a small green hut that was indeed just round the corner in the middle of the street. It smelled marvellously of frying bacon, and a pall of cigarette smoke also hung in the warm air. Bemusedly he heard his guide greet the other customers as if she knew them one and all, and explain that she'd brought the Guv'nor along for breakfast.

'I hope you can drink strong tea,' she murmured, 'coffee here is reckoned for the nobs, but the food is very good.'

'Should I ask how you come to be on visiting terms with London's taxi-driving fraternity?'

She grinned more easily now that the whiteness had faded

from his mouth and he sounded like the Macdonald she was accustomed to.

'The proprietor's a Trotter . . . Bert gave me an introduction.' She joined tactfully for a moment or two in the general conversation, and then returned to Angus and what he'd said before they left the theatre.

'I saw Bert's *Daily Mirror* this morning – that review wasn't worth losing any sleep over; it was just silly and spiteful.'

'Perhaps, but they aren't all stupid, and they can't find much that's good to say of something we've sweated blood over for weeks. I'm afraid they "damn with faint praise", Kate, and "without sneering, teach the rest to sneer".' He made an effort to sound unconcerned and knew by her compassionate gaze that he failed. 'Do you think I've grown too accustomed to success to accept criticism . . . expect only rave reviews and behave like a sulky adolescent when I don't get them?'

She shook her head like a teacher disappointed in a backward pupil. 'That's just silly. You're worried about the cast getting depressed, and the audiences staying away. That's not very likely – according to Walter Fairbrass, the box-office telephone never stops ringing.'

'What about a demoralised cast?'

'They're professionals,' she said with certainty, 'more than capable of making every critic in London eat his words provided they're certain *you* haven't lost faith in them.'

Angus blinked at the loaded plate put in front of him, but she was right about the excellence of the food, and he was suddenly ravenously hungry. While he ate she sipped tea the colour of mahogany and chatted to her friends.

'Do you bring Jem here?' he asked between mouthfuls.

Kate shook her head again. 'He wouldn't enjoy it. Sam might, only we're a bit frosty with each other nowadays.' She smiled to show that it didn't matter.

'It seems a long time ago that I pointed out to you Gil Forrest's duty to get love-struck over his leading lady,' Angus said suddenly.

'It seems a long time ago that it mattered,' she agreed with a faint smile.

Angus took a breath of smoky air and tried again with a subject that seemed damnably difficult.

'A theatre critic sharper than the others suggested that Jem and Anna were pulling the play out of the shape the playwright intended. I think he's right. However much I've tried to smother the electric charge it still sparks between them, like a bush fire – stamp on it in one place and it breaks out somewhere else.'

'I know,' Kate answered after a moment or two. 'It's what makes audiences love them; they're exciting to watch.' She looked up to meet his glance with eyes that were the most candid he'd ever known. 'It's painful for the people close to them like you and me, but I'm afraid it's painful for *them* as well. We all have to realise that, and just do the best we can . . . don't you think?'

The earnest suggestion was made for *his* comfort, he realised, because she thought she now understood what had thrown him off balance at the theatre. His face relaxed into a smile that would have astonished his colleagues by its sweetness.

'Yes, I think so.'

She glanced at her watch and looked guilty. 'I ought to be back at the studio. With Maitland out for most of the day, Cavendish is supposed to be in, not lolling about in idle conversation.'

Her hand lifted in a little farewell gesture, but Macdonald suddenly imprisoned it in his own.

'Thank you for coming to the rescue this morning, Kate.'

For once he wasn't hiding behind his usual mask of self-containment, and she felt shy of him.

'Hunger doth make c . . . cowards of us all,' she managed to misquote breathlessly; then turned and hurried out of the hut, leaving him still standing there.

She'd misspent much of the morning already when there was work urgently needing to be done, but still her mind was filled with the memory of Macdonald's face when she'd walked into him at the theatre. 'We must just do the best we can,' she'd said, and meant it; but at that moment he'd surely been confronting a situation for which good intentions weren't enough. Understanding and patience might hold his marriage and his company together, but he was far from certain of it.

She passionately wanted him to be wrong . . . lamented to an empty studio the mindless, hurtful stupidity of physical desire, that drove even intelligent human beings to risk everything else that made for happiness. Anna, being strong and selfish at heart, would probably survive disaster, but Jeremy would not; and now Kate wasn't even sure about the Guv'nor, either. Somewhere amid the wreckage there would also be herself, but not destroyed entirely – because hadn't she grown up determined never, *never* to be like Marguerite Cavendish?

In her agitated walk about the room she was halted by the sight of sketches on Sam's table, spread out there to dry. He must have spent most of the past night working on them. Meticulously drawn and coloured as usual, they were worth lingering over, but it was the notation underneath that made her frown: 'Costume designs for *Tristan and Isolde*, prepared for the Theater an der Wien.' It was another reminder, scarcely needed, that Sam Maitland's horizons were becoming wider than her own. She still found the familiar theatre world of London exciting enough, knew that she was fortunate to be in it, believed with reason that her reputation as a designer was growing steadily. But it would be a long time yet before any Continental director came begging for her services.

It was different for Sam. Thorough-going Englishmen would probably prefer to stay at home, but 'abroad' held no terrors for a half-Scottish, half-Viennese hybrid who knew the languages and ways of foreigners. Already she felt lonely, as if he were leaving her behind. But the sudden recollection that she was a hybrid herself was a curse, not a comfort. She would go on refusing to acknowledge that unwanted foreign fraction; she was a Londoner through and through.

With this clear in her mind once more she forced herself to settle down to the work in hand – a world away from Eliza Doolittle's flower-girl rags was the evening gown in which the heroine of *Private Lives*, on a terrace overlooking the Mediterranean, would accidentally meet her former husband. Macdonald had decreed that they must remain true to the period in which Noël Coward had set the play. So Anna would make her entrance as Amanda Prynne in a dress as redolent of the thirties' sinuous, silken glamour as a fifties' designer could possibly devise.

Absorbed in the task at last, Kate was jolted out of

concentration by the ringing of the telephone. She hurried over to Sam's desk to answer it, dislodged a folder balanced on a pile of books, and watched it empty itself at her feet. When the caller had been dealt with she swept together the papers on the floor, but almost failed to notice the smallest item that had slid furthest away. When it finally caught her eye she stooped to pick it up, and seemed for a moment to stop breathing.

> Dott. Arturo Contini
> Via Cavour 7, e Ponte Vecchio,
> Firenze.

Inscribed in an unfamiliar hand, the thick black strokes of the pen imprinted themselves on her brain. She could tear the paper into a thousand pieces, hurl them out of the window for the river to float them down to the sea . . . it would make no difference. Sam knew her father's whereabouts and so, now, did she.

With the paper back inside the folder again, she went back to her interrupted work, but anger lay coiled like a spring beneath the surface of her mind. She would get through the rest of the day by ignoring it – she ignored her usual brief lunch-break as well, and worked with such a charge of sheer nervous energy that the results took her by surprise. The designs were good . . . better than good; in fact they might be the best she'd ever done.

She was still brooding over this strange fact when Sam walked in. Cold damp air came with him, and raindrops shone on his hair in the bright lights of the studio. She noticed these things as if he were a stranger who needed to be assessed carefully.

'Sorry to be so late, partner . . . I wasn't expecting you to wait for me, though.'

She didn't answer or even smile to indicate that she'd listened to what he'd said, and so Sam tried again. 'For once I've got a little progress to report.' Her aloof expression didn't change, but he went on anyway, wondering what was amiss. 'Our bloody-minded labourers seem to have got tired of being on strike, so until the next storm in a teacup blows up, there's actually some work being done on the festival site.'

'A relief to Gerald Barry,' she agreed minimally.

'But *you* don't care one way or the other,' Sam suggested. 'What's wrong, Kate? Are you feeling put upon because the festival takes up so much of my time? It's only in these crucial planning stages, you know.'

'And when the design group no longer need you no doubt you'll be in Vienna.'

She heard her own hostile voice and thought she sounded like a petulant child excluded from a treat it didn't really want.

Sam thought she sounded hurt, and spoke gently to her. 'There hasn't been time to tell you . . . the theatre director only rang last night to say that their resident designer had fallen sick. I'm a stop-gap, but it's still flattering to be asked.' He leaned over her table as he talked, scanning the designs she'd been working on, and then looked at her. 'Is it safe to say that these are more than just very good, or will you get still crosser and think I'm patronising you?'

'I'm cross because I'm tired.' She pushed trembling fingers through her hair, then contradicted herself. 'No, I'm not – I'm sick with rage because of something else. I wasn't prying, but I knocked your Milan folder on the floor when I answered the telephone.'

'And you saw Arturo Contini's address – I should have thought of that.' He took her cold hands in his warm ones and gripped them harder when she tried to release herself. 'By the merest chance someone I worked with at La Scala happened to know of him – was even related to his family by marriage, as it turned out. I'd meant to try and find him if I could, but my very first enquiry led me straight to the man himself.'

Kate wrenched her hands away and stood confronting him, eyes bright with angry tears in the whiteness of her face, chest heaving as if she'd been running in a race. But she found breath to shout at him.

'You had no right to interfere – I hate *you* for it, and I hate this man . . . I *won't* have him for a father . . .'

Sam banged his fist on the table – for him so violent a gesture that she was halted in mid-flight.

'Listen . . . just *listen*, Kate. I brought back his address, that's all. I was going to give it to you if there ever looked like being a moment when you'd consider it rationally – my first mistake; that moment will never come. My second mistake was to think you might feel a grain of pity for the man. His only other child, a son, was killed in the closing stages of the war. His wife still blames *him* – she reckons a Resistance leader could have risked other people but kept his own child out of harm's way.'

Kate knuckled her wet eyes because, as usual, her handkerchief was smeared with paint. 'I'm sorry about his son, but you're mad if you think that hearing from *me* would help them. "By the way, my dear, I forgot to mention that I fathered a daughter twenty years ago in London. Her mother's dead – no problem there; but the girl might make some claim on me." Well, I *wouldn't*, not if I was starving. I've been loved by William and Aunt Lou, and trained with Elsie's savings. I don't *need* anyone else.'

'I've been thinking that he might need you,' Sam said quietly, 'but that isn't why I wanted to find him.'

'Don't bother to explain why . . . I don't want to know.'

'I shall tell you all the same. You can't forget that you were an illegitimate child, and you're afraid of physical love between a man and a woman because it seems to lead only to unhappiness or disgrace or disaster. So you ignore Gil Forrest, who adores you, to dance attendance on Jeremy, because he's *safe*. He may need you to hold his hand and bolster him up night after night, but it's Anna that he's hopelessly in love with. No danger *there* to Kate Cavendish's independent spirit and precious purity!'

She opened her mouth to rage at him, but no words came, because in that measured, annihilating way, he'd put his finger on the truth. Instead she took a deep breath, hoped she was being dignified and feared that she merely sounded defiant.

'I shall ignore or bolster up whomever I please, and my purity is strictly my own business. I don't need your advice . . . only a promise that you'll never interfere again or get in touch with my father.'

It seemed a long time before he lifted his hands in a little gesture of defeat. 'I give you my promise, Kate.'

She nodded, accepting what he said, and went to fetch her jacket. He watched while she pulled it on, but got to the door before her and stood blocking her way. Something that wasn't quite amusement twitched his mouth and glimmered in his eyes as he stared at her.

'You missed an opportunity back there, partner. Why didn't you ask me how I came to be such an expert at diagnosing what frightens you?'

'You're half-Austrian – reared on Sigmund Freud, I suppose.'

'No . . . the simple truth is that I'm frightened too. My father went to a medical conference in Vienna and fell fathoms deep in love with a girl who was in every way unsuited to marry him – but she allowed herself to be caught and put in his middle-class Calvinist cage because she was ill and desperate at the time. I watched them doing their best, but only managing to destroy each other, and I grew up determined to avoid the trap myself. You see . . . it takes a coward to recognise another coward!'

She felt inclined suddenly to burst into tears, because this interminable day that seemed to have held altogether too much sadness and bitter truth wasn't over yet – there was still her post-performance visit to Jeremy to come. But tears, she remembered just in time, were something she despised.

'You needn't have owned up. I'm used to thinking of you and the Guv'nor as men who're a match for anything, but today has blown that comforting theory sky-high. I'm going now before anything else happens.'

He opened the door and watched her bolt down the staircase to the street. Alone again, it was time to prepare the supper he didn't want; but instead he stared at the darkening river, marvelling at his own extraordinary confession and wondering how it was that Macdonald had also given himself away.

Chapter 16

Anna stared at the battered straw hat that would soon have to be skewered on top of her piled-up hair again. She hated the ugly hat, hated the streaks of black grease-paint on her face that failed to turn her into an unwashed Cockney flower-girl. She'd regretted agreeing to the part of Eliza Doolitle even before rehearsals began, but the possibility of disaster hadn't occurred to her. Now, after an unsuccessful opening and some cruelly unflattering reviews, it was time to face the truth – there were some weak spots in her armoury after all, and *Pygmalion* had found them.

When Jeremy's familiar knock sounded at the dressing-room door she was still sitting at her table, aimlessly stabbing at the straw with the fearsome hat-pin that would anchor it to her hair. She stared at him in the mirror and he saw the depth of her wretchedness. It was every actor's nightmare, losing confidence just before curtain-up. Beautiful, brilliant Anna should have been immune, but he could feel in his own blood and bones the weight of her reluctance to go on again in half an hour's time. His hands rested on her shoulders for a moment, briefly offering comfort, before he moved away again and propped himself up against a wall.

'Who was it you'd got under your bare bodkin just then – the theatre critic of *The Times*?' He tried to make a joke of it but she watched him with huge, tragic eyes.

'There were worse notices than his.'

Jeremy shook his head. 'I don't think so – his had the awkward merit of being true. He said what Angus has been saying to us for weeks as well.'

Suddenly lifted out of despair, she snapped her fingers in a gesture that dismissed her husband and the critic equally. 'They're both wrong. People come to the theatre to laugh and cry and be given a happy ending to take home with them, not a dehumanised social tract on the evils of a class-ridden society. You and I are right to play it as we do.' She watched him for a moment before adding softly, 'In any case, right or wrong, we can't play it in any other way, can we? The chemistry is too strong!'

Her meaning was clear, and it was the truth they'd been dodging for months. She waited for him to agree, to smile with gratitude or delight, even to drop the guard he kept on himself to the extent of wrapping his arms around her. Instead he stayed where he was, hands thrust in the pockets of his coat, as if that was the only safe place for them to be. There was silence in the hot, bright, little room, and time to register something more than his startling good looks. On stage he could still easily create the illusion of splendid youth. Here, under the cruel lights of the dressing-room, he looked tired and gaunt, and all of the forty-odd years she knew him to be.

It was time for them both to admit their predicament. Playing together on stage they were magically outside the rules that applied in real life; then she couldn't even remember what the rules were. But because Jeremy *was* now remembering them, so must she. She had a husband who deserved love and loyalty, and he happened also to be Jeremy's friend. Male friendships could be taken for granted, but not lightly betrayed. Anna hesitated over whether to include Kate Cavendish in her swift, sad survey, and decided not to; it was a pity that Kate should be a complication at all, but she wasn't important enough in herself to worry about.

The silence had lasted too long, but it was only interrupted by the call-boy knocking at the door and shouting 'quarter-hour, Miss Sheridan'.

'What are we going to do?' she asked quietly when the boy had gone.

Jeremy pushed himself upright and achieved a smile as he looked at her. It was unfair and almost unbearable that in her present absurd costume, face daubed in black grease-paint and framed in wisps of red hair, she should look so beautiful and so desirable. But he knew the answer he must give to her question.

'Do? What we do is play this damned play as we've never played it before, sweetheart. Tonight we'll have the audience cheering in their seats or die in the attempt.'

It wasn't the answer she had hoped for, but it didn't matter because he couldn't hide the expression in his eyes. It didn't even matter that for the moment the rules still held. She accepted his lead with her own slow, devastating smile.

'Into battle then, my darling. But if we don't win tonight I shall never play Eliza Doolittle again.'

Jeremy nodded, aware that for both of them the night had become a watershed; a change had been made that couldn't be reversed. He blew a kiss across the space between them, and then walked out of the room.

Calm again, Anna carefully repowdered her face to remove any trace of shine, and waited for the final call: 'Beginners, please.' She was ready now.

Three hours later if he'd troubled himself to come again, *The Times'* critic would have been certain of his previous verdict. And any carping purist in the audience could still have maintained that even if Jeremy Barrington had successfully turned himself into the ingratiating bully who was Professor Higgins, the termagant heroine of the piece had *still* been miscast. But the cheering, clapping masses cared neither for critics nor specialists in the mother-tongue of Hoxton. They didn't even care what kind of play George Bernard Shaw supposed he'd written. What they'd been given was a glorious, adult version of *Cinderella*. Having been transformed herself, the Cockney heroine was clearly going to transform Henry Higgins into a reluctant but captivated lover.

Kate sat through the curtain-calls, glowered at by her neighbour, who thought she didn't clap with sufficient enthusiasm. But she was comparing this ovation with the previous night's cool reception of the same play, same settings and costumes, same Shavian wit and sparkle. The difference was surely in the undisguised sexual charge that now set the stage alight whenever the two leading players faced one another. With this provocative Eliza and this not quite irredeemable monster of a professor Kate thought the audience knew perfectly well that the real battle wasn't over Hoxton vowels and the elegant handling of a teacup. For all Shaw's worthy social theorising, it was the age-old struggle between man and woman that they'd been watching with so much delight.

*   *   *

The house lights went up to persuade a still-cheering audience into leaving the theatre. With a final, smiling curtsey and a kiss blown to the gallery, Anna led the way off the stage, followed by Jeremy and the rest of the cast. In the wings, tired but triumphant, she stopped to look at him for a moment.

'You said we'd do it, Henry Higgins, and we did!'

'Oh, with knobs on, my darling.' His smile was so brilliant that she didn't sense his despair. Indeed they'd done it, but how in God's name was the trick to be done again and again and again, for as long as Angus said the show had to run? And how was such high success to be followed for a cruelly adoring public that always wanted more? Not knowing any answers, he climbed the stairs after Anna and plunged into the throng of visitors already milling around outside their doors. Soon, like a drink of cool, sweet water to a man dying of thirst, Kate would come to rescue him. For the space of an hour or two he might even manage to forget that he was Jeremy Barrington and become poor, plain John Bagg instead.

Anna frowned momentarily as he allowed himself to be enveloped in the crowd, but recovered at once to smile at her admirers and beg for a few minutes' grace – she disliked being seen off-stage in theatrical make-up. Cleaned off and natural-looking again, her dresser put her into a tailored wrap of heavy cream silk that Margot Stein had sent over from New York . . . *now* she would receive visitors.

Dora opened the door, but found herself looking at just one man, who said a firm good night and waited for her to walk away down the corridor. Then he went inside Anna's dressing-room and closed the door. His reticent face told her nothing as usual, except that praise for a miraculous performance didn't seem likely to be forthcoming. She smiled at him but sounded cool.

'My dear Angus, I'm delighted to see you, of course, but where is everyone else? There was the usual crowd when I came in.'

'I told them to leave – said you were sick to death of screamed compliments and phony kisses.' He saw her face change, and relented a little. 'Well not quite that! I suggested with more civility than I can usually manage that it would be kind to let you go home in peace for once.'

'Then you suggested far too much.' She spoke quietly, mindful of the thin dressing-room walls, but her voice had taken on the cold edge of steel. 'Don't *ever* send my friends away again, and spare me the nauseating lie that you were protecting me. You just dislike them.'

Anger held under fierce control made him look more remote than ever, but he answered as quietly as she. 'It wouldn't have been a lie – I'm very concerned about you.'

'Concerned?' She considered the word as if she hadn't heard it before, repeated it again with a stronger note of sarcasm. Then her mouth curled into a contemptuous smile. 'Any other man would have been overflowing with praise and gratitude and delight tonight, but my dear husband can only manage to be "concerned". Perhaps I should be thankful for *that*, and allow myself to be shut up in my cage until it's time to perform for him again.'

His face was very white now, but he spoke in the same level conversational tone. 'Get dressed, Anna; we'll finish this at home.'

For a moment or two he thought she was going to refuse;

214

then she changed her mind, flung off the wrap and pulled on the street clothes that Dora had put ready for her. They walked out past the barrage of conversation and laughter still coming from Jeremy's room, and left the theatre with a hoarse 'G'night, Guv, g'night M'um' from Bert Trotter that fell on deaf ears.

The late-night traffic had thinned and they were back at Cheyne Walk before Angus had decided how to resume a conversation that might be crucial to them. But Anna, who had decided that it shouldn't be resumed at all, announced briefly that she was going to bed.

'Not until we've talked, please,' he said gently. 'This time we have to stop pretending that nothing's wrong.'

She turned to stare at him, eyes glinting like jewels in the dead whiteness of her face. Even in this extremity of anger and exhaustion he found her beautiful, and his heart was torn with sadness. They had loved one another so short a time ago . . . he loved her still, and probably always would, because she wasn't a woman to forget or recover from.

'*I*'ll tell you what's wrong, Angus,' she said with bitter emphasis. 'We must be a success, of course, but only on *your* terms. The damned play's the thing, but it has to be your vision of it, not ours. Well, Jeremy and I perform it as we must. If that makes you more jealous than you can bear, think of Walter Fairbrass gloating over the box-office takings . . . think of the critics who, like you, may have to eat their words because tonight I proved that I *can* play the part of Eliza Doolittle.'

She was enraged with him, but he thought it was still surface anger, scarcely touching the euphoria left behind by a triumphant night. It seemed cruel to shake her out of it but they'd gone too far to stop now.

'I didn't doubt that you could and would succeed in playing it brilliantly,' he said with certainty. 'But I still prefer my vision, as you call it, because it's true to the intentions of the play; yours and Jeremy's is not.'

'Very well then – withdraw it altogether and we'll start rehearsing *Private Lives* immediately – will that end this pointless argument?'

Angus shook his head, took a deep breath and spoke as dispassionately as he could. 'I think we should let *Pygmalion* run, but start rehearsing something else . . . not *Private Lives*.'

For a moment Anna was deprived of words, and he seized his advantage. 'My dear, we can do better than that brittle, superficial comedy. What does it amount to? Two completely thankless rôles for poor Jane Carlisle and Gilbert, who deserve something better, while you and Jeremy alternately drool over one another or have a fight.' He might, in a less desperate moment, have agreed that it was an unnecessarily ruthless summing-up of a play he didn't like; but not now, with Anna so icily cool while he was not.

'*Now* we come to it at last,' she said. 'It's not this play or that, not even our way of doing it or yours – this is just about me and Jeremy . . . isn't it?'

'I could say that it's about you and me,' he observed with care, 'but for the moment we'll concentrate on Jem. Anna . . . let him go, please. There are other fine actors to choose from – Clunes, Scofield, or any one of half-a-dozen others . . .'

'You're mad,' she said flatly. 'There's no need to recite me a string of names – I chose Jeremy Barrington, and we were born to play opposite each other.'

Angus stared at her, looking for some remaining trace of the ardent woman who had begged to stay with him in London, and welcomed him into her bed, and allowed herself to be taken in shared love and longing. He put out his hand in a little, unconscious gesture of pleading for her to remember these things too, but she ignored it and it dropped to his side again.

'You're my wife,' he said after a moment or two, 'and Jem is my friend. *He* can't ignore these awkward facts even if you can. Let him go, so that he can find peace with Kate Cavendish, and take on the great rôles he ought to be playing, not Noël Coward's trivial, glossy rubbish.'

Far from remembering that she'd loved Angus Macdonald, she was suddenly close to hating him. All the triumph and exhilaration of the evening had died, and she was left confronting an enemy who would destroy her if she wasn't strong enough to fight exhaustion and out-face him.

'I reminded you of the truth once before, but you've forgotten it. The Swan belongs as much to me as to you – perhaps a good deal *more* to me, Jacob might reasonably point out. So we shall put on plays that suit *me*, my dear Angus, at least for as long as they seem to suit the paying public as well. I'm not very concerned about Kate Cavendish, and I doubt if Jeremy is either. She's just a little diversion, and lucky to be that.'

She'd managed to remain strong, and she was almost convinced of the truth of what she'd just said. Kate Cavendish couldn't be denied altogether because Jeremy made no secret of his affection for her. But her gamine charm would fade soon enough, whereas Anna knew that her own beauty hadn't even reached its prime. In any case what was tepid affection compared with the attraction

217

that pulled Jeremy to *her* as inevitably as ocean tides responded to the moon? The awkwardness was that in a different way she needed Angus as well, but she felt confident that after a day or two's hurt silence he would accept a situation that he was realistic enough to know he couldn't change.

'Well, now that all *that*'s settled, I must really go to bed,' she said finally.

She passed so close to him that he could smell the perfume she always wore. He was aware of the slight warmth of her body, but still felt cold and dead inside himself. She could have stood naked in front of him now without arousing a spark of desire.

'It's not quite settled.' His voice halted her almost at the door. 'I'll see *Private Lives* through because everyone else is already committed to it. After that the summer break will give you time to appoint a new director for the autumn productions. By then I shall have handed my share of our wedding present back to Jacob. I'll look for that cottage in the country, too, so that you can have all *this* to yourself as well.'

For a moment she tried to pretend that she didn't believe what he said – he loved the Swan too much to give it up; in all but legal right it had been *his* theatre. But Angus had never acquired the actor's habit of saying what he didn't mean. She was almost brought to pleading with him . . . *would* have done but for his crucial, unforgivable error in not understanding that Jeremy needed as much as she did the dazzling success they could achieve *together*, not the lonely isolation of working his way through whatever 'great' parts his friend thought were good for him.

'Do as you please,' she said through stiff lips, 'but I think you'll change your mind.' Then she managed to walk out of the room – making an exit, they called it in the business; she was used to them, but no exit had ever been more difficult than this one.

Kate knew there was no hurry about going backstage. Jeremy didn't need her while he made the transition back from the character he'd just played to being himself again. There were always enough acquaintances and hangers-on to cushion the drop from stage 'high' to ground-level reality where she could join him. Tonight she loitered more than usual, making up her mind what she would say when he asked, as he always did, how the performance had gone. It would be easy enough to agree that the audience cramming the theatre had hugely enjoyed itself; she hoped it was all she need say, because her own dismayed reaction would be harder to explain. Some of her time had also been spent hoping that Angus Macdonald wasn't watching, but he'd walked past her on his way out with Anna, and from the expression on his face she judged that he had been there all the time.

There were the usual visitors making a crowd in Jeremy's dressing-room when she got there – no need to do anything but smile and allow herself to be kissed by people she didn't know. It was a noisy, extravagant, unreal world in which they swam like goldfish in a bowl, always in the expectation of being stared at from outside. But when the last of them had drifted away and she steeled herself for Jeremy's usual question, for once it didn't come – he just sat aimlessly playing with her fingers instead.

'You look dreadfully tired,' she murmured. 'Why don't

we skip supper tonight – then you could go straight home to bed.'

She realised that it was a mistake as soon as the words left her mouth. His sagging shoulders straightened, and one beautiful hand swept across his face, apparently wiping exhaustion away.

'Not on your sweet life, Katey – half-a-dozen curtain-calls tonight insist that we drink to the damnation of every sodding theatre critic in London!'

It was so rare for him to swear that she wondered if he'd already drunk more than usual, but he caught the question in her face and smiled unctuously.

'Sober as a judge – so far! Come on, sweetheart. It's time we got to Rule's or they'll be shutting the door, and I'm ravenous.'

But, hungry or not, she noticed that although he kept sipping wine, he ate very little of the food they ordered at the restaurant. He was recognised as usual, but for once seemed to go out of his way to charm rather than ignore the strangers who wanted to be able to claim acquaintance with Jeremy Barrington. These fawning people were what he needed tonight, she finally realised, because he hadn't left the theatre behind – he was still playing to the gallery. When they were left in peace at last he smiled at her, rueful, but too late and too insincere in his apology.

'Forgive me, Kate – but you know how it is; we phony little idols can't afford to offend our admirers!'

'I know exactly how it is,' she agreed crisply. 'You've performed brilliantly all the evening, but now you can't stop; the actor's curse, William calls it – an insatiable hunger for applause.'

He said nothing for so long that she was obliged to take back error on herself.

'Sorry . . . hell hath no fury like a boring woman rightly ignored by her supper companion. Dear Jeremy, there's no reason why you shouldn't go on acting your boots off for as long as you want to, but I'll just take myself home – it's been rather a long, full day.' The memory of just how full it had been made her give a wry grimace, but his hand closed fiercely on her wrist as she started to leave the table.

'I'm a bloody fool, Kate, and you're right to be angry with me. If I've got you I don't need anyone else. The trouble is – *have* I got you?' His eyes burned in the exhausted pallor of his face and, with a tremor at her heart, she knew what was coming next. 'Would you . . . would you come back and stay with me just this once . . . if I promise not to keep on asking? William didn't get it quite right – our course is an insatiable hunger for reassurance that we really exist.'

He'd said the same thing to her once before, but not with this heartbreaking intensity of need. Whatever had happened to spark off the evening's supercharged performance raged in him still like a fever. She felt exhausted herself, and cold with dread, but she'd grown to love him, and surely love meant giving what was needed if it meant anything at all? There was something else to remember, too – Sam Maitland's calm voice telling her that no cost was likely to be involved with Jeremy; he was a safe choice for a coward. If she had to prove sooner or later that she wasn't afraid . . . well, let it be now, to round off this interminable, already unforgettable day.

'Can we go before I have time to think about it?'

If it wasn't quite the response that a would-be lover might reasonably expect, Jeremy didn't seem to notice. He gulped down the rest of his wine, and pulled her up with him from the table.

'You're right, my blessed one – no being "sicklied o'er with the pale cast of thought" for *us*!' He smiled sweetly at the waiters who watched them leave, and led her with scarcely a stumble to the door. A cab already waited there, looking to her sick imagination more like a tumbril ready to take her to Madame La Guillotine than a London taxi about to make the brief journey to Piccadilly. But she smiled bravely as she climbed in because in some small, still-functioning corner of her brain one of Aunt Lou's favourite maxims repeated itself: 'Remember Kate – God loves a *cheerful* giver.' Even if Louisa Campbell had never thought of giving in these terms, surely the principle held good?

She tried to relax in the warmth of Jeremy's arm about her shoulders, and avoided looking out of the taxi at the various ladies of the night who went casually about their business in Piccadilly Circus. Such courage, she reckoned, to do for money what it seemed so difficult to do even for love. But the die had been cast; she felt resigned now, and faintly regretful that it wouldn't be seemly to tell Sam that he'd been wrong.

The discreetly lit corridors of the Albany were familiar to her now. It was almost possible to pretend that she and Jeremy were a staidly married couple returning home after an evening out; but she caught sight of her pale, strained face in a hall mirror as he fumbled with his key and the frail little pretence faded away. She didn't look or feel staid at all, but tired and confusedly excited, and sad that she was needed only to dull his ache of longing for someone else.

Inside his own apartment, as if he sensed her tension and regret, he wrapped his arms about her until the warmth of his body stilled her trembling. Then he smiled and gently kissed her mouth.

'I love you, dear, sweet Kate – does that seem to make it all right?' Her nod agreed that it did. 'There's nothing to be frightened of,' he promised. 'We'll talk and comfort one another, and comfort will turn naturally to love when you're feeling warm and happy.'

She nodded again, remembering with anguish her familiar attic room in Paradise Walk as she walked into his bedroom instead. It was ridiculous to be suddenly more troubled by the lack of a toothbrush and face-flannel than by what must happen next, but with these mundane items she could at least have pretended that life was normal. As if he understood, Jeremy rummaged in a drawer and produced them for her and the worst of her problems seemed to be over. Gratitude made her smile with such warmth that he kissed her again, but more urgently this time, thinking that the programme could now be revised a little – less talk, same comfort, but much more love now that she looked so definitely prepared for it. When he lifted his head she was breathless and trembling again, but no longer with fear.

'You're more expert at this than I am,' she said unevenly. 'I'm bound to be a disappointment . . . even if you could stop wishing all the time that I was some-one else.'

Something in the awkward honesty of that little speech – the essence of Kate Cavendish he dimly realised it to be – penetrated the trance of fevered exhaustion he was wrapped in. Brilliant blue eyes in a haggard face locked themselves with hers, insisting that she was wrong. 'No one else wished for, my sweet . . . no one in the whole wide world . . . so if you're about to disappear please don't keep me waiting long.'

She went into the adjoining bathroom in a breathless daze, fumbled with clothes that seemed to have acquired far more hooks and eyes than when she'd put them on, dropped the cap of Jeremy's toothpaste tube in her agitation and took too long searching for it again on the marble floor. Was this disintegrating mixture of shame and excitement something one got used to? She supposed so, or who would find it bearable? But she was ready at last, wrapped in Jeremy's silk dressing-gown because, cheerful giver that she'd promised herself to become, it wasn't going to be possible to walk back to him entirely naked.

He was waiting, but not quite as she expected. In fact more precisely he wasn't waiting for her at all. Still dressed except for the shoes he'd sat down on the bed to remove, he was stretched out already fathoms deep in the slumber of an exhausted man who'd drunk far too much wine on top of performing for hours on highly strung nerves. He didn't need talk, or even comfort, and certainly not the exhausting pleasures of making love. There crossed her disordered mind the suspicion that she ought to feel slighted and very angry, but mixed with the shivers of dying excitement in her blood was only huge relief. She could safely leave because Jeremy's face looked peaceful again. The same old torments would probably be at work soon enough, but for as long as he slept he was safe from them. She removed his tie, covered him with a blanket, and crept back to the bathroom again.

Struggling to fasten the dress she'd got out of with so much difficulty a few moments ago, she thought regretfully of Sam Maitland – nothing to boast of after all, because in common with Andrew Marvell's coy mistress, her 'long preserv'd virginity' was still intact. And with that thought came the one last thing that an extraordinary day had lacked – insane little bubbles of merriment began welling up inside her and breaking through the surface of her mind. Afraid of waking Jeremy, she hurriedly turned out lamps and fumbled her way to the door before a gust of laughter doubled her up against the wall of the corridor. She straightened up to find the night-porter watching her with so pained a stare that she was almost undone again. If he'd looked less disapproving she might have apologised, but as it was they walked to the front door in frigid silence. A cabby disgorging someone else outside in the yard agreed to take her home to Southwark provided she remembered it was double-fare after midnight.

'Cheap at the price,' Kate told him cheerfully, but she no longer felt like laughing. Kaleidoscopic images of the long day chased each other across her mind's eye – the sight of Macdonald eating his taxi-driver's breakfast, her father's name written in thick black ink, Sam's face describing his parents' failed marriage, and last of all tormented Jeremy . . . who loved her, but probably not enough to drown Anna's siren song. They were simply the pictures left behind by a chaotic day, she told herself, with so little connection and so little significance that nothing crucial had really happened at all. It was just that she'd chosen to chance her luck in the mad, emotional world of the theatre. But Aunt Lou had undoubtedly been right about life in a Civil Service typing-pool – it would have been less exciting, but much less tiring as well.

Chapter 17

The Sunday morning routine at Paradise Walk depended on Percival next door. When he was in the run of a play and recovering from two Saturday performances Milly insisted on staying at home to minister to him. Otherwise, dressed to catch the canon's eye, she sailed out with William and Kate to attend matins at Southwark cathedral. Louisa never went with them, preferring to read her Bible at home. One visit to the cathedral had been enough to convince her that the Anglicans hovered on the very edge of Popery.

Kate normally took pleasure in the lovely, familiar service, but there was no peace to be found in it this morning. Should she ask forgiveness for a sin that had certainly been intended, if not actually achieved? Was a watchful heaven to be thanked for saving her from error, or blamed for sending Jeremy to sleep just when he should have been seducing her? Instead of concentrating on the *Book of Common Prayer* she examined her growing certainty that everything that had or hadn't happened yesterday would turn out to be significant after all.

It would have been a relief to share her anxiety, but who with? Certainly not Sam Maitland, and Aunt Lou's simple philosophy was unhelpful too: the Almighty would have no fault to find with His servants if they acted always for the best. But what was a servant to do who couldn't be sure what the best was? Elsie had been a source of practical advice in the past but Kate suspected that her old friend might seriously lack experience in the sort of problem she was faced with now.

At the end of the service Kate separated from William and Milly saying that she needed a walk beside the river before tackling Aunt Lou's Sunday lunch.

'Though what does *that* amount to?' William asked despondently as she smiled and left them. 'Spam fritters! That's the best we can do five years after the end of the war. I tell you what, Milly, the Labour Party *deserved* to all but lose last month's General Election. They hoodwinked people in 1945 into thinking they were capable of running this country. We've had nothing but gloom and misery ever since.'

Milly decided not to mention the Government's forthcoming 'pat on the back'. Kate's friend, Sam, had told them about the festival, but she already knew William's opinion of its chief instigator, Herbert Morrison. Of course it *was* a pity that the new ungentlemanly breed of politicians kept dear, dashing Anthony Eden out of office, but otherwise she had no strong views on the running of the country. She also secretly enjoyed Spam fritters if only Louisa could be persuaded to make enough of them.

'Kate wasn't quite her usual self this morning, William,' she pointed out. 'The dear girl mixed up the Jubilate and the Benedictus, and then forgot to remain kneeling for the Absolution. If Mr Maitland didn't seem so very nice I should think he was overworking her.'

'Try thinking of Jeremy Barrington instead,' William suggested. 'She isn't toiling in the studio for Sam until all hours every night – she's holding Barrington's hand

and telling him what a wonderful performer he is. I can't blame him for that – I needed Fanny to do the same thing for me years ago.'

'Yes, dear, but Fanny was your wife,' Milly observed delicately. 'One can't help wondering where darling Kate's devotion is leading to.'

'Not to the altar, I hope. Actors shouldn't marry outside the profession – it never works. I hope Jeremy Barrington has enough sense to know that.'

They turned the corner of Thrale Street into Paradise Walk at last, unaware of narrowly missing the very man they'd been talking about. Jeremy had called to see Kate and been told that she was unlikely to be back until lunchtime.

'She goes walking by herself for a bit of peace and quiet after the mad-house she works in,' Louisa had explained with more vigour than tact.

Jeremy, hollow-eyed and pale, had looked upset. 'I *need* to see her, Miss Campbell . . . otherwise I promise you I wouldn't make a nuisance of myself. We left something unfinished last night . . . something rather important.'

Louisa could believe it, remembering Kate's efforts at the breakfast-table to answer coherently anything that was said to her.

'Well, she'll be somewhere along the river after church – it's where she's always taken her troubles to ever since she was a wee girl. I doubt you'll miss her bright green jacket.'

He hadn't made the mistake of showering Louisa with thanks – the habits of his world didn't suit this stern Scottish lady; but his kiss on her cheek had been genuinely grateful.

The green jacket wasn't hard to find. Kate was in her usual attitude, arms folded on the balustrade, watching the river hurry by. Some of its eddies were dashed against the wall she was leaning on and spent in a little froth of foam; others escaped and went dancing on towards the sea, and only pure chance seemed to dictate which of them survived. Observing it she thought the same could be said of people; they liked to think they were in charge, but 'as flies to wanton boys are we to the gods – they kill us for their sport' was surely nearer the mark?

Someone, unwanted, came to stand beside her. She turned to murmur 'good morning' and walk on, but it was Jeremy's bright head the sunlight was glinting on. She hadn't expected him to appear . . . thought he would have decided to ignore the fiasco of the previous night. Heart thumping at twice its normal rate, she was still able to register his condition in the morning light. His ready smile was missing for once, and the network of fine lines about his eyes and mouth was clearly visible. No self-assured matinee idol now; instead she saw a tired, unhappy man who wasn't sure that he was welcome.

'Aunt Lou told me you'd be here,' he said abruptly. 'I'm afraid it's last night making you look troubled, dearest Kate, and I'm so very sorry.'

He couldn't see her eyes because she'd gone back to staring at the water, but her profile was etched against the black metal upright of the lamp-post beside her – nondescript nose, delicately carved lips above a firm chin, long line of slender throat. Her brown hair, cut almost as short as a boy's, was ruffled by the breeze. It marked her out from other women, nowadays all head-deep in elaborate waves and curls. But there was nothing elaborate about Kate at all – no opulent beauty to attract, and account for his certainty that she was someone he mustn't lose.

'I'm not troubled.' She said it cheerfully, but knew that the awkwardness between them would have to be dealt with.

'Last night was my fault . . . I lost the cap of your toothpaste tube – no wonder you gave up waiting for me!'

They normally found a shared pleasure in the ludicrous, but Jeremy still looked tragic, not amused. 'I was nearly half-dead and more than half-drunk . . . quite incapable, in fact, of making love to you at all. But that should have been *my* humiliation, Kate, not yours.'

Allowing something for an actor's imperishable need to dramatise, she still knew that his self-reproach was genuine. But at the risk of offending his dignity, she could only meet the moment with her usual candour. 'I might have *tried* to feel angry, only it suddenly struck me as being very funny instead. If your commissionaire stares at you rather oddly it's because he found me outside your door helpless with laughter.'

Jeremy's hand covered hers where it rested on the parapet, but he took so long to answer that she feared he *was* offended until he said unsteadily, 'Fly away shame, embarrassment drop dead! As usual, my darling, you've made everything all right.'

It was her turn to hesitate, wondering how to explain that nothing could be quite 'all right' again. Before she could make up her mind he hurried on himself.

'Kate, I know I'm far too old for you, and actors are famous for making rotten husbands, but do you think you could consider marrying me? I'd try so hard to make you happy.' Aware of having taken her breath away, his own strained face broke into an entrancing smile. 'Will you say yes, provided I don't give you time to think about it?'

She remembered the moment when she'd said that herself, smiled, and then grew serious again. 'Your age and your

profession . . . I can't see that *they* matter; but there are other
. . . other things that do.'

'Anna, you mean, or if not her, some future leading
lady?'

'Not any future ones . . . I might be able to cope with them;
it's Anna I'm not equipped to deal with.' Kate did her best
to make a joke of it. 'Fight someone your own weight . . .
that's a rule of life that Southwark street-children teach one
another.'

His grip on her hand tightened, as if he was afraid that
she might decide to end the conversation and walk away
from him.

'I'd deny it if I could, sweetheart, but the communication
between me and Anna on stage is obvious to anyone who
watches us. The theatre is one thing, though; reality is
another. In real life she belongs to Angus while you are
my "ever-fixed mark".'

For once Kate's face gave him no hint of what she was
thinking, but a firm rejection seemed so likely that he rushed
on before she could put it into words. 'I've signed a contract
. . . must honour it . . . but I'll leave the company as soon
as the present season ends. We could go on a much-needed
holiday, my love, and forget that Anna Sheridan exists.'

Kate gravely searched his face but found in it no vestige
of regret for what he proposed to give up.

'Macdonald won't let you go,' she said slowly. 'He'd be
mad to, even if he wasn't your friend.'

Jeremy was on surer ground now. 'All wrong, my darling one. What Angus always wanted for the Swan was
a true repertory company, with players swopping leads
and bit parts around. I don't know what he can do about
Anna, who probably won't ever agree to it, but he'll reckon

that my leaving is a step in the right direction, I promise you.'

His hand under her chin tipped up her mouth to be kissed. Her lips quivered under his, and suddenly happiness seemed possible. When he released her she smiled at him shyly.

'I'd like you to leave the company, but for *your* sake, not mine. I want you to do such things that even giants like Olivier and Gielgud must stand to applaud.'

'I'll do them, sweet Kate, if you'd only agree to marry me. Will you . . . please?'

She stared at him with grave eyes. 'Anna isn't the only problem,' she admitted after a moment or two. 'Sam thinks I'm a cripple where love is concerned. I grew up, you see, determined not to fall into the same trap as my mother, who loved a man too much to go on living without him. He also didn't stay long enough to marry her, so I was a bastard child. That might do for plain John Bagg, but not for Jeremy Barrington!'

His hands gripped her hard, almost hurting her. 'I *am* John Bagg, my dearest, and I don't care a fig about your father. More fool he if he never knew his "lass unparalleled"!'

She smiled then, remembering how he'd gone long ago to New York to play the part of Mark Antony. 'I think I'd *like* to be married to you,' she said finally.

The drained, unhappy-looking man who'd come in search of her was suddenly transfigured with relief, and she believed that she saw in his eager face enough love to make their marriage work.

She was caught and held in a fierce hug, kissed again, and finally released. Then, as she caught sight of his watch, her own smile disappeared.

'Oh, Lord . . . is it really *that* late? I'm afraid we'd better run.'

'Late for what?' he managed to gasp while they were galloping along.

'Aunt Lou's lunch. Poor Milly is very partial to Spam fritters, but she won't be allowed to start on them until we arrive.'

Jeremy did his best to laugh and run at the same time, but had to give up in the end to lean helplessly against a lamp-post. Trying not to laugh herself, Kate besought him to try to keep moving, and he finally managed it. But loping along beside her, he thought he must find a more suitable moment than this to explain that John Bagg's childhood – short on absurdity as well as on love – hadn't quite prepared him for the likely richness of life with Kate Cavendish.

Sam allowed himself sneaking glances across the room whenever his silent companion wasn't looking . . . no outward change, but he was ready to swear that for once she wasn't concentrating on the work in hand. It wasn't likely to be their turn-up about her father that kept her so quiet, because she never sulked once a quarrel was over. And if she'd thought about his own stupid confession, it would only be to wonder what it had to do with her. Then, while he was still staring, she suddenly lifted her head and caught him at it.

'Jeremy asked me to marry him yesterday,' she confessed in a sudden rush. 'I thought I'd better tell you because I . . . said I would!'

After a moment's silence he found something to say. 'Does that mean the end of Cavendish & Maitland?'

While he waited for her to answer he breathed on his

spectacles and then polished them on his shirt. It was a gesture she'd seen him make countless times; only now did it seem worth noticing because she saw that what the job really required was a nice, clean hankie, and what *he* surely required was a nice, kind wife who would see to it that he always had one in his pocket. She knew of women who'd jump at the chance – Jane Carlisle for one – but he'd made it clear that the trap of trusting his contentment to someone else was not for him. For a moment sadness pierced her . . . she would have wished him to be happy.

'I'd like to stay with Maitland, if that's all right with him,' she said at last.

He looked so grave that she half-expected him to say it wasn't all right at all; but then he nodded. 'He'll tell you when it *isn't* right,' he promised. Silence reigned for a moment until Sam remembered something left unsaid.

'I'm sorry, Kate – I should have wished you happy with Jeremy . . . I hope you will be.'

It seemed very formal, like the little bow that went with it. She could see his doubts, though, and thought he might have worried less if she could have told him that his friend would soon be leaving the Sheridan company; but it was Jeremy's news to give, not hers.

'Are William and Louisa pleased?' Sam next asked politely.

Kate's small frown reappeared. 'I think so, although with Aunt Lou it's especially hard to tell – because she likes to work at being inscrutable. At least they'll see more of me until the Swan's present season ends. Jeremy has decided that he doesn't need me and a late supper now after every performance – he feels happy enough, he says, to go straight home to bed.'

'A reformed character,' Sam observed with a touch of Louisa's Scottish dryness. He could have added that it was about time too, but Kate would certainly have pretended that she enjoyed watching Jeremy playing against Anna every night. She was loyal to the point of madness once she'd chosen where loyalty was to lie. There seemed to be nothing else that could safely be said about the news she'd just sprung on him, and he indicated with a brief little smile that the conversation was over. He went back to sketching the Mediterranean backdrop for a balcony scene in *Private Lives* instead. Kate resumed her own work, but continued to ponder in some unengaged part of her mind the scene in which her fiancé would tell Anna about the future.

It was occupying Jeremy's mind considerably as well. Angus must know soon that he would be leaving the company, but not until Anna had heard that Kate and he planned to marry when the season ended. His first inclination, to get the confession over and done with immediately, weakened as it grew time to set out for the theatre . . . better to choose a moment *after* the performance when she was happy and surrounded by admiring friends. But afterwards he realised his mistake – life's critical moments always chose themselves, without the slightest reference to good timing.

Anna walked into his dressing-room so soon after he arrived that he thought she must have been listening for him. She looked pale, and perhaps intended him to notice a general air of wistfulness.

'I should let you prepare in peace, shouldn't I,' she said gently, 'but I so needed a little company, dear Jem.'

'I suppose that means Angus is doing his usual thing

– juggling half-a-dozen different balls in the air,' Jeremy suggested with a smile.

'He isn't working for once, but he certainly left the flat early this morning – in search of a weekend country retreat. I can't say that a tumbledown rustic cottage is *my* idea of heaven, but he wants to be able to escape from London occasionally.'

It was scarcely a complete account of their quarrel, but Anna had finally decided on this limited version of it. She'd convinced herself that Angus had been trying to frighten her . . . he'd never be able to relinquish the Swan. Life in future wouldn't follow her first fine plan, but there was no reason why it shouldn't still be workable. He wouldn't allow sentiment, or the lack of it, to stand in the way of good theatre. In the country he'd finish dramatising *Anna Karenina* more quickly, and nothing would blind him to the fact that only she and Jeremy could become the perfect Anna and Captain Vronsky. But, watching Jeremy's thoughtful expression, she made one more confession.

'You must have guessed by now, my dear, that the Macdonald marriage isn't the wonderful arrangement it's generally supposed to be. I'm certain now of what I suspected years ago . . . Angus is too self-sufficient a man to really need a wife. But it's my fault as well, of course – I'm not a good enough actress to hide feelings that a loyal, conventional wife shouldn't have!'

Her smile asked him to admit that she spoke about *them*, but he knew that he must speak only about himself – must speak and smile and pretend that she wasn't going to mind.

'Anna darling, this is no time to be telling me about the pitfalls of marriage . . . you see I've just asked Kate to take *me* on and, incredible as it seems, she's been brave enough to say yes.'

Silence and stillness held time suspended. He couldn't decide whether to pray for someone to interrupt them, or for them to be left alone until that look of total blankness had faded from Anna's face and she came alive again. Then, finally, she smiled and he could tell himself that she understood – what happened to them on stage was outside what common sense, survival even, dictated in real life. 'My dear Jeremy, was there really a grain of doubt in your mind that she *wouldn't* agree? Surely not! When is the happy event to be . . . before you and I launch ourselves into Noël Coward's little frolic on the pitfalls of matrimony?'

'Afterwards,' Jeremy said with a smile of relief, 'when the season ends and we can all take a much-needed holiday.'

She nodded approvingly, and he was aware that relief was now mixed with a feeling of anti-climax . . . he'd been a fool to dread telling her about Kate. But the very next moment she managed to tighten his nerves again.

'Darling, we shall have to choose *next* season's pro-gramme very carefully. New little brides, I believe, are easily upset. We must be *most* circumspect – definitely *no* passionate love-scenes on stage . . . but it's a pity when I had a strong fancy to play the siren of the Nile!'

He hovered on the very edge of agreeing . . . would almost certainly have done so except for a sudden picture in his mind's eye of Kate looking at him with clear, candid eyes. An occasional small subterfuge sometimes saved hurt feelings but he knew in his soul that it wasn't going to be permissible now.

'I didn't finish giving you my news,' he said slowly. 'Anna, I'm going to leave the company when the season ends. It will have been the best time of my life, working with you and Angus, but now I must move on . . . it's only fair to Gil Forrest, too . . . he's earned the key rôles – deserves them; he's a fine actor, and you played against him marvellously in *The Portrait*.'

Jeremy thought he was talking too much . . . chattering like an idiot who loved the sound of his own voice; but anything was better than a silence that Anna seemed to refuse to break.

At last, very pale but completely composed, she spoke in a cool, clear voice. 'Do whatever you like, except take me for a fool. If Gilbert *can* find a better shop than the Sheridan company, he's free to go; but he's got more sense. Don't make *him* your excuse . . . just admit that you're leaving to stop our poor little Kate going mad with jealousy about you and me.' She glanced down at the watch on her wrist, pleased to see that her hand wasn't trembling. 'Time for both of us to get dressed . . . see you in Covent Garden as usual, my darling!'

An hour later, on one of the periodic visits he always made during the run of a production, to check that scenery and costumes were standing up to nightly wear and tear, Sam watched the opening scene and thought, 'Oh, Christ, Anna *knows* about Jem and Kate.' He was tempted to walk out as soon as he could, but found himself staying until the end, mesmerised by the battle taking place on stage. Eliza, sharp and bright and dangerous as a naked blade, began by stealing every scene; then, aware of being deliberately out-played, Jeremy geared up his own performance to match. The result brought the audience to the edge of their seats, afraid of missing the slightest word or glance, because *here* was theatre legend in the making.

When it was over Sam walked all the way home to Southwark, trying to drive out of his mind the smile that Anna and Jeremy had exchanged as they stood acknowledging the applause. For the moment, at least, with the battle over, they were released into some fulfilled communion that the rest of the world couldn't share in. Perhaps Angus had already learned to accept that it existed, or no longer cared – but dear God, what about Kate? She seemed ready at last to forget Marguerite Cavendish and gladly give away heart and soul and body. But would Jem understand that she'd require loyalty in return? And even if he understood, would Anna ever permit it to be possible?

Chapter 18

Sam had no idea what might happen next but in the real-life play he seemed to be watching from a ringside seat he was certain of one thing: his cast of actors had no choice now. Whatever happened, the game was afoot and they must play it to the end. He was scarcely surprised, therefore, when Macdonald arrived on his doorstep late one evening.

'Sorry . . . I know it's an odd time for a social call, but I thought I'd chance finding you at home.'

Sam didn't comment on his friend's grey, exhausted face, or on the luggage he'd brought with him – a large tan-coloured canvas grip that proclaimed it ex-naval issue, and a bundle of manuscript paper under one arm. Instead, he merely waved Angus up the stairs.

'I'm only just back myself. Pour yourself a dram while I get some supper. Now you're here you can help me eat the herrings that arrived from Scotland this morning. My father's housekeeper has a brother who has a fishing-boat, and since Morag believes in keeping trade in the family, consignments turn up from time to time.'

Sam looked at his friend's taut face and added a rider. 'They're good herrings and I shall cook them very well. Apart from that, you look as if it's days since you remembered to eat a square meal.' He walked away to his galley at the end of the room without waiting for an answer, but it was a moment or two before Angus appeared in the doorway with a helping of whisky for both of them.

'Inherited flair, I suppose,' he commented, watching Sam delicately removing backbones from the fish. 'I can just see you carving up some victim on the operating table, too.'

Sam smiled but shook his head. 'No, it didn't need war service in the RAMC to convince me that I wasn't cut out for a medical career. My father would have liked it, of course, just as yours probably hoped *you*'d grow up to be the next Procurator-Fiscal!'

Angus nodded, watching the fish now being carefully rolled in oatmeal. 'Proper man's work, administering the law – not like our theatrical nonsense. My dear family don't say so but they can scarcely believe that what I do is work at all.' He took a sip from his glass before he went on. 'Perhaps nonsense is what it is – fantasies played out by people who can't come to grips with real life.'

Sam looked up and saw the despair in his friend's face. 'Is that what life *is* at the moment . . . painfully real?'

'It's a complete mess, if you want the truth. Anna and I have had one row too many. Jem is leaving the company after *Private Lives*, and she can't decide whether to blame it on my jealousy or Kate's. He, by the way, is going to marry your partner.'

'Kate told me that,' Sam said slowly, 'but not about Jem leaving. Does it worry you so much? I had the feeling that you'd like to be able to swop your leading players around.'

Angus gave a little shrug. 'The question's academic now . . . I shall be leaving the Swan, too, at the end of this season.'

'Whatever for?' Sam almost shouted. 'It's as much yours as Anna's, surely?'

'Not really; I've been reminded several times that my share only comes with marrying into the Stein family, so I've written to Jacob to give it back to him. I don't think I'm entirely to blame for the fact that our marriage is on the rocks, but God knows if it matters in the end whose fault it is – the result is the same.'

'I'm very sorry, Angus,' Sam said, and meant it, 'but I'm glad Jem is going to make a completely fresh start with Kate . . . I wouldn't have credited him with so much sense. What will happen to the Swan?'

'We'll finish this season as planned, even though I'm moving out of Cheyne Walk. After that Anna can choose a new director and tell *him* which plays she's prepared to appear in. Whatever they are she'll be a huge success, having that thing we call "star quality" pressed down and brimming over.'

He managed to speak dispassionately – a man of the theatre passing experienced judgement on one more actress; only this one was his wife . . . the woman he'd given his stubborn heart to. Sam looked away from Macdonald's face before he asked his next question.

'What about you, Angus . . . what will *you* do?'

'Get out of London for a bit, as soon as I can. I've found a small cottage to rent furnished. It's on the edge of an upland village in Wiltshire. Nothing fancy, but lovely clean winds blow there, and the views are breathtaking too. I shall have to go to Edinburgh at the beginning of August, but for a month or so I'll be able to work on *Anna Karenina* in peace.'

'You'll need a bed in London as well,' Sam pointed out,

'from tonight onwards, by the look of the grip you brought with you.'

'Yes – I'll find a room in some small hotel for the time being – get a flat of my own again eventually, I suppose.'

'You used to turn up your nose a bit at Southwark, but one thing an ex-warehouse doesn't lack is space. There's a room off the studio you're welcome to look on as yours – "nothing fancy", to quote your own words; but the bed's comfortable, and we aren't likely to get under each other's feet too much.'

Macdonald tried to smile. 'You're by way of being psychic as well as a very good friend – how did you guess I was dreading that damned hotel room?'

'Hate 'em myself,' Sam explained briefly. 'Now whisht, laddie, while I concentrate on these herrings. Unlike Morag, I can't cook and talk at the same time. Come to think of it, *she* can do anything and talk at the same time.'

When the meal was over, Angus chose not to speak of personal things; instead he talked about the production of *The Cherry Orchard* that he must go to Edinburgh to direct for the festival. 'It's not only a marvellous play to do, but nicely timed as well,' he commented. 'After weeks of living with Tolstoy I'll be suitably steeped in the Russian mentality by then – childlike gaiety one moment, slavonic gloom the next.' He smiled at the idea, then looked serious again. 'Puts me in mind of Jem, as a matter of fact. I hope young Kate is going to be able to cope with a complicated character nearly twice her age.'

'I think we must assume that she can,' Sam said quietly. 'She's had quite a lot of practice at it in recent months'. Finding himself disinclined to go on discussing Kate and Jeremy, it was his turn to switch the conversation. 'Sad to think we're all now longing for this season to end. We started out with such high hopes to get the Swan afloat again.'

'It will survive well enough without me and Jeremy,' Angus pointed out. Then he said good night, but stopped in the doorway, having thought of something else. 'Just as well Kate will be too caught up in the business of getting married, though, to worry about William's old theatre. I can't see Anna not persuading Jacob *now* to change its name to the Sheridan – can you?'

He went away to bed, leaving Sam still folded up in his favourite seat overlooking the river. The spring night had fallen and the crescent of a new moon hung low in the sky downstream. Below sky and moon was the great, lit sprawl of London . . . millions of other human beings, sleeping or wakeful, loving and loved or lonely, laughing or enduring their own private sadnesses. Compared with that huge weight of humanity, the handful of people who occupied his thoughts could scarcely be said to matter. And one insignificant dot labelled Sam Maitland certainly didn't matter at all. If they kept their heads no disaster would occur before the Swan's season ended. After that the only small difficulty left would be his own – recognising in his partner a girl who was no longer Kate Cavendish but the wife of Jeremy Barrington . . . yes, that *would* take a little getting used to.

Breakfast in the Stein apartment in New York was a private, leisurely meal that Margot cherished. For as long as it could be made to last Jacob remained entirely hers, but once the magic circle was broken a new day would come rushing in, and there would be the usual queue of people wanting her husband's attention. After ten years of marriage it still mattered, and she still marvelled that it should. This ugly, forceful, not quite wholly Americanised European had become the core of her life, and her only private grief was that she hadn't been able to bear him a child. It was too late now, and control of the huge network of family enterprises would pass in time to his younger brother and sisters, and their children. Margot knew exactly what their affectionate attitude towards her concealed – one part contempt that she'd turned out to be infertile; three parts relief. They were all aware of the delight that Jacob took in his brilliant step-daughter, but Anna wasn't a family threat and nor, thanks be to God, was a husband who kept her safely in London.

On a morning at the end of April Margot skimmed through an airmailed letter, and looked up to find Jacob watching her across the breakfast table.

'It's just Anna's usual hurried scrawl,' she reported. 'Dreadful weather still, but at least petrol rationing is coming to an end. *Pygmalion*'s going very well, after a sticky start, and they've begun rehearsing the Noël Coward play that finishes the season.' She put down the letter and made a wry face at her husband. 'The interesting item is left for the P.S. – Jeremy has decided to take a wife! Didn't we meet her in London . . . a girl called Kate Cavendish? I seem to remember that she wore a stunningly elegant dress, and rather stole Anna's thunder!'

Jacob smiled, remembering the occasion very well. 'When I met her first in her work-room she was wearing a pair of overalls, and we discussed the virtue of fitting behaviour as practised by her grandfather! She made a rather vivid impression, as a matter of fact.' His smile broadened as he saw Margot considering this; it pleased him, although he wouldn't say so, that she would have preferred him not to remember other women. But there was a more serious matter occupying his mind as well.

'Is that all Anna says?' he asked next. 'Nothing about Angus, or the theatre?'

Margot shook her head. 'No mention at all, apart from the rehearsals. I suppose there's nothing else *to* mention.'

'Only that he's leaving the Swan when it closes for the summer,' Jacob said drily. 'You'd think that might be worth a post-script.'

'In heaven's name *why*? I thought he loved that theatre . . . saw it as the place where they would do great things together. Darling, are you sure you're not mistaken?'

'His note was courteous but entirely unmistakable – the perfect business letter, in fact. I am to take back his share of the theatre because he no longer feels entitled to keep so valuable a wedding present. The Swan is only one of the things, I gather, they disagree about, but an important one – they can't both be in charge, so he's leaving it to her. Their marriage is also effectively over.'

'How *can* it be, Jacob? They loved each other. I was certain of it, even on our last visit. I know she feels close to Jeremy as well, but Angus must surely have made allowances for that – he knows how actors are. Kate Cavendish will have to learn to understand as well.' She looked at her husband with large, troubled eyes. 'Why do you think she *didn't* mention it – because she's expecting Angus to change his mind?'

'He won't,' Jacob said with certainty, 'at least, not about his marriage; it either works or it doesn't for someone like him. I don't feel justified in trying to change his mind about that, but I should like to persuade him to stay on at the Swan if I can.'

Anxiety made her angry for a moment. Even her near-perfect Jacob couldn't help thinking like a man. He would exert himself over the theatre, but broken lives could be left to their own mending.

'It's Angus who must go, surely, if Anna chooses to stay,' she pointed out sharply. 'There are *other* directors, after all.'

'But none so good.' He thought the words but didn't speak them, aware of the unusual edge to his wife's voice. He gave a little sigh and kissed her goodbye just as the hall-porter's call from downstairs announced the arrival of his driver.

'They're rehearsing a new play together,' Margot said as she walked with him to the door. 'Don't you think that must mean they still need each other? Jacob, I shall have to answer her letter – am I to say that I know they're in difficulties, or wait for *her* to tell me?'

'Wait, my darling,' he suggested after a moment's thought. 'Nothing can change until they get to the end of the season – Angus says so himself. Give them time to get on with the new rehearsals. You'll think I'm being harsh if I say this, but creating performances is what they live for.'

She agreed doubtfully, tried to smile, and was kissed again before he took their own private elevator down to the hall.

Rehearsals for a play containing only four characters were likely to be painful if the actors were strangers, or trying to upstage each other in some way. Watching them unobserved from the back of the house, Kate was experienced enough by now to know that that wasn't happening here. Nevertheless there was something that Gil Forrest and Jane Carlisle, struggling to redeem their thankless supporting rôles, didn't expect, and it was causing them to falter. Noël Coward had composed a brilliantly comic, destructive dance in which the four characters kept changing partners. Played as Anna and Jeremy were playing it, it was becoming a bitter-sweet, tragi-comical romance, with the onlooker left in no doubt of real passion and heartbreak beneath the surface sparkle. Kate was there to watch the rehearsal with a practical object in view – her costume designs must allow the players to breathe and talk and move about as they were required to; but it was hard to concentrate on her own job when she was engrossed in what was happening on stage.

Back in the studio alone, towards the end of the afternoon, she heard footsteps on the stairs and expected Sam to appear, but it was Angus Macdonald who walked in instead.

'I'm staying here for the moment,' he explained briefly. Both voice and unsmiling expression dared her to comment on his situation, much less to pour over him the syrup of pity that he would instantly reject.

'I know . . . Sam told me to expect you.' She said it with equal brevity, and that seemed to be that, but when he hesitated, deprived of something to take exception to, she was suddenly aware of his extreme loneliness. It seemed inhumanly detached to go on with her work as if he wasn't there; and in any case there was a sense in which his problems were also hers.

'I won't go on about it,' she promised diffidently, 'but I have to say that I'm sorry things haven't worked out for you and Anna.'

A smile that she didn't enjoy touched his mouth, then faded again. 'Thank you . . . you managed that very nicely. Now I hope we're free to talk about the weather.'

His tone of voice whipped colour into her face and she

was about to suggest that they needn't talk at all. But with the unexpectedness that she'd noticed in him before, his expression suddenly relaxed into gentleness. 'No, we'll talk about *you* instead. Kate . . . don't worry, please. Anna and I are coming unstuck simply because we made the mistake that we narrowly avoided making years ago. There's no mistake about you and Jem . . . *you*'ll be all right.'

Her irritation with him melted into sadness. The Guv'nor was known to those who worked for him as a fair but hard taskmaster; not a man whose heart was easily touched, or whose patience could be tried for long. Her own start with him had certainly been unfriendly, but since then she had met him more than once on an altogether deeper level of understanding. He lacked Jeremy's easy charm, or the warmth of heart that contributed to Sam Maitland's odd brand of attractiveness; but still he was the axis round which they'd all revolved. She wondered how they would manage without him.

'I was at the theatre this morning, watching the rehearsal,' she said suddenly. 'It isn't my favourite play by a long chalk, but it no longer seemed to be the play I thought it was.'

'Did you like it any better that way?' Angus asked, with his eyes on her face.

She thought before she answered, but could see no alternative to being truthful.

'I suppose it worried me. Did Noël Coward *mean* it to be played in that heart-wrenching way . . . or is it just that Anna and Jeremy can't help playing themselves?' She met Macdonald's searching glance steadily. 'It's not to say that he doesn't love *me*; I know he does. But when they're on stage together I lose contact with him.'

'And at such times you wonder whether he can ever manage without her?'

She answered the question with a nod, knowing that it reached the heart of her anxiety. Angus came to stand beside her, and again she sensed his unexpected kindness.

'Listen, Kate . . . he must, for his own good, manage without her. Audiences love seeing them strike sparks off each other, but from now on what they'd appear in would always be Anna's choice of play. Wasting the God-given talent he possesses converting sophisticated comedy into a tear-jerker *isn't* what Jem ought to be doing. Marry him and make him feel secure enough to go it alone again . . . that's all *you* have to do.'

After a moment she nodded, and a transfiguring smile lit her face. 'That's what I think, too,' she agreed.

She felt no need after that to question the future, even though it probably meant separation from the Swan for herself as well as Jeremy. Anna would make certain that her new director had nothing to do with a designer who by then would be Jeremy Barrington's wife. It didn't matter very much – the important thing was that William's precious theatre had been rescued and was alive again. If Jeremy's going meant that Gil Forrest would step into the limelight there, well, that was something he deserved.

Kate had the uncomfortable sensation, though, of treading water . . . and for the first time in her life the days seemed to pass almost too slowly. They waited for the summer and the end of the season to come; they were all tired, but there was still the hurdle of the final production in front of them. She saw less of Jeremy now that her evenings weren't spent at the theatre. Their Sundays were shared, but he'd never again begged her to stay the night with him. They would marry as soon as the theatre closed for the summer; until then it was understood that she would sleep in her attic bedroom alone. Her strong impression was that all his stamina was needed to get him through the days of rehearsal and the evening performances. He looked fine-drawn and, when he forgot to smile, completely exhausted.

Occasionally he wandered into the studio in time to share her picnic lunch, and one day she raised the subject of the *Private Lives* rehearsals.

'It's too much to ask of you,' she said, made cross by anxiety, 'rehearsing one play and still performing another at night.'

If she sounded sharp, Jeremy's voice was sharper. 'You don't understand – having to switch concentration keeps us fresh. Ask William if you don't believe me.'

It wasn't the first time she'd felt excluded from the private world that only actors inhabited, but the reprimand was still painful. His apology came with a quick, rueful smile.

'Sorry, my sweet . . . I think I just proved your point for you – working two plays in tandem *is* a strain. Even so, it *is* better than getting bored and stale during a long run.'

'Then I'll stop worrying about you,' she said with an answering smile. 'I suppose it's easier, too, if what you're rehearsing is something you want to perform.' She intended not to hint at her own opinion of *Private Lives*, but it was Jeremy who suddenly went on talking about it.

'Angus tries to hide the fact, but it's obvious that he would rather we *weren't* doing the Coward play. He can't seem to see that it's just the thing to follow *Pygmalion*. Everything about it makes a marvellous contrast.'

'Perhaps,' Kate agreed cheerfully, 'but the costumes are

beasts to make, Elsie would tell you. Yards of bias-cut slipper satin to be sewn, and trimmed with sequins and fragile ostrich-feathers! Still, though I says it as shouldn't, the dresses are going to look beautiful.'

Jeremy caught her hand and kissed it. 'Damn the Swan for a moment . . . let's think about *us*. Sweetheart, will you mind living in Piccadilly for a bit – until we have time to find something you'd prefer?'

The truth was that she still felt ill at ease in his grand Albany rooms, seemed to become whenever she went there the gauche creature whom the hall porter had so clearly despised. But instead of saying so she touched his cheek in her familiar tender gesture.

'Piccadilly's not quite what I'm used to, but I can put up with it if I have to.' Then she added more seriously, 'Perhaps we could find a little hide-away as well, like Macdonald's. Don't you think a taste of the real world outside the theatre would be good for us?'

'A dyed-in-the-wool Londoner asking for farmyard smells and farmyard noises? I don't believe it!'

She smiled because he expected her to, but realised that he'd deliberately avoided giving a real answer, perhaps because he still didn't quite trust the world outside his goldfish bowl.

'Do you see much of Angus here?' he asked casually.

'I don't, because I've usually gone home by the time he gets back; Sam sees him, of course.' Then she had to force herself to ask a question that seemed dangerous but necessary. 'I don't see Anna nowadays, because Elsie does the fittings at the theatre . . . is she all right?'

Jeremy's face grew sombre. 'She's being very brave, but if Angus was making up his mind to walk out on her he could damn well have had the decency to wait until the end of the season. It's a colossal strain for the poor girl, still having to work with him, knowing all the time that everyone is watching them.'

'It's a strain for Macdonald too,' Kate pointed out, remembering his gaunt face. 'And if he doesn't like the play, it's mostly on *your* account – not worthy of you, he thinks.'

'I don't bloody well care *what* he thinks,' Jeremy suddenly shouted. 'Anna and I can do without him.'

The sight of Kate's white face made him apologise and quickly kiss her. But the visit had gone sour, and she didn't press him to stay longer when he got up to leave.

That night, for the first time, he didn't go straight home after the performance. When Anna invited him back to Cheyne Walk for a sandwich and a drink he decided that it would be less than kind not to go with her. The poor girl was lonely, as he himself of course was lonely without Kate. It wouldn't do to make a habit of it but he wasn't yet 'Benedick, the married man'. For a little while longer he could still do as he liked.

Chapter 19

The evening was fine and clear for London – an apple-green sky that merged into apricot in the west, and eastwards was already deepening to indigo. Outside the door of the studio Sam's chimney pots spilled a tangle of gold and bronze-coloured wallflowers. Kate watered them each evening, sniffed the perfume they released into the air, and commiserated with them as well – the poor things ought, she told them, to have the freedom of some country-cottage garden. Between the flowers and the exquisitely tinted sky, she scarcely noticed the taxi that slowed down as it came towards her. But when it stopped outside Sam's door she stood waiting for its passenger to appear.

A stranger stepped out, dapper in a light-coloured suit and hat – foreign was her first impression. It wasn't surprising, because her partner's friends were many and varied, and he was even now upstairs completing the designs that must soon be sent to Vienna. The visitor looked doubtfully at the barn-like building in front of him, then raised his hat to the girl who stood watching him.

'Good evening . . . I look for a Mr Maitland at . . . at Wharfside, I think . . . but perhaps this is not where he lives.'

The visitor's voice was pleasant, with an inflection in it

that she couldn't identify but, remembering Sam's Austrian connections, she guessed that here was someone who would turn out to be a maternal relative. She smiled at him in her usual friendly fashion.

'This is Wharfside and, appearances to the contrary, Mr Maitland does live here! I'll show you where to find him.'

He didn't return her smile, but she supposed that the scrap-yard-cum-junk-shop that was Sam's ground floor was enough to take any visitor aback. She led him quickly through the muddle to the stairs. 'The studio is up above,' she explained cheerfully. 'It's a bit more tidy there.'

Her companion acknowledged this with a nod, but still seemed reluctant to converse. She tried again, as they climbed the stairs, to make the occasion more sociable.

'Is Mr Maitland expecting you?'

'No . . . not at all; I come without appunt . . . appointment,' he corrected himself.

She couldn't help but feel that he came also without any apparent friendliness, but that wasn't her problem; needing only to clear up her table for the night, she would soon be going home. Sam turned round from his drawing-board as they walked in, and she thought with a twinge of amusement how well he matched the impression his elegantly turned-out visitor must already have received. Thick hair standing on end where he'd run his fingers through it, paint-splashed sweater, and baggy corduroys – scarcely the picture of an internationally known designer whose services were sought by all and sundry.

'A visitor for you, Sam . . . his taxi arrived while I was outside.' Then she spoke to the newcomer. 'This is Mr Maitland.'

Still miserly with words, he bowed and then handed Sam a

card. There was a moment of silence so profound in the room that her ever-ready imagination took flight – it wasn't a mere visiting-card at all. The stranger had brought some crucial secret message that held her partner locked in stillness while he tried to make sense of it. Amused again by the absurd idea, she nevertheless wondered why Sam didn't find something to say – he was instantly at ease with people as a rule. But when he spoke at last it was in a voice she scarcely recognised.

'I must introduce you to one another – Dottore Arturo Contini . . . meet Miss Kate Cavendish.'

The crash of the watering-can dropping from her hand was nerve-wrackingly loud, then there was silence again. Sam stared from the man's rigid face to the ashen girl. 'They bleed on *both* sides' . . . the useless words still hammered in his brain – they bleed, poor things . . . oh God, *how* they bleed. Then Kate suddenly made a dash for the cloakroom on the landing outside the door.

At last Arturo Contini spoke in a slow, dragging voice. 'Who is that girl . . . *Cavendish*, you said?'

Sam took off his spectacles and noticed without surprise that his fingers were unsteady.

'She is my partner here. Her mother was called Marguerite Cavendish . . . Kate was given her family name.'

'Having no father?' Contini asked hoarsely.

'No father that she has ever known. He belonged in Italy apparently, and went back there before Kate was born.'

'Holy Mother of God.' The Italian's ragged voice wavered and failed altogether as he collapsed into the nearest chair and buried his face in his hands. When Sam touched him gently, offering him a glass of brandy, his face was wet with tears.

'She is *my* daughter, isn't she?' he asked. '*That*'s why you looked for me in Milan.' He took a gulp from the glass.

'Why did she run from the room . . . because she knows who I am?'

'She knows, and I expect she was feeling sick with anger,' Sam admitted. 'She has grown up thinking of you as a man who abandoned her mother and caused her to commit suicide. Now, to make matters a little worse, she is thinking of me as a man who's broken a solemn promise not to get in touch with you. When I brought your address back from Milan I said that she must decide whether or not to use it.'

'And she chose not to. *Certo* . . . of course, believing what she does.' He stared at Sam with haunted eyes. 'We should help her, no, if she is unwell?'

'My almost certain guess is that she's already out of the front door – she lives with her grandfather, quite close by.'

'William Cavendish,' Contini remembered slowly. 'Marguerite was very proud of him.'

'So is Kate. William's theatre was bombed during the war, but it's recently been restored. One of the productions that Kate and I have worked on together is running there now. She's a very gifted stage-designer.'

Contini drank the last of his brandy, then stared at the empty glass while he framed in unaccustomed English all that he needed to say. Before he was ready to begin the door opened and Kate, white-faced but composed, walked in.

'I decided to get this meeting over with,' she said distinctly, 'but I hope my part in it needn't take long. Then the two of you can entertain each other.'

For a moment Sam thought she was going to stay standing by the door, ready to leave, and very unready to come anywhere near her father. But as if the strain was more than she could bear, she suddenly moved towards a chair and sat down with her hands gripping its arms. There were beads of perspiration on her upper lip, and Sam went to bring her a glass in which brandy was diluted with water.

'You'll feel better for this, partner,' he said gently.

She took it with no word of thanks . . . without even acknowledging that he was there. Uncertain whether or not he *should* be there, he finally decided that things would be worse if he left them alone together. He took up his usual position by a window overlooking the river, but watching them, not the moving water outside.

Arturo Contini began at the end rathcr than at the beginning. 'Mr Maitland did not invite me here,' he said, speaking to Kate. 'My nephew's wife told me that an English visitor had been asking about me – someone who knew that I'd lived in London long before the war. I was . . . curious, of course, especially when the visitor who wanted my address did not appear. A jewellery exhibition took me to Paris this week, but instead of going home I suddenly found myself in a train for Calais . . . on the way to a city I hadn't seen for more than twenty years.' He took a sip from the glass that Sam had refilled, and talked to the girl whose huge, dark eyes never left his face.

'I met and fell in love with Marguerite Cavendish on that first visit. I had no right to – I was already promised to the girl my father had picked out for me to marry; but Marguerite was everything my future wife was not – divinely fair and pretty, full of grace and sweetness. I knew that I would have to go back – my elder brother was in poor health, my family duty obliged me to go back to Milan. But I offered to explain to my father that I couldn't marry Lucia if Marguerite would agree to go with me. She refused even to consider it – she was certain that she would die in a foreign city, among people who were bound to hate her. When my father summoned me,

I went back alone, not knowing that she was going to bear my child. I never knew afterwards that she was dead.' He stopped talking and stared at Kate. 'There is no reason why you should believe me.'

It seemed to Sam, watching them both, an eternity before she decided to answer the question that Contini hadn't brought himself to ask.

'There's no reason, but I *do* believe you. My grandfather didn't know the whole story . . . he could only tell me what he knew, so I grew up hating you.'

Still father and daughter looked at one another, almost unaware that Sam was in the room.

'You're not like Marguerite,' Arturo murmured. 'I couldn't speak when you smiled at me out in the street, because you reminded me of my son, Alessandro. I didn't know why then. He would be almost twenty now if the Germans hadn't killed him.'

Kate closed her eyes for a moment, unable to bear the desolation in his face. Then she stood up, and so did he.

'I'm very, very sorry about your son,' she said gently. 'It's a pity about *us* too, but I'm afraid it's too late to be friends.'

There was another silence before he spoke again. 'Yes, it's too late, Katerina.' His hand lifted as if it couldn't help touching her cheek, then fell to his side again. 'But will you go on hating me?'

The simple directness of the question was such as Kate herself might have used, Sam thought. In one way and another they were much alike.

'No, I shan't hate you any more,' she said gravely. 'For that, at least, I'm glad you came.' Then she walked over to the door, but swung round again to look at Sam. 'I thought you'd broken a promise . . . I suppose I ought to have known better.' A smile that wavered perilously on the edge of tears was offered to both of them before she bolted for the stairs and disappeared.

Sam stared at the necklace of lights along the Embankment across the river. Dusk had fallen, and only a patrolling policeboat disturbed the quietness of the water. But nothing, he thought, would disturb the silence left in the room by Kate's departure unless he found something to say.

'There's no need to worry about her,' he muttered at last. 'She's always been much loved . . . is much loved still . . . and she's very gifted as well.'

He glanced at the Italian's face and looked away again. Arturo Contini perhaps imagined that he smiled, but to Sam it seemed a rictus grin, concealing almost intolerable pain.

Wharfside looked as usual the next morning – a dismal prospect of mostly empty or demolished warehouses, redeemed by glimpses in between of sparkling river, and the sight of Sam's brave, yellow door. The studio was unchanged, too, in its ordered clutter of sketches, stage models, stacks of coloured board, and swatches of material. But Kate knew that she would never be able to come here again without remembering the face of a man who'd asked if she must go on hating him.

Sam was eating a late breakfast when she went in, having been up and at work since sunrise. She refused the offer of food but helped herself to coffee from the pot. It was an excuse to sit down at the kitchen table with him – easier there to say what was in her mind.

'What's happened to my . . . my father?'

Sam glanced at the clock on the wall. 'If by some miracle

it leaves on time, his boat-train is even now pulling out of Victoria Station. He didn't see much point in lingering in London.'

That said, her partner returned to the task of spreading a very small piece of butter as far as it would go on a slice of bread. It seemed to interest him more than the conversation. There had been times before when she'd been made sharply aware of the gap of twelve years between them. It gave him an unfair advantage – years of acquired knowledge and experience that she didn't have. Now, when he was without the useful screen of his spectacles and still munching bread, she thought she ought to have been able to deal with him. But his face looked unfamiliar; the untidy, shambling, gentle man she supposed she knew was hidden behind this cool-voiced stranger who suddenly provoked her to anger.

'Why not say what you're thinking?' It came out so nearly a shout that she was forced to start again more quietly. 'Why not say I should have fallen on an unknown Italian's neck and thanked him for coming, even if it *was* twenty years too late?' Sam didn't answer and her voice rose again. 'Don't tell me it's nothing to do with you – he wouldn't have come at all but for you asking about him.'

'It has *that* much to do with me,' the man opposite her admitted, 'and I don't regret it, Kate. But what I think about you and your father . . . that has nothing to do with you.'

She picked up the mug of coffee and had to put it down again because her hands were trembling. It was a dreadful moment to realise that what she wanted most in life was to burst into tears and have Sam Maitland promise her that last night she hadn't been wickedly stupid and needlessly cruel.

'I told William,' she muttered. 'He needed to know that . . . that things *could* have been different. But until

I marry Jeremy I'm still Cavendish, not Contini; after that
Marguerite's sad little story really *will* be over.'

'So it will,' Sam agreed obligingly.

She eyed him in silence for a moment but knew that he
would give her no more help. At almost twenty-one, she
was a paid-up adult member of the human race, and hadn't
she always been in any case a self-opinionated piece who'd
made a habit of not being told what to do?

'I shall now get on with some work,' she announced, and
did so. There was no need to confess that, as the morning
wore on, there hovered between her and the sketch in front
of her the image of a sad-eyed man she hadn't been able
to hate at all. Nor did she tell Sam of a decision that had
quietly lodged itself in her mind. One day she would go to
Florence . . . not to see its treasures but to find the grave of
a boy whose smile had been like hers.

There was one other person to tell about her father's visit
before she could bury it in some dim corner of her memory.
Jeremy must be the sharer of her burden of sadness, not
Sam.

She walked into the Swan as the audience were taking
their seats after the interval. Walter Fairbrass, still working
in his cubby-hole behind the box-office, spotted her as she
went past and waved to her to come in.

'Haven't clapped eyes on you in weeks, Kate . . . the great
man keeps you to himself, and who can blame him!' Walter
sounded jovial and smiled at her with approval. He wasn't a
follower of female fashions – middle-aged bachelors weren't
required to be – but he was aware that she always managed
to look different from other women. It was something to
do with her boyish hair, of course, but also to do with the

extreme simplicity of her clothes and the singing colours she always wore.

'I don't come every evening now because the "great man" is better off going home to sleep after the show,' she explained. 'How is it going, Walter . . . people still flocking to see Professor Higgins and Eliza?'

'Always a full house – would be for months to come, too. It's a pity to take it off if you ask me. But the Guv'nor knows what he's doing, of course, and *Private Lives* is bound to be a knock-out as well.' Walter smiled again at his visitor. 'Can't complain, Kate . . . the Swan couldn't have a better boss or a better company.'

For once, she thought, the theatre grapevine along which there normally travelled every vestige of news or innuendo couldn't be functioning, if even Walter didn't yet know that both Macdonald and its leading man would soon be leaving the Swan. She remembered that Jeremy had said how bravely Anna contended with the curious glances from people who knew that her marriage was over. If the few who did know were being discreet, the glances couldn't be very many, but allowance had always to be made for an actor's need to elaborate on the truth a little.

She watched the last scene or two from the back of the dress-circle and realised that what Walter had said was true – it *was* a pity that a production so enchanting would be coming off the boards. Especially in these later stages of the play Anna was a marvellous Eliza Doolittle, but Jeremy performed a greater miracle: he was Henry Higgins to the life – bully, egoist, and charmer, all at the same time.

Anxious not to appear at his door too soon, Kate took refuge after the performance in Elsie's work-room. A half-finished dress for *Private Lives* was hanging up, and it was a pleasure to admire her friend's workmanship. Then as the sound of voices calling out good night suggested that the theatre was beginning to empty backstage, she climbed the stairs to Jeremy's dressing-room. He was normally the last to leave; tonight, it seemed, he must have been the first. Even his dresser had gone as well, and the room was already in darkness. Feeling disproportionately upset at missing him, she was still standing in the corridor when Bert Trotter came lumbering along, making one of his many rounds.

''Ee's gawn, Kate . . . went orf sharpish with 'er ladyship, good ten minutes ago, I'd say, same as usual.'

Bert's eyes were rheumy but still sharp, and although there was kindness in him, there was an incurable love of gossip as well.

She did her best to smile. 'Stupid of me . . . I expect I've muddled up our arrangements. Good night, Bert, and my greetings to Mrs Trotter.'

He insisted on walking downstairs with her, but an enquiry about the state of his health lasted them to the stage door. She clambered onto a bus as it was pulling away from the kerb, and pretended to look grateful for a lecture from a kindly conductor all the way to Southwark on the perils of leaping on a moving vehicle. Jeremy might appear one morning at Wharfside; if not, she must wait until Sunday to see him after all. It was quite clear in her mind that she mustn't go to the theatre again when he wasn't expecting her and feel ill-used if he'd decided to keep a lonely woman company. Anna needed his help, probably, in the same way that Macdonald was being helped by Sam. Friends rallied round in time of adversity . . . it was what friends were for.

When Sunday came she didn't mention her visit to the theatre, and nor did Jeremy speak at all of Anna. He was quiet and abstracted altogether, and she waited until they were on Hampstead Heath eating the picnic provided by Aunt Lou before she embarked on an account of her father's visit.

At the end of it he simply said, 'Poor bastard!' and then smiled at the startled expression on her face. 'Not *you*, sweetheart . . . I was thinking of Contini.'

'You sounded as if you were sorry for my father,' she commented. 'Sam was, too – in fact he made it quite clear, as usual, that I'd been a disappointment to him. But no amount of war-time bravery or pity for his loss alters the fact that Arturo Contini seduced my poor little Marguerite when he was already promised to another girl.'

Jeremy's mouth twisted in a strangely rueful smile. 'No extenuating circumstances allowed, sweetheart? No forgiveness for a genuine mistake . . . a trap that he couldn't see any way out of? Perhaps not; perhaps we just like to pretend that there are *ever* any extenuating circumstances.' He suddenly got to his feet and pulled her up as well. 'Shall we go home? It's getting too cold for al fresco dalliance.'

It wasn't cold and there hadn't been any dalliance, but she sensed that his mood had changed. He wasn't a man who could be happy for long away from the familiar sights and sounds of the city. She knew that about him now, and had abandoned in her mind the idea of a secluded cottage in the country. A house in London it would have to be for Jeremy, but she would insist on a little patch of garden – she wasn't going to grow her wallflowers in chimney pots if she could help it.

Chapter 20

Anna had finally nerved herself to include in her regular letter to New York the news that her marriage to Angus was a failure. Margot Stein laid the letter down and stared at her husband.

'It's not *quite* a postscript that she's suddenly remembered to include, but almost! And she sounds astonishingly calm for a girl whose husband has abandoned her. I don't understand it, Jacob – least of all the fact that she finds it possible to go on working with him. Are theatre people really so different from the rest of us that what happens on the stage is more important than what happens to them in real life?'

Jacob considered the question before he shook his head. 'Not more important, but perhaps what happens on the stage becomes the part of them that is real.' He saw the sudden distress in his wife's face and smiled lovingly at her. 'Don't let it upset you, my heart. Anna wouldn't want to change things even if she could; for as long as she's working it means that she's far more often happy than she is unhappy, and I doubt if many people can say as much.'

Margot almost smiled herself because the sane and reasoned answer was so entirely typical of Jacob Stein. But she still had an objection to make.

'What about Angus . . . does *he* muddle real and unreal in the same way?'

'Probably not, and therein lies their difficulty, I expect. It doesn't matter when they're working; only when they're trying to share what's left of life together.'

'So what is going to happen to the Swan?' Margot asked next.

'I don't know yet.' Jacob's heavy brows drew together in a frown. To be in the position of not knowing was, for him, so rare and unpalatable that he'd postponed admitting it until now.

'I wrote to Angus as formally as he'd written to me . . . said I relied on him not to leave at least until I could go to London and talk to him about the theatre's future. It spiked his guns for the time being, but did no more than that, I'm afraid.'

Margot smiled sadly. 'What did you expect? He's a thrawn Scot, my dear – they take pride in being stubborn.' She stared at her daughter's letter again, and then at Jacob. 'Anna is proud, too, and probably much more hurt than I realised at first. Why not just let Angus go if he can't share the theatre with her? She loves it quite as much as he does, if you are worried about what might become of it – though I can't see why you should be; it's just another playhouse after all.'

Unbidden there appeared in her husband's mind the image of a tired-faced girl in shabby overalls whose smile had thanked him for preserving the name of the Swan.

'*Not* just another playhouse,' he corrected. 'Kate Cavendish would tell you that it's her grandfather's theatre – part of London's history!'

He flew to London a week later, officially a member of

an important trade delegation, but Margot had no doubt that he would find time while he was there to settle the future of the Swan, even if he could do nothing to mend his step-daughter's marriage.

It was nearly lunchtime when Kate heard footsteps on the stairs – not Sam's, she could always recognise *them*, and not Macdonald's more impatient stride; but a male visitor, certainly. Expecting one of Sam's festival committee colleagues, she opened the door and found there the thick-set, immaculately suited figure of Macdonald's step-father-in-law.

'You don't remember me,' he said a little sadly. 'It is the penalty, alas, of growing old.'

The smile he found he'd recollected so vividly lit her thin face. 'You aren't anywhere near growing old . . . and of course I remember you, Mr Stein!'

Amusement wiped away his look of bloodhound mournfulness, and he gave a snort of laughter in which she happily joined. But she grew serious again, remembering the awkwardness of the situation about which he'd presumably come to tackle Macdonald.

'No one's here but me . . . Sam *might* be back in an hour or so, but Angus not until this evening,' she explained regretfully.

'Then I shall give *you* lunch,' Jacob announced. He thought he saw that she frowned and his mouth twitched again. 'My dear Kate, may I have the pleasure of taking you to luncheon at the Savoy? That's what I should have said, but I forgot my manners!'

'It's my get-up that's wrong, not your manners,' she explained. 'The commissionaire at the Savoy Hotel would think I'd come to mend something.' She hesitated for a moment and then decided to trust her new friend – for friend was what she felt him to be. 'It's not much of a walk if you'd like to meet my grandfather and Aunt Lou instead.'

She took him by the shortest route, alongside the grey bulk of the cathedral and through the rich smells of the Borough Market, most of whose inhabitants she seemed to know.

When Jacob stopped to stare she asked an anxious question. 'Do you mind coming this way? Aunt Lou, of course, would say that I should have thought of that before.'

'Then we must convince your dear aunt that she'd be wrong.' He shot away, having glimpsed among the heaps of cabbages and bananas the bright colours of a flower-stall. A few moments later he was back, with an armful of narcissi and golden irises. He had, it seemed, enjoyed a stimulating exchange of compliments with the trilby-hatted matriarch who kept the stall. 'I like this place,' he said simply, and looking at his face Kate saw that it was so.

Once under the archway, with the roar of Thrale Street's traffic suddenly left behind, Jacob had the sensation of walking back in time. They should have been arriving in a sedan-chair at this hidden cluster of shabby, elegantly bow-windowed houses. And even though he was greeted by a host who looked more Edwardian dandy than Regency beau, there still persisted the feeling that mid-twentieth-century London had been left behind.

William, in blazer and cravat, with every silver hair in place as if he'd been expecting a distinguished visitor, made him welcome. Louisa – just as neat, but much less colourful – thanked him calmly for the flowers. Beside her sat a different sort of lady, on the ample side and hung about with disconnected chiffon scarves; but she spoke in the beautifully rounded vowels of a trained actress. Milly saw William bringing out the best sherry glasses, and smiled warmly on their visitor. She explained with graceful gestures that two members of the household – Elsie and Percival – were absent . . . 'alas and alack, toiling in the vineyard'. Jacob, who was enjoying himself very much, said with complete truthfulness that he was sorry to be missing them.

Lunch, though frugal, went merrily as a marriage-bell and Kate felt reluctant to part company with their watchful, compassionate guest. She had no doubt that he observed their oddities, but with pleasure, not derision. Milly also got up regretfully to return next door – it was a long time since she'd felt she was making such an impression on a male visitor – but at last William led Jacob into his conservatory to smoke, apologising for the lack of a cigar to offer him.

'Days of peace perhaps, but not of plenty! Still, we shall not go short of marrows by the look of things. An uninspiring vegetable, I'm afraid, but Kate has persuaded them to sprawl over the air-raid shelter very prettily.'

Jacob admired the rampant greenery, but thought for a moment of the nights they had spent in that dark refuge. By the look of the bombed spaces around Sam Maitland's warehouse, shelters hadn't just been required for prettiness in Southwark. Then abruptly, he changed the subject of conversation.

'Do you know how things are at the Swan?'

William hesitated, but decided that what he was being asked for was the truth. 'I *think* I know,' he admitted cautiously. 'Two productions so far, both huge successes, and a third one soon about to start. A splendid company, adorned by Anna and Jeremy and brilliantly directed by Angus Macdonald. That's more than enough, of course, but they even have the best two designers in London as well, in Sam and my dear Kate.'

'All true,' Jacob agreed with a faint smile, 'but all threatened now because Anna and Angus can't share their marriage or the theatre happily. I can do nothing about their personal problems, but I *am* involved in what happens to the Swan. Who do you think should be left in charge?'

Impaled on Jacob's rapier glance, William lifted his hands in a graceful, apologetic gesture. 'Forgive me if I say it should be Angus, not your step-daughter. If the theatre is to be entirely hers, any new director would be in an impossible position. Without a director at all, I think it would fail. Let her remain what she is – the most enchanting of actresses.'

Jacob nodded, thanked William for his opinion, but omitted to say whether he shared it or not. Ten minutes later he was out in Thrale Street again, looking for a coasting taxi.

Anna welcomed him at Cheyne Walk with almost feverish pleasure. She poured wine for him that he didn't want, reproached him for coming without Margot, and enquired after friends in New York in an excited flow of questions that didn't wait for answers. But, like a mechanical toy that someone had forgotten to rewind, she finally ran down into silence.

Jacob spoke with the gentleness he kept only for Margot and for her. 'You've been lonely without Angus.'

She gave a little shrug, and smiled again. 'Lonely, yes . . . but very peaceful. It *wasn't* peaceful when we were trying to live together. We *can't* live together, it seems.'

The note of finality in her voice was too familiar for him to argue with. She wasn't a woman who could be persuaded to change her mind. 'I haven't come to interfere – only to suggest a plan for the future. Do you feel like listening to it?' he asked instead.

She nodded, and he began – expecting rejection, outburst, histrionics even, since she was, above all things, an actress. But she said nothing until he'd finished, and from being excessively excited seemed now to have become excessively calm.

'You've forgotten one thing. Even though I may agree, Angus may not – he's an obstinate devil.'

'"Thrawn" was your mother's word for him. My only hope is that he loves the Swan enough to want the best for it – which he must believe is himself.'

Anna's lovely mouth sketched a grimace – of doubt or wry agreement? Jacob wasn't sure which, but he was grateful for her unexpected self-restraint. It wasn't a quality that the acting profession usually instilled in its members.

'Having put *us* to rights, more or less, what's next on your agenda?' she asked. 'Can you stay until Saturday? It's the last night of *Pygmalion*.'

Jacob's shoulders lifted in a gesture of regret. 'The delegation is due in Paris tomorrow evening . . . and afterwards we're scheduled to go to Rome and Bonn. But I also have a fancy to see where the Steins sprang from. However many *nyet*-muttering Russians stand in the way, I'm determined to visit Warsaw before I let them usher me onto an aircraft back to New York.'

Anna smiled at him. 'Do that, but be careful – Margot would be heartbroken if you got thrown into some Communist gaol.'

He waved the possibility aside and fixed her with eyes that had always seen more than she wanted them to. 'Are *you* going to be all right, Anna? You're happy about what we've arranged?'

'Content, let's say . . . although I do have one regret. Angus spends a lot of time on some windswept, godforsaken hill-top dramatising *Anna Karenina*. The part is bound to go to someone else now, and for *that* I may never quite forgive you!'

She smiled brilliantly as she said it and he knew it would be useless to ask again – the humiliation of a failed marriage, the loss of Angus . . . these were real-life things, destructive only if she let them inside her make-believe world of the theatre.

'I wish I could see the performance tonight at least, but we're obliged to attend some official ministerial dinner,' he said sadly. 'I expect it will be an awkward evening, even leaving aside the food on offer. Whether we deserved to or not, America grew fat on the war; this country grew very thin – it doesn't make for easy conversation over the dinner-table.'

'Poor Jacob . . . and before that you must beard the Highlander in his den! He's staying with Sam Maitland at the moment, but I expect you know that.'

He nodded, and kissed her goodbye, but left uncomfortably aware that something important about the conversation had remained hidden behind her smile. He was also aware of not having mentioned his visit to Paradise Walk. But Kate Cavendish was engaged to marry Jeremy Barrington and what Anna felt about *that* was something else she had kept hidden behind her façade of bright, fragile self-control.

*   *   *

With the last performance of *Pygmalion* safely over, there was almost an end-of-term gaiety about the theatre backstage. Even Ernie Williams, climbing down from the light-bridge, whistled cheerfully at the prospect of several nights in a row at home, and John Clarke ruled off the prompt book with an extra, jaunty, red line. 'Last performance ended dead on time, seven curtain-calls.'

The Guv'nor had mellowed to the extent of allowing them nearly a week off. Then there'd be the dress-rehearsal for *Private Lives*, and, unless it fell flat on its face, a run of six weeks; after that a month's summer holiday stretched in front of them before work started on the autumn season.

Kate had been anticipating that Jeremy would haunt the studio, unable to decide what else to do with himself while an empty week slowly passed. But his early telephone call on Sunday morning revealed that he had something quite different in mind.

'Kate love, I've decided to do what I ought to have done years ago . . . I'm . . . I'm going to Birmingham, to see my mother. Well, I mean I'm going to try, but it's more likely that she'll slam the door in my face.' The words tumbled over one another in a breathless rush, and his voice sounded strained. Kate understood now why he'd seemed unlike himself for the past week, with this weighing on his mind.

'Oh, Jem, I'm very glad,' she said quickly, 'even though I can see what an ordeal it is. Would it help if I came too – or make things worse?'

'Much worse, I think.' The refusal came so sharply that she had to struggle not to feel rebuffed by it, and to remind herself that there would be easier times to meet his mother than during this painful reunion.

'Darling Kate . . . don't mind me leaving you behind.' As

always, he was quick to sense hurt, and now – also as usual – was being extravagantly remorseful. 'It's just that things are better this way . . . believe me.'

'All right – much better your way,' she agreed cheerfully. 'Dear Jem, I hope it won't be nearly as painful as you think. No one, least of all your mother, could resist you for long, so I shan't worry *too* much about you!'

She expected some attempt at raillery in return, but the prospect ahead seemed to fill him with too much dread. Instead, he reminded her almost brusquely that he loved her and then rang off before she could ask when to expect him back in London. The following Wednesday evening when she rang his Albany number, there was still no reply, but she refused to feel anxious. It surely meant that the reunion was going well after all and Jeremy was staying to make it last as long as possible.

The next day Angus Macdonald returned from his Wiltshire cottage and called in at the Swan on the way back to Wharfside. There was no real need to do so; Bert Trotter knew perfectly well that a dress-rehearsal had been called for the following morning. Angus knew what the truth was – he just wanted to be in the theatre by himself, while it was expectant but still peaceful. By tomorrow it would be filled again with the noise and confusion brought in by other people. For the moment it was entirely his – by the grace of Jacob Stein, and Anna. It was hard to believe, even now, that she hadn't objected to Jacob's astounding gift. He'd had to refuse to accept it until she'd told him herself that he was welcome to the Swan.

'We were wiser than we knew all those years ago,' she'd said coolly. 'We *should* have done better to stay on different sides of the Atlantic! Never mind . . . it hasn't been all loss. I hope you agree with that, at least, Angus?'

Her haunting smile had challenged him not to remember moments that had been anything but loss. She was so beautiful, and now so gallant and generous in defeat, that his heart was riven by more sadness and sense of waste than he could put into words.

'It doesn't seem remotely fair for me to have the Swan, and for you to have to start again. Are you *quite* sure, Anna?'

She'd merely nodded, and glanced at the clock as if the conversation no longer interested her very much. As usual he was being too earnest for a woman who refused to treat life with his Scottish seriousness. Her marriage and her London adventure had been a mistake; well, she would extricate herself gracefully from both, as and when she could, with no fuss or loss of dignity. And if she shared any of his grief, he wouldn't be allowed to know about it.

'Even if I *weren't* sure, Jacob has arranged it all,' she'd said with a sweet absent smile. 'We should know better by now than to argue with him.'

He walked into the deserted theatre still remembering that conversation. If she needed help in starting again in New York, Jacob would certainly provide it without a second thought; but a failed husband could do one last thing for her. However little he liked it, the play that ended the season *must* permit her to go in triumph. Between them they would mount a production of *Private Lives* that would even blot out memories of Gertrude Lawrence and Coward himself. He owed it to Anna to make sure that London never forgot her.

'Very glad you've come, Guv,' said Bert Trotter's hoarse

voice suddenly behind him. 'What you might call providential-like, seein' as I wasn't expectin' you.'

Angus roused himself to listen to the latest plaint – the theatre cat wasn't on top of the mouse problem, perhaps, or Ada Trotter's twinges were playing up again. But Bert was looking more seriously glum than usual.

'Miss M's dahnstairs, raisin' Cain . . . says someone's pinched 'er wardrobe! Place bin locked up since larst Saturday night, so you can search *me* what's 'appened to it.'

With Bert labouring behind him, Angus sprinted down the basement stairs and into the wardrobe room. A white-faced Elsie Manners stood leaning against the table, as if she needed its support. She showed no surprise that the Guv'nor should walk in, and was so far jerked out of normality as to forget to offer him her usual restrained greeting.

'Dress rehearsal tomorrow and nothing's here,' she said baldly. 'Every one of Miss Sheridan's dresses gone.'

'Nonsense, Elsie . . . The dresser will have put them ready in her room.'

'They aren't there . . . I've looked.' Elsie's flat London voice rose almost to a shout. Worse than the nightmare of having to start work all over again on the beautiful, elaborate dresses Kate had designed, was the fact of knowing that there simply wasn't time . . . inferior replacements would have to be begged, borrowed, or bought in. Without knowing how she could be, she felt to blame. She was in charge here; the wardrobe room was her kingdom.

'I came to . . . to finish an alteration to one of Miss Carlisle's dresses. Then I walked in here . . .'

Angus put his warm hands over her cold ones that were gripped tightly together.

'Elsie dear, don't take on so . . . there's certain to be some simple explanation. Anna probably took the dresses home with her . . . I've heard her say before now that she likes to get used to wearing them before she has to play in them. She just forgot to mention it, that's all.'

A smile touched Elsie's pallid mouth. 'Didn't think of that, stupid old fool that I am! Got all worked up about nothing. Well, I've done what I came for, so I'll go home and calm down.'

'I'm going in your direction; we'll share a taxi,' Angus said, wondering whether she knew that his living quarters in London were now at Wharfside, not Cheyne Walk. She almost certainly did know, but it wouldn't occur to her to comment on the fact. Among the people who made up their world she was a resolutely independent figure, and her only human weaknesses – as far as he knew – were keen professional pride and her affection for Kate Cavendish. What she learned about other people's lives she saw no reason to discuss, and what she didn't know she saw no reason to guess at. Angus thought her a strange but estimable woman.

At her own request the taxi dropped her at the entrance to Paradise Walk – otherwise Milly would be sure to spot her and want to know what was what. Angus helped her out, climbed back in again, and went on to Wharfside. His mind was full of tomorrow's vital rehearsal, and the matter of Anna's dresses had almost faded from his mind.

Chapter 21

Only Kate was in the studio, but this afternoon she wasn't absorbed in drawing. Sitting by the window, she seemed only to be intent on the river view outside. She turned a pale face towards him when he went in, and like Elsie Manners, she forgot to greet him as well.

'I tried to reach you in Wiltshire, but you didn't answer.' Her voice was faintly accusing . . . held low by an effort of will. 'Sam's out too, until later on. I didn't know what to do.'

'Do about what?'

'Tomorrow's dress rehearsal. Anna's letter only arrived this morning – by the way, she liked the dresses so much that she's taken them with her . . . to New York. They were too beautiful, she said, to leave behind – she seemed to think I'd be glad to know that.'

Kate's voice, normally coloured by anything she happened to be feeling, was now a calm, flat monotone. Angus stared at her for a moment, then strode into what had become his bedroom. Among a pile of envelopes waiting for him, one addressed in Anna's flowing hand stood out.

My dear Angus,

If you hadn't deserted London so quickly on Saturday night I should have given you this news in person.

My 'fresh start' begins at once, I'm afraid. Jacob pulls the puppets' strings, but at least I insist on choosing *when* to dance, and I choose now – not when our London season was supposed to end. It might even come as a relief to you . . . you hated doing *Private Lives*, and now you won't have to!

By the way, Jeremy is coming with me. Another relief, perhaps; you'll be rid of *both* your starry leading players and can have the repertory company you always wanted. I think I've persuaded him not to feel *too* badly about his little dress-designer friend. There was really no hope of them living happily together, so it was kinder not to let them get entrapped in marriage – *such* a mistake, as you and I both know.

We are sailing for New York on Monday . . . then a much-needed holiday, I think, before we take Broadway by storm. We *shall* do that, of course, but we shall live together in complete contentment as well; we're two of a kind, you see.

I'm afraid this letter may sound hard, but the truth is that I don't mean it so. We're doing what we must for ourselves, but in the end you may even come to admit that it's right for *everybody* else as well.

     Yours ever,
     Anna

When Angus walked back into the studio Kate was still where he had left her, watching the river but not seeing it. She wore some kind of pinafore dress, and the blouse beneath it left her arms bare. They looked childishly fragile – she was too thin altogether; but she wasn't a child, and the pain she struggled with was an adult pain.

'I expect you know that Jem's gone with Anna,' Angus said. He didn't make a question of it – for certain, she already knew.

'*His* letter arrived this morning as well. I should think they asked the Albany porter to post them together last night, wouldn't you? The man didn't like me very much . . . which is only fair, I suppose, considering that I never cared for him.' The idea of the porter seemed to absorb her mind, or at least to be something bearable to think about when so much else was not. 'Jem said he was going to Birmingham,' she murmured in the same quiet voice, 'to stop me wondering where he was, I suppose.'

The immediate future lay in ruins and, for his own relief, Angus wanted to rage at a monstrously selfish couple who'd broken the theatre's one sacred taboo. But for the moment the only thing that mattered was the hurt done to the girl in front of him, and he doubted if raging would help her. She sensed his helpless longing to give comfort and turned round to look at him.

'Jem apologised very nicely – I'm not sure why he should bother when I've known all along that it was Anna he really wanted, not me. But he'll never do the great things now that he might have done – don't *you* feel that too?'

About to say that he didn't at the moment care if Jeremy Barrington ended his career damned in hell or playing the Demon King in pantomime, he didn't get the chance. Kate was speaking again in the same quiet, reflective voice.

'Still, he could just have *said* that he'd changed his mind about marrying me . . . that way he wouldn't have let the Swan down so badly.'

Angus walked over to her and took her hands in a grip that

hurt. 'Dear Kate, shall I tell you what really happened? Jem wasn't using what passes for his mind at all. He was simply besotted . . . physically enthralled by a woman who used on him every one of the weapons she had. Suddenly everything that she thought was hers was slipping away – I'd gone, Jacob Stein had insisted on giving *me* the theatre, and, worst of all, Jeremy was on the verge of belonging to you. It was time to remind us that *she* still called the tune.'

The ghost of a sad smile touched Kate's mouth. 'Alfred Doolittle was right about "middle-class morality"! But for that Jem and I would have been as good as married by now, and Anna might have called in vain. Sam saw it all more clearly than I did . . . he even tried to cure me of being such a coward about love.'

Her smile crumpled because the combined assault of recent months was suddenly more than she could bear – Anna's hatred, her father's arrival, Jeremy's needs, and her own uncertainties were all muddled up now with sheer exhaustion. Like a child unable to hold out any longer, she turned her face against Macdonald's shoulder and wept. She was still cradled in his arms when Sam walked in – cheerfully fulminating about something that had seemed important until he caught sight of them. Then he stopped dead, but couldn't control the expression on his face.

Kate smeared away her tears and glared at him. 'I was just having a little weep, that's all,' she announced with dignity. 'Now I think I shall go home instead.' Her eyes thanked Macdonald for his kindness and then she left the room, forgetting to say goodbye to them.

'What was all that about?' Sam asked when the door had closed behind her. 'Kate *never* weeps unless she's angry.' He found himself wanting to shout – but that wouldn't do;

observers like him were obliged to stay cool and uninvolved. 'What the hell is going *on*, Angus?' It came out as a shout after all.

Macdonald handed him Anna's letter. 'Kate did better than me, she heard from both of them this morning. Perhaps Jem's apologies to me will follow.'

When Sam looked up from reading he saw the sombreness in his friend's face. 'I almost refused when Jacob offered me the theatre,' Angus muttered, 'but Anna seemed to be taking it so well that in the end I didn't.' Then he lifted his hands in a helpless, angry gesture. 'Now I'm blaming myself, and Jacob; and Kate is afraid she wasn't quite fast enough to keep Jem safe from Anna. Why can't we just say that a bloody selfish unprincipled pair don't care what damage they inflict on other people?'

Sam thought of the wreckage the two of them had left behind – no, they wouldn't have cared about that; at least, Jem *had* cared about Kate, and he'd probably hated letting Macdonald down, but he hadn't been strong enough to withstand a woman with a will more resolute than his own. He stared at the ceiling, and spoke almost to himself.

'I can't help remembering that line in *Private Lives* – Elyot Chase asks Amanda, "What shall we do in time of crisis?" and she replies—'

'"Behave exquisitely!"' Angus finished the quotation himself with a roar of rage and mingled, helpless laughter. 'Oh, Christ almighty, Sam . . . I expect that's just what Anna *did* say to Jem. She was probably got up in one of Kate's dresses at the time – she took them with her, by the way.'

Sam nodded. 'Our only mistake was ever to take them seriously . . . they're *actors*, not real people. But I'm afraid my Kate didn't quite believe that.' He roused himself from thinking about her to ask another question.

'What happens tomorrow?'

'What *can* happen? Instead of a dress rehearsal I announce to the assembled company that the last production of the season is cancelled. We put notices in the press, and Walter, poor sod, is left to cope with the mess at the box-office. The stage crew will have to be paid off, but somehow I must keep Pat O'Donovan and Ernie Williams on the strength . . . they're too good to lose.'

'If you can decide on your first play for the autumn we'll be ready for them to start work on that after an earlier holiday than they expected.'

Macdonald's mouth twisted. 'No Anna Sheridan, no Jem Barrington, setting each other and the stage alight. Will the customers still come, I wonder?'

'We shall have to wait and find out,' Sam said calmly. 'What you must do is go and finish *Anna Karenina*, and then groom Jane Carlisle for the leading rôle. It's high time she had her chance, and for a start *she*'s got Madame Karenina's black hair.'

Angus smiled more naturally this time. 'So she has.' He lapsed into silence again, then stared at his friend. 'A little while ago I wanted to rail and curse to high heaven, I could have throttled Anna, and kicked Jem from here to the Swan; but Kate's reaction was probably the only right one.'

'You needn't tell me what it was,' Sam muttered, 'just pure grief, because Jem had upset things at the theatre and chucked overboard a great career to play second fiddle to Anna from now on. My partner really loves the stupid chap, you see.'

Then, with no more to be said, he walked over to his

table and began to study the sketches he'd left there to dry.

Kate could scarcely remember afterwards how she got through the long, empty summer. There was always work, of course, and a holiday in Cornwall that Sam insisted it would be a kindness if she shared with Jane Carlisle. Jane was to star in the play that would be the attraction of the coming season. It would be her first leading rôle, and she was by turns wildly excited and desperate about it. Sam himself went abroad, and Kate now found it easier to work in the studio without him. She was perfectly at ease with Angus Macdonald whenever he came to London from his Wiltshire hideaway; they had something in common – a sense of failure and hurt that must be overcome. But Sam, Kate reckoned, had no knowledge of these things. Worse still, he'd been right all along, and that was harder to forgive.

When he came back from Italy she made up her mind not to ask about his visit beyond the minimal enquiry that courtesy required. She had no intention of showing the slightest interest in knowing if he'd even been to Florence, much less seen her father. In any case, there was news of her own to give, and it burst out of her while he was unloading papers from his briefcase.

'Sam, you'll never guess . . . William and Milly are taking to the boards. They can't stop smiling at each other at the thought of acting again.'

'In whose play, partner?'

'Macdonald's, of course – *Anna Karenina*. William is to be Prince Shcherbatsky and Milly will be his wife. Angus said they both read the parts beautifully.' She saw no answering pleasure in Sam's face and felt deeply disappointed in him. 'You could at least look a *little* happy. Try imagining what it means to William to appear at the Swan again – even if it weren't going to be in the most exciting new opening of the entire winter.'

But Sam still registered only unflattering surprise. 'Macdonald considered your grandfather once before and turned him down. What caused the sudden change of mind?'

She couldn't help blushing a little for the suspicion that had several times occurred to her – that Macdonald was being very kind, and doing what he thought would please her.

Sam saw the colour in her face and misunderstood it. 'It seems I shouldn't have asked,' he said coolly. 'Macdonald can cast his plays whichever way he likes . . . *I*'ll say that before *you* throw it at me, partner . . . but I hope he realises that Milly probably sees herself as a cross between Catherine the Great and the last unfortunate Tzarina.'

An unwilling grin rescued Kate from embarrassment. 'He says she *may* need a little reining-in!' she admitted reluctantly.

Sam smiled too, and a moment of awkwardness seemed to be over. He picked up a theatre programme and held it out to her. 'This was waiting for me in my mail . . . Jem sent it over, because he thought we ought to see it.'

The programme was of a Broadway production of *Private Lives*, starring Anna and Jeremy. The designers mentioned were unknown to Kate, but she stared at a separate acknowledgement at the bottom of the page: 'Miss Sheridan's dresses by Kate Cavendish, London.'

She looked back for a moment at the past before she answered. 'I suppose it's her way of playing fair . . . the "little seamstress" is given her due. Still, the American sets can't be nearly as beautiful as the ones *you'd* created for them.'

Sam bowed gracefully, amused by the note of satisfaction in her voice. 'I suppose we should have guessed that Anna would choose that play – they'd already rehearsed the damn thing enough to be able to play it in their sleep.'

'What comes next, do you think?' Kate asked. 'A full-blooded bash at *Macbeth*? Jeremy might not enjoy it very much, but I can see Anna letting rip as Lady M.'

The suggestion was made solemnly, and perhaps for that reason surprised a chuckle out of Sam that grew into a guffaw. She held out for a moment but had to join in, and the next moment they were both helpless with laughter. Wiping her wet eyes, she wondered how long it was since they'd felt so at ease with each other . . . months, probably.

'Every actor seems to believe the old superstition that *Macbeth* is a very unlucky play, so I can't really see Jeremy agreeing to it,' she managed to say at last. 'How did his letter sound . . . happy?'

'All right, but a bit subdued, I thought. Margot has obviously done her best for them, and Jacob was bound to help – giving the Swan entirely to Angus was certain to mean that Anna would go back to New York; but I doubt if he was happy about the way they *both* reappeared, and he wouldn't be Jacob Stein if he hadn't told them so.'

'Then he doesn't understand, just as *I* didn't to begin with. Jem had old friends like you and Angus to shape his career, and me to . . . to bolster him up, and I thought that would be enough. But I see now that he simply couldn't do without Anna – she's his fatal weakness; the flaw that all Shakespeare's tragic heroes have. So if *she* went back to New York, he was bound to go as well – whatever mess it made of the rest of his life.' Her hands sketched an expressive gesture. '*My* little share in it was futile . . . I think perhaps I always knew that it didn't quite ring true – me alongside Jeremy Barrington.'

Sam nodded, wondering whether she felt as calm about it now as she managed to sound. If not, what he was about to say next would bring that new-found tranquillity crashing about their ears. He knew what a high-wire performer felt like setting out without a safety-net.

'Kate, we've got a hard slog in front of us, getting two productions ready for the Swan. After that we've been commissioned to do the sets and costumes for a new production of *Tosca* in Milan – we must deliver complete designs early in the New Year. I shall need you to come with me this time.'

She regarded him steadily for a moment, noting the small changes that only became apparent when someone normally seen every day returned after even a brief absence. She'd been accustomed to Jeremy's golden beauty, and even against Macdonald's hawk-like good looks Sam had seemed to be at a disadvantage. But now she was aware of having missed something important that others more perceptive than herself had managed *not* to miss. Tanned by Italian sunshine, his face looked suddenly well worth a second glance. Intelligence and humour were not such common merits that they deserved to be underrated, but strength of character was there as well. His unruly mop of hair was already flecked with silver, but she knew with surprising certainty that he would become more, not less, attractive as he grew older. By then, of course, they would have parted company; partnerships didn't last for ever. But she was suddenly stabbed with pain at the thought of managing without him.

'It's kind of you to include me in the commission,' she said at last, 'but I'm sure the management of La Scala didn't. It's Maitland they'll have asked for.'

'It's Cavendish & Maitland they're contracted to get. And if Cavendish still doesn't want to throw herself over the hurdle of setting foot in Italy, I shall remind her brutally that we have a *shared* business to run.'

The angry disquiet that he'd anticipated was in her face now, although he mistook the reason for it. Kate struggled with the temptation to shout at him, but rage was getting the upper hand. No matter what had happened he still regarded her as the coward who must be persuaded, blackmailed, or hauled by brute force to confront what crippled her emotionally. She had meant to find the moment to confess that dread of the past no longer needed exorcising because it had been overcome. But he wouldn't believe her if she said it now, because he didn't know that she'd already made up her own mind to go to Italy one day.

'I don't see why I should have to fall in with whatever *you* care to arrange,' she said fiercely. 'Suppose it doesn't suit *my* plans to go away?'

Sam remembered her earlier blush and again mistook the reason for it. 'Angus isn't another Jem Barrington, Kate – you don't have to hold *his* hand if things go wrong, and smooth *his* ruffled self-esteem. He's a man who can manage on his own, and probably prefers to do so.'

'Well, it doesn't stop him enjoying *my* company,' she said rashly. Too late she was aware of giving an unfair picture of Macdonald's kindness. But Sam must be made aware once and for all that she was her own woman now, seasoned survivor of emotional storms, and if not the knock-down, drag-out femme fatale that was Anna Sheridan, at least someone who had charms worth taking seriously. She waited expectantly to hear what he would say . . . at last feared that he might not bother to say anything at all because the conversation seemed to have lost interest for him. But just when she was about to shout at him to say *something*, he answered with cold, annihilating courtesy.

'Far be it for me to interfere with your private life, partner, but we *are* committed to delivering complete set and costume designs in person soon after Christmas. Macdonald will probably understand that your company must be foregone in the cause of not letting La Scala down.'

He didn't wait for her to reply, but after a glance at the relentless downpour of rain outside shrugged himself into a raincoat. 'Now, before I start work here, I'd better go and see whether the bloody little pleasure domes I'm supposed to be decorating for Gerald Barry and the festival committee are still there or not; with any luck they'll have collapsed into the Thames mud again. *Arrivederci*, Kate!'

As the door closed behind him she sat down hastily because her legs were trembling. It would have been a relief to burst into tears, but she only cried when she was angry and anger had unfortunately been replaced by something that felt much more like grief. After a while she picked up her brush, stared at it, and laid it down again. Then she got up and went to the bookshelves that lined the end wall of the studio. She found easily what she was looking for – a fat volume that she'd sometimes seen Sam consult. Kobbé's *Complete Opera Book* had a great deal to say, it seemed, on the subject of the lady whose life had become fatally intertwined with a painter and a sinister Chief of Police. *Tosca* was going to take a great deal of designing.

Chapter 22

The Swan's autumn season opened with Shaw's tongue-in-cheek Ruritanian comedy, *Arms and the Man*. The critics were kind, and the public didn't stay away. The past débâcle seemed to have been forgotten, and Angus and Walter Fairbrass heaved sighs of relief – the theatre was still afloat, and, without its former star players, even seemed to have relaxed into smoother and happier running.

Gilbert took a minor rôle in the Shaw comedy, but heart and mind wrestled with the challenge ahead – becoming Tolstoy's Captain Vronsky. He wanted the opening of *Anna Karenina* to come more than he'd wanted anything else in life; and he dreaded it with an equal terror that turned his bones to water. Angus saw nothing to worry about in that, but he felt a good deal more anxious about Jane Carlisle, faced with the huge ordeal of stepping into Anna's shoes. In her he thought he detected too great a dread and not enough anticipation.

She was given no part in the opening production, being required to steep herself in all things Russian for the rôle of Madame Karenina. But when not rehearsing, it seemed to Kate that she haunted the studio, looking for Sam.

'He keeps me calm,' she admitted one afternoon. 'Angus *tries* to be patient, but only Sam really understands how desperate I feel sometimes.' The gesture that accompanied this – hand held to brow – was undeniably theatrical, but Kate realised that Jane had something to be dramatic about. Creating the woman Angus had drawn out of Tolstoy's tragic heroine was enough to test the most experienced actress, and this girl had also for the first time to emerge from the shadow of Anna Sheridan.

'I expect you're sick of being told what a chance you've got,' Kate said, 'but there isn't an actress in London who wouldn't give her eye-teeth for it. Think of *that* whenever Macdonald seems to be asking too much of you.'

It was too-bracing advice for someone hoping to be treated tenderly, and Jane was attractively flushed with irritation when Sam walked in.

'I'm being given a lecture,' she said with a bravely rueful smile for him. 'Kate's right – I *am* a bore, hanging round here and feeling sorry for myself. But she doesn't quite understand that opening night isn't some little hilltop that I've got to take by storm . . . it's more like being told to climb Mount Everest!'

Her voice trembled a little and made its desired effect on Sam, who was now frowning at his partner.

'Long before opening night we shall all . . . *all*,' he repeated with another minatory look at Kate, 'have convinced you that you can even take Mount Everest by storm.'

Jane stretched out her hand to him in a graceful gesture, and Kate struggled with herself again not to think that it had been borrowed from Anna Sheridan. She liked Jane Carlisle, and thought she deserved her great chance. But still and all she *was* becoming a bore, with her vapours and leading-lady mannerisms, and it was a relief when she got up to leave.

'Dear Sam, I must fly . . . but I'm looking forward so

much to this evening.' Her husky voice managed to hint at such delicious, even illicit, delights to be shared later on that Sam felt obliged to explain when the door had closed behind her.

'Renata Tebaldi is in London, making her Covent Garden début tonight. I thought it would take Jane's mind off rehearsals to rub shoulders with the glittering mob in the crush bar.'

'Nice for her,' Kate agreed politely. 'She might even enjoy the music as well.'

'I very much doubt it . . . the poor girl sings the national anthem just about as off-key as you do.'

She considered this in silence and, for no good reason that she could think of, felt more kindly towards Jane Carlisle until Sam spoilt it again.

'Macdonald's driving her hard at the moment, Kate. She needs support from the rest of us, not well-intentioned lectures.'

'Anything you say, partner,' she agreed sweetly. 'While she waits for you here in future I shall be like Brer Fox and say nuffin.'

His glance raked her face, and he was aware that it was time to abandon the cause of Jane Carlisle. Beneath his partner's surface cheerfulness he sensed the effort she had had to make not to be ground down between the millstones of Anna and Jeremy. The truth was that she was in the wrong world. She belonged where people didn't hurt others even without noticing that they did so, and where promises once given had to be kept. He couldn't tell her so, remembering how fiercely she had rejected his attempts at offering advice in the past, and abruptly changed tack instead.

'William enjoying himself?'

As always when she thought about her grandfather, affection lit her face. 'He's like a war-horse listening to the kettle drums and sniffing the scent of battle. When Milly comes sailing over to breakfast the pair of them are suddenly in Moscow, not Paradise Walk at all, and our humble earthenware teapot becomes the Princess Shcherbatsky's samovar!' She thought of something else that gave her pleasure as well. 'William says that Gil is going to be *very* good – I'm so glad about that.'

Sam nodded, aware that it was an opinion Macdonald shared. He was tempted to ask what William thought of Jane, but decided against it, remembering the beginning of their conversation. Instead, he made a point of calling at the Swan when he was certain to find Angus there, but chose a moment when the Guv'nor was bawling out a stage-hand for a clumsy scene-change the previous evening.

'Wasn't that rather a sledgehammer to crack a nut?' he asked when the man had been sent away.

'Mind your own bloody business,' Macdonald snapped, and immediately apologised. 'Sorry, Sam . . . nerves getting the better of me. Haven't seen you around lately.'

'We're busy . . . conjuring up elaborate St Petersburg and Moscow interiors, in case you've forgotten. It's an ambitious production – in every way.'

Macdonald's mouth twisted in a grin that lacked amusement. 'Foolhardy, you mean! God knows why I ever thought it could be done – Tolstoy's huge canvas of life hacked down to fit into three hours and the dimensions of a theatre stage. *There*'s "o'er-vaulting ambition", if you like.'

Sam heard the unusual tremor in his friend's voice and tried to sound very matter-of-fact himself. 'Agonise if you must, but there isn't any need. What remains after your hacking gives us the essence of Anna's story. The rest of us just have to make it come alive.'

'And therein lies my real anxiety,' Angus finally admitted. 'This play's like a musical score – even the smallest part contributes something important, but in the end it must stand or fall by Jane's performance, and at the moment I'm terribly afraid it's going to fall. It won't be *her* fault, but my error of judgement. She's a good enough actress technically, but it may be that she's just too young, or too inexperienced in suffering to portray Anna's tragedy.'

Sam thought of Jane's frightened eyes when she forgot to smile, and her borrowed airs and graces that were to convince herself as much as anyone that she *was* the leading lady Angus required.

'The Swan couldn't survive another last-minute upset,' he said slowly. 'Nor could Jane's self-confidence recover from being fired now. We must somehow nurse her along to opening night. *That*'s the terrifying hurdle; after that I'm sure she'll settle down.' He saw that he hadn't convinced Angus and tried again. 'She's got the support of fine, experienced players who want her to succeed – they'll carry her if they have to until she finds her feet.'

Macdonald nodded at last. 'Gilbert's so excellent as Vronsky that I couldn't ask for better. In fact they're *all* good, with old William steady as a rock holding them together. Even Milly has calmed down nicely, and there's a sort of sweet, inspired dottiness about her that keeps the rest of them happy.'

The thought of Mildred Pearce had made Angus smile but Sam knew about his friend, as he knew about Kate, that happiness had forsaken him. Macdonald hated fail-ure, but Anna and Jeremy between them had rubbed his nose in that demoralising condition. Sam found himself sending up a little prayer that the play Angus had poured all his own pent-up longing and heartbreak into would bring him at least the salvation of a huge success for the Swan.

The tempo grew steadily more fierce – rehearsals, fittings, ceaseless hammering backstage, and voices for ever shouting instructions that other disembodied voices seemed to disagree with; the customary pandemonium, in fact, out of which the miracle of a smooth-running, coherent, wonderful production might eventually emerge.

Opening night was a fortnight away, and the first complete run-through had been called, when for once Jane failed to appear on time. It was frowned upon, to be late for a rehearsal that involved the entire company, but Angus merely shouted for John Clarke to telephone Jane's flat.

'No reply . . . she must be on her way here,' John reported when he came back.

Fifteen minutes later an irritated director began the rehearsal, with Jane's understudy reading her part. After another half-hour Sam walked in, spotted Macdonald sitting in the auditorium, and slid in beside him. Angus turned to grin savagely at him. 'As you see, we are rehearsing *without* Anna Karenina – this rather vital run-through seems to have escaped her memory.'

'Jane hasn't forgotten . . . she's funked it, I'm afraid,' Sam said quietly. 'I'm here because she telephoned me from Victoria Station. She's on her way to Brighton . . . where her people live.'

The house-lights were on and he could see rage, but not yet despair, in Macdonald's face. 'Dear God . . . what a time to choose; couldn't she have waited till the weekend for a little dose of parental reassurance? I'll flay her when she gets back.'

'She's not coming back,' Sam said in the same level voice. 'I spent all last evening persuading her that playing the part of Anna wouldn't mean that *she'd* end up dead under a train as well. When I left her she seemed calm, but this morning she was incoherent on the telephone . . . just kept repeating over and over again what her doctor had said – she must abandon the part or ruin her health.'

Macdonald let out a long shuddering sigh, then stood up and interrupted the rehearsal. Jane was indisposed, he announced with heroic calm; they would postpone the run-through for forty-eight hours to give her time to recover. The rest of the cast slowly drifted away, curious, and not altogether reassured that some whiff of crisis wasn't hanging in the air. Back in his own office, Angus poured whisky for himself and Sam.

'We need something stronger than Bert Trotter's appalling coffee,' he said. 'Now before I do anything else I shall have to go charging down to Brighton after that bloody tiresome girl.'

As usual when deeply troubled, Sam took off his spectacles and stared at them. 'She won't come back with you – hysteria will set in if you try to force her.' He looked away from the despair in Macdonald's face, but tried to apologise.

'I'm sorry, old friend . . . I egged you on to giving her the part, and I've kept on insisting that she'd be all right once we'd got her past the ordeal of opening night.'

Angus swept the words aside. '*My* fault, not yours . . . I liked the idea of playing Svengali; I saw myself creating a great new star! Oh Christ, Sam, what are we going to do?

Her understudy could manage for a night or two once the play was running, but ask her to *create* the part and *she'd* go to pieces as well. I'm beginning to think Jacob should have left the Swan a ruin – it's jinxed now, but at least there was no shame in being a victim of war.' He wiped a hand across his face and produced a travesty of a smile. 'I do know that there are worse things to worry about – Russia's built an atomic bomb, and the war that's already going on in Korea may be the beginning of the end of this poor, frightened planet.'

'And the Labour Government's made rather a mess of things here, and we're sick to death of being told that better days are round the corner,' Sam agreed. 'All quite true, but we aren't absolved from trying to repair our own quite small disaster. There are other good actresses in London, and they can't all be working.'

'Oh sure, and any of them can master *this* part among parts in the next ten days or so, I suppose. My dear Sam, we need a miracle-worker, not a good actress who happens to be free.'

It was true, of course, and Sam was aware that the idea just sliding into his brain might plunge them into even more complete disaster. But desperate ills called for desperate remedies.

'Don't do anything for the moment, Angus,' he said firmly. 'Give me an hour or two; then I'll ring you here.'

Anna left New York the following night. As a first-class passenger on a Pan-American Constellation she was provided with a comfortable bunk, and in it with the self-discipline of a trained actress she forced herself to relax into sleep.

Sam was waiting for her at the airport and of the two of them it was he who looked as if he'd just flown the Atlantic. Anna emerged from customs exquisitely groomed, ready to be looked at and admired. With all his private reservations about her, Sam had to acknowledge to himself that here was a diamond of the first water, perfectly cut and perfectly set.

'There'll be some dreadful coffee on offer in the cafeteria – shall we sample it before we leave?' he suggested.

It proved to be undrinkable, but Anna had grasped the reason for the hiatus.

'I suppose Angus didn't want me to come. You should have let me walk in unannounced.'

'He behaved like a maddened bull when I said I'd telephoned you,' Sam admitted. 'In fact when I spoke to him an hour ago he was still insisting that he'd rather close the Swan than have *you* salvage him. The man's a pig-headed Highlander, you understand.' He watched her face anxiously for signs that she regretted coming, even for a hint that she might take the next aeroplane home, but it was still more worrying to see her smile. In the past nine months she'd had time to forget the self-defeating stubbornness of which her husband was capable.

'Leaving Angus himself aside, can you learn the part in time? It's a gruelling one, Anna.'

Her hands sketched a gesture that he remembered. 'Of course I can cope with the lines – the more difficult thing is to feel myself into the mentality of that other Anna. If Angus can put his grudges aside and work with me, we'll manage – we understand one another very well in the theatre.'

Sam nodded and hoped that she was now sufficiently prepared for the meeting at Wharfside that Macdonald had promised to attend. 'How's Jem?' he asked politely as they drove towards London.

'Very well . . . he's coming back, too, quite soon. It's an ordeal for the poor love, steeling himself to face Angus.'

'He'll have to face Kate as well – that might require even more courage,' Sam suggested in a neutral voice.

He felt Anna's little shrug in the seat beside him. 'All right, my dear Sam, I'll admit it if it makes you any happier – we behaved very badly by the standards of people like Kate Cavendish.'

'But such boring, old-fashioned standards,' Sam said gently, 'and how silly of us to expect people like you and Jem to abide by them.'

After a little silence she managed to answer him. 'It's very irritating . . . you're all so damnably concerned about Kate. Jeremy doesn't say so but he's been haunted about leaving her, and Jacob, I'll swear, goes out of his way to remind us of her existence. Angus is probably besotted with her as well by now. She never gave *me* the impression that she couldn't perfectly well take care of herself – quite the reverse, in fact.'

Anna stared out of the window as she spoke, but the sight of her unsteady hands gripped together in her lap made Sam suddenly take pity on her.

'It's Jem I should be having a go at, not you. I should just be grateful to you for coming over – I am *very* grateful, Anna.'

'Angus isn't, however,' she said almost forlornly. 'He'd obviously rather believe that I'm here because I can't bear to see another actress take the part of Tolstoy's Anna. Perhaps it's what *you* really think as well.'

'I think you've come to help,' Sam heard himself say, and hoped it was true. 'God knows help is what we need.'

She turned to look at him and smiled. 'I think so, too!' Then she grew serious again. 'What happens if Angus won't have me at any price? I can just go home, of course; but what about the Swan?'

'The Shaw play that's on now *could* be kept running until he can find the actress he needs, but there's been a lot of advance publicity and talk about what was going to be *the* production of the season. After what happened before, to postpone this one would expose him to really damaging ridicule. On the other hand, an understudy attempting *Anna* would certainly bring it to disaster, so he's damned either way.'

Anna nodded but said nothing more and they drove the rest of the way to Wharfside in silence.

Kate was waiting in her favourite window seat at the studio – watching the river as usual, and trying not to be aware of Macdonald pacing up and down like a caged lion. She'd disagreed strongly that she should be there at all, and been told that she was needed. Half-afraid that he might renege on the meeting before Sam and Anna arrived, she finally stayed.

She reckoned that for once Anna was bound to feel at a disadvantage. It was going to be hard enough for her to confront them at all; harder still to have to face them not at her best, feeling tired and dishevelled after a night in an aeroplane.

But when the door opened and she walked in, it took thirty seconds to realise that no sneaking female sympathy was required. As always, Anna was exquisitely dressed and made-up – the perfect professional, Kate decided as ungrudgingly as Sam had done. But a different realisation also dawned: perhaps for the first time in her life, this apparently self-possessed woman was nervous.

Sam broke the awkward silence. 'Anna assures me that she slept on the plane; she's even ready to start work at once, since we're so desperately short of time.'

It was a brave, or rash, attempt to force Macdonald's hand, and Kate wondered if Sam had just thought of it in desperation, or planned in advance what his opening gambit would be. But the dark frown on his friend's face seemed to offer no chance of success. Angus would choose to go down now rather than be rescued by his wife, because pride, however inconvenient, had become the rock he must cling to.

'There *is* time to say hello,' she said diffidently, 'or am I in such dire disgrace that you can't even do that?'

'We've got all the time in the world,' he answered. 'It was kind of you to take this rather extravagant amount of pity on us, but I'm afraid you've had a wasted journey, Anna. Sam didn't wait long enough before ringing you to be told that I've decided to postpone the production.'

His cold deliberate voice suggested that the conversation was now over. Kate saw Sam take a deep breath to say something that would probably make Angus more angry still, and seized the only opportunity she would get. She moved nearer to Macdonald so that she could link her arm through his in a gesture she feared they would all misunderstand, but it was necessary because she needed to be facing Anna, not him.

'Darling Guv, bless your trusting heart, but I'm afraid you've missed the point. Anna hasn't come out of pity – oh dear me, no! She just wants *this* part more than anything else. However long you postpone things she'll stay, and hope to convince you that she can do it better than any other actress in London. She may be right, but we shall have no way of knowing whether she is or not.'

Silence greeted this speech. Sam wondered whether he could bring himself to believe that Anna deserved such cruelty or that Kate was capable of it. Angus considered a view of Anna's arrival that he had entirely overlooked, and *she* stared at Kate. Trying to drag a denial together in her mind, she was suddenly confused by the wordless message she was being sent. A little shake of her mentor's head warned her not to interrupt – there was more to come.

'I suppose an experienced leading lady like Anna might even pretend that she could learn the part quickly enough for the play to open on schedule.' Kate shrugged and allowed the absurd idea to languish, and Anna grasped the cue she'd now been offered.

'Angus knows there's no pretence about that,' she said proudly. 'I'm a quick study . . . I can learn whatever I have to.'

Fascinated by this female duel, and fancying that he could see the helpless body of Jeremy Barrington lying between them, Sam watched Anna approach her opponent.

'I suppose I should say I'm sorry for all that happened . . . but it wouldn't be true. It would never have done for you to marry Jem; he understood that himself, even though he did hate jilting you at the last minute.'

Sam found that he was holding his breath, unable to guess what Kate would say next; he thought he should have guessed it would concern the theatre rather than herself.

'The worst thing Jeremy did was to let the Swan down. It doesn't deserve *another* betrayal, but Jane Carlisle seems to have caught the miserable infection from both of *you*. William was going to have a part in the play . . . Milly, too. It's despicable, I reckon, not to care what happens to other people.'

Angus heard the tremor in her voice, and suddenly took charge of the conversation.

'I suppose you've got a reservation at the Ritz as usual?' he said to Anna, and saw her nod. 'Then I'll deliver you there. These hard-worked people will probably be glad to see the back of us.' He nodded goodbye to Sam, smiled at Kate, and then held the door open. Feeling discouraged by an interview that seemed to have gone badly wrong, Anna allowed herself to be taken away.

When the door closed behind them Kate sat down hurriedly in the nearest chair and ducked her head. Sam stared at her for a moment and then disappeared into the kitchen. When he returned with mugs of coffee she smiled her thanks, but still looked so sad that he offered what comfort he could.

'Well done, partner! I almost made a mess of things, but *you* didn't.'

'Angus isn't going to change his mind, though. We've wasted a day, and still not found anyone.'

He shook his head. 'Wrong, my dear girl. I'll take a bet with you that even now Angus is describing the opening scene. But I hope Anna understands that if she walks out on *this* play, he will certainly break her lovely neck!'

He watched doubt and then shining relief light Kate's face, but found himself wanting to ask a question. 'Did you mean what you said to Angus – about Anna just coming because she wanted the part?'

'No – I think she'd have come if it was only to play Charley's Aunt,' Kate muttered after a moment's thought, 'but it didn't seem the right tactic to tell Angus so. As Aunt Lou would say, he's "unco' thrawn when the de'il takes him".'

Sam sipped his coffee and smiled, and didn't explain what he was smiling about.

Chapter 23

Sam was proved right. Anna was to stay, and come hell or high water the play would open on time. Rehearsals were feverishly resumed, Elsie muttered to herself in the wardrobe room over dresses that had to be altered to fit a different leading lady, and William returned with Milly to Paradise Walk each night expressing delight about the change of cast.

'Poor little Jane did her best,' he explained more than once, 'but the part just wasn't *in* her as it is in Anna Macdonald.'

'Very true,' Louisa observed tartly. 'I dare say it helps to have had practice in the rôle of an adulterous woman, but I hope you can hush your rhapsodies when Kate's about; she lost a fiancé to the creature, remember.'

William wrapped himself in professional dignity. 'I speak, naturally, of Anna the actress, who is by any standard superb, not of the woman who is Macdonald's wife.'

'They're two sides of the same coin, if you ask me, but I'm not an impressionable man, nor an actor, thank God.'

Refreshed by having had the last word, Louisa retired from the subject in good order. 'Have you given a thought to Kate's birthday, William? When I reminded her all she could say was that it falls on the day of the dress rehearsal –

she'd think about celebrating *after* opening night. The truth is that she's just as besotted with that theatre as you are. I knew I was right all along to want to keep her out of the madhouse that you and Fanny lived in.'

'No, my dear Lou, you'd have been quite wrong. The blood of the Cavendishes is in her veins and so, I'm bound to say, is her father's. Try making a clerk in the Inland Revenue out of that mixture!' A regal wave of his hand dismissed the idea and Louisa snorted with disgust – he was *living* the part of Prince Shcherbatsky now, and Milly Pearce was giving herself the same aristocratic airs and graces.

The question of Kate's birthday seemed to have been shelved, and she assumed that no one outside Paradise Walk knew about it. There seemed in any case to be no particular merit in becoming twenty-one – it happened to most people; what was important now was knowing whether between them she and Sam had recreated the elaborate, exotic world of pre-revolutionary Russian high society.

After a breakfast of presents and kisses at home, she went to the studio earlier than usual, with the intention of getting some work done before it was time to go to the theatre. Yesterday's sketch of a costume for *Tosca* was still pinned to her drawing-board but she was distracted from examining it. A package, carefully wrapped, lay balanced on top of another smaller one on her table. Sam, she realised, had known about her birthday after all.

By the time he walked into the room she had unwrapped his gift and was still staring entranced at a small, perfect water-colour of the view from the studio window.

'When you're very famous I expect this will be very valuable, but I shan't ever part with it,' she said unsteadily. 'It's beautiful, Sam.'

He smiled, but merely blew her a little kiss. 'Happy birthday, Kate! The other package arrived some while ago, but there were instructions to keep it for today.'

Her mind leapt to Jeremy . . . perhaps *he*'d known and remembered. But placed on top of a jeweller's box inside the wrapping was a card that said simply, 'For Katerina'; in one corner were the initials A.C. She sat down, aware that her legs were trembling as much as the fingers that lifted the lid of the box. Lying on a bed of crimson velvet was a bracelet worked in gold – each of its links fashioned in the shape of a tiny, perfect rose.

'It's . . . it's being quite a day for . . . for precious gifts,' she muttered. 'Did *you* tell my father? Is that how he knew?'

'He asked me when he came here, and by the look of *that* he's been working on it ever since. No wonder I was told in Milan that other goldsmiths can only try to copy what he does.'

'They might *try*,' Kate agreed slowly, 'but I don't see how they can succeed.' She touched the bracelet very gently – stroked it, Sam thought – and then closed the box again. 'Now I shall have to write to him . . .' Her voice trailed into silence but her eyes asked instead the desperate question that occurred to her.

'"*Caro Padre*" will do nicely,' said Sam.

Even a dress rehearsal seemed, after that, almost a trivial affair, but gradually the powerful effect of Macdonald's play asserted itself and she was caught up in what was happening on the stage. Angus took the rehearsal straight through without interruptions, to Anna's despairing suicide. It was not, Kate knew, how Tolstoy had ended his novel, but anything more on the stage would have blunted the powerful impact of the drama.

At the end of the rehearsal the tired players waited for Macdonald's verdict, but one person was missing amid the usual backstage confusion. It suddenly seemed necessary to Kate to go and find her.

Anna was in her dressing-room, still costumed and made-up as she had finished the last act – not yet released, it seemed, from the tragic spell of the play. She looked up as Kate went in, and stared at her in the mirror.

'Well? Shall we let the Swan down the day after tomorrow?'

'No,' Kate answered baldly. It was hard to find words to comment on what she'd just watched, but she was acutely aware that the woman in front of her waited for a more convincing answer. 'You might have been studying the part for months, instead of a few days; the result is spellbinding.'

She registered the fact as she spoke that Anna's dresser seemed not to be there, and found herself automatically undoing the row of tiny buttons that fastened the back of Madame Karenina's black velvet dress. When Anna stepped out of it and sank back into her chair again, tense and tired, Kate began to massage her shoulders and neck just as she'd done often enough for Jeremy after a performance.

She finally moved away and Anna began to smear cold-cream on her face and wipe it clean of make-up. They were not friends – probably never would be; but they met on equal terms now. Their lives had become linked in the small, enclosed world of the theatre – they would probably remain so.

'I told Angus you'd come for the part, and I told Sam you'd come to rescue us,' Kate said suddenly. 'Even now

I'm not sure which was true. Perhaps it doesn't even matter any more, but one likes to get at the truth if one can.'

Anna turned to meet her direct gaze and recognised that all along she had underestimated the spare, elusive appeal that belonged to the girl in front of her. It had nothing in common with her own rich beauty, but it explained why Jeremy had never quite been able to forget Kate Cavendish.

'All right – here's the truth you seem to value so much, although it often does more harm than good in my opinion. I came to show Angus that in the theatre he still couldn't manage without me. But it will be a point of honour with him to show me that I'm not needed in any other capacity.'

Unable to say for certain that she was wrong, Kate muttered instead, 'You still have Jeremy; isn't that enough?'

Anna's face, bare of make-up now but still beautiful, was touched fleetingly with an expression Kate couldn't interpret.

'I'll offer you some more of the truth you like so much. For a few months after we left London Jem and I lived entirely for each other. Ignoring the rest of the world, we consumed love . . . on stage and off it. It was marvellous while it lasted, but that sort of marvel *can't* last. I gradually discovered that I still wanted the rest of the world after all.'

'What about Jeremy?' Kate asked hoarsely. 'What did *he* want?'

Anna gave a little shrug. 'Oh, what he'd left behind, I expect – his friends here, perhaps even *you*.' Malice edged her smile. 'He's coming to London, so you'll have to make up your mind whether you want him back or not.'

If the taunt was meant to hurt it almost passed Kate by. She was seeing clearly for the first time the real woman who still existed inside Anna Macdonald, and, like any other, the woman was vulnerable to pain. Jeremy hadn't been entirely won after all, and Angus could only be had back on terms she might never find acceptable.

Anna suddenly stood up and wrapped herself in one of her beautiful silk robes. 'Well, I suppose I must go and listen to my dear husband pointing out all the things I did wrong.'

Kate shook her head. 'I saw his face at the end of the rehearsal and I can tell you that nothing was wrong at all. He's probably waiting to thank you on bended knee.'

Anna gave a real smile at last. 'A new experience for Macdonald – in that case I shall keep him waiting a little longer!'

Jeremy was back in London but not part of the crowd swarming into the Swan on opening night. It was something to be thankful for, Angus reckoned. Jem attracted attention as inevitably as sparks flew upward – he always had, even before he'd decamped with another man's wife instead of marrying the girl he was engaged to.

'At least he's had the minimal decency to stay away tonight,' Angus grunted to Sam while they dragged out the minutes until curtain-up. 'There's been enough gossip and speculation about the cast change and Anna's arrival as it is. I want people to watch the damned play, not sit wondering whether the returned prodigal is about to leap over the footlights and seize the part of Captain Vronsky from Gil.'

'He'll have thought of that,' Sam murmured. 'Jem's wonderfully considerate . . . in small things!'

The dryness made Macdonald's face relax into a grin, but only for a moment. 'What do you suppose Kate thinks about seeing him again? I haven't felt like asking her myself.'

'I haven't even considered asking her,' Sam admitted. 'I used to have the strange idea that I was qualified to give her advice on matters far removed from stage design, but I learned my lesson in the end. She's entitled to find her own way now without any more well-meant interference from me.'

Angus frowned over the stubbing-out of another half-smoked cigarette. 'I hope Jem isn't coming back in the rôle of contrite sinner to ensnare her all over again, but it's quite likely to happen. Anna doesn't enlarge on the subject, naturally, but a hint is occasionally left lying in the air that their first, fine, careless rapture is over. They're both quite capable of believing that it can be forgotten if that's what now suits them best.'

Sam nodded but chose not to reply and looked at his watch instead. 'Time to move, thank God – you hide at the back of the stalls; I'll lurk upstairs. Here's hoping, old friend!'

They had still a few minutes to endure before the house lights dimmed and the tabs swung open, but there was only one place to be now – out where they could see the culmination of all the past weeks – the grindingly hard work, the setbacks and disasters, and the rare moments of delight that had kept them labouring over something that might bring honour and glory to the Swan after all.

But it *was* a glorious evening, and to make sure that nothing was lacking William was led back onto the stage by Macdonald after the curtain calls. He spoke simply of his joy at playing there again, and then summoned Anna, Gilbert, and Angus back to share in the tumult of applause. Milly wept copiously as the entire company bowed again, and even Elsie Manners forgot for a moment to mutter that old actors lived and died playing to the gallery.

Kate stayed well out of sight, knowing that her congratulations wouldn't be needed for a little while. There had been no time recently to think quietly by herself, but she was strongly of the opinion that some thinking needed to be done. Jeremy's return to London seemed to make this the moment when she must start putting her muddled life in order, but the difficulty was to know where to begin. Then, astonished by the first decision that had just lodged itself in her mind, she spoke out loud.

'Yes, *that's* it, of course; why on earth didn't I think of it before?'

'Think of *what*, may one ask?' Sam's voice said politely behind her.

She swung round, and smiled involuntarily at the sight of him. 'What a swell you look!'

'First-night fine feathers – it's the same old me underneath. You didn't answer my question, by the way.'

'I'm not going to! Nothing personal, Sam – it's just that I don't know whether what I'm going to do will work or not. But I need to take a day off tomorrow. Is that all right?'

He nodded, wondering again what he would do when she smiled at him for the last time and finally walked out of his life. It was bound to happen . . . even in the unlikely event that she had managed to outgrow Jeremy Barrington, some other dashing fellow would eventually sweep her away from him.

'Jem's back in London,' he said abruptly, 'but not here tonight.'

'I know . . . Anna told me. It seems that they're on the best of terms still, but no longer quite ready to die for love.

I can't help feeling that Aunt Lou may be right about theatre people . . . they don't seem *able* to be constant. Perhaps we shouldn't expect them to be, but it's a pity they put such spells on the rest of us.'

'William was constant to his Fanny, by the sound of it.'

Kate's transfiguring grin appeared at the thought of her grandfather. 'He was good tonight, wasn't he? I almost burst with pride, and so did Aunt Lou, although she'd rather die on the rack than say so.'

Sam nodded, aware that he'd been side-tracked from the subject of Jem.

'It's time we went, I think – allow me to escort you to the shindig upstairs, Miss Cavendish.'

She gave a mock curtsey and they left the wardrobe room together, both remembering another opening-night party when she had made her entrance with the bright-haired, charming man who couldn't help but edge his way into their thoughts even when he wasn't there.

She saw him materialise three days later, caught sight of him from the window as he walked along Wharfside. But he came slowly, and then stopped altogether to stare at the grey, impersonal river glimpsed between one building and the next. It almost seemed as if that was all he'd come to see and, afraid that he might decide in the end just to walk away, she suddenly ran down the stairs out into the biting December air. He spun round when she called his name, but stood watching her.

'I was waiting for you to come in . . . and then I thought you might be making up your mind not to,' she said gravely.

He stared at her, identifying changes – she was nearly a year older, she was mistress of herself, and she seemed to have become entirely beautiful, even in her old working clothes.

'Dear, sweet Kate, I was trying to decide what to say,' he admitted. 'Should I begin by apologising all over again, or simply assume that you'd lost interest long ago in old, stale history?'

She smiled at him with real amusement. 'I think we should at least go inside while you're making up your mind. It's perishing out here!'

He followed her up the stairs into the empty studio, while she eased the awkwardness of the moment by explaining that Sam was out at another South Bank site meeting.

'They're in a state of barely controlled panic now, poor things; it's touch and go whether the festival will be ready by the time the King is due to go to St Paul's next May and declare it open. Too many cuts in the budget, much too much rain, and not enough zeal among the workmen. But I dare say things will come right in the end; it seems to be our way – a heroic last-minute determination to stop messing about when things get really desperate!'

She saw Jeremy's strained face try to smile, but the effort was painful. It wasn't how Jeremy Barrington ought to be, she thought sadly. He was meant to charm people out of their dull, ordinary lives . . . they required him to smile and enchant, not leave them racked with concern about him.

'Why don't we just agree to forget old history?' she suggested gently. 'We're old friends who haven't met for a long time . . . a bit out of touch, but friends still. Don't you remember us promising we always would be?'

His mouth crumpled suddenly, and he held out his arms. She went into them because it seemed impossible to do anything else, but in the shared embrace there was only a wordless exchange of affection and reassurance. When he released her and they stood looking at one another, he finally measured the change in her – there couldn't be any going back, because she had left him behind now, much more completely than he had left her to indulge his mindless passion for Anna. It was a dreadful moment to discover that what he'd really wanted all along was here.

'Have you come back to stay?' she asked, wishing he would take his turn at helping the conversation along.

'Yes . . . I hope so, Kate.' He made an expressive gesture with his hands that seemed to put mistakes aside. 'New York isn't where I want to live; I know that for certain now. Anna probably will go back when this run finishes – she loves Manhattan, and of course Margot and Jacob are there. I've been offered *Hamlet* at Stratford – just before I get too old to do it at all. It's probably more than I deserve, and God knows whether I can pull it off without Angus keeping an eye on me.' An echo of the old, charmingly rueful smile lifted the corners of his mouth. 'What I really mean, of course, is without *you* to hold my hand.'

She hesitated for a moment, then plunged. 'There's something else that might help – a ghost from the past finally laid to rest. Jem, two days ago when I knew for certain that you were back in London, I went to Birmingham. The stage manager at the City Rep was kind enough to hunt through their records, and he found for me what had been young John Bagg's home-address. I went there next, more than half-afraid that it would lead me to a dead end. But your mother still lives in that little terraced house, with trains rattling past the end of the garden.'

'You went to Chamberlain Street? Dear God, Kate, you *saw* my mother?' He caught hold of her again and she could feel his hands trembling. 'She slammed the door in your face, I expect. She did that to me more than once.'

Kate covered his hands with her own warm ones. 'I'm bound to say she wasn't very welcoming, but despite Aunt Lou's best efforts to make a lady of me, I had a street-upbringing as well. When she could see that she wasn't going to get rid of me she eventually asked me in.'

'What in God's name did you talk about?' Jeremy muttered.

'You, of course! She was very tempted to refuse to listen, but lonely enough not to despise a visitor altogether. In the end she even made me a cup of tea and seemed to understand when I tried to explain that the great Jem Barrington was still her son, in need of roots and reassurance.' There was a long silence before the question Kate waited for was forced out of him at last.

'How was she?'

'Handicapped by arthritis, but still managing to keep her house shining as a new pin. It would do her a great deal of good to be able to boast about you to her neighbours – but she hasn't felt entitled to do that. I don't think she'd shut the door in your face if you went now.'

Instead of answering he seemed to be staring at a past that had become no less vivid for all the long years in between. She watched his face anxiously, but for once its lack of expression defeated her until he turned her hands over and lifted them to his mouth.

'Thank you, my dearest dear. I'm terribly tempted to say all kinds of foolish things, but I expect they're better left unsaid.' He stared at her face and knew in advance the answer to the question he still must ask. 'It's too late now, isn't it? I had my chance and threw it away.'

Tears stung her eyelids because for all her longing to take away his sadness she couldn't mistake deep affection for love any more.

'Yes, dear Jem, I'm afraid it *is* too late for going back to where we were. But it wasn't all your fault. I was a mixed-up mess of a girl, and that didn't help.' The moment might have made good theatre, she thought, but it seemed increasingly unbearable when it was real. 'Don't regret coming back, though. This is where you belong . . . with *us*, always.'

He leaned forward to leave a little farewell kiss on her mouth. 'Thank you, Kate. Now I shall go to Stratford and become the Prince of Denmark, and God knows what else thereafter. I shall enjoy my work, and probably all my leading ladies as well, but I'm afraid I shall regret losing you until I die.'

It was a superb exit line but for once it wasn't calculated. When he had gone she wept a little, fearing that what he'd said might be entirely true.

Chapter 24

Having brought Anna back to London, Sam performed the same service for Jane Carlisle and even talked Macdonald into agreeing to accept her in the company again. Observing this behaviour, Kate told herself that it was high time the detached observer got embroiled in the muddles that everyone else made of their lives. There was no doubt that Sam was involved now. Putting Jane together again took most of the spare time he had, but Anna leaned on him too, and for all Kate knew there were other women as well who required his love and comfort. She was happy to think they didn't include her; she and Sam were merely business partners who would be visiting Italy together in the new year. That die was cast but she refused to confess to him how much the prospect weighed on her. Instead she hid behind outward indifference, but late into the night at home wrestled with Italian verbs, and the blood-soaked history of her father's country. Her carefully worded letter of thanks for his birthday gift had received no reply, and she couldn't decide whether this silence came as a relief or a hurt too painful to admit to.

Christmas had nearly arrived when she returned to the studio one day after an even wetter excursion than usual. Once again she was laying out sodden shoes, gloves, and

scarf to dry round Sam's wood-burning stove when Jane
Carlisle walked in.

'You've chosen a miserable afternoon for a social call, and
Sam's not even here,' she observed, doing her best to sound
cordial. 'His father's unwell and he took the night train to
Edinburgh.'

'I know . . . that's why I came now. I wanted to bring
something while he was away.' Jane undid her dripping
cape and produced a small, wrapped package that she'd been
sheltering from the rain. 'Will you give it to him, please,
when he gets back? We've got a week off from rehearsals,
and I'm going home for Christmas.' Another volley of rain
flung itself against the windows like grapeshot and it seemed
impossible not to invite her to stay.

'Hadn't you better wait and see if it eases off? There won't
be any sugar, but we can have a cup of tea.'

Jane's smile accepted an invitation she hadn't expected
and she was sitting on the floor by the stove when Kate came
back with the tea, wet hair drying in a dark cloud around her
face. She had, her hostess supposed, been born pretty; now
she was a small, perfectly shaped girl with the sinuous grace
of a cat. Kate was aware of lacking charity towards her and
could find no saving excuse for it.

'You might have posted the parcel and saved yourself a
soaking,' she suggested as they sipped their tea.

'No, it was too fragile for that.' Jane turned a flushed face
towards her and smiled with reminiscent pleasure. 'It's a
little dog carved out of Chinese jade – the only thing of
value I possess. That's why I want to give it to Sam.'

'Very generous,' Kate muttered. No need to wonder
whether it would take him by surprise. He must know
that their friendship had reached the stage when valuable

presents were exchanged. She felt depressed by the thought, and then still more depressed by her own lack of generosity. 'Your little dog couldn't have come to a better home – Sam will cherish it,' she managed to say.

Her visitor nodded, then hesitated. The expression on Kate's face, though not unfriendly, didn't invite her to linger, but no actress could easily pass up a chance to talk about herself.

'I expect you think I behaved very badly,' Jane began. 'Well, I *know* you do; so of course did Angus, and I can't blame either of you. That's why it's been so wonderful to have darling Sam still keeping his faith in me. Kate, I wanted to be an actress from the time I first watched Peggy Ashcroft play at the Old Vic. I was ten years old and in that one marvellous year I saw her as four Shakespearian heroines – Cleopatra, Imogen, Rosalind and Portia. I doubt if I understood a quarter of the words, but I knew the magic of what I was seeing.' She interrupted herself to stare at Kate. 'With William for a grandfather didn't *you* know it, too?'

'Yes, but what I do now was the nearest I could get to it,' Kate admitted. 'An actress who can't perform in front of an audience is liable to get howled off the stage.'

Jane nodded sympathetically and went on. 'My parents didn't understand, but they were too kind to put me off. I was allowed to go to RADA, and finally I could call myself an actress. Getting taken on by Angus for *The Portrait* was my first glimpse of success; then I became part of his Swan company, happy to be playing second fiddle to someone as glorious as Anna Macdonald. I was *good* at that – good enough to think that one day it would be *my* turn to be the leading lady. When Anna left so suddenly, I didn't really believe my turn had come, but

Sam thought I'd earned it, and persuaded Angus to let me be Anna Karenina.

'I think I knew almost at once that it wasn't going to work; the Guv'nor suspected it too, but couldn't quite bring himself to give me the sack. You probably think that it was unforgivable to just run away, but I'd have ruined the play for everyone else if I'd stayed.'

It had been very nearly ruined in any case, Kate thought; but, still clinging hard to the spirit of the season of the nativity, she managed not to say so.

'When I fled home to Brighton I thought it was the end of my career,' Jane went on, enjoying a monologue that was so exclusively about herself. 'I was certain I should never have the nerve to set foot on a stage again, even if a theatre management was brave enough to risk offering me a part.'

'Then along came Sam, riding to the rescue on his white charger,' Kate suggested, watching Jane blush very prettily.

'Yes . . . having bribed or bludgeoned Angus into giving me another chance. Dearest Sam even pretended that it was *his* fault – for pushing me before I was ready to be pushed. He's such a heavenly man – so strong, but so gentle. I'd rather *die* than let him down again . . . but I shan't, now. The part of Celia in *As You Like It* was made for me, and I shall play it with all my heart, just for him.'

She would too, Kate thought. It was an important but supporting rôle; she would wear the costumes beautifully, speak the verse intelligently with Macdonald's help, and have her gentil, parfit knight, Sam Maitland, always at hand to tell her how well she was doing.

'I'm glad,' Kate said, firmly enough to persuade herself that she meant it. 'You'll be just right for Celia.'

'Your grandfather said that, too,' Jane admitted with a

pleased smile. 'I was *dreading* the thought of walking into the theatre and facing them all again, and there was an awful moment when nobody uttered a word. Then William came up to me and said, "Welcome back, dear child"! I burst into tears, and after that they were all wonderfully kind. It's a pity you can't know what it feels like to belong to the theatre, Kate . . . I mean I know you're *involved*, but it's not quite the same thing, is it?'

There was no malice in her face – only genuine regret for someone excluded from their magic world. Actors couldn't help knowing that other people were like children forced to stand for ever outside the sweetshop window, noses pressed against the glass, staring at the delights they would never taste.

Deciding that the season of goodwill had lasted long enough, Kate pointed out that, though only so slightly involved, it was time all the same that she got back to painting Celia's Forest of Arden.

Jane donned shoes and mac again but, looking round the studio, had one more shot in her locker. 'It's very cosy for you working here, but don't you sometimes feel a trifle *de trop*? I mean it *is* Sam's home – awkward if he wants to stay in bed late, or take a wife!'

She smiled with a maddening hint of pity in her face, and finally went away. Kate returned to the drawing-board, but discovered ten minutes later that the sheet of paper in front of her was covered with drawings of a pekinese . . . like the little lion dog of China, carved in cool, translucent jade, that waited to be discovered on Sam's table. Unaware of what her hand was doing, her mind wrestled with the thought that Jane had just so helpfully lodged in it – she had taken for granted her right to be there. But Sam's wife, when he took one, would see it as no right at all.

Christmas falling on a Friday gave Angus the chance to declare a weekend holiday for cast and theatre-crew. William could relax and shepherd his household to the cathedral on Christmas morning, pleasantly aware that the Southwark congregation realised Prince Shcherbatsky was in its midst. Milly came crowned with the new fur toque Kate had made for her – not quite Russian sable, but who would know the difference? – and even Aunt Lou was prevailed upon to attend, and listen once more to the story of the nativity. Kate heard the Gospel words she knew by heart, sang the carols with her usual off-key gusto, and tried to recapture the joy that had always come with Christmas. She thought she was succeeding quite well until Elsie asked a question as they walked home after the service.

'Which of your lame dogs are you fretting about?'

Kate made an effort to smile. 'Sorry – was I looking glum? There was no reason to. Jeremy's spending today with his mother, which is cause for joy, not gloom. Gil is having an American-style Christmas with Anna and her friends, and Macdonald – scarcely anyone's idea of a lame dog – is enjoying *not* being sociable in his country retreat!'

'Sam still visiting his father?' Elsie asked next, noticing who hadn't been mentioned.

'Yes, which is rather sad for him because he dislikes Edinburgh. I'm sure he'd much rather be down in Brighton with Jane Carlisle.'

'Well, you don't care one way or the other about that, so what *is* troubling you?'

Kate turned to look at her friend, wishing that the unease

. . . no, the unhappiness . . . she suffered from could be simply told and dealt with. But the reply she produced had at least some part of the truth in it.

'I expect I'm in a bit of a state about going to Milan next week.'

'Will you go and see your father?'

'How can I?' Kate cried, as if a painful nerve had been touched on. 'I doubt if his wife knows I even exist.' She frowned over the stone she kicked into the gutter with the practised aim of childhood. 'He didn't answer my letter so his birthday present was probably just a way of saying goodbye. I wish Sam hadn't interfered. We were better off not knowing about each other.'

'I dare say you'll know what to do when you get there,' Elsie suggested firmly, with no grounds for such a supposition, and only the longing to give comfort to a girl whose face looked full of strain.

Kate didn't reply and they walked the rest of the way home in silence.

The journey was to be made by boat and train, because in winter Milan was a notoriously fog-prone city, said Sam. She agreed that a channel crossing and a night in a train would be novelties enough for her; she didn't mind keeping aeroplanes for another occasion.

On the morning of their departure she arrived at Wharfside wearing a scarlet coat of dashingly military cut, with a pill-box hat of the same colour clinging to her dark hair. There had been admiring whistles as she walked through the market, with Percival Pearce gallantly carrying her suitcase, but Sam's welcome wasn't fulsome.

'Well, it's going to be hard to mislay you, partner.'

'That's what I thought,' she agreed, dampened but trying to sound cheerful. It was his own fault that she was going at all, and not her fault that she wasn't Jane Carlisle.

But he was an experienced travelling-companion who always had the right tickets to hand, seemed to know by instinct where their seats and sleeping-berths were likely to be, and whose gentle courtesy extracted pleasantness in return, even from people who were tired and surly. Jem, she thought, would have made a *deliberate* effort to charm them, and Macdonald none at all. Perhaps Jane had been right, though needlessly theatrical; there was something special about Sam Maitland.

For January the Channel was unseasonably calm; Normandy looked remarkably like Kent; and all she saw of Paris were some lights and the railway line that linked the Gare du Nord with the Gare St Lazare. Foreign travel scarcely seemed exciting after all, despite the disembodied voices she listened to, calling out strange names in the darkness as the train occasionally stopped on its night journey across France.

But daybreak brought a moment she was never to forget. They emerged from a mountain tunnel . . . into Italy. She stood at a corridor window, marvelling at the completeness of the change. Landscape, people, houses, all were different now. They had even left behind the bitter weather of the north, because the Lombardy countryside was washed in pale, winter sunlight instead of rain. The first shock of surprise was lost in a stranger shock of recognition – this tranquil, poplar-studded landscape didn't seem foreign to her and, could she have jumped off the train at any way-side village, she thought the inhabitants would have been familiar too.

Milan at noon-time *was* bewildering, with throngs of hurrying, intent-faced citizens – going home, Sam explained, for the long, serious, midday meal.

'I shan't be allowed to stand still long enough to read the street names,' Kate said anxiously.

'No need – from our hotel just keep walking, *sempre diretto* as they say here! Via Manzoni will lead you straight into the Piazza della Scala. Between that and the Duomo is the famous Gallería, where all Milan goes to study the news, drink coffee, and exchange the gossip of the day. Throw in the castle of the Sforzas and you'll have seen all that most visitors remember of the city!'

She was prepared for him to say that work must start immediately, but waiting at the hotel were a charming nosegay of flowers for her, and a note for Sam.

'This afternoon we are to repose ourselves after the journey,' he explained with a smile, 'before we dine with the *Direttore* and his wife tonight; work begins tomorrow. Now, since we have the next few hours to ourselves, what's it to be?'

'A glimpse of *The Last Supper* before it fades into the total invisibility everyone says it's threatened with, then the paintings in the Pinacoteca Brera, and perhaps a call at the cathedral on the way back.'

He smiled at the programme, but had no fault to find with it beyond suggesting that the winter dusk would have set in before they had time to climb to the terraces that snaked around the roof of the cathedral. 'A pity because on a clear day you can see as far as the Alps; still, the nearer views are extraordinary too – it's like playing hide and seek in a white, petrified forest of spires and pinnacles.'

They did all these things and ended up watching the world

go by over coffee under the glass dome of the Gallería. Sam also watched his companion, thinking that Italy seemed to agree with her quite as obviously as she pleased the predatory Italian males who found occasion to amble past their table.

'Sharks, every one of them,' he pointed out helpfully, 'ever on the watch for some new and appetising mouthful.'

Kate smiled, accepting both compliment and warning, but her mind was on the discovery that it had been the very best afternoon she could remember. She would have liked to tell him so, and in the past would have done it unthinkingly, but such frankness was inhibited now by the thought of Jane Carlisle. Instead, she concentrated on what must concern her most.

'Sam, I've been dithering but I shall have to see my father before we leave for home. His card had the shop address of the Ponte Vecchio on it, and I shall go there – but it means a weekday visit when it will be open.' She anticipated the question in his face and answered it. 'There's no need for you to offer to come with me; it's something I must do alone.'

'Then go tomorrow and get it over,' he suggested slowly. 'I'll present our designs at La Scala, and they can have the rest of the day to argue about them. Then, if they want changes, we shall be able to work on them together when you get back.' She nodded, wondering why she'd thought he would be surprised. He'd probably banked on the certainty all along that if she came to Italy she would decide to visit Florence. He pointed across the marble floor in front of them to the windows of a travel agency.

'There you are – any *viaggio* instantly arranged . . . what could be neater?'

She admitted that it was altogether neat, but kept to herself as they walked back to the hotel afterwards how altogether unnerving as well was the prospect of the journey ahead of her. If she'd understood a little more of the Italian talk that was hurled at her . . . if she'd been sure of her father's welcome . . . if only she'd refused to come to Italy at all.

The evening was unexpectedly enjoyable, once she'd been appraised by two pairs of dark eyes and been, for varying reasons, approved of. It also revealed to her how completely at home Sam felt among these charmingly sophisticated people. She found herself feeling proud about that, and only realised afterwards how absurd it was. When they parted company for the night she assured him firmly that she was quite capable of hiring a taxi to take her to the station; but at seven-thirty the next morning when she went downstairs he was in the hall studying a wall-map of Italy.

'It's the small boy in all grown men,' he explained, 'you can't keep us away from trains and railway stations.'

With his usual competence she was guided to her seat on the Rome express, and found a lump in her throat as she watched him wave her away. It seemed an appropriate start to a day that threatened to be emotional.

At half-past ten the train pulled into Florence station, and a quarter of an hour later she was standing in a stone recess on the Ponte Vecchio, staring at a view familiar from a hundred paintings and photographs. The yellow-green Arno that Mark Twain had been so contemptuous about – 'they call it a river, do these dark and bloody Florentines' – threaded a city of umber, faded rose, and brown, huddled about the matchless russet dome of the Cathedral. For a moment longer she lingered there, pretending that this was what she had come to see. Then she crossed the road and walked into one of the tiny shops that lined the bridge like jewel caskets, all gleaming with the richness of gold.

A stumbling enquiry in Italian for '*il dottore* Arturo Contini, *per favore*' received only the gravest of stares. Her next request, for English to be spoken if possible, brought a courteous bow. This could certainly be managed but, alas, *il dottore* was not there.

'It's very important,' Kate explained earnestly, 'I've come from London. If he is at Via Cavour instead could you possibly telephone for me, and say that . . . that Katerina is here?'

Now that she was actually in Florence the thought of not seeing her father seemed to have become unbearable, but how was she to explain that to this incongruously dark-suited and elderly custodian of so much bright treasure? He still stared at her, wondering what could be important about a young Englishwoman's need to see the *padrone*. He reckoned himself a judge of people now – there had been long years in which to study the men and women who could afford to buy Arturo Contini's jewellery. Most of them seemed unworthy of what they bought, but this girl's face and manner pleased him.

At last he made up his mind. 'The *Dottore* is not here or at Via Cavour, *signorina* . . . you will find him at the Convento della Santa Maddalena. He is unwell, you understand, but it is possible that the good sisters would permit you to see him.'

'Can I walk there?' she asked briefly.

'Better a taxi.' He called instructions to someone in a back room, then turned to Kate again. 'You are a stranger here, I think – Luigi will take you to the place where taxis wait.'

She held out her hand, unaware that the gesture surprised and pleased him. 'Thank you . . . you've been very kind.'

Her small youthful escort seemed anxious to assure himself in every window that his dark hair remained as smooth as a seal's pelt, but he shot sidelong glances at her as well as they turned off the bridge onto the Lungarno. The scarlet coat and hat were worth admiring, and so were the inglese's long, slender legs – in fact she was *molto appetitosa* altogether, and he prided himself on his judgement in such matters, leaving less interesting studies to old Signor Filippo. A taxi was found, directions given to the driver, and Kate handed in with a flourish that might in other circumstances have tempted her to smile. But she thanked him gravely and he walked back to the shop pleasantly conscious of having conducted himself well – as was the duty of every true-born Italian male.

Chapter 25

The hospital looked forbidding on the outside, more prison than convent, but the young nun who admitted her had a reassuringly gentle smile. Kate gave haltingly the name of the '*infermo*' she hoped to visit, but it brought a look of doubt to the girl's face.

'*Aspetta un momento, signorina. Devo domandare . . . la suor' Angelica parla inglese.*'

She glided away, making no noise even on the stone floor. The ancient building seemed wrapped altogether in the silence of the dead, and Kate shivered as the thought came to her. The little room she waited in felt cold, too – the only addition to its starkly white-washed walls being the carving of an anguished Christ on the cross to remind visitors of the sins that had needed so terrible a redemption.

She was still staring at it when an older nun arrived dressed in a white nursing habit. Sister Angelica's face, framed severely in its starched wimple, was unsmiling although she greeted Kate pleasantly.

'It would have been better to telephone,' she said in a voice that still hadn't entirely lost its soft Irish lilt. 'Then we could have told you that only the closest relatives would be admitted even if *il dottore* Contini wished for visitors.'

'I'm his daughter – is that close enough?' Kate saw the

nun's frown. Had she shouted in this hushed place? Her next question came almost in a whisper. 'Why is my father here, Sister?' But her earlier query was still being grappled with. 'The Signora Contini didn't speak of a daughter, only of their son who was killed.' Sister Angelica lived in a state of grace that forbade anger with another human being, but her worn face expressed reproach for a claim that seemed to be false.

'I am not the Signora's daughter,' Kate explained in a low voice, 'nor does she know me. My mother was English. I was born after the *Dottore* returned to Italy from London. If his wife is here with him I'll go away; if not, will you ask him if he will see me, please? My name is Katerina.'

The nun stared at her for so long that she had given up hope of being admitted when finally the answer came. 'Child, your father is very ill – beyond saving by human skill,' she admitted gently. 'A cancer of the liver still defeats us, I am afraid, but at least his suffering will have been mercifully brief.'

Kate knew a moment's terrible temptation to shatter the stillness around her, to disturb the nun's serene acceptance of death, and shout that her father *couldn't* die because she needed him. But the words didn't leave her mouth. The woman in front of her probably saw earthly needs as irrelevant; happiness lay in life eternal.

'If you don't distress him there's no reason for you not to stay,' the nun said after a moment's consideration. 'His wife no longer comes.'

She led the way along a cloister that bordered an inner courtyard. Lemon trees grew in tubs round the ancient cistern in the centre, and urns filled with herbs released fragrance into the air as Kate brushed her fingers against them. The pungent scent of rosemary reminded her of Aunt Lou's herb patch at home, insisting that life and all familiar things still went on outside this place of death and unearthly love and promised salvation.

Her father's changed condition drew a stifled gasp from her, and for a moment it seemed more than she could manage to walk forward and kneel beside the bed. No distress, the nun had said . . . but oh, dear God, the pain of coming so much too late, either to know or help her father. She took the skeletal hand lying on the counterpane in both of hers as if to will into it some transfusion of her own youth and strength. Unaware of Sister Angelica leaving the cell-like little room, she tried to pray, and almost missed the moment when her father's eyes opened and focused on her.

'It's me, Father . . . Katerina,' she managed to murmur. 'I'm sorry I haven't come before.'

His head moved slightly on the pillow; it didn't matter, the faint gesture said – she was there now.

'I've been waiting for you,' he said in a thread of a voice, and his pale mouth sketched a smile.

There would be time later, she realised, to be haunted by the thought of how easily she might have disappointed him. Now, she must just hold his hand and find something to say. She told him about William's appearance behind the footlights again, and about the costumes she'd designed for *Tosca*. Then, because it seemed very necessary now, she explained that she was glad she'd finally come to Italy.

'I was stupid about it for a long time. My clever partner, Sam Maitland, made me do it in the end, but I'm sorry it took me so long.'

Arturo's eyes never left her face, as if he needed every moment of the time that was left just to look at his daughter.

'You are here now,' he whispered. 'Nothing else matters.'

Kate held up her free hand so that the light shone on the bracelet she wore. 'It's the most beautiful thing I shall ever own – I tried to say that in my letter, but I don't suppose I said it very well.'

Her father's gaunt face smiled. 'Well enough for me you said it.' Then overcome by weakness and the drugs that dulled his pain, he sank into sleep again, still holding her hand.

She had no idea how much later it was that the door opened quietly and Sister Angelica's hand touched her shoulder.

'Come away now, child. Your father is sleeping, and you must have something to eat. He won't be alone – one of the novices will stay with him.'

Food was brought to her in the austere little room she had been shown to first, and she had sense enough left not to refuse the good soup and bread. Her Irish friend reappeared just as she was finishing it.

'I was hoping you'd come back,' Kate said. 'I wanted to thank you, and to . . . to ask what will happen now.'

'Your father made his wishes clear – the Signora understands that he is to be buried next to his son.'

'May I stay . . . until the end?' She saw pity in the nun's face, but the serenity that came from absolute faith as well.

'My dear, this is the end. Your father's sleep now is the final coma the doctor told us to expect. He won't wake again; there is no fear of him missing you.'

'But I nearly missed *him*,' Kate whispered, 'so very nearly.' She closed her eyes against the pain of knowing how close she'd come to it, but tears trickled down her face nevertheless, warm against the coldness of her skin. The nun let her weep but began to talk quietly herself.

'People imagine that we who live by a strict rule relinquish choices once we've opted for the enclosed life, but we remain human; still make mistakes, still either learn or choose not to learn, finally discover how to defeat regret by accepting its necessity.'

'My father lost happiness through someone else's choice – I don't think he ever found it again,' Kate muttered.

'Perhaps not, my dear, but he learned to accept loss without bitterness – that is a kind of joy in itself.'

Kate didn't query the comfort she was being offered even though the joy that Sister Angelica spoke of was surely too rarefied for most ordinary human beings. Instead she stood up, holding out her hand. 'I shall always remember today, and be grateful that he had you to look after him.'

She kissed the nun's cheek, and five minutes later the heavy, iron-barred door of the convent closed behind her. She was far from the railway station and found a free taxi too late to catch the express she had been booked on. Instead, there was a stopping train for Milan leaving in another hour. It was a long, tedious journey but she sat through it in an isolation so complete that she seemed to have become invisible. If anyone spoke to her she didn't hear them; heart and mind still clung to that cell-like room and the gaunt face of the man who had smiled at her with love.

At last the lights of Milan stabbed the rainy darkness outside, but she didn't move until a fellow-passenger touched her, penetrating the haze of exhaustion she was wrapped in.

'*Ecco Milano, signorina . . . siamo arrivati.*'

She stumbled down from the train, trying to call to mind the name of the hotel she must give a taxi-driver; but at the gate leading from the platform into the huge station hall a man searching the crowd for her called her name, and she turned to find Sam standing there. For a heart-stopping moment of time she saw his familiar figure haloed in light; this was a Sam Maitland transfigured, beautiful and infinitely dear. There was even nothing strange about this new vision of him – it was as if her heart had always known what she was now seeing clearly.

'I missed the *rapido*,' she said unsteadily when she could talk at all.

'I know – that's what I came to meet. They said there was only one other train from Florence tonight. I've been trying to bribe the gods with all sorts of rash promises if only they'd see to it that you stepped off it safely.' He didn't smile as he spoke but she was familiar with his habit of saying what he didn't mean with a grave face. 'Kate, when I saw Giorgio di Palma at the theatre this morning he told me that your father has been ill since last summer. If I'd known I wouldn't have let you go to Florence alone.'

'He's dying . . . is perhaps dead by now . . . but at least he knew that I'd come. If you hadn't made me go today it would have been too late.'

'Should you have stayed . . . to attend his funeral?'

She stared at him with eyes that looked intensely dark in the pallor of her face. The accumulated emotions of the day had been overwhelming enough; that splendid vision of a moment ago and what it might mean when she could stop and think about it seemed now almost more than she could bear.

'No,' she stammered at last. 'I said goodbye to him at the convent. It's all arranged for him to be buried next to Alessandro. There's no need to distress his widow still more by having her learn about me.'

Sam touched her face with a gentle hand. He wanted more than anything in life to enfold her in his arms, but

340

she had wrapped herself instead in a garment of lonely, private sadness.

He tried to smile and almost succeeded. 'Shall we go? I'm beginning to hate this blasted railway station.'

The wet weather blew away during the night, leaving the morning streets rain-washed and the air unusually clear. Kate braved its rawness to stand on her little balcony, astonished to remember that this was only her third awakening in Italy. It seemed to be an appropriate word to come to mind; she might have been anywhere else for years and still have learned less than she'd discovered here. Her lessons had brought more pain than joy, but she clung to what Sister Angelica had insisted upon. The choice of how to deal with life was hers. Acceptance of mistakes, instead of a blind refusal to admit her errors, would be a start. It was too late for more than that where her father was concerned; she must learn to do without what had been found and lost almost in the same moment. But Sam offered a lesson that promised to be even harder to learn. Somehow she must put away that moment at the railway station when she'd seen him nimbused in light. Once again she'd been too late, and perhaps it was to be the story of her life.

He was already at breakfast when she went downstairs, and deep in conversation with the waiter who was serving him. He probably knew the man's family history by now – she'd noticed before how readily people seemed to confide in him. Her legs felt weak and unreliable but she forced herself to walk forward and wish him good morning.

'You're looking better, partner,' he said after inspecting her, 'so I'm going to get my news over and done with. Giorgio telephoned early this morning to say that your father died last night. I haven't ever mentioned your name in that connection, so di Palma doesn't know of the relationship and won't talk about Arturo to you.'

She nodded, unable to speak, trying to remember what Sister Angelica would say – that her father was safely reunited with God and Alessandro. 'Hadn't you better tell me how yesterday went at the theatre?' she managed to suggest eventually, and Sam followed the lead she gave him.

'It went rather well on the whole, but there are some changes we must make,' he said with regret. 'The Scala stage is so huge that the subtle effects we pride ourselves on tend to get lost. It's flourish, not finesse, that counts here.'

She was able to smile at the typical Maitland comment, and from then on forced mind and imagination to return to the work in hand. Rather to her surprise she not only survived the hectic day in the opera house, but even found herself enjoying it. Perhaps it was an unexpected inheritance from her father that she should feel at ease among these volatile, imaginative people. Only as Sam and she left the theatre to walk back to the hotel did she heave a sigh of relief.

'Tired, Kate?' he asked, as they stood at a street corner, waiting for traffic-lights to change. 'Our colleagues here are charming but I doubt if anyone has ever found them restful.'

'Well, I can't help wondering how the work gets done,' she confessed. 'Does everything require that much talk and argument?'

'Always, in my experience, but they're more flexible than we are. If there's a union rule that says, having argued all day, they can't work all night, they just ignore it. So things *do* get done.' He turned to smile at her. 'Never mind . . . we'll soon be back in the cloistered calm of Wharfside.'

'So we shall,' she agreed, with a slight hesitation he failed for once to notice. But he was aware that the day had been a strain for her, and that she looked and sounded very tired.

'There's no need to buckle on your armour again tonight. Shall I make your excuses to Giorgio and his sister?' he suggested gently as the lights changed and they could move at last.

'Yes . . . yes, please,' she muttered finally. 'I wanted to go to the Opera to experience something my father probably enjoyed, but I shall spare you a companion bathed in tears throughout the performance. Italy is having a strange effect on me, I'm afraid – all my nerve-ends seem exposed, and pleasure is as hard to bear as pain.'

'In that case I'll stay with you,' said Sam. 'It's been a long day – we'll just have dinner quietly together.'

'We'll do nothing of the kind,' she almost shouted with a change of tone that halted him in mid-stride. 'I'm going to spend the evening alone.' The expression on his face said that, even making allowances for her emotional state, she was behaving badly. He'd expected better of her – even a Southwark brat had had time by now to learn the rudiments of good manners. Well, she must go on behaving badly or break down and weep out her heart's grief. 'Go to the opera, please,' she said more quietly. 'It's kind of you to offer, but I don't need you, Sam.'

He left her at the doors of the hotel without another word, and she didn't see him again until the following morning. She had reached her second cup of coffee before he appeared in the hotel restaurant.

'I hope you slept well,' she said politely.

'Very well, thank you, though for not nearly long enough.' She poured more coffee that she didn't want while she considered what to say next. The subject was hard to broach, but Sam obligingly led into it himself.

'Much as I enjoy working here, I shan't be sorry to go home tomorrow . . . and I don't suppose you will, either.'

She took a deep breath to steady a suddenly racing heart and began what she must say. 'Sam . . . unless you insist that there's too much work waiting for us in London, I should like to stay here – well, not *here*, in Florence.'

His face was expressionless, but when he spoke she thought she detected anger only just held in check beneath the flatness of his voice.

'You do rather spring surprises on me, partner. Your grandfather will expect me to deliver you back to Paradise Walk intact, not leave you here, more or less without money or friends.'

'I'll write to William and Aunt Lou, and explain.'

'Explain *what*?'

'That if I leave now I shall go with the past still tying me up in knots. Sorting it out is something I have to do sooner or later, but I'd much rather get it over with.'

Her eyes stared gravely at him, and in the midst of a lamentable mixture of anger and fear he was well aware that what she'd said was true. She would stay because she had to, not because this was a whim that it would amuse her to indulge.

'You have next to no money, and in Florence no friends at all. How can you possibly stay?' he asked roughly.

She still watched him, wondering why concern about her should blind him to the obvious advantage of what she proposed. He must want his studio to himself by now.

'I'm hoping that my share of the Scala fee could be paid to me here, in lire. I'd live on it for a month or two in some cheap *pensione*.' There was one more terrible hurdle to jump, but the memory of Jane Carlisle drove her over it. 'I'm not expecting you to wait for me to return to London. This is your chance to find another partner, and you'll be glad of a change. In . . . in fact we both shall.'

He didn't even try to deny it, just kept breaking into ever-smaller pieces a roll he seemed to have no interest in eating.

'Leaving Cavendish & Maitland aside, aren't you leaving some other loose ends in London?' he enquired at last. 'Or is Jem to be punished for going off with Anna and kept waiting until you decide to forgive him?'

It was so wide of the mark and also so bitterly unfair that, even in a public room, she was hard put to it not to rage at him. He saw the blaze of anger in her eyes but she forced herself to speak quietly, and he was aware again of the change in her – his protégée had gone for good; she was her own woman now.

'Jeremy and I understand one another,' she said at last. 'He needn't concern you.'

'Then that seems to conclude our discussion.' If he'd come to the dining-room with breakfast in mind, he seemed to have forgotten it, because he stood up and waved away a hovering waiter. 'Now, if you can force yourself to think of work there's a lot to be done before we earn the fee you're relying on.'

They were ready to leave on time, because they stayed at the theatre late into the night. It seemed strange to Kate that she could still work with him when heart and mind and body shrank from being so near to him that she was afraid of giving herself away. They talked only of the work in hand, and it was a help to sense that he wanted it to be finished as desperately as she did.

'Not exactly wealth beyond the dreams of avarice, but this will keep you housed and fed for a while,' he said the following morning, handing her a wad of unfamiliar bank-notes.

She longed for him to say he understood her need to stay, but they travelled in silence to the station. Winter fog had settled on the streets, and she was grateful for it. The grey blanket reminded her of London, and helped to muffle the strangeness of this different city around her.

The Paris train was due to leave first, and she couldn't walk away even though she sensed clearly how little Sam wanted her to stay there. At last the huge express appeared to be gathering itself for departure amid a final crescendo of whistle-blowing, flag-waving, and the excited cries of encouragement that seemed to be necessary to get it moving. Kate reached up to kiss Sam's cheek, and his remote expression suddenly changed. She saw him shout but could make out nothing above the noise. He clambered up the steps, and there was still a moment when he could have leaned down and touched her hand. Then even that was gone. Unaware of the crowd and the commotion around her, she stood in a trance of stillness. Perhaps one day memory would allow her to forget the moment when Sam finally travelled out of her life, but until then she must learn the lesson Sister Angelica had offered her.

Chapter 26

Florence is not huge; it can still be explored on foot. After a week or so Kate no longer felt a stranger there; she had a room in a modest *pensione* that overlooked the Ponte Vecchio, and she could find her way about without consulting a map at every street corner. She wasn't aware of feeling lonely, only of a nagging sense that time was being wasted, because an inspection of the Florentine sights, lovely though they were, wasn't accomplishing the purpose she was there for. Then one morning instead of making a careful study of the cloisters of Santa Croce, she suddenly retraced her steps to the little shop she'd been to once before. Luigi, about to go home to lunch, threw open the door for her with one of the operatic gestures that he favoured.

'*Ecco l'inglese, Signor Filippo . . . lei ricorda?*'

Kate had no choice now but to go in, apologising for her late arrival. 'I'm afraid I'm not even a customer, either . . . I only wanted to talk to you.'

'To talk about what, Signorina?' His voice was polite, but she sensed that she wasn't welcome, because since her first visit a calamity had befallen them. His sadness was something she could feel; and in some way that he could only guess at, she was connected with it. She knew that he would have preferred to ask her to leave.

She revised the order of her questions, hoping that the second of them would cause him less distress.

'I wanted to ask if I might visit the Contini workshops . . . in the Via Cavour. I'm not a goldsmith, Signore, but it would . . . would interest me very much to go there.'

His elderly hands trembled on the counter between them, but he still managed a composed reply.

'You ask for permission in the wrong place, I am afraid. The head of the firm, Marco-Tullio Contini, is in Milan now. The *padrone* here is dead . . . but perhaps you already knew that, after your first visit.'

'Yes, I knew it,' she agreed quietly. 'In fact my other purpose in coming was to ask if you could tell me where he is buried.'

This time his voice was unsteady. 'Still you ask in the wrong place. It is for the Signora Contini to tell you that, not me. Now, permit me to close the shop . . . the shutters should be down by now and I have to obey the orders from Milan.'

Her own disappointment was acute, but Kate wanted to weep for him – such grief was in his voice for the *padrone* he had lost, and such unhappiness with a new régime into which he was now too old to fit.

'I'm sorry . . . I shouldn't have come troubling you,' she said gently. '*Scusami*, Signore.'

Even then he might still have resisted, but she held out her hand to say goodbye and, automatically, his glance fell on the bracelet she wore. After a long moment his eyes lifted from the exquisite chain of roses about her wrist.

'I see you own a Contini piece,' he said slowly.

'My father gave it to me . . . it was a special birthday present.'

'It wasn't bought here – a private sale perhaps.'

'It wasn't bought at all.' She smiled suddenly, proudly, and he blinked at the transformation in her strained face. 'My father made it for me. That's why I wanted to see his workshop in the Via Cavour.'

Another silence followed, but at last she got an answer. 'Then you came to the right place after all . . . the *padrone* made that here, in his little atelier upstairs, when he already knew that he was ill. He didn't tell me who it was for, you understand – only that he would refuse to die until he finished it.'

Kate felt the hot prick of tears behind her eyelids, but there was comfort as well in knowing that this old and gentle man could help her to understand the truth about her father.

'I didn't mean to come here because Signora Contini still doesn't know about me,' Kate explained unevenly. 'When I saw my father at Santa Maddalena that day it was only the second time I ever met him. Until he came to London last spring he didn't know he had a daughter.'

Filippo slowly nodded his neat, grey head. 'So, now I understand. I was taken on here when your father came back from London to settle in Florence and open the workshops in the Via Cavour. His father and elder brother were still alive then, but he was the finest goldsmith of the three of them. Are you perhaps a jeweller too, signorina?' he asked suddenly.

'No. I design for the theatre, and stage costumes sometimes need jewellery, but it's sham stuff, nothing like these beautiful pieces.' Kate stared at a brooch in the case beside her – a little gold peacock, whose filigree tail held a tiny diamond as the centre of each eye. Cellini himself couldn't have fashioned anything lovelier. She returned her attention to the man in front of her. 'Tell me about my father, please . . . was he happy here?'

Filippo weighed his answer carefully. 'He was contented with his work, of course . . . but something was missing for happiness. He hated the Fascisti, and blamed Mussolini for dragging us into the war, hated the Nazis even more, and became a leading member of the Resistance committee. But when Alessandro was killed the light was blown out of his life.'

'And out of the Signora's,' Kate felt obliged to point out.

'Of course, and Lucia Contini never forgave him. It must have been a strange and wonderful thing for the *padrone* . . . to learn that he still had a child after all.'

'Will you tell me now where he is buried?'

'At Fiesole, close to where he lived. A No. 7 bus from the Piazza San Marco will take you there. The cemetery belongs to the convent and church of San Francesco, at the top of a very steep hill looking down over Florence; it's peaceful there for him, and very beautiful.'

'Thank you.' Kate smiled gratefully but held out her hand again. 'I've stayed too long and you should be eating your lunch. But I'd like to come back if I may. I can stay in Florence for as long as my little stock of lire holds out.'

'Come when you like. If I am busy you can sit upstairs . . . no one uses the atelier now. The new head of the firm is a business man, not a goldsmith.'

She heard again the note of sadness for a changed order of things an old man couldn't approve of; but, promising to come back, she finally left him to the task of winding down the steel shutters.

The next morning she waited for the bus he had said would take her to Fiesole. She was familiar with the system now, knew that to board the bus at all she must push like everyone else. Even then the battle wasn't done – it was always an equal fight to reach the front of the bus in order to get off again. She thought wistfully of London bus-journeys that hadn't been a trial of strength, but homesickness lay in wait for her there and she studied instead the villas that still lined the road up to Fiesole – the home of a once-thriving English colony. How many of those ancient inhabitants survived and clung to a way of life that must have seemed paradisiacal in the sunset glow of Victorian days?

The hill she was to climb at Fiesole was steep, but the view at the top worth a few aching leg muscles. It was impossible to tire of and at its heart, as always, was the white-ribbed, russet dome of the cathedral.

At last she turned away to intercept the black-gowned *sagrestano*, hurrying about some burial task. He listened to her careful enquiry for the Contini graves and led her to them himself. There was no headstone at the moment, he explained; it had been removed for a new name to be added. Kate thanked him, aware of his curiosity about her. As a rule *stranieri* came to admire the convent cloisters and the view, not to bring flowers to decorate a burial plot. But he had to leave her there, and take away a memory of her smile, and of her slender, red-coated figure kneeling by Arturo Contini's grave.

She went often after that, always with a posy of fresh flowers to leave for Alessandro and her father. One day the headstone had been re-erected, and she was grateful for its simple marble dignity. Weeping angels and cherubs decked in wreaths of monstrous artificial flowers seemed to be the preferred Italian commemoration; but she thought they would have been ill-chosen for the man whose sure taste had governed what was made in the Contini workshops.

On one of her frequent visits to the Ponte Vecchio Kate

asked about the future. 'You said that Marco-Tullio wasn't an artist,' she reminded Filippo.

'No, but his brother, Enrico, is – they are Paolo Contini's sons, you understand. The *padrone* taught Enrico, and there are other craftsmen in the workshops – not as good as their teacher, but still better than most.'

The old man watched her face, as he always did, for fleeting reminders of her father. The resemblance didn't lie in features, only in their shared colouring, and an occasional expression that he couldn't bear to miss.

'You could stay and learn. No – you don't even need to learn, I think . . . the knowledge is already in your blood.'

They always spoke together in Italian now, and in that language what Filippo had just said seemed to take on an added resonance and richness. Kate smiled at him, knowing that her sketches of some jewellery on the table had prompted his suggestion. One was a delicate design for a necklace that perhaps even Arturo would have approved of. She did her best nowadays to remember what Sister Angelica had said: resignation and acceptance brought peace of mind – a partial state of grace that even her father had reached after much grief. She was still a beginner, still regretting what she had missed here, and aware that she might never recover from needing Sam Maitland for true happiness. But there was some comfort in working in this tiny room where her father had laboured over her bracelet. The goldsmith's equipment was familiar to her now, scarcely changed over centuries – the ancient machines for rolling gold into wire or finest thread, the tiny crucibles of glazed crockery, and the piece of hollowed charcoal used for melting silver. She knew about the Precious Metals Bank where Arturo had bought gold and silver, and she'd listened to Filippo's stories – their gems had been bought in Amsterdam, but turquoise and lapis had come from Persia, and coral from Torre del Greco near Naples.

'I can't stay,' she said at last in answer to him, 'but I shall come back to Italy as often as I can.'

'Why not? Already you're at home here,' Filippo persisted. 'You speak, look, seem, more Italian every day. The *padrone* told me England was a cold, wet country where people always said what they didn't mean.' But in case this sounded too harsh, he added something else as well. 'That doesn't mean he didn't admire them, you understand. In the First War we fought with England against the Austrians – that was how it should have been against the Nazis, he said.'

'It's how it *was* in the end,' she pointed out gently.

Filippo nodded, remembering dreadful times that were already passing into history. 'The Germans blew up all the bridges except this one – Hitler admired the Ponte Vecchio, apparently. But they destroyed the buildings at each end so that it couldn't be used. The poor fools didn't know that the *padrone* and his *resistenza* friends had a telephone line across the bridge that kept them in touch with the British Army.'

He smiled at the memory, but then grew serious again. 'Why did you come, if not to stay?'

She thought that even in English it would have been a difficult question to answer. 'To learn about my father, and myself,' she said haltingly. 'I was in a muddle because of all I didn't understand . . . had been ever since I could remember, and so I kept on making mistakes. I think I shall be able to do better when I go home – but London *is* still my home. It's where I belong.'

That truth was clear in her mind now, but still some conviction that she couldn't have explained kept her where she was. It wasn't yet time to make a dash for Paradise Walk, to see the flag flying above the stage-house of the Swan again, and St Paul's grey head nudging the London sky. She was becoming almost more lonely than she could bear, but the feeling persisted that something was left unfinished that must be dealt with before she could leave Florence. Then she would go home to face the fact that Sam had tied up his own loose end with Jane Carlisle and that Cavendish & Maitland existed no longer.

Trying to understand her own state of mind, she came to the conclusion at last that what seemed to be keeping her there was no more than a reluctance to turn her back on the little plot at Fiesole. She would go this very morning and explain to her gentle ghosts that she was bringing them a posy of jonquils and freesias for the last time. It didn't matter about leaving then because she would take away with her the knowledge that she'd had a father and a brother – and even their dying couldn't now alter that.

She walked away from the grave at last but stopped for a final look at the city spread out below her. The past weeks had been wet, but today the sky was clear, and even a foretaste of spring was in the softer air. This view, and the picture of her father's little room above the shop, would be the memories she would most vividly take home with her.

'Signorina . . . the *sagrestano* pointed you out to me,' said a harsh voice behind her.

Kate registered again a strange fact about Italians: the women often sounded strident while their menfolk did not; then she turned to confront a stranger – of middle age, dressed entirely in black. The woman's sallow face looked drawn and lifeless, but her dark, deep-set eyes burned with anger.

'It is *you* who brings flowers to my family's grave . . . the *sagrestano* said so. I don't want you there – it belongs to me, Lucia Contini.' Not only the grief of bereavement thickened her voice, but the conviction that she was wronged as well, by the unpardonable intrusion of a stranger.

'I shall bring no more flowers, Signora,' Kate said slowly. 'I am leaving Florence soon.'

'Leave *now*. I don't want you here. I've thrown your flowers away.'

Kate's instinctive pity for her vanished in a bright, pure flame of rage. 'You had no right to touch them,' she said sharply. 'They were *my* gift.'

The woman stepped towards her, so quickly that she seemed about to inflict a blow. But her hands only fastened on Kate's arms, holding her there so that the Signora's eyes could examine her face. It seemed to tell her nothing and her grip relaxed, but she gestured instead towards the gate. 'It is my son who lies here; he doesn't need the flowers of a stranger.'

'Perhaps not, but I brought them for my father as well.'

The words, torn out of her, dropped into a well of silence – no echo, even, came back to disturb the stillness of death around them; no bird sang from a cypress tree, no other human voice insisted that somewhere life went on.

At last sounds forced themselves through Lucia Contini's pale lips. 'I don't believe you,' she managed to say, but her anguished eyes denied the lie.

Kate fumbled for Italian words that would explain and, if possible, lessen the woman's hurt. 'When Arturo Contini lived in London as a young man he fell deeply in love with an English dancer. She refused to go back with him to Italy and he returned to marry you instead. My mother killed herself soon afterwards. Until last spring my father didn't know that

I'd been born, or that Marguerite was long since dead. I met him once then in London, and again here on the day he died. Is that so much for you to have to share with me?'

She thought for a moment that she was to be left standing there without an answer, but at last Lucia spoke. Anger had been mastered with a huge effort of self-control, but it still laced her voice, as corrosive as acid.

'I had nothing of him to share with you. Arturo went to London while I grew up enough to marry him, but by the time I was ready for him, he was no longer ready for me. He pretended, but I always knew. I became his wife, but never the woman he wanted. Then when Alessandro was born it mattered less. I could love *him* instead. *Dio mio*, how I loved him.'

Her voice cracked again with such pain that Kate would have held out her hands to offer comfort. But for Lucia grief was like Alessandro's grave, entirely hers and the only possession now that mattered.

'The Germans killed my boy – Arturo let them kill him when he was still a child. There was nothing left then. Now I don't know why I remain alive . . . to go on suffering, I think.'

After a while Kate found something to say. 'It might be to go on learning as well.' She doubted if her murmured suggestion was even heard. This woman was deaf to everything but the sound of her own sorrow. Sister Angelica, though, would surely say that even *she* still had choices to make.

'What have I to learn? That "God's in His Heaven and all's right with the world"?' A glimmer of malice shone in her ravaged face for a moment as she spat out the English words. 'That surprises you, but my husband always kept books of English verse by his bed. That poet of yours, a man called Browning, even lived here, but I don't know why Arturo bothered with what he wrote. Who now can believe in God and all that stupid nonsense about heaven?'

'The nun who nursed my father believes in Him,' Kate pointed out. 'Her life is lived serenely in that certainty, but she doesn't feel entitled to blame God for what goes wrong – He doesn't create evil and unhappiness; *we* do, she would tell you.'

She waited for another raging denial, but none came at all; instead, tears that Lucia Contini seemed unaware of began to trickle down her face.

'Please listen,' Kate asked gently. 'So far it's been nothing but waste. My mother killed herself for grief, and my father lost not only her but the contentment of a real marriage with you. My grandparents lost an only daughter, just as you and my father lost a son. You have been a victim, but not the only one. If you choose to hate the memory of your husband, and now me as well, all you do is go on keeping tragedy alive.'

They stared at one another in silence until Lucia let out her breath on a long, shuddering sigh. 'I shouldn't have thrown the flowers away,' she muttered at last. 'I don't know why I did that.'

'It doesn't matter now.' Kate smiled to reassure her, unaware of her mistake until Lucia suddenly let out a cry of animal pain.

Her clawlike hands fastened on Kate again, feverishly shaking her. 'No – you mustn't look like Alessandro . . . that I cannot bear.'

With her own heart breaking, Kate offered the only comfort she could find. 'I'm afraid you're imagining the resemblance . . . I take after my English mother,' she lied.

'Yes . . . yes, perhaps that's true . . . but you must go

away now and not come back; I don't want you here again.' Huge despairing eyes looked out of Lucia's gaunt face, and although she released her grip she stood waiting. She wouldn't leave until she was certain that she was the one left there alone with the past.

Kate lifted her own hands in a gesture of pain that wouldn't go into words, and then stumbled past. She walked blindly down the steep hill and kept walking, all the long way back to Florence. There was only one coherent thought in her mind – she could go home now . . . in fact it was long past the time for going home.

Chapter 27

Along with Sunday evening silence, darkness had settled over the deserted stretches of the Chelsea Embankment. A cold March wind blew off the river but in Anna's drawing-room there was warmth and light. She was stretched out gracefully on a velvet chaise-longue – personifying for Jeremy the glamour that ordinary people associated with the theatre. He smiled at the word, but saw nothing wrong with it; the rest of the world *was* ordinary compared with them.

He lifted his glass to her but the gesture reminded him of his mother's complaint on one of his recent visits to Birmingham – he was always playing a part, she'd said. It was probably true – even now, old friends that they were, he and Anna behaved as if they waited for invisible curtains to swing open.

'What are you smiling at?' she asked suddenly.

'Us,' he admitted, 'sniffing hot-house lilac and sipping Chateau Yquem in front of the log fire we've just switched on. Angus, on the other hand, is probably crouched in front of a blazing tree-trunk after a day spent fighting the elements on the Wiltshire hills.'

'Even if he is, does it make him any more virtuous?' Anna wanted to know.

'No, but I think it makes him more real.' Jeremy's

beautiful features composed themselves in an expression of deep thought. 'Anna, do you ever stop to wonder who we really are? At the moment you're supposed to be a tragic Russian heroine and I'm a half-mad Danish prince. Next week I might have become a Roman general and it'll be your turn to go mad as one of Tennessee Williams's despairing prostitutes. But when we're *not* these people, are we anything at all?'

'Darling, an English Sunday evening is making you morbid,' she said briskly. 'What we *are* is exceptionally talented, civilised people. We've even managed the feat of staying friends at the end of a wonderful love-affair.' She waved away a laughing protest. 'I'm serious, Jem. You and I lived on the mountain-top for a while, and came down to the valley afterwards with affection and respect intact. I don't know who else could have managed that.'

His charming smile reappeared at the note of satisfaction in her voice. 'True, dear Anna, and I shall always count myself privileged to have been both lover *and* friend.'

'Thank you, but don't make it sound like a Roman general's farewell!' she protested. 'The transfer to New York is only for a limited run, thank God. Then I shall be back, expecting Angus to find me something less harrowing than *Karenina*.'

'Every management here and on Broadway will be fighting over you – no need to depend on our awkward friend.'

She considered the golden wine in her glass before answering. 'No need at all, but it happens that I trust Angus professionally.'

'And you don't want him offering plum parts to actresses who don't deserve them! Darling one, it was Sam who led him into that mistake with Jane Carlisle, you know.

Macdonald wasn't lured into rashness by Jane's charms, self-evident though they are.'

'I'm well aware of that,' Anna said calmly. 'The only woman who has ever lured him into rashness was *me*. There was a moment when I thought he might be too aware of Kate Cavendish's less evident charms, but then I realised that she'd merely tapped an unsuspected vein of kindness in my flinty husband. He was trying to make up to her for *us*.'

She offered Jeremy a beautiful, rueful smile, that admitted they'd both behaved badly but insisted at the same time on their release from the rules that other people were supposed to follow. It was a line of reasoning that he'd used often enough himself – whatever they did was bound to be excusable. How could the Danish prince or Roman general walk off-stage and become a dutiful suburban husband ready to mow the lawn and not covet his neighbour's wife? But he'd asked the wrong question a moment ago. What they needed to know was how to live off-stage without harming normal people. Perhaps the punishment of the gods was that they must never try, and were doomed to go lonely.

Anna stared at his sombre face, half-guessing what made him look so sad.

'My dear, there's no need for such crushing guilt. Kate is clearly enjoying herself in Italy too much to come home, and Angus is too busy not to be happy. We didn't do either of them any lasting damage.'

Jeremy lifted haunted eyes to look at her. 'No, but we might have done and we didn't care. Instead, we did the damage to ourselves, if we're honest enough to admit it. We had the intoxicating delight of making love morning, noon, and night; we were a famous couple in New York, fawned over by the people who like to collect celebrities. But we burned passion out, and even got sick of our own power to attract.'

Anna looked away from the anguish in his face, but the flames she stared at in the grate came from artificial logs – they were make-believe too, like the rest of their lives.

'You still love Kate Cavendish,' she said at last, not making a question of it.

'Yes . . . as you love Angus, I think.'

She lifted her hands in a little helpless gesture that admitted the truth of what she could scarcely bear. 'I used to dread every day that he would ask me for a divorce,' she said in a low voice. 'Now it seems almost worse that he doesn't even bother, because he can do without a woman in his life. For the moment, at least, I'm the *actress* he wants most, but even that may change. If it does I don't quite know what I shall do.'

She tried to smile but her huge eyes were suddenly so full of fear that he wrapped his arms about her for the first time in a long while. But no desire leapt between them now; they were like two frightened children, he thought, clinging together for comfort in the dark.

In Paradise Walk again, Kate came to the conclusion that only she had changed. William and Milly, still appearing at the Swan, continued to enjoy the status of neighbourhood celebrities; Aunt Lou struggled to feed her household; and Elsie bemoaned the madness of a director who'd decided to dress the *Two Gentlemen of Verona* in the costumes of Edwardian England.

They all wept a little to have Kate restored to them, and then talked of everything but where she'd been. It seemed such strange behaviour that she commented on it when she and Elsie were washing dishes after the others had gone to bed.

'It was William's idea . . . I *told* him it was daft,' Elsie snorted. 'We were all to pretend that Italy wasn't worth a mention – then you'd forget about it and not want to go back.'

Kate smiled as she scoured a plate – it sounded like a piece of her grandfather's logic. But when she didn't answer Elsie's sharp eyes fastened on her.

'Italy *was* important, wasn't it? Well, bound to have been, considering what happened there.'

Kate nodded. 'Yes, very important – but it's over now. Time to find myself another job.'

'What happened to the one you had?'

'I think it came to an end in Milan railway station. Sam naturally didn't approve of me walking out on him for a couple of months.' She disposed carefully of the last plate before going on with the conversation. 'Your letters haven't said, but I expect he's got a new partner by now – he only has to take his pick. Perhaps he's got a wife as well, though surely you *would* have remembered to mention that!'

'No wife, no partner, as far as I know. Jane Carlisle's doing very well, apparently, in *As You Like It*, so for the moment she doesn't need Sam to hold her hand. Actors – no wonder I can't stand 'em.'

Kate understood the meaning of that last sentence. Her friend excluded Sam Maitland from the wholesale dislike she reserved for the rest of the gender male. If any man could be said to do no wrong, he was her chosen candidate. It followed as the night the day that poor Jane Carlisle had no right to keep Sam waiting while she revelled in the limelight of success.

'Do you know about Macdonald taking *Anna Karenina* to New York?' Elsie asked next, and saw Kate nod. 'He was kind enough to ask William and Milly if they wanted to go too. For once even *she* had a glimmer of sense and understood that it was too late to become the toast of Broadway, but William declined straightaway. He'll be glad when the London run finishes. It's been the perfect final curtain to his years at the Swan, but he's tired now, and frightened of forgetting his lines, poor dear old fool.'

Kate suddenly wrapped her arms round Elsie in a warm hug. 'Oh, I'm glad to be back . . . I needed to stay away, but you can't imagine how much I missed you all.'

'So I should hope,' said Elsie, trying not to smile.

It was one thing to decide that she must do what Sam so far hadn't done – make a formal end of Cavendish & Maitland; it was another to force herself to walk to Wharfside. When she eventually managed it the only person she found there was a freckle-faced, very young man. She was first aware of his extreme youth compared with her own advanced age, but then took in something else about him; he also looked feverishly unwell.

'I know who *you* are,' he said in a hoarse voice. 'I'm Sam's new junior, Jamie Gilmour. He's in Vienna and I'm trying to look after things here, but not managing very well at the moment.'

'Because you ought to be in bed,' Kate pointed out severely. 'Is there someone at home to cosset you?'

Jamie admitted to a mother only too ready to cosset given half a chance, and after a little more persuasion agreed that Sam's erstwhile partner could be trusted to mind the shop while he took his influenza home to bed.

Left alone, Kate stared round the studio – once so familiar, but now changed by the decorative bamboo screen that separated the studio from what had obviously become Sam's private sitting-room. Perhaps Jane had insisted on that, and it surely wasn't unreasonable. No new wife would expect to share her home with the collection of people who drifted in and out of the studio all day long. It wasn't unreasonable, but Kate found herself deeply depressed by changes that could scarcely have made the truth more clear. With a brand-new assistant and a neat little private life as well, Sam Maitland certainly didn't need Cavendish any more.

She went to watch *Anna Karenina* for the last time before Angus took the production to New York. The warmth of everyone's welcome at the Swan melted for a moment the terrible coldness that had settled about her heart, but the truth was that she didn't belong there either any more. Even Anna would be able to come back, but Kate Cavendish would be excluded in future, being no longer part of the firm.

She managed to promise Macdonald cheerfully enough that she'd keep an eye on things while Sam was away, but his glance at her was searching, and it was a relief when Gilbert interrupted them.

'Dear, darling Kate . . . we've missed you, but how gorgeously Continental you look!'

'You must blame the Italian barber who cut my hair. The ladies' hairdressers out there like more flowing locks to work on.'

Gilbert smiled but his mind, she sensed, was not on fashions in hair. 'It seems a long time ago, doesn't it,' he asked tentatively, 'that spring morning on the Malvern Hills?'

'We exchanged information about our fathers,' she said after a moment's thought. 'Yours seemed to come off better at the time, but only because I didn't know mine then.'

Gilbert let the comment pass, having steeled himself for what must come next. 'I think I sort of asked you to . . . to take me on, but it was quite wrong of me, Kate. Marry within the profession – that's our golden rule. Who else could put up with us?'

He didn't believe it, of course; none of them did, these dragon-fly creatures kept airborne by the certainty that ordinary mortals found them irresistible. But she smilingly agreed that they should remain as they were, devoted but unmarried to one another, and saw that he looked unexpectedly relieved.

Sam came back from the Staatsoper in Vienna two days later. The studio lights were shining through the murk of a wet March evening, and he went in congratulating himself on having found so conscientious an assistant. Then he opened the door and his heart seemed to stop beating . . . after too much work and travelling he was hallucinating, conjuring out of desperate need the vision of a crop-haired, slender girl who couldn't really be there at all – except that the next moment the vision spoke to him.

'Hello, Sam . . . had a good trip?'

'Vienna was spring-like,' he managed to say, 'and the Austrians charming as usual. What the hell are *you* doing here?'

She wanted to weep for the happiness of seeing him and the grief of knowing that she wasn't welcome. He was her only source of joy, but he'd become this tired-faced, hostile stranger.

'I suppose I'm minding the shop,' she explained with difficulty. 'I came to see you and found Jamie struggling to stay on his feet. He finally agreed to give in and go home when I promised to stay until you came back.'

'How very kind, but now you mustn't put yourself out any longer,' Sam said politely. 'I expect you're getting ready to leave again. Is it to be holding Macdonald's hand in New York this time, or Jem's in Stratford?'

Both were so wide of the mark that she stared at him, trying to make sense of what he'd asked.

'All right – what *are* you going to do?' he suddenly shouted, stung by her composure when his own self-control was slipping away. Italy had changed her, or else memory had lied and she'd always been as beautiful and quietly sure of herself as this.

'I'm going to set up on my own – I've had enough experience now, and the best of teachers.' His grim expression didn't relax and she knew that what she was going to say next must surely be a waste of time. 'There's no hurry, though, if you'll let me help with an SOS that came from Glyndebourne yesterday. Their new production of *The Magic Flute* needs a replacement designer – someone made the mistake of going skiing and got himself smashed up. I promised we'd rescue them.'

'A prestigious start for Cavendish's new career,' said Sam. 'You should have mentioned that "we" don't exist any more, but I don't suppose that matters.'

'Of *course* it matters,' she cried. 'They think they're

getting you as well – and in any case you *love* doing operas.'

'You accepted the commission, Kate. It's yours.'

She'd known it all along; there was no reason why it should hurt so much that she could scarcely breathe.

'We left your things untouched,' he said next. 'I thought you'd prefer to clear them out yourself.' Then he sat down at his own desk, pretending to make sense of what he saw there.

With the terrible feeling of having been dismissed, she began heaping pens and brushes together, but suddenly threw them down again. 'Sam – please say you understand why I had to stay in Italy.'

He took so long to answer that there was time to stare at him, registering changes – there were more flecks of silver in his mop of dark hair and a new gauntness about his face. He looked older than he should, and the fear that he might be getting ill again caught at her heart. How could she bear to leave at all, doubting that he would ever take care of himself? But then she remembered the bamboo screen and Jane Carlisle.

He answered at last, and suddenly his voice was as it used to be – slow and gentle. 'I understood, Kate, even in Milan. But leaving you there alone made me very afraid, and I was angry as well, because you didn't need me.'

'I wasn't alone for long. I found a friend – the dear old man who had loved and served my father. I found an enemy, too; a tormented woman called Lucia Contini who believes that my mother cheated her of a real marriage.' She took a deep breath and pointed at the far end of the room. 'I hope *you*'ll be truly happy here with

Jane. It's such a terrible thing to waste the chance of happiness.'

A glimmer of amusement about his mouth made him look familiar again.

'You're right in general, but adrift on particulars, I'm afraid. An announcement of Jane and Gilbert's engagement is to be in tomorrow's *Times*.'

'It *can't* be,' Kate shouted. 'She was *yours* . . . she haunted this place, depended on you.' An angry sob choked her for a moment and she banged the table instead. 'She has no *right* to marry Gilbert.'

Sam was looking solemn again now. 'He let me down very gently – explained how deeply grateful he was, they *both* were, for my fatherly kindness to Jane . . .'

'Fatherly *nothing*,' Kate interrupted furiously. 'She's lusciously pretty – what Filippo's assistant in Florence calls *molto appetitosa*. How could you *not* have lusted after her, as well as wanting to be kind?'

'My poor taste, I expect,' Sam said apologetically. 'Now who's telling this story, me or you?'

'You,' she agreed, 'but first I have to tell you where you went wrong. Covent Garden was a serious mistake with a girl who only likes Ivor Novello.'

Sam shook his head. 'A much worse error was to mention that my mother's parents had been Austrian Jews – not the sort of people Jane's family were accustomed to, she delicately pointed out.'

Bermondsey suddenly got the upper hand. 'Then she's a stupid cow!' Kate shouted. 'You mustn't be hurt – she doesn't know any better.' Too overwrought to read his expression, she was thankful to hear the sudden sharp ring of the telephone. Sam picked up the receiver and, not wanting to have to listen to his conversation, she walked past the screen, forgetful of the fact that this might now be out-of-bounds to her.

It had been made into a charming sitting-room, with its own marvellous view of the river, but something was still familiar – the wistful portrait of his mother, looking down from the white-washed wall. She too, it seemed to say, had been mistaken in the choice she'd made, but Kate disagreed with a woman who'd been given Sam to love – surely not such a bad choice after all?

Then she saw what hung next to the portrait – a small, framed drawing that sent her heart leaping into her mouth. Not seen for a long time, it was still instantly recognised. Looking at the view of Southwark Cathedral she was ten years old again, a dreadful war was about to start, and on a seat beside her a shy young man was sketching in charcoal. While her heart alternately faltered or raced, her mind struggled to measure the difference between the child she'd been then and the adult she'd grown into, burdened with a legacy of fear, self-doubt, and sheer confusion. Had she simply been blind all along, or was she about to make another mistake that would end in the worst humiliation of all? Whichever it turned out to be, she must at least try to become again that clear-sighted Southwark brat, intent on doing what instinct said was right; if not, she would brand herself the coward that Marguerite had been.

When Sam walked into the room he propped himself against the window as usual, giving her no help.

'I don't want to be paid for staying in Jamie's absence,' she said with heroic calm. 'But I'd like you to give me *that* instead.' Her hand pointed at the little charcoal drawing. 'I always reckoned it was half-mine anyway.'

She thought she could hear the silence in the room, so heavy was it and fraught with suspense.

'Not the smallest fraction of it is yours,' Sam said flatly. 'Take anything else you like, but that belongs here.'

He couldn't have been more brutal if he'd tried, but she didn't look crushed or angry; in fact he had the strange feeling that she was trying not to smile. But she seemed to have lost interest in the drawing.

'Gilbert thought of marrying me at one time, but the idea of offering his father a bastard daughter-in-law rather put him off. Aunt Lou says the Scots are very choosy too, so I expect it would put *your* father off as well.'

The stillness in the room was now so profound that she feared they might both have stopped breathing. Then a tug hooted on the river and Sam's paralysis was broken.

'It scarcely matters, does it?' he asked when he could speak. 'There are your other suitors to choose from.'

'If you mean Angus, he was kind when he thought I needed help,' she said simply, 'but he doesn't *see* any other woman – only Anna. If she could have understood that she wouldn't have disliked me so much.'

'And Jem? Are you going to say *he* doesn't count, either?'

'Of course he counts – friendship's like marriage, for better or for worse, and that's what we are: true friends. I never did love him in the way that marriage requires, but that was something I couldn't understand when I was in such a muddle about everything.'

Her little candle of hope was flickering out, because the question she had made herself ask was still lying ignored, forgotten even, in the air between them. It couldn't be asked again; her bolt was shot now. She went back to the task of stacking things together, but her head was bowed over what she was doing because she was mortally afraid of bursting into tears. Then Sam moved so quietly that she didn't hear him, but from behind his hands pulled her out of the chair to turn and face him. He looked grave, but suddenly her candle was aflame again.

'My father's only difficult in small things, Kate, like the right amount of salt in his porridge. He'd welcome a Hottentot or even a Roman Catholic as a daughter-in-law if I loved her enough to marry her. I think he'd reckon he'd got off lightly with you.'

He saw her mouth tremble and the shine of tears in her eyes, but she tried to smile. 'I thought you were going to turn me down – either because it *was* Jane you'd wanted, or because life still looked safer without anyone at all.'

'Sweetheart, a Cockney urchin once offered me an acid-drop and showed me where angels are to be found – the battle has been lost since then!' His hands pulled her against him and she could feel the thudding of his heart. 'Dear love, I've been waiting such a long, long time for you to get round to *me*. I was afraid you never would – that's why I kept pretending that I wasn't in the contest at all.'

She pulled away from him a little so that she could look at his face. No vision born of tiredness and desolation this time; he *was* Sam, beautifully real and familiar, though now transfigured with happiness.

'I'm not sure what to do next,' she confessed. 'Sing, turn cartwheels, thank heaven on my knees . . . ?'

'Not sing, my dearest,' Sam entreated. 'Anything but that!'

She began to laugh, because laughing was suddenly so easy, but his mouth found the little mole above her upper lip, and then moved on to her own mouth, and laughter was swallowed up in the leap of desire, running like wildfire from his body to hers. *This* was the mad delight that Marguerite had lived and died for. She understood it at last, and was no longer afraid. But Sam lifted his head, and the ghost of a smile was on his face.

'Light of my life, history isn't going to repeat itself. We shall stop while I still can and walk sedately round to Paradise Walk. Lovely as it would be to possess you this very minute, I think the episcopalian spirit of Aunt Lou might hover around the bed, insisting that a marriage ceremony comes first.'

But Kate was looking troubled now. 'Sam, will you promise not to mind that I'm still so shamefully chaste? It wasn't Aunt Lou's upbringing – only the cowardice you once accused me of. Jeremy tried to cure me of it, but I took so long to get ready that he fell asleep instead. Do you . . . do you think you'll be able to manage it?'

The anxious question tried him very hard but he gasped that he would do his best, then gave way to a great shout of laughter. She waited for him to recover, still feeling irrationally sad.

'Sam, the nun who nursed my father lived a secluded life, but she seemed to understand that we blame God or each other for the choices we make when we should be blaming ourselves – my parents did that, and so perhaps did yours. If I hadn't seen your little drawing I'd have made a dreadful mistake myself – chosen to pretend that I could walk away from you without breaking my heart.'

Sam touched her lips with a gentle finger. 'Your mouth is sad because you're thinking of the others, aren't you? Anna and Angus choosing to hurt even though they need to love

373

each other; Jem pretending that his lonely see-saw of elation and despair will do; even Gilbert, too intelligent not to know that his lovely Jane will make him a self-centred, ambitious, actress-wife.'

Kate nodded, grieving for them all. 'There's someone worse, too – the poor woman who watches by my brother's grave at Fiesole. She told me never to go back, but one day we'll go together so that you can meet old Filippo as well.' Then another thought wiped sadness from her face. 'Lucia's an Italian woman who needs children to love. Sam, how would it be if we offered her ours . . . as her godchildren, I mean? We should have to get started *soon*, of course.'

Seriously, he agreed, the sooner the better; there was only one small obstacle to overcome. 'I hope you haven't forgotten Glyndebourne, partner. Perhaps we should tackle that together first.'

'Cavendish & Maitland again,' she announced with huge satisfaction, and saw him shake his head.

'Maitland & Maitland, I rather thought instead,' Sam said.

Maggie's Market

Dee Williams

It's 1935 and Maggie Ross loves her life in Kelvin Market, where her husband Tony has a bric-a-brac stall and where she lives, with her young family, above Mr Goldman's bespoke tailors. But one fine spring day, her husband vanishes into thin air and her world collapses.

The last anyone saw of Tony is at Rotherhithe station, where Mr Goldman glimpsed him boarding a train, though Maggie can only guess at her husband's destination. And she has no way of telling what prompted him to leave so suddenly – especially when she's got a new baby on the way. What she can tell is who her real friends are as she struggles to bring up her children alone. There's outspoken, gold-hearted Winnie, whose cheerful chatter hides a sad past, and cheeky Eve, whom she's known since they were girls. And there's also Inspector Matthews, the policeman sent to investigate her husband's disappearance. A man who, to the Kelvin Market stallholders, is on the wrong side of the law, but a man to whom Maggie is increasingly drawn . . .

'A brilliant story, full of surprises' *Woman's Realm*

'A moving story, full of intrigue and suspense . . . a wam and appealing cast of characters . . . an excellent treat' *Bolton Evening News*

0 7472 5536 9

HEADLINE

When Tomorrow Dawns

Lyn Andrews

1945. The people of Liverpool, after six years of terror and grief and getting by, are making the best of the hard-won peace, none more so than the ebullient O'Sheas. They welcome widowed Mary O'Malley from Dublin, her young son Kevin, and Breda, her bold strap of a sister, with open arms and hearts.

Mary is determined to make a fresh start for her family, despite Breda, who is soon up to her old tricks. At first all goes well, and Mary begins to build up an understanding with their new neighbour Chris Kennedy – until events take a dramatic turn that puts Chris beyond her reach. Forced to leave the shelter of the O'Sheas' home, humiliated and bereft, Mary faces a future that is suddenly uncertain once more. But she knows that life has to go on . . .

'Lyn Andrews presents her readers with more than just another saga of romance and family strife. She has a realism that is almost tangible' *Liverpool Echo*

0 7472 5806 6

HEADLINE